CRITICS' PR

REVOLUTION

Book 3 of the America Series

"An adventure through America's rich and compelling history." – *Movies, Shows & Books*

"A vivid world for the reader to get caught up in." – *Books And More*

"A memorable read." – *St. Louis Post-Dispatch*

"The characters are so vivid and alive, you think you're reading about old friends." – *The Times-News Online*

"Mike Bond is a masterful storyteller." – *Sacramento Bee*

"A testament to the effect the politics and moral revolution have had on America." – *Miami Times*

"Truly beautiful writing." *Bookbites*

"An extraordinary and deftly crafted novel that combines interesting characters within the context of an historically detailed background." – *Midwest Book Review*

"Truly beautiful writing … A coming-of-Age Masterpiece." – *BookTrib*

FREEDOM

Book 2 of the America Series

"A simply riveting and deftly crafted read from an author with a genuine flair for narrative driven storytelling and an impressive attention to historical detail." – *Midwest Book Review*

"A memorable read." – *St. Louis Post-Dispatch*

AMERICA
Book 1 of the America Series

"Mike Bond has done it again, focusing his formidable talents on yet another genre: the historical novel." – *The Daily News*

"Brings to mind classic coming-of-age masterpieces such as *Look Homeward, Angel*." – *BookTrib*

"An involving, thoughtful tale that explores America's tectonic shifts leading to Vietnam." – *Kirkus*

"This book is a winner because it introduces our tumultuous history with characters we can identify with, admire and root for." – *Goodreads*

"I was intrigued and engrossed the entire time… a vivid world for the reader to get caught up in. – *Books And More*

"The most beautiful prose I have ever read." – *NetGalley*

"We wonder if the youth of today will have to fight the same fights for the same rights all over again. It would behoove them to read this book." – *Arizona Daily Star*

SNOW

"An action-packed adventure, but also a morality tale of what happens when two men who should know better get entangled in a crime from which they can't escape." – *Denver Post*

"More than just a thriller, *Snow* lights up the complexities of American culture, the tensions of morality and obligation and the human search for love and freedom, all of which makes it clear Bond is a masterful storyteller." – *Sacramento Bee*

"A captivating story of three friends on opposing sides of a betrayal… a well-paced tale with intricate storylines." – *Kirkus*

"A complex interplay of fascinating characters." – *Culture Buzz*

"Exploring the psyche and the depths of human reasoning and drive, *Snow* is a captivating story." – *BookTrib*

"An action-packed thriller that wouldn't let go. The heart-pounding scenes kept me on the edge of my seat." – *Goodreads*

"A simple story at its heart that warps into a splendid morality tale." – *Providence Sunday Journal*

ASSASSINS

"An exhilarating spy novel that offers equal amounts of ingenuity and intrigue." – *Kirkus*

"An epic spy story... Bond often writes with a staccato beat, in sentence fragments with the effect of bullet fire. His dialogue is sharp and his description of combat is tactical and detached, professional as a soldier's debriefing. Yet this terseness is rife with tension and feeling... A cohesive and compelling story of political intrigue, religious fanaticism, love, brotherhood and the ultimate pursuit of peace." – *Honolulu Star-Advertiser*

"Packs one thrilling punch after the other... A first-rate thriller." – *Book Chase*

"Powerful, true to life, and explosive... A story that could be ripped right out of the headlines." – *Just Reviews*

"Bond is one of America's best thriller writers... You need to get this book... It's an eye-opener, a page-turner... very strongly based in reality." – *Culture Buzz*

"Riveting, thrilling... so realistic and fast-paced that the reader felt as if they were actually there." – *NetGalley*

"The action is outstanding and realistic ... The background is provided by recent events we have all lived through. The flow of the writing is almost musical as romance and horrors share equal billing... I wish everyone could read and understand this book." – *Goodreads*

SAVING PARADISE
Book 1 of the Pono Hawkins Series

KILLING MAINE
Book 2 of the Pono Hawkins Series

"Quite a ride for those who love good crime thrillers... I can't recommend this one strongly enough." – *Book Chase*

"Bond returns with another winner in *Killing Maine*. Bond's ability to infuse his real-world experiences into a fast-paced story is unequaled." – *Culture Buzz*

"A twisting mystery with enough suspicious characters and red herrings to keep you guessing. It's also a dire warning about the power of big industry and a commentary on our modern ecological responsibilities. A great read for the socially and environmentally conscious mystery lover." – *Honolulu Star-Advertiser*

"Sucks in the reader and makes it difficult to put the book down until the very last page... A winner of a thriller." – *Mystery Maven*

"Another stellar ride from Bond; checking out Pono's first adventure isn't a prerequisite, but this will make readers want to." – *Kirkus*

GOODBYE PARIS
Book 3 of the Pono Hawkins Series

"There's tension, turmoil and drama on every page that's hot enough to singe your fingers." – *New York Times* Bestseller, Steve Berry

"A rip-roaring page-turner, edgy and brilliantly realistic." – *Culture Buzz*

"Exhilarating." – *Kirkus*

"Another non-stop thriller of a novel by a master of the genre." – *Midwest Book Review*

"A stunning thriller, entrancing love story and exciting account of anti-terror operations." – *BookTrib*

"Doesn't stop until it has delivered every possible ounce of intelligent excitement." – *Miami Times*

"Fast and twisty, and you don't know how it's going to end." – *Arizona Daily Sun*

"Mike Bond is my favorite author... and his books are nothing short of works of art… I could not put this book down once I started reading it." – *Goodreads*

"A great book with normal special forces action and thrills, but what makes it great is the integration of Islamic terrorism." – *Basingstone Reviews*

"An action-packed story culminates in an exciting ending." – *The Bookworm*

THE LAST SAVANNA

FIRST PRIZE FOR FICTION, *Los Angeles Book Festival*: "One of the best books yet on Africa, a stunning tale of love and loss amid a magnificent wilderness and its myriad animals, and a deadly manhunt through savage jungles, steep mountains and fierce deserts as an SAS commando tries to save the elephants, the woman he loves and the soul of Africa itself."

"A gripping thriller." – *Liverpool Daily Post (UK)*

"One of the most realistic portrayals of Africa yet… Dynamic, heart-breaking and timely to current events… a must-read." – *Yahoo Reviews*

"Sheer intensity, depicting the immense, arid land and never-ending scenes… but it's the volatile nature of nature itself that gives the story its greatest distinction." – *Kirkus*

"One of the most darkly beautiful books you will ever read." – *WordDreams*

"Exciting, action-packed… A nightmarish vision of Africa." – *Manchester Evening News (UK)*

"A powerful love story set in the savage jungles and deserts of East Africa." – *Daily Examiner (UK)*

"The central figure is not human; it is the barren, terrifying landscape of Northern Kenya and the deadly creatures who inhabit it." – *Daily Telegraph (UK)*

"An entrancing, terrifying vision of Africa." – *BBC*

"A manhunt through crocodile-infested jungle, sun-scorched savannah, and impenetrable mountains as a former SAS man tries to save the life of the woman he loves but cannot have." – *Evening Telegraph (UK)*

"Tragic and beautiful, sentimental and ruthless, *The Last Savanna* is a vast and wonderful book." – *NetGalley*

"From the opening page maintains an exhilarating pace until the closing line ... A highly entertaining and gripping read." – *East African Wild Life Society*

HOLY WAR

"Action-filled thriller." – *Manchester Evening News (UK)*

"This suspense-laden novel has a never-ending sense of impending doom... An unyielding tension leaves a lasting impression." – *Kirkus*

"A profound tale of war... Impossible to stop reading." – *British Armed Forces Broadcasting*

"A terrific book... The smells, taste, noise, dust, and fear are communicated so clearly." – *Great Book Escapes*

"A supercharged thriller... A story to chill and haunt you." – *Peterborough Evening Telegraph (UK)*

"A tale of fear, hatred, revenge, and desire, flicking between bloody Beirut and the lesser battles of London and Paris." – *Evening Herald (UK)*

"If you are looking to get a driver's seat look at the landscape of modern conflict, holy wars, and the Middle East then this is the perfect book to do so." – *Masterful Book Reviews*

A gripping tale of passion, hostage- taking and war, set against a war-ravaged Beirut." – *Evening News (UK)*

"A stunning novel of love and loss, good and evil, of real people who live in our hearts after the last page is done...Unusual and profound." – *Greater London Radio*

HOUSE OF JAGUAR

"A riveting thriller of murder, politics, and lies." – *London Broadcasting*

"Tough and tense thriller." – *Manchester Evening News (UK)*

"A high-octane story rife with action, from U.S. streets to Guatemalan jungles." – *Kirkus*

"A terrifying depiction of one man's battle against the CIA and Latin American death squads." – *BBC*

"Vicious thriller of drugs and revolution in the wilds of Guatemala." – *Liverpool Daily Post (UK)*

"With detailed descriptions of actual jungle battles and manhunts, vanishing rain forests and the ferocity of guerrilla war, *House of Jaguar* also reveals the CIA's role in both death squads and drug running, twin scourges of Central America." – *Newton Chronicle (UK)*

"Grips the reader from the very first page. An ideal thriller for the beach, but be prepared to be there when the sun goes down." – *Herald Express (UK)*

TIBETAN CROSS

"Bond's deft thriller will reinforce your worst fears... A taut, tense tale of pursuit through exotic and unsavory locales." – *Publishers Weekly*

"Grips the reader from the very first chapter until the climactic ending." – *UPI*

"One of the most exciting in recent fiction... An astonishing thriller." – *San Francisco Examiner*

"A tautly written study of one man's descent into living hell... a mood of near claustrophobic intensity." – *Spokane Chronicle*

"It *is* a thriller... Incredible, but also believable." – *Associated Press*

"A thriller that everyone should go out and buy right away. The writing is wonderful throughout... Bond working that fatalistic margin where life and death are one and the existential reality leaves one caring only to survive." – *Sunday Oregonian*

"Murderous intensity... A tense and graphically written story." – *Richmond Times*

"The most jaundiced adventure fan will be held by *Tibetan Cross*." – *Sacramento Bee*

"Grips the reader from the opening chapter and never lets go." – *Miami Herald*

THE DRUM THAT BEATS WITHIN US
Poetry

"The poetry is sometimes raw, painful, exquisite but there is always the sense that it was written from the heart." – *LibraryThing*

"A collection of poetry that explores the elements of nature, what nature can provide, what nature can take away, and how humans are connected to it all." – *Book Review Bin*

"Passionately felt emotional connections, particularly to Western landscapes and Native American culture... compellingly linking the great cycles of stars with little, common lives... to create a powerful sense of loss... a muscular poignancy." – *Kirkus*

"An exploration of self and nature... that asks us to look at our environment through the eyes of animals... and the poetry that has been with us since the dawn of time... comforting, challenging, and thought provoking." – *Bound2Books*

"His poetry courses, rhythmic and true through his works. His words serve as an important alarm for readers to wake from their contented slumber of self-absorbed thought and notice the changes around them. Eye-opening and a joy to read, the master of the existential thriller can add another winning title to his accolades." – *BookTrib*

"The language is beautiful, heartbreaking, romantic, sad, savvy, and nostalgic all at once. From longer poems to very short, thought-provoking poems, the lines of each take the reader to a world the poet has experienced or given much thought to. Truly beautiful." – *Goodreads*

"This is such a beautiful book of poetry... the imagery is vibrant, devastating, and haunting... A thoroughly modern 21st century collection that revisits and revises classic themes. Highly recommended." – *NetGalley*

"The poems are beautiful and range from the long lyrical expressions of love and nature to the brief expressions of a moments insight into a sudden feeling, expressed with a few words that capture the moment and the feeling perfectly." – *Metapsychology Reviews*

"*The Drum That Beats Within Us* presents us with a world gone awry, a world in which the warrior poet has fought, and a world in which only love survives." – *Vine Reviews*

JOY
Poetry

-

"Exquisite… written from the heart." – *Library Thing*

"Beautiful … expressed with a few words that capture the moment and the feeling perfectly." – *Metapsychology Reviews*

An exploration of self and nature... Comforting, challenging, and thought provoking." – *Bound2Books*

"A world gone awry, a world in which the warrior poet has fought, and a world in which only love survives." – *Vine Reviews*

"Eye-opening and a joy to read." – *BookTrib*

"An amazing find … Highly 5/5" – *RokinRev Review*

"An incredible collection … The language is beautiful, heartbreaking, romantic, sad, savvy, and nostalgic all at once... Truly beautiful." – *Goodreads*

"A fabulous read ... His poetry dances between reflections on the majesty of wilderness, the joys and sorrows of love, and passionate expressions of life's greatest existential questions. It's a book I'd suggest to all poetry lovers out there." – *An Exquisite Endeavour Book Review*

ALSO BY MIKE BOND

NOVELS

Revolution

Freedom

America

Snow

Assassins

Saving Paradise

Killing Maine

Goodbye Paris

The Last Savanna

Holy War

House of Jaguar

Tibetan Cross

POETRY

Joy

The Drum That Beats Within Us

CRUDE

For all the children,
that they may live,
and earth survive.

Nothing is so firmly believed
as what we least know.
– *Michel de Montaigne*

One believes things because one has been conditioned to
believe them.
– *Aldous Huxley*

Humans prefer only one thing to freedom,
and that is slavery.
– *Fyodor Dostoyevsky*

A great civilization is not conquered from without
until it has destroyed itself from within.
– *Will Durant*

We will all go together when we go,
all suffused with an incandescent glow.
– *Tom Lehrer*

MIKE BOND

BOND

CRUDE

BIG CITY PRESS

Published in the United States by Big City Press, New York.

ISBN PAPERBACK: 978-1-949751-32-1

ISBN EBOOK: 978-1-949751-33-8

ISBN AUDIOBOOK: 978-1-949751-34-5

CONTENTS

1

BLOOD IN THE WATER

THE SHARK HIT so hard he thought it was a ship keel out of the deep, its gritty hide rasping his thigh and its huge tail ripping a dive fin off his foot. He yanked a repellant tube from his divepack, fumbled and lost it, couldn't see it in his headlamp, faced the shark but it wasn't there, was above him, to the left, below, grinning jaws.

He dove, grabbing for the repellant, watching the shark. It attacked, feinted and dodged, the biggest tiger shark he'd ever seen. His hand bumped the repellant, knocking it away. He grasped for it, trying to circle to face the shark, to stay upright despite the missing fin. *Don't panic.*

The shark dove, then rose toward him, teeth glinting in his headlamp. His wrist grazed the repellant, driving it lower. He snapped on his Orca torch, looked around frantically for Two, but the other diver wasn't there.

Don't panic.

He sank deeper. His face touched the tube. He grabbed and squeezed it, repellant blinding his mask. The shark circled once, slid into the depths.

The repellant faded. He coughed, realized he had spit out his mouthpiece. He shoved it in, gurgled water, coughed and spit it out.

His legs and feet were still there. The shark had just nicked him, tested him. Maybe it had smelled blood from when he'd torn his knee climbing out of the sub.

Or blood from someone else?

Where was Two?

The shark darted beneath him. He wanted to shine his torch at it, but that might attract it, anger it. He pulled in his legs and yanked out a second tube. Black repellant spurted out.

Don't panic.

One tube left. The rebreather thundered with his panting. Larger and larger, the shark nosed toward him through clouds of repellant, crunching its jaws.

He ripped off his divepack, the rebreather hissing, and smashed the shark's snout. It dove, tail slamming him sideways, swung round and began to circle him, closer and closer.

Don't panic.

Faster the shark circled. With only one fin he couldn't keep up; it would get him. He fired the last repellant.

It clouded the water and he couldn't see the shark, only felt the crush of water as it smashed past, couldn't hear over his own frantic gasps. Choking and crying, he shoved his arms back through the divepack straps, tugged up his legs against his body.

Beyond his torch light the watery darkness expanded forever. Without Two, how could he finish? Should he return to the sub? Maybe Two was already there, had abandoned the mission because of the shark? There'd been no message from the sub.

The water grew colder, darker; he was sinking too deep. The repellant was gone. With tiger sharks, he remembered, when there's one, there's many.

His watch showed 38 feet. He couldn't see the shark. Fish schooled past, fusiliers or jacks.

01:52, the watch said. One hour left. If one diver didn't reach the platform, the other had to do it alone. He turned to 347 degrees and began to swim, slowly kicking the one fin.

Above him the black waves glinted with light. He ached to go up, but the shark would attack if he rose to the top like a dying fish. He swam toward the light till it brightened the wavetops, then surfaced quickly to check his approach.

Before him, a wide platform of brilliant lights towered ten stories into the night, a glittering city on pylons over the waves, its gas flare blazing across the black sky.

A school of barracuda shot like missiles beneath him. He checked his watch: *02:03*. He sank back into the gloom and swam northeast toward a huge metal strut descending into the sea. His first position – the southeast corner pylon.

In the oily rushing darkness there was no sign of Two. For an instant, he wondered who Two was – on missions like this you never knew the others' names, you just had numbers.

Waves roiled round the pylon, greasy and oil-turbid, slamming him against the barnacles and clams on the steel. Bounced back and forth, he tried to set his course northwest at 320 degrees and almost swam into another strut of the pylon, so big it took him half a minute to go around it.

Fish struck his face – butterflies and angels and little trash feeders drawn to his headlamp.

The platform's light dissolved down through the oily water. *02:19*. He sank below it, watching for the shark, for sea snakes and scorpion fish.

At the platform's center, a huge cluster of four pipes descended straight down. They roared with the gas rushing up them toward the platform above.

Easy part now. He touched a pipe, then yanked back his hand. That gas comes out of the earth at boiling point. And a burn attracts sharks just like blood.

He was losing it, too worried about the shark, about Two.

Don't panic.

Above him, waves lashed the pylons, fell back on themselves and raveled on. Oil streaked the surface, distorting the light from the plat-form's flare. How strange, he thought, to bore into the earth. Suck life from the past. And burn it in the sky.

He dove down the pipes to fifty feet, where a great steel ring clamped the four pipes together. The bolts on each flange were big as his head. He unslung the divepack and took out a heavy package. It was solid, malleable, crescent-shaped, as long as his forearm. He pinned it into place under the lower flange, near one of the four hot pipes.

He placed a second charge against the upper flange. Unrolling the coil of wire that linked them to two other charges from his pack, he swam a third of the way around the pipes till the wire grew taut, and fitted the two other charges above and below the flange.

On the unrolled wire midway between the two pairs of charges was a water-sealed box like a soap dish that he tucked under the flange. He ran his finger and thumb along each wire; there were no kinks, no cuts.

02:47 – ahead of schedule, despite the shark. Even without Two.

When his watch hit *02:55,* he pushed a two-inch button on the right side of the water-sealed box, then swam up to twenty feet below surface and southward from the platform, rechecking his watch often for depth and direction. He craved to shine down his torch to check for the shark, but that would only attract it.

Don't panic.

You can do this in your sleep. In seven minutes you'll be back in the sub. Fuck Two.

Far below, a huge shape crossed the deep. *No,* he begged. *Please no.* He lit the torch. The shape undulated onward, trailing phosphores-cence. A giant squid.

But now he'd turned on his torch.

2
SOUTHERN CROSS

O N THE CATWALK of the Makassar gas platform's third deck, Liz Chaplin leaned her elbows on the damp rail, watching the Southern Cross sink toward the western horizon.

How distant the planets were, yet so close. How far more distant were the stars. Space so endlessly deep, inconceivably far. And what you see now had happened millions of years ago, had taken all that time for their light to get here. And all that time like space, unending.

Below the catwalk, the moonlit waves rolled steadily southward, breaking whitely around the platform pylons. The warm wind out of the Celebes fifty miles to the east tasted of jungle, fruit, and flowers. It eddied round her ankles and rose under her loose dress up the insides of her thighs.

When you see the Southern Cross for the first time, the song goes, you'll understand why you came this way. She'd always loved the pure beauty of the song but now felt she understood its meaning as the songwriter had said: *using the power of the universe to heal your wounds.*

Out here in the middle of the ocean, you *felt* the power of the universe. But *what* was this power? What wounds was she trying to heal?

03:14. At 04:30 on the mainland the mosques would turn on the first tape of the day: *Wake up and pray*. You could almost hear them, way out here.

She distracted herself thinking what time it was in Anchorage. How funny that back there it was still yesterday, barely noon.

Anchorage in October, sidewalks slippery with icy slush, a white fog roiling off the water. Fourteen hours of darkness a day.

She hugged her arms, chafing them with cold palms, and ran a finger along the rail, raking off dew that splattered at her feet. She glanced along the fluorescent gangway to the crew quarters. The blue aura of a television flickered against a wall, the men from the late shift watching baseball playoffs. Those who had replaced them in the control room overhead sat at computer banks studying the constant stream of data on gas volumes, pipe pressures, temperatures, CO_2 and water content, glycol supply, and the thousands of other fluctuating parameters of this towering industrial city, along with the great Gencom printers that spit every fact and figure out in black and white. A wall of transmitters pulsed it up to the stars, the satellites sending it instantly to Jakarta and to the world headquarters of Rawhide Energy in New York.

The gas platform was one life, off-platform another. You could feel so close to people on the platform, but know so little of their other lives. The men seemed more solitary; the women were more confiding in each other. But there were only four other women: two engineers, the assistant chef in the kitchen, and a tattooed computer techie so introverted she could go for days without speaking.

After a few weeks here, you no longer even heard the howl of gas rushing up the pipes from far below the sea, the rumbling thunder of the huge separators sucking oil and water from the gas and forcing the gas into the monstrous intestines of pipe that snaked, humming with power, up to the jet compressor trains that scrubbed, recompressed, chilled, dehydrated, and punched it into another pipeline down across the seabed to Borneo.

Nor did she even notice anymore the constant roar of flames far overhead – the gas flare atop the stack – bright enough to be seen from orbit – burning methane but creating millions of tons of CO2, and used as a potential escape valve for the gas if something went wrong on the platform.

But nothing ever went wrong on the platform. It made her feel pride for the human genius that had built this three-billion-dollar, ten-thousand-ton colossus like a skyscraper on the sea floor, its eight gas wells driving down two miles through the earth, able to find a reservoir of gas or oil in a space as small as a suitcase up to a depth of three miles.

That was her job. As a Rawhide senior geologist, she analyzed the seismic data and well logs and told her bosses where to find oil and gas. They spent millions of dollars to drill exactly where she told them. Nearly always she was right.

Three-fifteen in the morning here meant eight-fifteen p.m. yesterday in London, the cold wind biting down the Thames. In four hours, she'd be on the 07:05 chopper across the Makassar Strait to Kalimantan, the 09:30 Garuda Airlines flight to Jakarta, noon out of Jakarta on Singapore Airlines, London by nine p.m. tomorrow. A few weeks in the cold mists of London to remind her why she lived in Indonesia. Or if she'd wanted, a few weeks in the Caribbean, Réunion, anywhere.

She could go anywhere but was damned if she cared.

"WE'RE ABOUT TO HAVE A NUCLEAR WAR." ROSS BULLOCK looked out at the journalists crowded into Rawhide Energy's Wall Street press auditorium.

There was a shocked silence, then a rustling of chairs as the journalists faced him. This wasn't just another Wall Street dog-and-pony show worth five paras in tomorrow's business news. Ross, the CEO of Rawhide Energy and the son of its founder, had invited members of every prominent news organization in the country to hear him make the most important announcement he had ever, *would* ever, make as both an international business leader and an American.

"The US-Russian war in Ukraine will soon go nuclear. Ukraine has clearly lost, but the White House refuses to admit it or to agree to peace talks. And now with war escalating in the Middle East, the likelihood of it all becoming nuclear is so obvious that at Rawhide Energy we feel it essential for human survival to raise this issue as publicly as we can.

"As you probably know, we have refused to comply with sanctions against Russia. Among all the people we've ever worked with, all over the world, the Russians are probably the most like us Americans. They're friendly, hard-working, cooperative, and kind. They very much love their families and their country. They are world leaders in science, engineering, medicine, space research, music, literature, art, and many other fields. They've been honorable partners in a number of our international projects. And about this war and its horrendous dangers for the world, our government bears much of the responsibility."

The journalists shuffled papers, glanced at one another, looked back to him.

"And now that this Third World War has expanded to the Middle East, if we don't stop now, it will soon kill us all. We *can* stop it; we can avoid destroying nearly all of life on Earth." He paused for a sip of water to let the words sink in.

"Again, as most of you know, the real cause of the US-Russian war in Ukraine goes back to the 1990s, when we promised Russia there would be no NATO expansion into Eastern Europe. Instead we have expanded NATO to Russia's boundaries, surrounded Russia with nuclear missiles, built bioweapons labs and CIA training camps on its borders, and have turned the Ukrainians into mercenaries against their own kin. Every attempt by Russia to resolve this problem, at the UN and other forums, has been ignored. Every Russian request for friendship or closer alliances with the West has been rejected by the U.S. In the spring of 2014, Russia invaded Crimea because we had instructed Ukraine to cut off Russia's access to Sebastopol, Russia's most essential historic port. We spent five billion dollars in our 2014 coup that overthrew Ukraine's popularly elected, pro-Russian government. This warlike, illegal coup was ordered by president Obama and engineered by Victoria Nuland, who in way back in 2003 engineered with Bush and Cheney the tragic invasion of Iraq. At that point she should have been arrested for war crimes, but instead was appointed by president Biden as Undersecretary of State, and only recently fired. She is responsible, worldwide, for over two million civilian deaths, plus a hundred thousand U.S. military deaths. You can look it up. In the entire history of the United States, no woman has killed more people than Victoria Nuland."

The journalists watched him, silent and disinterested.

"These are but a few of our U.S. provocations against Russia since we promised them peace at the end of the Cold War – provocations contrary to every agreement we ever signed with them. Most of you know this, so why not speak about it? Isn't that what journalists are supposed to do?"

He stared at them, hoping for a response. There was nothing. "If we had kept our promises, kept our side of the bargain, we wouldn't be facing nuclear annihilation today.

"Our lives, our families, our civilization, and all life on earth may soon be destroyed. The U.S. and Russia have more than 11,000 nuclear weapons, which will kill all life on this planet many times over. In a nuclear war, every city and town in the U.S., Europe and Asia will be vaporized in a fire five times hotter than the center of the sun, exploding at warp speed incinerating everything. Billions of people atomized, billions more dying in agony from burns and radiation . . . Countless trillions of tons of fiery radioactive debris – tiny bits of people, cities, highways, forests, farms – choking the skies for decades and turning most of the earth into a darkened frozen ball. With no survivors."

THREE STORIES BENEATH THE METAL GRID AT LIZ'S FEET, THE dark sea rippled, supple and restless. She imagined it down to the bottom, then down through two more miles of sand, boulders, mud, and dead vegetation to a coastal river she had discovered that had been buried for over a hundred million years. And then the ancient sea floors below it, that had been built over eons from infinite skeletons of diatoms and other microorganisms. And that made crude, which ran the world.

I can read the depths of the earth, she thought. *Why can't I see inside myself?*

Who is there?

The deck snapped sideways, knocked her head into the rail, and smashed her up into the catwalk above. A horrible explosion crushed her ears, flashed the night red, and blew struts of blazing steel into the sky. Flames and boiling steam howled through the crew quarters. Someone dashed out the door toward her. His body exploded off the catwalk.

Rivers of oil blazed over the sea; streams of fire pirouetted into the sky. People dove out windows and tumbled in flames off the catwalks into the ocean far below.

Her hair afire, she ran toward the crew quarters. Its walls convulsed then blew outward and spun into the sea. She stumbled across the compressor deck, metal chunks crashing down, globs of molten condensate. Someone lay under a hot steel wall; she pulled his hand but his arm fell off and she could not drag him out.

Metal beams screeched, wrenched apart and collapsed, seething, into the sea. A cast iron compressor wall came crunching down.

From this deck it was two decks down to the wellheads, where the gas coming up from the sea might possibly be shut off. She ran to the stairwell but the stairs were gone, and the catwalks below. A siren was howling *Abandon Platform.* Gas-filled pipes were blowing like bombs, the air humming with flying metal. *If the main gas lines go,* she realized, *it all explodes.*

She slid down a hot girder to the deck below. The wellhead deck was gone, columns of flame roaring out of the sea. There were no wellheads left to shut off. She leaped down a hundred feet into the red, roaring sea.

3

EXTINCTION

"**F**OR BILLIONS OF YEARS,** life has evolved here on this planet," Ross told the journalists. "From the first microbes to single cells, to ocean life, land creatures, dinosaurs, mammals, birds, insects, reptiles – billions of different creatures living over millions and millions of years. Till only a couple of million years ago when our ancestors climbed down from the trees and started on the long path we're still on today. This entire planet throbs with the miracle of life. Are we now going to exterminate it all?"

"But isn't that unpatriotic?" yelled a tall, silver-haired guy in the fourth row of seats: *Neal Callan, CNN*, "when the president and our allies have called for a united front against Russia?"

"I've spent much time in Russia, been in every one of its eleven time zones. They've always welcomed Americans, and been excited to work with us. Our two countries have decades of superb cooperation in science, medicine, everything from space to paleontology. How can we desert an honorable partner when it's clear that U.S. and NATO share a major part of the guilt for this war?"

"That's just Russian propaganda!" someone called; Ross couldn't see him.

"Do you know how many times," he asked them, "Russia has been invaded from the West? Napoleon's French army invaded all of western Russia and burned Moscow. Then Britain, France, and the U.S. attacked Russia from three sides in the Crimean War. The German invasion in World War One destroyed all of western Russia and killed nearly three million people. Then right after World War One, Britain, the U.S., and France invaded western Russia and almost captured Moscow, also attacking from the Baltic, Pacific and Black Sea . . . Did you know all this?"

No one spoke.

"Once again, the Russians healed their wounds and rebuilt their country. Then the German World War Two invasion killed 27 million Russians, including eighty percent of the young men. Everything between the Russian border and Moscow was destroyed. One of every four Russians was either killed or wounded."

He looked out at them. "Can you imagine, if one out of every four Americans was either killed or wounded? In World War Two, we lost 290 thousand people, and our ally, Russia, lost 27 million – nearly 100 times more."

They were silent.

"Then, after Russia had suffered so much, the United States repeatedly harassed and attacked it and surrounded it with nuclear missiles, promising nuclear death for all Russians at any moment, only seconds away –"

He stopped to sip some water. "What if, after we and the Russians agreed on peace, they put nuclear missiles and biolabs on our borders with Canada and Mexico? Wouldn't we respond?"

"But aren't you just trying to make money?" someone called. "Taking advantage of a crisis?"

Nat Reedy – Ross remembered – *MSNBC*. A spindly, cantankerous guy with a grudge against everything, which had earned him a small but devoted audience.

"This is not *any* crisis. By poisoning the closeness between brothers, we may destroy nearly all life on earth, which, as far as astrophysicists know, *may be the only life in the universe.* And the only people making money on this ghastly war are the U.S. and European war industries, and the politicians, bankers, and media who work for them."

"But you're bound to lose shareholders," Reedy protested.

"Eighty percent of Americans are terrified that a nuclear war is about to happen. Rawhide has the support of our biggest investors – the mutual funds, banking partnerships, insurance companies, and others. And we've polled a broad section of all our shareholders. Nearly everyone's on board. The few that weren't we offered a premium buyback, but nearly all refused. These are people who like to make money. And you can't make money if everybody's dead."

"What is the position of your Board?"

"They believe we're heading to a nuclear war. They see Rawhide's stand as a small way to impede this. Perhaps as a wake-up call."

"What about the average 401(k) investor?"

"They fear nuclear war too, and see that Rawhide is trying to stop it."

"What about your employees?"

"We're a team; we don't *have* employees. Twenty-seven thousand people who've made Rawhide what it is today – from Betsy Lincoln, our VP of Human Relations, who's helped grow the company since we were a two-room office in Billings, Montana, and Mitch Carter, our head financial genius, and Victor Minh, our engineering guru, down to the tanker drivers and LNG crews," and on and on he listed them, "and we've all thought it through, very carefully."

"You're not afraid of a media backlash?" Reedy cautioned.

"Most of the politicians and media work for the war machine. They don't realize how many Americans are terrified a nuclear war's about to happen. And there seems no way to stop the homicidal maniacs who are creating it."

They were standing now and peering over each other's shoulders, phones aimed at him.

"If you want to understand this Ukraine war," Ross added, "think of Cicero: *Cui bono: Who benefits?*

"Rawhide," he continued, "has its roots in North Dakota, Montana, and Wyoming. We're a tough, hard people, and we don't betray our friends. And we don't automatically do what we're told; we think about things carefully then do what we think is right. And deserting our relationships with our Russian partners would be to chicken out on a friend.

"However, the president keeps insanely escalating this perilous conflict between the world's *two largest and most dangerous nuclear arsenals*" – he waved a hand in disbelief – "that has put us already in the Third World War. And now with the White House's dangerous Iran payoffs and concessions, the whole Middle East is aflame. Unless we stop this, it will soon kill us all, not only us humans who have caused it, but nearly all life on earth."

"If this were true," someone called, "how could we stop it?"

"How to stop it? We are ruled by very powerful interests over which *we the people* have no control. This hideous, fatal Ukraine war and the Middle Eastern conflict that has grown from it – all this has been imposed on us, not by our own choice, but by the world's most powerful war machine. This coming election may not save us. And the war machine has so much economic, political, and media power they may win the election anyway.

"Do we hide our heads and hope our rulers let us live? Or like Rawhide, do we confront the pro-war mob in the White House, Congress, and media? Do we refuse to abandon loyal partners, neither Russia nor Ukraine, amidst this totally unnecessary war between brethren, created largely by the United States?"

They began to stir uneasily, as if embarrassed.

"In the unlikely event," Ross added, "that we don't have a nuclear war now, we have nonetheless created decades of sorrow and hatred toward the United States among the Russian and Ukrainian people. What could have been decades of peace and cooperation, economic growth and world harmony will now be decades of escalating danger as all sides continue to build faster and more explosive nuclear weapons in a spiral that will irrevocably lead to world death."

He looked out at them. Did anyone care?

LIZ THRASHED THROUGH BURNING OIL DRAGGING AN injured man behind her. He was babbling in Malay, half-conscious, face and head charred, arm broken. She reached a chunk of blistered polyurethane bobbing on the waves, two men clinging to it.

"Grab him!" she yelled in Malay, pulling the injured man onto the foam.

"*Leuka berat,*" one screamed. "He too bad hurt."

She swam back toward the flames, as close as she could get, seeking survivors, and turned toward a glint of light but it was just a burning tennis shoe. *New Balance*, it said; near it bobbed a tinfoil package, a chunk of wood, a visored cap with the words *Rawhide Indonesia*, a plastic cup.

Something rough-skinned and hard whacked her leg; she thought it was a burnt body, a broken beam, and ducked underwater but could see only fire-shadows and darkness.

"PUTIN CAUSED IT," SOMEONE CALLED. "YOU THINK WE SHOULDN'T make him suffer?" It was the linebacker lady from *NPR*, cell phone clutched like an amulet to her chest.

"This war was started long ago, intentionally," Ross answered. *How much,* he wondered, *would they listen to, be willing to consider?* "And the people suffering from it are the million Ukrainian and Russian dead or maimed for life, and their many millions of grieving families. Even worse, the complete reversal of decades of growing peace, prosperity, and world connectivity. And not one of those people who've died, or lost a loved one, would say it was worth it."

"But you're a family-owned corporation, so it's easier for you," called a chubby, crewcut CBS woman with a nose ring. "And you inherited your position –"

"My father was a wildcat driller in Montana, Wyoming, and North Dakota. I learned the business all the way up, from pipefitter and welder to CEO. I've negotiated billion-dollar deals and I've cleaned the restrooms in our offices. And everything in between. But we're not family-owned now; we're owned by thousands of investors, all over the world."

"Is this related," another woman called, "to your background in astrophysics? Your commitment to outer space, getting us off the planet?"

"Looking at the universe makes us aware of the unique magnificence of life. And the insanity of destroying it."

She seemed in her thirties, slender, a slightly Asian face. *Lily something*, the *Times*. She glanced at her notes. "You *are* an astrophysicist, have a PhD, worked at the Jet Propulsion Laboratory?"

The happiest days of my life – with Mary. "But after my father's unfortunate early death, I had to either take over Rawhide or see it sold to competitors with no interest in maintaining our wonderful team of people. Or all the investments we'd made in creating a better world . . ."

"And you see your refusal to comply with Russian sanctions as creating a better world?"

"Or at least saving the one we've got."

AS SHE WATCHED ROSS BULLOCK SPEAK, LILY HSIU WAS SURPRISED by two conflicting ideas. She'd read his past comments on climate change, that oil companies do cause climate change and pollution and enormous environmental damage, not even considering the secondary effects of automobiles, highways, roads and the entire asphalt and concrete world.

But he explained that in the short term there seemed no alternative: to shut off all these many billions of gallons of crude pumping each day out of the earth, was, in his words, to take us back to a more primitive world of whale oil, wood fires, and horse-drawn carriages. He'd argued strongly for nuclear power, but wasn't that because Rawhide owned nine percent of the world's uranium? Wasn't he, like all powerful men, surreptitiously pushing his own agenda?

And now he stood at the podium talking about nuclear war – what agenda was this? That was easy: Rawhide had contracts with Russian energy companies and was making billions of dollars a year from them. Wasn't he just protecting his own interests at the expense of world harmony? Hadn't the Russians – hadn't Putin – invaded Ukraine for no reason but to expand their hold over that poor country? To threaten the world?

It was clear: under the cloak of masculine fidelity to friends, Ross was protecting his own assets, his own multi-billion-dollar cash flow.

She would have to check on what he was saying had happened in the last thirty-plus years since the dissolution of the Soviet Union. That the U.S. had made all these non-aggression agreements with the Russians – no NATO expansion, no nuclear missiles on Russia's borders, no takeovers of Eastern European governments – but the U.S. had since then abrogated every promise, repeatedly betrayed the peace agreements it had signed. She couldn't remember this ever being covered in the *Times.*

None of this mattered anyway; it was just part of his excuse. Her article, her editor had made clear, was to debunk Ross's conspiracy statements about the dangers of nuclear war. The *Times,* he'd added, doesn't want the subject even raised, as it might hurt the president's odds of reelection. Therefore her job was to invalidate Bullock's claims, his sources, his ideas. "The view from the top," he'd said, "is this Bullock guy is dangerous, and in our own subliminal way we must make that clear."

Funny, she thought ironically, Ross didn't seem that dangerous . . . *Smart, yes, passionate, yes . . . But don't give him a break just because he's good-looking.*

She'd base her article on the Russian invasion as an assault on rules-based international order. That was the White House position. But Ross had just pointed out that the U.S. had a long history of assaults on international order, having engendered over eighty coups, wars, and invasions, overturning popularly elected governments, since the sordid devastation of Vietnam and the deaths of millions across Indochina, then followed by two invasions of Iraq, both for oil, and a twenty-year occupation of Afghanistan and other places in the

Middle East. No other country, and certainly not Russia, had killed anywhere near as many people.

Had to be bullshit.

The "US war machine," as Ross had called it, "spends more money on killing people than the next eleven countries together, and twelve times more than Russia. And has been working for years to create this Ukraine war."

Sounded crazy, but she would look it up.

Her own family's tragic memories – did she really want to disinter them now? Hadn't America been, for her, life-saving? What would have happened to her in China?

Through a gap between several people's heads, she scanned Ross. Tall and lithe, handsome in a quiet way, but a bit of a geek. A wounded veteran of the Bush 2 Iraq invasion and afterwards supposedly an astrophysicist. Then his father's death had catapulted him to president and chief operating officer of a Northern Rockies wildcatter that he soon turned into one of the world's most powerful energy companies? Had to be more to it than that.

He seemed too young, too lonely, disconnected. And now by refusing to join the sanctions and by warning of nuclear war, he'd permanently cut himself off from the world of brotherhood, patriotism and good feelings.

She felt a shiver of sorrow for him – and instantly killed it – for this self-annihilating gauntlet he'd cast down before the president. They were going to finish him off. He'd be called a conspiracy theorist, a traitor. They'd have him killed.

But who was *they*? She felt frustrated, uncertain, didn't like it.

Write the damn article, and get on with your life.

What life was that?

FROM THE BACK OF THE ROOM SOMEONE YELLED, "BUT WE'VE SEEN how the Russians interfered in our 2016 elections –"

Ross cut in. "Numerous investigations by government attorneys from both parties found no evidence, despite wanting to, of any such interference. The entire scam seems to have come from the Clinton campaign via a discredited British spy. But the Russians, who had done nothing, felt unjustly blamed, and this put one more nail in the coffin of world peace."

"Aren't you just a defeatist, pro-Russian?"

He tried not to grimace. "It's the ancient question: Do I defend my country right or wrong, which has gotten us into so many ghastly wars over many years, including one I've been in? Or can we force our government to stop when it leads us and the world down the path of destruction?

"The world . . ." He stopped to look at them, trying to reach each one, "depends on *you* – the media – to speak the truth. One of the reasons public confidence in the media – in *you* – is the lowest in history is because you often *don't* say the truth. And the truth right now is that we are facing nuclear annihilation. So it's time for you to say it."

Mitch Carter barged to the microphone. "Mr. Bullock's got a plane to catch. We'll cut the questions now and ask you to refer to your press kits." Snatching Ross's elbow, he propelled him from the lectern, the other vice presidents closing round him as if he were a defeated boxer being escorted from the ring. "Hold it!" Ross said. "I don't have to catch any damn plane!"

"Yeah, you do." Mitch's cherubic face was flushed. Ross wondered if he'd been drinking. "See what all your fancy talk brings us?" Mitch snapped.

Ross didn't understand. "What?"

"Makassar just blew."

4

THEY

"SELL US SHORT, all you can!" Mitch Carter hissed into his phone.

"No!" Ross snapped. "Not one share!" he yelled. "Betsy! What do I tell these jackals?"

"It just hit Reuters," someone called.

"Tell them the truth," Betsy answered.

"Say nothing," Mitch said in his rough voice. "Show grief and distress, say we're on top of it."

"The shutoff valves on the lower pipes have stopped it," Victor Minh said, "no more gas is escaping."

"Where's my plane?" Ross called.

"Hong Kong."

"Get a rental. Something fast. We'll meet them with the chopper –"

Beyond the glass walls of his office the sun was sinking between cliffs of concrete, glass and steel. "The markets," he yelled at Mitch. "Don't pull *any*thing!"

"Play it your way." Mitch snapped. "We'll only lose thirty a share."

"And when it hits bottom, we start a buyback. That's our story."

"Buyback? With what?"

Ross glanced through the two round windows in the leather-padded door leading into the press auditorium, where journalists milled like disaffected sheep. "Betsy, please get my overnight bag. You, too," he said to Mitch, "you're going, and you too, Betsy – get your things. Victor! I need you too."

Victor Minh was trembling, running skinny fingers through his lank hair. *The platform's his baby,* Ross thought, conscious of Minh wanting a cigarette, some way to deal with this tragedy that nothing could deal with.

Ross shoved through the doors into the auditorium and snapped on the mike. A few journalists glanced up, others still on their phones. "We've just had an explosion."

They flocked like chickens to corn. "One of our gas platforms in the Makassar Strait between Borneo and Sulawesi. We don't know yet about our people. I'm going there now. Nadine Kowalski, our VP Communications, will keep you informed."

"Soon as we know anything –" he fought down the tears in his throat "– so will you."

The journalists headed for the doors. Ross, Mitch, Victor, and Betsy took the red-carpeted elevator to the garage and a limo to the Downtown Heliport. Hands over ears, they ducked under the chopper's whirring blades, its downblast flaying their clothes.

Ross climbed in beside the pilot. The Sikorsky rose, spinning slightly as it soared up from the East River and the Staten Island Ferry terminal toward Newark, around the gray, grim towers of Wall Street, the emptiness where the World Trade Center had stood, the peaks of Chrysler and Empire State to starboard, cars thronging like a million bright ants in the streets below.

Endless windows gleamed in thousands of streets of apartments and office skyscrapers; steam rose from many thousands of furnaces, from power plants and cogenerators; the entire region below throbbed with light and movement. *How,* he wondered briefly, *can we shut this down? What can we find to replace it?*

His mind turned back to Makassar. There'd be no survivors – how could there be, if the thing blew?

But how could it blow?

He turned to the helicopter pilot. "What we got?"

"Dassault Elan. Two pilots and a stew. Refuel and crew change at Sigonella Naval Air Station in Sicily. Arrival Kalimantan in sixteen hours." The pilot eased the stick forward as the chopper crossed the glittering black Hudson to New Jersey.

"It's that goddamn valve cluster," Mitch Carter yelled over the chopper roar.

"That wouldn't blow," Victor snapped. "Not like this."

"How many times," Mitch's said angrily, "did I ask you? *Beg* you?"

"The shutoff valves in the lower pipes and the sea lines should cut all oil and gas flow instantaneously," Ross said, "before the valve cluster would blow."

"These journalists," Betsy said. "They're human when we're on top, but the instant we start going down, they'll rip us apart."

Ross broke from trying to imagine the explosion, how it might have happened. "We're not *going* down."

HALF-BLIND AND CHOKING ON OIL AND SMOKE, LIZ SWAM IN circles around the smoldering platform but found only one person, a shivering Scotsman named Callister. She towed him to the floating polyester. The first man she'd brought was gone.

"He die," one of the two Malays said. "We push him off."

"No room," the other Malay said, prying away Callister's hands. He had a head wound, waves washing his blood. She thought of sharks and pulled up her legs.

"Burnt," Callister hoarsed. "Burnt lungs inside."

A wave knocked him off the foam. She dragged him back. "Burnt lungs," he gasped. "God help." The Malay with the head wound blinked through his blood, chunks of foam breaking off in his hands, waves crashing over him.

Soon choppers had to come. The Balikpapan base was only an hour away. The Emergency Management System would've instantly alerted the base; they'd have known anyway from the pressure drop in the pipeline. They'd have known from the sudden stop in the data stream up to the satellites or when they tried to connect. They'd know.

Or would they? For a moment she almost recognized the hammering beat of a chopper, but it was just new flames bursting from the molten platform.

The bleeding Malay screeched and leaped up from the foam, clawing at the sky, fell back, and was dragged off in a thrash of water.

"Chuchut!" the other screamed. "Shark!"

A gritty beam smashed into her legs. The Malay fought to climb on the foam, shoving her and Callister under. She came up choking, the foam tipped and dumped them off, the Malay's knees smashing her face. A wave knocked her back under.

She fought to the surface. The Malay scrambled over her, pushing her down, his elbow cracking her nose. Her hand hit a head. Callister.

In a great sucking splash the Malay and the foam vanished.

The sea frothed with foam and flesh. Callister yanked her down by the hair, air bursting from her lungs. She broke free; he snatched her ankle. Through thunder and sudden light came a roar flattening the waves. A rope snaked down out of the light and smacked the water.

Callister's fingers clamped her throat. She pried them loose, got behind him, and swam him toward the rope. The shark hit, knocking them apart. Someone hanging from the rope reached for her.

She turned Callister toward the sling. "Here!" she yelled, coughing water.

Callister went down. She couldn't pull him up. A wave yanked him away. She could not find him. Hands pulled her into the sling. "Callister!" she screamed. "Callister!"

His head sloshed up. She grabbed him; the sling tightened. The waves split apart, and a huge dark maw roared up and tore him from her arms. The sling spun her up into the helicopter's open door.

THE DASSAULT RACED DOWN THE RUNWAY PAST THE QUEUED airliners with their flashing tails and wingtips, and rocketed nearly straight up into the night, the yellow blotch of New York and the East Coast vanishing westward behind them. When it levelled out, Ross went into the master bedroom and lay down.

Beyond the plexiglass, the early night blazed with stars. He thought of the oily sun sinking between the buildings and how he'd kept it in his mind when he spoke to the reporters, that it brought peace to focus on something. Like the burning platform.

He changed into a sweatshirt, jeans and running shoes, washed his face, and went back to the living room. "You guys all call home?"

"Done," Betsy said.

He took a beer from the reefer and sat in a leather armchair with the bottle cold against his thigh. Betsy, still in her gray suit, silk blouse, and silver nylons, was cross-checking computer lists of employees on the platform. Victor knelt on the carpet amid blueprints and engineering drawings. Mitch was hunched over the phone, talking to Jakarta.

Mitch waved them over. On his computer was an aerial shot of a twisted, blazing pile of metal in a flaming sea. Underneath was written, *First flyover by Indonesian Air Force. No survivors sighted.*

"Strange," Victor said, "it happened in the middle of your press conference."

"Don't blame a tragedy due to poor design," Mitch snapped, "on a press conference."

"Maybe it's what we get," Victor countered, "for messing with the big guys."

"Going forward," Ross said, "we suspend dividends, investments and expansions, any budgeted items we can postpone, all that."

"That shows we're weak," Mitch snapped. "That we've been hurt."

"Of course we've been hurt. This shows the financial markets that we're taking the steps to deal with it, that we're fighting back."

Mitch shook his head. "I don't agree."

"And over the next few days, we're going to start raising funds from under-leveraged assets all over the world. Billions in cash, to deal with this."

They were in clouds, out the window only darkness. The engines raised pitch as the pilot climbed above the clouds. The fuel in this plane, Ross thought, that would carry them half way around the world – came from deep in the earth. Or under the sea. "If they hit this plane," he said, "you realize they get us all?"

"Don't be silly," Betsy said. "Anyway, who's *they?*"

5

TRAPS

LIZ ROSE from the depths to warm sunlight. Someone was near, protective. She enjoyed this feeling for a moment, floated to consciousness.

A chunky man in a tight blue blazer sat beside her hospital bed. Pouched lips, half-bald with a fringe of graying curly hair, unshaven sagging cheeks, a frazzled air. "What *is* this?" she whispered, shocked by her hoarseness.

"Jakarta," he said. "Hospital. I just dropped by to . . ."

"It blew up? The platform?"

He looked at her. "Yes."

"I don't know *how* . . ." She drifted away.

"We don't either."

"I know you, can't remember –"

"Mitch Carter. Our CFO." He patted her hand. "Tell me, what happened?"

"I was standing on the third deck . . ." Talking hurt her burnt throat. " . . . It was about three a.m."

"Why were you there?"

"Looking at the stars."

He laid a gentle hand on her shoulder. "And you thought the fire came out of the water?"

"Where it started, below the valve cluster –"

The hand withdrew. "My dear, it couldn't have started *under*water."

"It *did*."

He shook her arm, rattling her intravenous tubes. "Think more carefully. We need your help. The accident would've started on the first deck."

"No!" She yanked her arm away, searing her burns.

Ross Bullock came in. He was taller and younger than in the photos. He wore black-framed glasses and seemed sad and lonely. "I'm glad to see you."

"She's pretty mixed up," Mitch said. "Doesn't remember much. At three a.m. she was out on Deck Three."

"I like to go up there," she husked. "Before dawn, the Southern Cross –"

"You sure you weren't on the first deck, above the valve cluster?" Mitch said.

"Why would I be down there?"

"You tell me."

"There's plenty of time," Ross said, "to get into this."

"I want out of here," she croaked.

"We're working on that."

"Working on it? What's the problem?"

"The Indonesians," Mitch said. "Pulling their usual crap . . ."

She rose up on her elbows. "You tell them . . ."

"Lie down," Ross said softly. "You've got some nasty burns, a sprained ankle, multiple abrasions. You need rest."

"Try to remember the sequence," Mitch put in. "How it happened. Not just when it blew on the low deck, but anything you remember before that. Any unimportant little detail, anything strikes your mind –"

"I've told you," Liz said, "what strikes my mind."

From the foot of the bed, Ross smiled wearily down at her. Three pens were clipped in his shirt pocket. He wore a wedding ring. She remembered hearing that his wife had died five years ago. He seemed a vital man, but washed-out, exhausted.

"We have to meet the Indonesian families," he said. "Then the Ministry, Pertamina. Betsy Lincoln, VP of Human Relations, she'll be by to see you."

In the corridor, carts of stained bedding and empty wheelchairs slowed the way. Mitch took Ross's arm. "Like I said, she just doesn't remember. And I don't buy this looking at the stars crap. Interesting that she's the only one who escaped."

Ross shook his head. "For the moment, we take her word."

Mitch stopped him. "I didn't want to say in there, but we got the results of the computer simulation. It's consistent with a low deck explosion."

"Above waterline?"

"Or at it."

"And what caused it?"

"That's what I want to know. And what she was doing on the third deck. If that's where she was."

THE ARMORED BLACK MERCEDES WAITED FOR THEM OUTSIDE the hospital with A/C full on. As they slipped into the cool rear seat, Ross took a folded sheet from his pocket. "Victor and I've called nearly half the families of the people on the platform. Another sixty to go."

"We only got eighteen minutes to get to the chopper." Mitch glanced at his phone. "Fucking Jesus, sixty-four point two-nine. Our stock drops any more, the sharks start gathering."

Ross's phone was vibrating constantly. He let them all go except his media director Bruce Sullivan's private phone. It was 3:21 a.m. in New York, so this was serious. "The latest news," Sullivan husked, "we're getting destroyed on social media . . ."

"Who?"

"Our Thread feed suddenly has seven million people hating us. They're going to shut us down, won't even let us respond."

"What the fuck for?"

"They say we're disseminating false information about the accident –"

"That's nuts! We've been completely open, expressing our sorrow, promising to get to the bottom of this!"

"Doesn't matter. Most of the media are calling us an environmental menace, don't even want to hear our side. It's crazy, if they all drop the boom on us, we're done."

"They'll get over it," Ross said, an optimism he didn't feel.

"Subsea gas pipe pressure ratings –" Victor Minh was quoting from *The Subsea Engineering Handbook* – "are incorporated into the pipe size factor, as shown here: Base Cost C0 ($\times$106 USD); Min. = 2.0 | Avg. = 3.0 | Max. = 4.0; Base Materials: Carbon steel; Pressure: 10 ksi."

"What the fuck," Mitch sighed, "is ksi?"

"One thousand pounds per square inch. So if those pipes were carbon steel . . ."

Ross glanced up from the list of families he had to call. "They *were* carbon steel."

"Ten ksi," Victor added patiently, "means they can withstand pressures of ten thousand pounds per square inch. So there's no way those pipes would have blown without some external force . . ."

"External force?" Mitch smiled.

"A bomb."

"Bullshit."

Victor stared out the limo's darkened window at the city. No matter how many times he'd run these numbers through his head, there was no way that corrosion or other natural processes had doomed those carbon steel pipes. He'd explained this to the insurance pool, given them the analysis from the *Subsea Handbook*: "Cost of a typical subsea manifold can be estimated by *(6-7)C=fs ·fn ·ft ·C0+Cmisc,* where *C*= cost of the manifold; f_t= manifold type factor (cluster, PLEM); f_n= number-of-slot factor; f_s = pipe size factor; and C_0= basic cost; and C_{misc}: *miscellaneous cost not common to all manifolds.*"

What the hell did that mean – "miscellaneous cost not common to all manifolds"?

He pushed back, worrying, against the limo's glossy seat.

FROM THE CHOPPER'S PLEXIGLASS WINDOW, THE RUINED platform looked like a half-sunk battleship trailing a purple sheen, salvage boats scurrying around it. Ross pulled off his ear protectors and bent forward to the pilot. "Go lower."

The rotor pitch deepened as the chopper dropped. The blackened towers rose nearer, the hulking charred machines and blasted windows. Shreds of burnt catwalk drooped in the sea; the platform's Kodiaks and lifeboats had melted in their racks. Above the caved-in chopper pad a fire nozzle jutted up, a stump of hose dangling from it.

"Like I said," the pilot told them, "nowhere to land."

"You see how those pipes burst?" Victor called. "It wouldn't blow there. Not naturally."

"That was downward pressure," Mitch yelled. "From the first deck."

A diver surfaced, his yellow tanks bright against the swell. "Those are the guys," Victor said, "who found where the valves blew below the platform. Now they're cutting off the damaged pipe at eighty deep and capping it. The ocean floor substructure is still good . . . all we have to do is –"

"Sell it," Mitch said.

"There's too much gas down there," Ross said, "to sell it."

"Either we rehab it, at a billion and a half, or sell the field."

"The insurance pool should cover everything, including revenue loss for five years," Victor said. "That gives us time to rebuild with not too much drop in cash flow."

The chopper climbed to five thousand feet and swung back north toward Borneo. The towering white clouds thinned, their shadows shark-like across the blue sea.

In his mind Ross, could see nothing but the shattered, charred platform, could think only of the lives that had been lost there, many in agony, the thousands of grieving families and friends.

How, despite ironclad safety precautions, had this happened?

The pilot slid a clipboard log onto his knee and began to write; Ross felt envy for such straightforward tasks. Mitch was tapping fingers on his seat and staring out the window. Victor was bent over engineering drawings of the valve cluster and punching numbers into his phone.

Tiny fishing boats trailed hairline wakes across the velvet sea. Borneo's dark coast widened toward them across the horizon.

They started to descend. Along the coast, wide arrowheads of fish traps pointed out to sea. Fish swam in with the tide but when it went out they kept swimming with the tide, instead of turning back, as the nets funneled them toward the narrowing closed ends. And when the tide turned, the fishermen came out and got them.

The altimeter began to dip, its little dial racing backwards, making Ross wish one could reverse time.

Borneo's coast rose in a muddy green carpet toward far peaks patched with remnants of rain forest. Most of the jungle had been clearcut and shipped to Chinese furniture makers or to mills to make decks, countertops and toilet paper in America and Europe, and now the great Mahakam River spilled its guts of brown eroded earth into the sea, and the few remaining orangutans starved as the palm oil corporations razed their last retreats.

Before he'd seen it, Ross had imagined the Mahakam as a mysterious dark river out of Conrad, an impenetrable jungle of dreams and dangers. *If you take away the jungle, does the heart of darkness vanish too?*

The chopper landed in a spray of mud at Balikpapan, the major city on Kalimantan, on the Indonesian side of Borneo. New rain had left great puddles on the red earth in which blue sky and white cumulus fluttered. Bulldozers rumbled and clanked, building a new runway. A Garuda Indonesia Airbus thundered past, two others waiting behind it.

It seemed impossible that only decades ago these people were shrinking each other's heads and nailing them over their doors. Now they drove SUVs to malls with Paris and New York fashions, with iPhones and Facebook and all that other shit.

RAWHIDE'S BALIKPAPAN OFFICE SAT ON A SIDE STREET BEHIND the Islamic Center. "Let's keep this," Mitch said, "to half an hour, max."

"Calm down," Ross said. "We need to stay as long as they want."

"You say too much," Victor interrupted, "they take it as weakness."

Over two hundred dark somber faces awaited them in the conference room. Hands clasped before him, he stood in front, next to Victor. "There is nothing I or anyone can say," he began, waiting for Victor to translate into Malay, "to help you in your sorrow. I would trade my own life" – *is that true*, he wondered, *would I?* – "to have stopped this horrible accident –"

"No accident!" a woman yelled in English.

"We'll soon know. And if . . ."

"*You* did it!" called out a man with a round pocked face and black hair over his brows.

"Ignore him!" Victor whispered.

"Rawhide has always been one family," Ross said. "Those of you who've worked in our other operations – the U.S., Europe, South America – you know this. So we've all lost sons, brothers . . ."

While Victor translated Ross watched the grim, unresponsive faces, trying to see into dark eyes that stared back with hatred.

Why, he wondered, *do they hate? Has someone told them to?*

"As you know," he said, "Rawhide has been one of the world's fastest growing companies. But no success is worth a single person's life. This platform on which your loved-ones worked had great value for the world. It gave energy, and growth . . ." Again he waited for Victor to translate. "I promise we'll find the cause of this accident and that everyone who has lost a wage earner will be kept at that wage."

"No accident!"

Ross scanned the crowd and caught out a small, dark-haired man with bushy eyebrows.

"*You* blew it up!" This one was taller, curly-haired, hands in the pockets of a tan leather jacket.

The loudening rumble of Malay filled the room. "I lose my husband!" a short woman in a ragged black sweater screamed in English. "And you not care!"

Ross raised a hand to hold back the noise. "Anyone who thinks that, come see me."

Something flashed under the lights and a bottle smacked the edge of the stage and spun back into the crowd. *"You!"* Ross yelled. "You by the aisle there!"

A muscular man in an orange T-shirt, a round bull head, elbowed toward the back door. "Stop him!" Ross called.

"What you care?" said the woman in the black sweater. "Take you insurance money. Go home!"

He stepped toward her. *"What* insurance money?"

The faces staring at him were closed, unreadable. He felt a horrible chagrin for intruding on their sorrow. As he turned toward Victor, an awful pain cracked open his forehead, knocking him back, and he fought to keep from falling as the room roared and spun around him.

Victor was yelling in Malay and everyone was screaming. Warmth spilled down Ross's face. A bottle smashed against the wall, glass tinkling down.

"It's not true," Ross yelled. "You mustn't think this!"

A pretty young woman surged to the front, dark glasses, hair hidden by a Muslim scarf. She reached inside her gown, and he tried to block what he thought was a gun but it was a cup of black liquid she threw on him.

Mitch hustled him through the door past a double line of police, rocks and bottles hitting around them, one policeman struck on a cheek by a rock but not flinching as blood spurted down his face. Ross raised his hand to smell the black liquid the woman had thrown at him.

Crude.

The driver raced at the crowd that split apart, stones crashing off the windows. "Hustle!" Mitch yelled. "Hospital!"

"No," Victor answered. "Don't let them see he's hurt. Doctor. Hotel."

In the courtesy mirror, Ross's face was black with blood down one side, the yellow coronas of streetlights flashing past. "They didn't fight back, those cops," he said. "They could have stopped it."

"Those people yelling," Victor said, "they vanish. They come to only make everyone angry. Then they disappear."

"That woman – what'd she say about insurance?" Mitch glanced back at Ross. "Oh Christ, look at you. How you gonna meet the minister tomorrow?"

Ross remembered the fish traps along the coast, the ranks of netted pylons like arrows narrowing toward the sea. *Like a fish,* he thought. *To get out of a trap, you have to swim against the tide.*

But what was the trap? Which way was the tide?

6

LORD DURVON ST. MILES

S INCE THE U.S.-RUSSIAN WAR IN UKRAINE began, Durvon St. Miles had made a lot more money. His shares in Lockheed Martin, Honeywell, Raytheon, Boeing, General Dynamics, and Northrop Grumman had more than doubled, and he'd made another fortune buying and selling these weapons directly to the same markets.

After years of unprofitable peace, the merchants of death had revived the Cold War and escalated it into an even deadlier Third World War all over the globe, sparking the greatest explosion of weapon and nuclear warhead production in the eighty years since the Second World War.

Ukraine offered endless black market deals on U.S. weapons at substantial discounts. Very few U.S. weapons were tracked, and Ukraine had always been a hotbed of corruption. Not only were American weapons companies doing huge deals, but also their politicians, lawyers, subcontractors, PR firms, and media were helping every way they could.

And with the Middle East aflame and wars all over Africa and elsewhere, everybody was buying weapons. While the big guys were threatening each other with nuclear war.

"They should be more careful what they wish for," St. Miles chuckled to his pug, Winston. "They may get more war than they plan for." Winston licked his nose and sniffled, watching St. Miles' pocket for a treat.

Learning history, St. Miles had several times told Winston, quickly disabuses one of any notion that humans are loving and good. Instead, humans were often horribly evil, while considering themselves good.

And though humans fussed a lot about peace, what they really loved was war. Driven by their media (*If it bleeds, it leads*), war was the full-time livelihood of many politicians, corporations, lobbyists, universities, think tanks, and others who gamble with human lives.

Because their love for killing was rooted in the most ancient corners of their brains, they were unlikely to change. Thus it was wiser to see humans as they really were, rather than what they thought they were. Wiser to recognize that war is a constant, no matter what you say or do. You just have to pick the best wars, nurture and grow them. Because any year of war is more profitable than many years of peace.

He'd often wondered why some people acted distressed about all the earnest young souls who went off to war and died, often in great agony and horror. But weren't they fools, for swallowing the lie?

If your country wants you to die, find another country.

In a similar vein, it can be profitable to first ruin a company then take it over. A good way is a futures short stock contract on it, a bet that it will decline in value. This meant that at a specific time in the future, you can sell the stock and profit from the difference between what it was and its new lower price.

Then you start talking the stock down, suggest to analysts they give it a warning, and people begin dumping their shares. Like a landslide the momentum builds, more and more investors hear your warning, the stop-loss orders start kicking in, others see the stock dropping, get nervous and sell too. It's helpful at this point to pull in the media, which is always happy to make things worse. When the stock drops as far as you think it'll go, you unload your short position, use those funds to buy even more of the stock, take a long position on it as it rises, and exit your long position once the stock climbs to where it was to start with.

As a result, a lot of dumb fuckers lose their life's investments, but that's democracy for you.

A famous example was how George Soros broke the British pound. He borrowed a lot of money to buy pounds, then talked the pound down till the government was forced to devalue it. He then bought the pound again after it had been devalued and repaid the money he'd borrowed, making billions for himself while destroying the savings of millions of people.

And then used some of his billions to try to destroy America by encouraging crime everywhere – but what was he going to do as the country fell apart – buy it?

But it isn't always that easy, the voice in the back of his head reminded him. If you sell short but the stock doesn't drop, you have to keep putting in money to cover your position. If the price stays high, you can lose your money. Lots of it.

The trick is to borrow enough to cover your margins.

Funny that all it takes to make money is money.

He swung his feet off his desk and stared absently through the window at the rainy London dusk. Early headlights on Trafalgar Square trickled down the ancient glass. He scowled at the computer screens lined across his desk. Rawhide had fallen to sixty-one and change, still dropping. The Moscow woman had called to tell him to watch it, and she'd been a good source in the past, happy to get her fifteen percent of every deal she turned him on to.

He reached to press the intercom but didn't, got up and took three ice cubes from the freezer, poured four fingers of thirty-two-year-old Talisker into a crystal glass, and gulped it down.

"Remember the good," Doctor Emry kept saying. "You've got more money than you can ever spend, a magnificent castle, and lovely properties all over the world, all the sexual escapades you want – *and* – you're up for a peerage – *Lord* Durvon St. Miles."

Such crap. Doctor Emry might be a famous psychologist, but he didn't know shit about what was good. About how it didn't exist.

39

Ironically, it *would* be good to tell these homicidal maniacs in Washington, Kiev, London, Paris and Moscow, *Be careful with this nuclear war stuff.*

How can we make money if we're all dead?

But like Doctor Emry and the other people who lived in their heads, the people who created these wars could invent reasons for anything.

That war is patriotic. That lies are true. Killing is good. Desire for someone is called love, when actually you just want to shove your prick up their ass and dominate them like they want to be dominated. And the moment you cut off the money, they go away, and you've got to buy someone else.

Just like war.

War's just capitalism, he'd always told Winston. Like the wars in Sudan and Yemen he'd made good money on. *Maybe now Myanmar. Maybe soon Iran, but that will be a big one. It will spark a cornucopia of small ones.,*

In recent years he'd made several billion pounds betting on small wars likely to need weapons. They'd been delightful, like infatuations that leave a smoldering memory. And in other wars, too, and in the crude oil markets so fatally linked to them. War, of course, was fabulous for crude markets, and many wars had been created solely to boost crude prices.

So when you saw a war coming, you bet long on crude.

No matter which way the needle moved, he'd usually figured it out beforehand. Or learned it from the scandalous fools who would tell him their dirtiest secrets for a few thousand quid.

The actual impact of these wars, and the misery and financial suffering they caused for the many while enriching the few, delighted him no end. He'd grown up smaller and more fearful than most other boys in his part of Brixton and the borough of Lambeth, and the local thugs hadn't let him forget it. Hadn't they called him "girly," the butt who played the grinning fool while his tormenters goaded him? A foot shorter and a stone lighter, how could he fight eight thugs? Even if he'd dared?

But he'd gotten them back. This vast London townhouse, the Cotswold castle, the 16th century palace on Île de la Cité, the Spanish olive farm and the Caribbean hideaway, the sleek Citation waiting in its London City hangar. While the thugs and their kin moldered beer-sodden in their mews and 'garden apts' in miserable corners of the increasingly-miserable and overflowing cities of what had once been Great Britain.

Again he turned to a computer screen. *These Rawhide guys*, the Moscow woman had said, *are going to be fed to the lions. You want to get in on the feast?*

Rawhide was still dropping. Somebody was going to smell blood in the water. Soon.

A dumb fuck, this Rawhide guy. Trying to make peace. He should be shot.

Weariness hit him, a sense of being old, of not wanting to fight any more. *When you stop fighting,* he reminded himself, *you die.*

The ancient sea captain's clock in the corner bonged four. If he listened he might hear Big Ben in the distance, but no, not with this rain. He could still have Malcolm tell Chet to ready the plane for Marbella tonight. No, that was a bore. The trouble with being so rich, he'd told Doctor Emry, is that nothing appeals to you anymore. Not that Emry would understand.

He reached for the buzzer but pulled back his hand. When you don't know what to do, Mom had always said, do nothing.

He poured himself more single malt, took a gold snuff box from his top drawer, spooned a line of coke on his desk and sucked it up with a silver straw, wet his finger, wiped up the last dust and licked it.

The rain beat harder against his window. He snuggled warmly into his chair. *Even if you're not happy, you're still better off than almost anybody else.*

In the penumbra of the window, he glimpsed the reflection of his top-floor office, the hand-detailed walnut wainscots and gleaming oak floors, the ebony desk big enough to park his Rolls, the antiques, the Turners on the walls, the Picasso of a naked boy from the rear, bending over . . .

Even if you're miserable you're better off than almost anybody else. He'd tried to make Doctor Emry understand that – Emry who only talked to him for five hundred an hour.

He caught his image in the window. Cadaverous, hanging jowls, gleaming skull and low-lidded eyes: *you're not the beauty you used to be.* "You've got turkey neck," Cavendish at the club had joked, "your neck skin hangs like wattles off your chin." He should have Plimpton take it in. But for all the money he'd paid Plimpton, his face still looked old.

And the little boys, the soft ones with silky skin and girlish laughter, they scorned men who looked old. Demanded more money.

No matter how many surgeries, how many injections and transfusions and pills and all-night sexcapades and watching what he ate and drank and all that rot, every day he was getting uglier and older.

Outside the window, it had turned cold and gray, the rain coming down hard. Why live here and not Marbella? His vineyards and olive trees in red rich soil under the golden sun, the white villa beneath ancient widespread trees . . . the Spanish boys. The young Moroccans, fresh from the Straits, their hairless genitals and velvet mouths.

Lord Durvon St. Miles.

The headlights on Trafalgar brightened as night fell. The cocaine spread delightfully through him. *Take anything you want.* But even *that* didn't matter. Even cocaine wasn't what it used to be. Even the testosterone and growth hormone and other bioidentical gunk they shoved in his veins wasn't keeping him young. But by the time Levitra didn't work anymore, there'd be something else. He raised his empty glass to human ingenuity, and pressed the buzzer.

"Yes, sir," Malcolm said instantly.

"Have Douglas put away the car. I'm staying in town tonight."

He'd been wanting to take a crude bet now but was afraid of the dollar. When the dollar climbed, crude dropped. The Fed couldn't help fucking things up.

Weapons, crude, cocaine, boys, and single malt.

When nuclear war came, was there a way to profit from that too?

THE HEAD DIVER WAS A TALL AUSTRALIAN WITH SHORT BLACK HAIR, tanned darker than a Malay. He smelled of crude; dried salt whitened the backs of his hands.

In the conference room at Rawhide's Balikpapan office, he opened his iPad to a row of underwater photos. "Those pipes blew all the way down to sixty feet."

"Where did it start?" Ross asked.

"Somewhere between sixty feet and just below the valve cluster. For now, that's all we can tell."

"It wouldn't look like this," Victor said, "if it started on the first deck."

"Not true." Mitch turned to Ross. "See what you did, your fucking announcement?"

"About the war?"

"We're right to take a stand," Betsy put in. "The White House has canceled its No First Strike agreement. All the treaties have been killed. There's no communication any more between us and Russia. At any moment, we could all die."

The doctor came and with small delicate hands sewed seven stitches in Ross's temple, under the hairline. "What would make people turn against us?" he asked her.

"Sorrow."

The police chief came clasping his visored cap over his ample belly. He had a gregarious full mouth, acne-scarred cheeks, and eyes like periwinkles. "Throwing bottles? Surely outside agitators. Have full confidence, we find."

Ross fingered his pounding temples. "How?"

The chief thought. "Have full confidence."

"Guy couldn't find his pecker," Mitch said when the chief left, "in his own pants."

"Hey," Betsy said, "I've known men like that."

"It'll be all over the Jakarta morning news, Ross. Then all over Wall Street," Mitch sighed, "you being attacked, chased out of that meeting. When it hits the Nikkei . . ."

"It's a distraction. The real issue is our platform's blown. We don't know how. We have a hundred thirty-one dead people plus one survivor in the hospital, but the Indonesians won't let her out."

"Using her as a pawn," Victor said.

"Our shares are down to fifty-nine." Mitch sat heavily. "And the bond market will trash our rating. There'll be months of negative cash flow till the insurance kicks in. If it even kicks in." He faced down, looking at his hands. "Because the damn insurance pool, they'll fuck with us."

"When you signed the contract, Mitch," Victor insisted, "you locked them in."

"If we postpone capex for three months," Ross said, "freeze expenditures, sell the Emirates leases, refi some low-leveraged assets, we can handle the cash flow."

Mitch pursed his lips. "If nothing else goes wrong."

"And we have the payments to the families," Victor said.

"The big ones hit later. After the insurance."

"Our stock keeps dropping –" Mitch said.

"We can survive this," Ross said.

"Not if it don't stop."

A BOARD OF DIRECTORS CAN BE HELPFUL OR DESTRUCTIVE. A helpful board works as a team to nourish, advise, and grow the company. A destructive board is made up of enemies who work together, when needed, to control, overturn and sometimes even rip a company apart.

It was the third video board meeting this week of Rawhide Holdings, Inc. (*Nasdaq 100: RWHD*). The screen automatically switched to whoever was speaking. If more than one person spoke, the screen would split. These meetings drove Ross crazy because now that everything was going to hell, everyone wanted to pick a fight, to show they were smarter than he was, than the others. But few of their imperative suggestions made sense, and they were clogging his time with expectations and demands. "We should do," they all kept saying. But none of them did.

It was one of the toughest things he'd had to do, early on, as the company grew, to switch from a small board of family members, just his father and mother, his uncle Ralph, and the family accountant and lawyer, all since deceased. But to expand, he had to sell shares in the company – he'd had to bring in shareholder members, often those "recommended by major investors: Jim Burleigh, a Texas oil engineer, Deborah Quinn, a senior McKinsey partner, Samsal Younane, an international financier, and Asa Chomsky, the math genius. And two months ago, they'd voted Jim Burleigh Chairman.

So now as Chief Executive Officer, CEO, as well as a Board member, Ross had to report to Jim, and to the Board, on how he was running his own family company. Luckily, he'd been able to appoint Mitch Carter and Victor Minh to the Board as allies if needed. But Mitch was growing more reticent by the day.

"It's time," Jim Burleigh said, "to rethink this."

Angry and tired, Ross snapped back, "Rethink *what?*"

"Your damn peace talk."

"Don't be an ass," Ross said, instantly wishing to take it back. "Jim, you lost a son in Iraq, I was wounded there – listen, please, we *have* to stop this war! Or it's the end. For everyone, life on Earth!"

"We're still with you on this," Deborah Quinn broke in. "But we have to step softly, stay out of the limelight . . . They're like a pack of hyenas out there, the moment they get you down."

THE SPIDER CREPT ACROSS THE TILE CEILING, KEEPING TO THE DARK mossy patches, toward the moth bumbling around the light. Tensing its long legs, it sprang and pinned the moth against the ceiling, but the moth broke free and the spider fell huge and hairy on Liz's face. She slapped it aside; it scrambled under the covers, and she leaped out of bed, grabbed a chair, and whacked the bed till the spider was a brown stain in the sheets.

She yanked on her robe and slippers, gasping from the pain in her sprained ankle. Outside the grimy window, the late-night lights of Jakarta flickered bleakly. In the corridor, hard-edged boots passed. She listened to them thunk down the stairs to the floor below.

If she left the hospital it could get Rawhide in trouble. As if they weren't already. But the Indonesians had no right to make her stay. She scowled at the flyspecked photo of President Widodo on the wall, and cracked open the door.

No one in the corridor. At the far end a flickering yellow light. A distant radio's tinny chant. Snores, groans, and mumbling from other rooms, the hazy buzz of neon.

Her slippers whispered across the gritty tiles; her ankle and the burnt skin of her thighs roaring with pain. The lockers were up ahead, with her clothes.

The thick yellow air stank of bleach, stale curry, and urine. An old woman jumped back from a doorway, white eyes staring.

No lockers at this end. Liz turned back, but the hard footsteps reached the top of the far stairs and thumped toward her down the hall. She ducked into a dark room, bumping a metal pan that clattered across the floor.

The boots clicked, nearer. Silence, then a man yelling. She edged to the door and looked out.

A soldier stood outside her room yelling into his radio. He had a shiny helmet and a rifle slung vertically. She ducked back from the doorway.

"Hah-ha!" A witch's harsh voice behind her, an old woman sitting on her bed.

"Please be quiet," Liz said in Malay, holding a finger to her lips, but the old woman didn't seem to hear or see, her white orbs fluttering. She spoke again, and Liz touched her dry, split lips; the woman reached up a feathery hand to feel Liz's face. The boots crunched nearer, flashlight dancing across the transom window.

The woman felt Liz's hair and hissed. Liz tried to pull away, but her hair caught in the woman's bracelets. Finally she tugged free, touched the woman's lips again, and slid under the bed.

The flashlight blazed in. A man's voice, imperious. Silence. The man repeated his question, the woman's voice quavering. The boots walked on to the next room, then the one beyond, then returned and passed by her room, back the way they'd come.

Liz took off her slippers and ran barefoot down the hall and stairs, clasping her robe tightly, past the empty admissions desk and out into the mucky, dark, cold street.

At the corner she put on her slippers and caught her breath. Ahead, a wide dark road was backed by low buildings, godowns, and shacks, dim streetlights like sentinels in the distance. Water gleamed dully in the potholes. The chill, wet air smelled of kerosene and rotten bananas.

She ran several blocks, slipping in muddy ruts. A cat sprinted across the road. Here and there among the tin-roofed huts and godowns, lantern lights glimmered. She hungered to knock on their doors.

She crossed the road into darkness on the other side. Something scrambled underfoot – a rat – she jumped back, slipped and fell, her robe and legs muddy, slippers filthy.

Her left foot hurt. A long red line across the sole pulsed blood. *"Damn!"* She glanced around for something to wrap it. Nothing but sodden leaves, cardboard and paper, rusting cans, scraps of tin, broken bottles, the foul, dark liquid trickling along the gutter.

"Damn!" She put on her slipper again and limped along the street till it diagonaled into an avenue with streetlights. In the hazy, damp distance shone the lights of taller buildings and the red beacons of radio towers.

A truck clattered past, tilting on its springs. She sat on a splintery bench under the tin roof of a shop, trying to catch her breath.

A car passed, then another. Two more, one the other way. A taxi came and she ran into the street waving, but it swerved around her and kept going.

More cars. Another taxi she waved at, but it swung past. She ran after it yelling. It stopped and backed up. The driver was a small dark man with a thin white moustache.

"American Embassy," she said in Malay. "Embassy – USA – America . . ."

He waved fingers downward for her to enter. She sat in front, and he waved her to the back but she shook her head.

He drove holding the gear stick and singing softly to himself. Foam dice swung from the mirror. A picture of Mohammed riding his white steed up to heaven was taped to the dash. Every so often the man glanced at her muddy knees and faced ahead, gripping the wheel.

The Marines at the white-pillared, steel-fenced Embassy gate made her wait while they called upstairs. She shivered and tried to wrap the robe tighter. "Sorry, Ma'am," a Marine said. "We have no proof you're American –"

"Can't you hear my *voice*, for Christ's sake? What do I sound like – Bangladeshi? I'm Liz Chaplin from 1811 Pierce Street in Anchorage, Alaska. Area code 907, cell number 739-1192. *Please*, I'm hurt and cold and scared and my foot's bleeding, and I need to see the Ambassador or somebody –"

The Marine talked more on his radio. The taxi driver revved his engine to show his displeasure at waiting. "Sorry Ma'am, but can you come back during office hours?"

She snatched his radio. "Who am I speaking to?" she yelled.

"This's Sergeant Trillin."

"Sergeant, either you tell this man to let me in and pay my taxi, or I'm going to snatch his bayonet and come back there and cut your balls off. Is that American enough for you?"

Sergeant Trillin chuckled. "Let me speak to the Marine."

The Marine talked on the radio, then signaled two others who walked her toward the Embassy compound past the reinforced concrete barbed-wired walls and truck bomb barriers to the wide bright doors where two more Marines waited.

Her heart surged. *Deliverance.*

7

TAKE YOU DOWN

"THE MEDIA'S GONE INSANE," Bruce Sullivan said from Rawhide's Wall Street office. "They're saying we intentionally blew Makassar for the insurance. Because it wasn't cash-flowing, we'd over-reached financially, needed the funds –"

"In the whole damn industry," Mitch growled, "we have the best cash position!"

"They don't care about the truth," Victor scoffed. "We must remember that."

"Facebook and Instagram," Sullivan said, "they've shut us down."

"Meta thinks they own us," Victor said.

"In a way," Sullivan answered, "they do."

Ross looked away from the screen, at the conference room of Rawhide's Jakarta office, out the window at the white mass of the Al-Azhar Great Mosque, and beyond it the glass and steel office towers of District 8 scintillating in late afternoon sun. He leaned back in his seat and turned to another screen. "Isaiah?"

"Yeah, that's right," Isaiah King said from his Wall Street office.

"So legally –"

"Legally you can't do shit. People believe what they're told to believe. They never even see the retraction that comes weeks later. If there even is one."

"I'm worried," Mitch interrupted, "about the pool."

Isaiah fingered his beard, a scratchy sound. "Bankers keep a low profile. For now, they'll wait and see."

"They'll want more collateral."

"And if you argue," Isaiah broke in, "they'll pull your lines."

"Already they're apeshit over Makassar," Mitch added. "And pissed we've refused to pull out of Russia."

"All by themselves," Isaiah said, "they can take you down."

THREE TRUCKS OF SOLDIERS HERDED THE MERCEDES NEXT morning through the armored gates of the Ministry of Energy and Mineral Resources Tower off Thamrin Circle in central Jakarta. Soldiers stood in rows on both sides as Ross and the others stepped from the sweltering morning through tinted doors into a palatial air-conditioned hall and up the fast elevator directly to the minister's office at the top.

For half an hour they waited in the minister's chilled anteroom. The leather couches squeaked uncomfortably. Jakarta's smoky enormity roiled beyond the tinted windows.

"We shouldn't take this," Mitch said.

Ross glanced through the plate glass at the traffic below throbbing on the boulevards and rotating around the Circle like an immense roulette wheel. "What do you suggest?"

A beautiful woman in a slit sarong brought them Bali tea and Surinam coffee. A deputy minister came in and shook hands wetly. "He's running late . . ."

Mitch glanced at his watch. "So are we."

"Not much longer."

Mitch stood. "Perhaps the minister can call us. In Singapore –"

Ross patted the couch. "Sit down, Mitch." He nodded at a stone Buddha who sat with legs folded and palms clasped in the corner.

"The only wisdom you can get from sitting like that," Mitch said, "is that life is a pain in the ass."

Minutes later the beautiful woman led them down a vast teak corridor to Minyak Kotor's office. Sunlight cast down through tinted skylights in the teak cathedral ceiling. The minister reached across the corner of his desk to shake hands, not standing, and nodded them to a low circle of chairs in front.

"Terrible, your explosion," the minister said. His desk was so large you could land a chopper on it, Ross thought, without even disturbing the obligatory pictures of family and home town, the empty calendar and the chunk of strange rock, basalt maybe, no doubt churned up by an oil drill from somewhere deep in the earth. The minister sighed. "We mourn the deaths."

"As do we," Ross said.

The minister glanced at Ross's bandaged forehead. "You had some trouble, with the people of Balikpapan?"

"It's understandable," Ross said. "The loss of loved ones."

"Professional agitators," Victor said.

"I hope your Internal Security is on it," Mitch said.

The minister tugged at his glossy silk suit and stroked his goatee. "You're a foreign company. You'll go on making money. We remain with the souls of our dead." He glanced around as if seeing the vast room for the first time, the filigree teak screens of ancient Indonesian warrior motifs, the rows of certificates down one gleaming mahogany wall, the gold-framed photos of the minister with so many smiling people. "We must of course sanction this. Very severely."

Ross thought of the two million people this man's predecessors had killed for oil, but for which they'd never been imprisoned, and instead had won renown and had accumulated vast fortunes, prestige, women and power. "We lost all our people on that platform. And an investment of two billion dollars."

"Which you insured for three billion."

"Replacement value –"

"You built a cheap plant and were running over capacity. You cut corners."

"That's not true, Excellency," Victor said.

"And you insured the production of gas, as well as the plant. This very morning I am called by the *Jakarta Post* editor. Yesterday the *Straights Times*. They ask me, did the platform blow up because you were pushing it too hard? Or for insurance?"

"That's crazy," Mitch said.

"Our newspapers are saying it – see the trouble I'm in?"

"Your government owns the newspapers," Mitch said.

"We have democracy here," the minister said. "Just like you."

"Exactly."

"It's because of the newspapers I have to take this action."

"What action?"

"We have to show we're doing something." The minister finished his tea and made a fussy show of finding his napkin. "Now don't we?" He brightened. "Mind you, as soon as things are normalized, you get them back."

"*What* back?"

"Your leases. We're forced to sequester your oil and gas production."

"You can't *do* that." Ross crossed his legs and settled back in his chair. "It's specifically prohibited in the contract . . ."

"We have a way. Remember, it's *our* gas and oil." The minister slapped his desk. "We're doing this for legal security. We can defend it in court. *Our* court. So let's resolve our differences on the platform problem."

"Differences?" Victor said.

"We'll sort them out in the coming weeks. Won't we?" The minister stood; his gray silk suit hissed with a metallic coldness, like fingers down a blackboard.

"Goddamn it, Minyak," Ross said. "Sit down."

"No time now."

"Remember where *you* were, when we started?"

The minister patted Ross's arm. "Haven't we both come a long way! And now you, not just president of a worldwide energy

52

company, but quite a fan, I hear, of stopping this war that is doing so good for keeping crude prices high."

"You know the real history, the NATO promises, the escalations, the American missile installations on Russia's borders, the 2014 U.S. coup that overthrew Ukraine's popularly elected government, this comedian Zelenskyy whose previous claim to fame was playing the piano with his dick in Moscow nightclubs – perhaps you've seen it on YouTube?"

"That is fake news."

"You know it's true, Minyak. I'm warning you –"

"*Warning* me? You who are looking at big trouble? With refusing to follow your own country's sanctions?"

"Hell, Jokowi himself said the sanctions will make things worse, hurt everybody!"

The minister flinched at the mention of President Joko Widodo's nickname, perhaps fearing Ross had a connection to him. He gripped Ross's elbow as he walked them to the elevator. "Remember, I'll always be your friend."

Outside the minister's office their armored black Mercedes shimmered in the heat. Traffic on the Boulevard roared in all directions. Heat and brown exhaust danced in the turbid light. A lone bird flapped over, crying.

"He's gonna take those leases?" Mitch swore. "Over my dead body."

"If they want our wells, what better way than this?"

"Would they blow us up? If we don't produce, they don't make money."

Jakarta's unending avenues and crowded streets floated past the limousine's tinted windows. Sewer stink seeped through the air conditioning. "The legal fees on this," Mitch said, "will be astronomical."

"OPEC won't let them steal our leases," Victor insisted. "Isn't that true, Ross? What about the CIA Jakarta station – Wally and Keith, they'll fight for us? They won't let them yank our oil?"

Ross thought of the fish traps on the coast. "We're being trapped.

Forced where we don't want to go. But how we get out is to go back the same way we came in. We have to swim against the tide."

"Yeah," Mitch said. "Right."

8

FLOTSAM

"**S**ABOTAGE?**"** Wally Singleton, the U.S. Ambassador to Indonesia, lit his cigarillo and stretched his long, slender legs in their silk slacks across his hand-carved desk. "Can't see it." He had wiry gray-copper hair, the flushed face of a country club drinker, and a Phi Beta Kappa ring on his wedding finger.

"We think it might be," Ross said.

"Always dangerous, this neck of the woods," Keith Ormsley, the CIA Jakarta Station Chief, put in. "You know that."

"They want their leases back."

Keith chuckled. "Not surprising." He had a big florid smile and a belly that implied, incorrectly, not to take him seriously.

"They're saying all the leases we signed with the previous government are fraudulent because of the twenty-three percent we had to pay them under the table."

"Those were market conditions back then." Keith eased back in his chair. "Lots of folks paid more."

"If they cancel those leases, they make billions." Ross turned to Wally. "Our last lease with them, crude was thirty-one. Now it's seventy-eight. Same with natgas. They cancel that one lease they make four billion."

Wally beamed at them across his desk. "And you're out four billion." He had a laconic smile, perhaps from years in Los Angeles commercial real estate and as a major bundler in the president's last election.

"They can screw us all, this way," Ross said.

"International law." Wally relit his cigarillo. "Might not let them."

"They can kill us with lawyers and bureaucracy. You know that."

"What's left of their reserves?" Keith sighed, "seven per cent?"

"Their proven reserves," Ross said, "are just six times their annual consumption. They're already importing nearly half their oil. Without these imports, they have about six years remaining."

"What would *you* do," Wally said, "if your cash cow was running out, after fifty years of payoffs and squandering? You're fat and lazy and need lots of money to pay the Army to control the people? Wouldn't *you* try to steal those leases back?"

Keith shrugged. "Lots of blood in this oil –"

Wally smiled. "Always is."

"They haven't forgotten 1966," Ross answered. "They still hate us."

"And love us too. Just like Argentina, Chile, all those places." Wally waved away smoke. "You kill all the left-wingers, and the whole country turns left-wing. Go figure."

Keith shook his head. "That was over-reported."

Ross watched him. "You CIA guys helped to kill two million Indonesians in four months – you think *that* was over-reported? An Operation Gladio, to get Indonesian oil into our hands?"

"If you see it that way."

"It *was* that way, Keith. You guys wrote the program."

"And you've done well by it." Wally smiled again. "Haven't you?"

"That was long before my time. As you know," Ross said. "So I need you to bring these peckerheads in line."

"We don't have them by the balls anymore," Keith said.

"I want BIN – those nasty bastards at Badan Intelijen Negara – to put their top hundred agents on this. Interrogating our onshore contractors, all seagoing traffic, anybody who's visited the platform the last months – that'd be in the chopper logs – anyone else who might have reason to hit us."

"Ross, you've gotta give it up," Keith said. "It was an accident! Bad maintenance, everyone's saying –"

"And I want *you guys* on it! Here, in D.C., Singapore, Saudi . . . And I want NSA on it too, and that" – he stared at Wally – "means you!" He turned to Keith, "And I want *you guys* cooperating with BIN. On every clue . . ."

"For Chrissake, we're not Dick Tracy."

"You're saying *no*? We're an American company, millions of American stockholders, mutual funds –"

"Lot of foreign money, too," Wally said.

"– retirement funds, millions of people depending on us, twenty-seven thousand employees – and we're getting screwed over by the Indonesians – which it's *your* job to prevent, and you're saying you won't help us?"

"You don't need help," Keith chuckled. "There's no sabotage. No conspiracy. They try to cancel those leases, they have years of legal suffering ahead."

"They'll make four billion canceling. What's a hundred million in lawyers?"

"Ross, you're overreacting."

"So why are they just hitting Rawhide?"

"Maybe" – Wally smiled – "you should stay out of politics?"

"We have every right to challenge those sanctions."

"This is trench warfare. You stick your head out of the trench, they shoot it off."

"You guys know of anyone else getting hit in any way? No news from EXXON, Chevron, BP, Total, any of the others?"

Wally shook his cigarillo into the wastebasket. "Nothing we've heard, have we, Keith?"

"Nothing" – Keith glanced at his watch – "that I've been informed of."

"That doesn't say much."

"You've a nasty turn of mind, Ross. You always have."

Ross stood. "That's why I'm where I am. And you're where you are."

"Precisely." Keith exhaled. "And where *you* are, is in deep shit."

"Oh, by the way, that girl," Wally cut in, "who survived the platform? Showed up at the Embassy four-thirty this morning. In a bathrobe. Said she 'escaped' from the hospital."

"What the hell's that mean?"

"Said the hospital wouldn't let her out. I think you got a crazy one there."

"We'll take her back to the States with us."

"Indo intelligence won't clear her."

"Don't worry" – Keith grinned – "BIN will take good care of her."

Ross stood, hating them. "I'm going over your head, Wally. Just so you know."

"The Big Guy?" The Ambassador smiled. "It won't do you any good. He won't even remember who you are."

"WHAT'D THEY SAY?" MITCH RASPED AS ROSS SLID INTO THE BACK of the Mercedes.

Ross settled himself into the cool leather. "They won't protect us on the leases."

"Ross," Mitch implored, "the markets are kicking our ass."

"What are we at?"

"Fifty-five point nine. Down two bucks in an hour . . ."

Ross let the car's acceleration soothe him back into the seat. "It'll bounce back –"

"And if S&P downgrades us? If the banks back out of the Thai leases, the Uzbekistan pipeline? And the Indonesians shaft us on these leases? What if some other goddamn disaster . . . I'm the fucking CFO, and it's driving me crazy, this drop in our stock. Ross, what if . . ."

"What if *what*?"

"What if we talked to a couple of folks, pulled in a partner?"

Ross snorted. "You whoring us out, Mitch?"

"Not a management share, Jesus. I'm talking board seat, joint ventures."

"You'd sell our ass in a joint venture?"

Mitch looked meaningfully at Victor. "We're going to need cash."

"What bothers me," Victor answered, "is why don't the Agency and the Ambassador have our back?"

"I'm calling the president," Ross said. "He'll know."

"WHY CAN'T I GO?" LIZ SLAPPED HER HAND ON THE IRONWOOD table in her new room at the Ritz Carlton.

"They want you as a witness." Mitch pulled his chair nearer hers. "Afraid if you leave, you might not come back for the inquest."

"If I say I'll come back," she scowled, "I will."

"We're working on getting you out," Mitch said. "In the meantime, we've rented you an apartment. In the Eternity Tower, in District 8, thirty-seventh floor, great views . . ."

"I don't like heights."

"Indoor and outdoor pools, sauna, jacuzzi, hammam, cinema, library, a big gym – you'll love it."

"Soon as you're ready to," Ross said, "we'd like to talk about what you want to do next. In Rawhide, the world."

"When you're ready," Mitch added.

"I'm so sorry." Ross squeezed her hand, then dropped it. "For what you've been through, and for all the families who've lost people . . ."

"And we still don't know how it happened," Mitch said.

She shook her head. "It was *no* accident."

"Come on now." Mitch smiled gently. "You're a PhD geologist, not an engineer –"

"My masters was ocean engineering."

"But still –"

"And they're holding *me* hostage? While you guys come and go?"

"You're the only one," Mitch said, "who was there. And survived." He tucked a creased trouser. "That's why what you testify is so important." He looked her in the eyes. "What I'm saying, Liz, is the fate of the company may rest on what you say."

"That's enough, Mitch," Ross said.

"C'mon, Ross, better she knows the truth."

"I have hideous dreams," she said. "Every night. The explosion, the fires, the ocean burning, everyone dying and drowning. The sharks."

"I do, too," Ross said. "Lots of us do."

"Though not like you," Victor added.

She stood, wincing. "I hate Jakarta. I want out of here."

"Where to?" Ross said.

"When I get to the airport, I'll decide."

"SHE'S TROUBLE," MITCH HUFFED AS THE MERCEDES HUSTLED them back to Jakarta HQ.

Ross glanced at him. "Nuts."

"Busting our balls because she can't get out of Indonesia. Christ, we're paying her full salary though she's not working, her hotel, now we're getting her this nice apartment –"

"Mitch, she's been in the hospital."

"Bought her new clothes, everything she lost on the platform . . . And we're risking bankruptcy while she'll get a nice settlement."

"She's still in shock. I'd want to leave, too."

"You're too soft-hearted, Ross. It does you harm."

"If the Indonesians don't free her, I'll have a buddy get her out."

"Buddy?" Mitch scratched at his thinning hair. "What buddy?"

"Guy I grew up with in North Dakota. Ex-Seal, does deepwater recon and rescues."

Mitch looked out at the skyscrapers shrouded in soiled air. "That would piss off the Indos even more. Make them more determined to steal our leases."

"You know what?" Ross looked at him steadily. "I don't give a damn about our leases."

"You're losing your grip." Mitch slapped Ross's shoulder. "Toughen up."

Ross nodded at the hazy gleam of Jakarta beyond the car window. "So what do you think about that filthy air? What do you think about all our dead people? And their families? All our goddamn oil in the ocean? What about it, Mitch – what do *you* think?"

"What do I think? I think the world's a dangerous place. There's no rules, no morals. Anybody speaking about morals is trying to corner a deal. Or planning a war –"

"Not always. It doesn't have to be that way."

RAWHIDE'S JAKARTA OFFICE MANAGER, NEIL DRUMMOND, MET them at the door, a photograph in his hand. "One of the choppers checking flotsam found something –"

Ross glared at him, exasperated by weariness, by Drummond's red hair, his contentious freckles. "Tons of stuff's floating out there."

"– diving equipment."

"So? How many divers we got out there?"

"None who've lost a mouthpiece and harness. Especially not one that's been all chewed up by a shark."

9

DAWN RAID

L ILY'S *TIMES* EDITOR, Ian Hamilton, had the habit of flicking his pen back and forth between the thumb and forefinger of his right hand, which sat atop her printed story, over a round coffee stain where he'd put down his cup.

Three generations ago, she knew, his family name had been Hamininski, and it made her proud that so many people had come from so many places to make America the great country it was.

"Lily," Ian was saying, "you've got to stop doing shit like this. You're going to lose your job."

Wow. She refocused on Ian jabbing his red pencil across lines in her story, lines she knew were true and had footnoted at the end. "You're going way out on a limb saying it's irrefutable that the virus came from the Wuhan lab –"

"It's a *biological weapons* lab. Researching how to kill people. Partially funded by Anthony Fauci and our government –"

"– and that the release was *intentional?* Are you crazy?"

"China had 4 deaths per million people from COVID. The U.S. had 3,500 deaths per million. China shut down internal travel but expanded it to the US. It's all in my piece! Have you even read it?"

"Lily, it doesn't matter! We just can't *say* these things," he snapped as if she should have known, and it was not to be challenged. He leaned back in his padded mahogany armchair. "You know the old truism: Nothing exists till the *Times* says so."

"Sounds like the Catholic church. In the fourteenth century."

"Whoa, we're not criticizing anybody." He smiled entreatingly. "Please, Lily? I've done everything I can for you. But I can't protect you anymore."

"I'm a reporter. I'm supposed to say the truth."

"Sometimes the truth will get you in trouble." He leaned forward, elbows on his desk. "Things have changed here. You know it."

"I try not to."

"I've been here twenty-two years, but we're not the *Times* anymore . . . almost a caricature." He stared out the window, as if wanting to say more.

"So that's why you're killing my piece? First you don't run my Rawhide nuclear war story, and now you shoot down my Wuhan piece?"

"Think this through, Lily. Suppose we do admit the virus came from the Wuhan lab. Right away we have egg on our face for having declared the exact opposite for years. Even worse, we attacked and silenced anyone who said it came from the lab. Then think what the repercussions would be: China owns over a trillion dollars in U.S. Treasuries. Second, many major U.S. corporations are financially dependent on China. Three, many U.S. politicians, including our president, have received billions of dollars from China. Four, the decision to make these Wuhan bioweapons came from deep inside the American power structure."

He sat back luxuriously in his chair, as if this explained everything.

"You're saying don't rock the boat."

"Don't *sink* the boat. What makes us the most powerful media presence in the world are the links we have with top levels of government and industry and the other power centers that run this country. The moment we go off the rails, we lose that."

He leaned forward amicably. "Our final position on COVID is no one is going to *ever* know where it came from. We will *never know!* Is that clear? No matter how much evidence links it to the Wuhan lab. So you can't just interfere and say it irrefutably came from the lab. And even worse, that it was intentional."

"Two months ago I spent five weeks in Wuhan and interviewed senior people – two in the lab's oversight division, who were both following the experiments, another who was in the gain of function group itself –"

"I know that. I *paid* for that trip."

"I speak perfect Chinese. Some people thought I was part of the government. They were honest . . ."

"That doesn't matter." He smiled encouragingly. "Look, we've got a *real* story for you."

She forced down the bile in her gut, the fierceness in her voice. "Mine was a real story. They both were."

"You're very lucky," he smiled, "because now I'm giving you a really big one. Something that can catapult you up the ladder."

This didn't sound like much fun, but she furiously bit her tongue.

"There's this guy named Dale Robichaud," Ian went on. "The Louisiana gas king. He's on the Commodities Futures Trading Commission, the CFTC. He called us, a big inside tip. He says the CFTC is going to charge Rawhide Energy with price manipulation of the Wyoming Basin crude market. And with false refining reports. There could be a lot of meat in this story. I want you to track it down."

"The CFTC? We studied them in grad school. They're the agency overseeing futures and options markets, specifically energy markets like crude. And they can shut Rawhide down any time they want."

"This guy Robichaud, as a member of the CFTC's Energy & Environmental Markets Advisory Committee, he's apparently supposed to oversee trading in U.S. natural gas markets. A lot of money. And he's close to the president, raised millions for him."

This gave Lily a quiver of disgust.

"See if this has legs," Ian added. "Call him, go interview him, see what he says. And this's an exclusive, so don't waste time."

"I didn't waste time on my Wuhan story."

Ian smiled avuncularly and tipped back in his chair. "You're going against all the top people here, Lily. It's putting you on thin ice."

"Is there an *angle*," she said acidly, "you want me to pursue on this?"

"Anything you learn about Rawhide," he smiled, "is grist for the mill."

"That's my *angle*?"

He tipped forward and flicked his pencil atop his stained blotter. "I've sent you my notes. Call Robichaud. Go to Louisiana and interview him if you have to; there's money for it. Do this right and it can help your future here."

Lily gathered her papers and stalked out. At the moment she wasn't sure, any longer, if she gave a damn about her future here.

"WE GOT TROUBLE," MITCH CAME INTO ROSS'S SUITE WITH whiskey and ice in a paper cup and sat heavily.

"I know that," Ross said peaceably.

"EastPac's putting a move on us."

Ross felt a suffocating heaviness. EastPac, Eastern Pacific Energy, was a fast-moving well-financed competitor backed by endless pools of Chinese corporate and government money partially channeled through Singapore. For a moment he couldn't deal with this. Couldn't deal with anything anymore. "How much?"

"They just picked up seven percent in a dawn raid on Nasdaq. Looking for more."

In a dawn raid, a competitor buys as much stock as they can as soon as markets open, before the target company can react. It was ten p.m. in Jakarta, so Nasdaq had opened a half hour ago. "We can beat them."

"If they get to ten percent? Twenty?"

Ross smiled ironically. "It'll drive up our stock –"

Mitch drained his whiskey and tossed the cup into a wicker basket. "And every time it drops back down, they'll buy more."

"We'll have to cut them off."

Mitch snatched a newspaper from the coffee table. "How?"

KNOWN FOR HIS SHARP BUSINESS DEALS AND THE METEORIC *rise of his energy company Rawhide, Ross Bullock is not only a hard-driving business leader, he is also a scientist, mountain climber, and conservationist. With an undergraduate degree in physics and a PhD in astrophysics, he is a fierce advocate for space exploration, or as he puts it, "getting off this little rock."*

He has purchased vast areas of wilderness to protect it from logging, and fought for cleaner rivers and lower pollution. His drive to make Rawhide and the world a greener place via nuclear energy has earned him fierce opposition from green energy advocates and other energy companies. His refusal to abide by U.S. and European Union sanctions against Russia has led to multiple attacks against him by the White House and a wide range of pro-war politicians and lobbyists on both sides of the aisle . . . And now the Indonesian gas platform catastrophe, probably due to bad maintenance, plus rumors of mismanagement at several of his other facilities, have knocked down Rawhide's stock price at the same time that a threatened hostile takeover by EastPac Energy should have driven it higher . . .

Mitch tossed the *Washington Post* back on the table. "Why do they always have to make stuff up?"

"That's their schtick," Betsy said. "Whenever there's good news that doesn't fit their agenda, either they don't report it or they say *but*, and then give you some cockamamie story about why the good news is actually bad . . ."

"Honesty doesn't sell clicks." Mitch gripped his head in his hands, massaging his temples. "But after all this crap we keep saying about the war, they should treat us fair."

"Come on, Mitch, the Democratic media loves this war."

"That's no reason to attack us."

Ross shrugged. "They've been told to."

Mitch grimaced. "By who?"

"That's what we have to find out."

10

MISSILES FROM UKRAINE

2:52 **IN BANGKOK.** Turk Holman scanned the gleaming, smoke-filled restaurant packed with loud voices and flashy people. The animated languages – English, Thai, French, Chinese – the sharp-eyed elegant young women, the hard-faced young men and prosperous older ones. Each would spend seven to ten thousand baht here tonight, two hundred to three hundred USD, of which Turk's costs averaged forty-seven.

But tonight something felt heavy, cold. Out of place. You have a sense, after all the years, when bad shit is coming. He had maybe learned it as a Seal or from other nasty stuff he'd done and since tried to forget.

Simone Li came through a beaded curtain, shoved her hip against him and slapped her cocktail tray down on the bar. "Table thirteen, they Myanmar. *De*-fense ministry."

Turk stepped around the bar for a look. Table thirteen, by the wall under the purple lanterns, five guys in dark suits, in the middle a heavy-set older man with gold teeth and gold-rimmed spectacles. "He's a deputy minister," Turk said. "It's on us. No matter what they drink."

"Already they talking Dom Perignon. I don't like that. Not for free."

"Give them the Chinese shit with the Dom label. They won't know the difference."

"Fuck no, I don't want to kill them."

When the phone vibrated in his pocket, he didn't want to take it.

"You busy?" Ross said.

"Where are you?"

"Jakarta."

"I know about the platform. Holy Jesus."

"What do you think?"

"Textbook. We learned it in underwater demo."

"Can you come down, take a look, talk to the divers? I can shoot you the pix. Also, there was just one survivor, an American geologist. She's a wonderful young woman, and I want to make sure she gets out of Indonesia in one piece."

"Ross, I don't rescue damsels in distress."

"Not anymore?"

"Fuck you."

"Fuck you, too."

"Look, I'm running a fuckin restaurant and bar –"

"Yeah, I wouldn't come either. If I was you."

"Send me the pix, you bastard."

When the bar closed at 3 a.m. he went upstairs and sat on the Persian rug in front of the big screen with his back against an ottoman, a glass of Roku and ice on one side, a hash pipe and black Zippo on the other, and ran the videos and blueprints Ross had sent him. Simone came in, tucked up her kimono, sat beside him and took the pipe.

"Got to go," he said. "First flight this morning."

"I know, soon as he call."

"You can move Cao up to chief bartender, and Tim can take my job."

"I can do your job."

"Of course. But yours is harder."

"Bad news, this platform. Trouble comes in three. You should not go."

"Ross and I grew up together. He watches out for me; I watch out for him."

"Yeah, but you do dangerous part; he makes money."

"The money to buy this place came from him."

"He give lots of people money."

"That's who he is."

"I just saying, don't go. I not your wife, not girlfriend anymore. Just partner, just friend. I worry you go."

"Do what you'd do if I was dead."

She spat. "Maybe you just have a look, talk to him, come back?"

"It never turns out that way."

She put down the pipe. "I'm not going back to old days, Turk."

He turned to the screen. "Neither am I." His words felt hollow. This was the trouble with women, why you should never live with just one. Especially while you're still young.

But he really wasn't that young anymore.

"They Myanmar *de*-fense minister and they others?" Simone snapped. "I hear when I am behind curtain, fixing drinks, they argue about bad things."

He smiled at her affectionately. "Bad things?"

"Buying missiles, mines to blow up when people step on them. From Ukraine."

BEYOND THE BALCONY OF ROSS'S SUITE, THE MAKASSAR STRAIT was turning lurid gold under the fast-rising sun, a line of dark tankers across its copper horizon. And out there a ruined platform with a hundred thirty-one dead and one saved. Could a crack in a carbon steel pipe really ignite that fast?

The numbers said no.

It was only 05:30 and already the Jakarta streets were roaring with cars, taxis, buses, trucks, motorcycles, scooters . . . Jets taking off in long lines, tankers, freighters, fishing boats, tugs, pleasure boats . . . In all the polluted cities and corners of the world, in the sea, the air, on every road and highway. All powered by a strange dark liquid sucked from the earth.

This brief flash of fossil energy before the long downward slope. Humans weren't going to make it into that expanding universe that was their only hope, their only future, their only heavenly salvation. Because the energy they needed to get there would soon be used up, and because they'd spent too much time and wealth killing each other.

By 07:00 Ross had gone through 441 new emails. Over a hundred had been internal – engineering, finance, accounting, field offices and other platforms. Another hundred had been forwarded by his press office, from journalists with questions or wanting interviews. Short messages from industry friends wishing him well and offering help. Queries from salvage companies, international lawyers, and all the other ambulance chasers of the world.

At seven-thirty Mitch came in, cold coffee in hand, scratching stubble, his shirt undone. "EastPac's eating us alive."

"They've got a long way to go," Ross said, "before I worry about it. For now, they're just driving up our stock."

"Yeah, what's the good of that?"

"Ten ksi carbon steel," Ross said. "No way it would blow from within."

"WE'RE GETTING YOU OUT," Ross told Liz when she came in his office door at 08:20.

She scowled. "Changed my mind."

"A friend of mine's coming, he can do it –"

"I've thought about it. I'm staying here."

"You wanted to leave –"

"I was on the third deck when it blew, saw it come up out of the water."

"That's what the pictures seem to say."

"I'm staying here till I find out who did it."

"We have hundreds of people working on that – the engineers who designed it, the contractors, our own engineers, the insurance under-writers, you name it . . . There'll be an independent commission, an accident report –"

"If it wasn't an accident?"

"We won't know, will we, till the reports are in?"

"Mr. Bullock, I'm the only one alive who saw it . . ."

He nodded, said nothing.

". . . and I know the geology of the ocean floor where the platform sat, the molecular composition of the pipeline steel, the chemical analysis of the gas, its flammability range, all that. I have a master's in ocean engineering, and I know how the platform was designed and built. So don't you dare tell me I can't help."

Ross looked at the young woman with the bruised face and singed hair, the white bandage on her right arm, another on her left leg, and he wondered how she could be walking around as if nothing had happened. She wasn't just tough; she was ruthless.

"Of course, you should help. We'll give you an office at HQ Jakarta, pay you out of Makassar LLC, and you study the whole thing, see what you can figure out."

"You shouldn'a done that," Mitch said when she left. "We don't know her part in this. How come she survived, and no one else?"

"What you got against her, Mitch?"

"I got nothing against her. Don't like lies, that's all."

"What else is there?" Ross grimaced. "Let's get back to New York –"

"Before EastPac eats us alive? Before the banks ditch us, our insurers drop us, our stock dies, the media runs us into a wall, and what the fuck else can go wrong?"

ROSS CALLED THE PRESIDENT ON THE WAY TO THE AIRPORT BUT got Nathan Coldmire.

"The president's very concerned," Coldmire said.

"I don't give a fuck about concerned. I want to talk to him."

"He's off radar. Delaware."

"Fuck Delaware. I want to talk to him. And I want the Agency on this. No more shit from Wally and Keith, the damn Jakarta Station. Tell him I want the Agency on it. Now!"

"He's stunned," Coldmire huffed. "We all are. Horrible, the deaths."

"We think it might have been a bomb. I sent you the pix."

"Yes, we're having them analyzed right now."

"Did you see those blast marks?" Ross said.

"Our people have."

"The Indonesians want to steal our leases."

"Understandable, in this context."

"*What* context?"

Coldmire sighed. "There's a world war in Ukraine, and the Middle East is on fire. Haven't you noticed?"

Ross bit down fury. "You guys are going to kill us all, Nathan. We had no choice but to oppose you. Eventually everyone will. Or we'll all die in your nuclear war."

"Look, I got a bunch of calls waiting. Let me review this. We won't let you down."

Ross shut off. "He won't let us down . . ."

Mitch laughed. "So they *are* going to fuck us."

Ross nodded. "But now we know."

AT 12:10 Turk landed at Jakarta's Soekarno Airport while Ross and the others were waiting to board their Gulfstream to New York.

"You look like shit," Turk said. "What happened to your face?"

"Got hit by a bottle. Some people not connected to anyone on the platform. They ranted a lot about how crooked we are, got everyone stirred up."

"You okay?" Turk's eyebrows raised. "You're in a tough place."

Ross nodded. "It's almost overwhelming."

"You can win this?"

"I think so."

"I want to see the platform," Turk said. "Go down for a look."

"The chief diver will meet you in Balikpapan."

"Who is he?"

"Ex-Australian Navy. Knows his stuff."

"What's he think?"

"All he can say for sure is that it blew somewhere between sixty feet and just below the valve cluster. Not sure if there was a bomb or if something went wrong inside the pipe."

"He couldn't tell by what's left? If it blew in or out?"

Ross shook his head. "Trouble is, even if there were an external explosive, the gas in the pipe would then ignite, and that explosion would blow everything outward again."

"And it all landed on the bottom five hundred feet down. At that depth, even if we can get there, what's left to find?"

11

SHARK REPELLANT

"**WE POISON THE BASTARDS**," Mitch said.

"They'll fight it off," Ross said. "We'll get hurt more than EastPac."

"Not if we hit them with a shareholder rights plan."

"You've been screaming about our stock price dropping, now you want to drive it even lower?"

"They just upped their hold to nine and change."

Ross glanced out the Gulfstream's window at the Saudi desert unrolling far below. "That won't kill us."

"It's the only thing propping up our stock price," Victor added, "this takeover thing."

"If they keep increasing their stake?" Mitch looked at them exasperatedly, a man at the end of his hopes. "Which of course they will?"

Easy to say we can deal with it, Ross reminded himself. *But if we can't?* "Till they hit twelve," he said, "we're good."

"We're in the middle of a hostile takeover," Mitch snapped. "They want to eat us, and we don't want to be eaten. It's time for shark repellant –"

"Too soon," Victor insisted.

"A quick board meeting, then we file the SEC 8K and pass a shareholder plan giving our present shareholders the right to buy more stock at a discount, so a lot of them do, which reduces EastPac's ownership percentage . . . You know all this . . ." Mitch gave a false grin. "Making ourselves so poisonous no one wants to eat us."

"It screws our investors," Ross said. "The retired teachers and cops and lots of other people who get diluted, and hurt when our price drops . . ."

"You saying they're better off if EastPac buys us?"

"It's funny, but it's true, Mitch. Our stock's at fifty-four, and EastPac is offering fifty-seven two."

"So we do a safe harbor –"

"That's cheating." Victor said. "We've never done it."

"It makes us look like shit," Mitch answered. "That's the point – so nobody wants us."

"Precisely." Ross sat back in his chair thinking of the fish traps in Borneo. To escape, you had to swim against the tide. Go back the way you came.

But here, now, which way was the tide?

"We increase our debt?" Mitch said. "Blow it out of the water?"

Ross sighed, not wanting to argue. "The banks are grabbing their balls already. The Boston Group, three times I've talked to them today . . ." He shook his head. "The Kuwait pool, guess what they're saying . . ."

"I don't want to," Mitch said tiredly.

"That's why we don't do shark repellant. Because the tide is driving us toward it."

"Tide? What tide?"

"They're pushing us toward it – why?" Ross went on, more to himself. "What's in it for them?"

"Everything for them," Victor said. "Nothing for us."

"Look how this all began," Mitch answered. "I've been saying this a long time. Who gives a royal flying rat's ass about nuclear war?"

"We all should. Then maybe we can avoid it."

"So we find a partner? That's what I keep saying. But I'm talking to the deaf and dumb."

"A white knight?" Ross smiled. "We get taken over, but just by someone not quite as bad as EastPac?"

"Either we poison pill them." Mitch leaned forward, hands clasped on his knees. "Or we find a better deal."

"Either way, Mitch, it's the people who believed in us who get poisoned."

"A BUNCH OF ENVIRO NGOs," Bruce Sullivan said, "have signed a letter to the media that we must be sanctioned, boycotted, and criminally charged for bad maintenance leading to an environmental disaster in the South China Sea –"

"Not true," Victor said. "We capped it, right away."

"– and, get *this*, that we are needlessly prolonging an environmentally destructive war by refusing to unite against the oppressors."

"It just showed up on Bloomberg," Mitch rasped.

"It'll destroy us on social media." Sullivan looked down, shook his head. "I can try to control it, but . . ."

Sullivan looked worn and sleepy on the screen, Ross thought. But of course, the plane was over Saudi now where it was early afternoon, so about five a.m. in New York, and Bruce had probably been up all night. "Do what you can," Ross said.

"And there's all these tweets, but no way to track them down. That we blew the platform for the insurance, that we're not helping the victims' families, that we're going to go bankrupt and EastPac's going to pick up the pieces . . . Meta won't answer us; they're just a big whorehouse full of talk and no responsibility for what gets said."

"Don't they have some rule? They take stuff down all the time –"

"Only stuff they don't like."

"Who's telling them what to like?"

"God knows. But instead, they've shut *us* down. We have no way to fight back."

Ross sat, tried to think. "Bruce, I need to know who's behind this. Who's sending these goddamn tweets or whatever they're called?"

"It's all behind firewalls. No way to tell."

STRONG HEADWINDS HAD MADE THEM BURN SO MUCH AVGAS they'd had to refuel in Abu Dhabi instead of Sicily, meaning another stop in Madrid before the last leg home to New York. Ross paced the narrow fuselage, glanced out at the clouds and deserts below, and paced some more.

Mitch and Victor sat glumly at the conference table amid engineering drawings and empty coffee cups as computer screens tracked the price of their stock down on every world exchange. "I can't think any more," Betsy said and went to bed. The cabin attendant sat dozing on a couch, hands folded in her lap.

Ross entered the cockpit and looked between the two pilots. The desert beyond the plane glowed with late sunlight, the sky above deep blue. The wall of instruments glowed sedately. "You guys fine?" Ross said.

"No sweat." The copilot looked back at him. "You should get some rest."

He wandered back to the conference table and checked his phone. If it was now three p.m. over Saudi, that meant nine p.m. in Tokyo. He pulled up a list of Nikkei analysts and punched in the first. "Good evening, Hirono. It's Ross Bullock . . . Yes, and to you too. It's late, but I wanted to bring you up to speed . . ."

There were eighteen of them, from Hirono Akutegawa to Shimono Sanzuri, and he wanted to talk to them all before the Tokyo futures markets opened in the morning. He left the same message for those he couldn't reach:

Our strength is what we have underground, our long-term contracts, our new ventures.

Now is the time to buy in. In a year, with all our new wells coming on, the new Nigerian fields, our Norwegian gas deals, once this has quieted down and our insurance pools have kicked in, covering our costs, our stock will be triple what it is today.

There will be no markets if there's a nuclear war.

It wasn't time to tell them, he'd decided, that the Indonesians were canceling their leases, that the Boston bank pool might pull their loans.

And that the White House didn't have their back.

No matter. Whatever it takes, we will dig our way out of this.

And stop EastPac. Maybe even slow down Armageddon.

ON LONG FLIGHTS LIKE THIS HE'D SOMETIMES THINK BACK THE twenty-one years to when he'd been a high school kid working winter weekends on his father's rigs in the North Dakota oil fields, the crude curdled in frozen puddles, the oily odors on the bitter wind, the crunch of boot heels through crusted ice, the cloying warmth of the operations trailer, its odors of burnt coffee and wet wool, the patient nodding donkeys, their slow steady sucking oil out of the earth.

Standing by his mother in a wood-smoky kitchen or in a bitterly cold schoolroom of chalked blackboards and students' artwork tacked to walls, the stars at night so white and thick it seemed almost day, that he could almost reach them. Summer's dusty ballfields and breezy prairies, the winter wind across the white, ravaged stubble, his father's Ford 150 with the rusty hole in its floor where wind and ice came through, the numbness in his fingers from working winter steel – gloves couldn't stop it – it was deeper, that life.

From age ten he'd worked every school vacation in the oil fields. To excavate a pit in the ravaging wind at thirty below, the sting of it, the grins of the older guys recognizing that *Okay, this kid may be the owner's son but holy shit he can work* . . . His power and pride when he beat the elements, did more than anyone else.

It seemed weird that this same kid now ran an international oil company. A billionaire. The same kid who sometimes couldn't drive the fourteen miles to Mandan because he was too broke to buy the gas – and who now had a stable of fast cars he never drove and his own airplanes to fly him all over the world. And the one thing he'd learned? He was happier back then.

Was it the optimistic anticipations of youth? Or, as he sometimes now thought, bucking oil pipes and roughing out a new forage were real *work*, something you physically did, and the doing of it and seeing the final product brought you pleasure.

And when you had no money, you didn't worry about losing it. Now he scanned the Gulfstream's rich interior, the paintings, leather living room, the oaken door leading to the posh master bedroom, sauna and bath, the classy kitchen and Victorian dining room and other lovely bedrooms – but all he did was worry about losing money.

He rubbed the back of his neck to make the soreness go away. *You can't always get what you want.*

But what did he want?

The bare wild lands of winter, the aching cold, had made him wonder how the deer and antelope survived, how the Mandans had survived, how anyone could. Yet the Mandans had prospered, and loved life, till in two years they all died of smallpox brought by white traders.

How do you rectify all the wrongs of time?

Growing up in North Dakota was a stroke of luck that few kids have – right out of high school full time in the oil fields at nine bucks an hour and in a month you could buy a used pickup and the girls all wanted to go out with you – except the ones who went away to college and only wanted to go out with college guys.

And working the oil fields had made him want more, and he'd soon saved enough money to go to Bozeman and get a physics degree in three years at Montana State, an amazing university that taught you exactly what you needed to know and nothing you didn't. And which gave him, absolutely for free, an abiding love of the stars, of astrophysics, the key to the universe.

From there the scholarship to Caltech, the PhD, then one year at NASA's Jet Propulsion Laboratory scanning the depths of space, till suddenly his father died and he'd faced the terrible choice that had haunted him ever since: wander deep space and abandon the company his parents had worked so hard to build? Or take Rawhide even further, out into the universe of high finance and international deals, maybe even beyond crude?

The choice was easy. Ross went back to the oil fields, and in a year Rawhide bought twenty new leases and traded for more. "That well's dry," an old foreman said of one, but Ross managed to drill a little deeper and broke into a huge reservoir, and with that money bought another forty-seven leases and in three more years, in the late 1990s, Rawhide was pumping 17,000 barrels a day, selling them at $23 a barrel, and paying all its costs at $16.

When he thought about the past it seemed as if he'd been fated to end up here. But back then it would have seemed a ridiculous fantasy. 17,000 barrels a day was nothing in the real world, but when the Billings refinery closed, Ross bought it for nearly nothing. The price of crude began to climb, and lots of Montana and North Dakota oil started flowing to Billings. In two more years he'd bought two Gulf Coast refineries for nothing down, then a rusty old tanker that was just right for shuttling jet fuel and other products from Louisiana up the East Coast.

Then meeting Mary, who made everything perfect. Then North Sea gas and combined cycle gas-fired power plants, electricity snaking its feelers out all over the world. *Rawhide is Energy* became its motto. *And Energy is Life.*

His dim reflection in the Perspex looked pale and weary – had he aged this much in just a few days, as Turk had said? It wasn't even a week since the press conference to announce Rawhide's warning on nuclear war. He'd known there'd be impacts, but not this.

Not a blown platform and 131 people dead.

He watched his reflected face stippled by the wingtip's flashing light: *You've been here before and got out. You will again.*

If nothing else goes wrong, we can still win this.

Had it been a mistake to refuse the sanctions? To warn of nuclear war? Every bone in his body said *no, we did the right thing.* He eased back and took a breath. No need to go all over this again tonight. He peered out the window. In six hours, Madrid.

THE CNN TALKING HEAD, EARNEST-LOOKING AND CAREFULLY coiffed and painted, intoned thoughtfully, "There have been safety infractions for months on the Makassar platform, Indonesian Minister of Energy and Mineral Resources Minyak Kotor said today."

"I don't believe these bastards." Victor thumbed off the TV.

"A great philosopher told me once," Ross said, "that we must cease trying to please the imbeciles."

"It goes deeper," Mitch snapped. "Someone wants our head."

"They can't have it," Ross said with false joviality. He went through the living room to the master bath and took a leak, pushed the button, and it was vacuumed into the Gulfstream's septic tank to be pumped later into the huge Newark sewage system and thence into the sea – how many billion tons of human excreta dumped hourly into the sea from which we came and cannot live without?

"It's all crap," he said to Victor when he returned.

"It's destroying us," Mitch said. "That's what you don't seem to understand."

"I CAN TAKE RAWHIDE DOWN," Dale Robichaud said when Lily called him. "They've tried to fix prices, they've lied to regulators, the list goes on and on . . ."

"Can you give me some examples?" she asked. "Some cases I can look into? That will improve my story. We can do a Zoom, if you want. I'll set it up."

"No Zoom, none of that stuff. And I won't give you all this over the phone. But hey, if the *Times* doesn't want it, I can sell it elsewhere."

"I never said we didn't want it."

"Then come on out here, and I'll give you the whole story. But do it quick, or it goes to someone else."

IT WAS TIME TO CALL SINGAPORE, BUT Ross WAS WEARING down. He stared out the Perspex at the white clouds and black night at fifty below zero, thinking of a North Dakota blizzard years ago that had been even colder.

Had to be the winter he'd turned four. Snow already above the windows, the old log house creaking and rattling in the vicious wind, and everyone stayed inside around the fireplace and read books or played cards and enjoyed not having to do anything.

He was lying on the soft thick braided rug hugging a yellow retriever named Trudi, and over her tawny shoulder watching the flames dance against the granite stones. He couldn't figure how fire happened, how the wood turned black then ashes as the flames pirouetted above it, how heat was made – what *was* heat, anyway?

Without fire we humans couldn't have evolved from African apes.

We'd be back there still. Or long gone.

Fire, this change from thing *to* heat, *makes us who we are.*

Like the oil Dad pumps out of the earth. Oil that runs cars and trucks and trains and heats houses and shops and factories and makes electricity all over America –

Wow. But where did that oil come from?

And how did it change from a stinky black sludge to what makes a plane go?

Dad sitting there in his old leather armchair, smiling and half-asleep, with his big-knuckled, scarred hands, his face weathered by a hundred blizzards, did he even know?

Mom, who'd braided this rug he was lying on, who ran this house and barns and ranch and the finances of a drilling company of twenty people. She who knew so much – did *she* know?

In that North Dakota blizzard he'd wanted to understand fire. Not to make money. To understand.

And now he had to understand who was plotting against him. Who their allies were across the world. And how to defeat them.

1 2

THE GLASS WALL

FIFTY FEET BELOW THE SURFACE, the cold, roiling black-green water was turgid with platform debris and gas and sediment bubbling up from the cutoff valves below.

Turk flipped on his Sea Dragon. Slivers of fish darted away from its glare. A platform pylon appeared out of the green-algae gloom. It was twisted sideways as if it had been struck from behind. By the force of the explosion that had ignited in the four huge gas pipes clustered under the center of the platform.

All four pipes had been ripped apart into huge tongues of splintered steel jabbing outward like leaves of a flower.

"Going down a bit," he said into his mic.

"Got you, mate," Clint the Aussie answered.

They drifted down another twenty and circled the pipes. Here you could see strain in the steel – stretch lines, cracks, discolorations that were visible if you rubbed off the new coat of algae. The algae that couldn't have lived here before because the pipes would have been too hot. And now it was their home. Maybe for generations to come.

He swam back up to where the splintered steel tongues had splayed out from the force of the blast. Carefully he rose toward where the raw edges of exploded steel curled toward him. He shone his Sea Dragon on the first. All the way around it, the arc of the bent steel splinters curled tighter and tighter toward their tips. "This one," he said to Clint, "it's an outie only."

Clint glanced at him. "Let's call this pipe Number One."

Pipe Two was the same, an outie. This didn't seem right. He'd been expecting that a device had blown the pipes; it was so old school, once you looked beneath the surface.

On Pipe Three, the tongues of splintered steel didn't bend so far, some barely at all. Holding down his elation, Turk swam to Pipe Four.

Like Pipe Three, its tongues of tortured steel were far less incurved. "The platform was blown," he rasped to Clint.

"Tiger behind you," Clint said. "Big one."

Turk spun to face the huge shark that swerved and glided past. "Let's take some samples and pix. And get out of here."

FROM THE GLASS WALL OF HIS MADISON AVENUE PENTHOUSE Ross watched the lights flicker on the MetLife Tower and the jagged peaks of lower Manhattan, the traffic rumble quieting in the streets far below.

His phone throbbed against his chest. Mitch again. "Yeah?"

"Forty-three. Forty-fucking-three point eight-seven."

"Relax, Mitch. It's going to get worse."

Mitch huffed despondently. "We gonna ride this all the way down?"

"It'll flatten eventually." Ross took a breath. "I promise."

"How the fuck would you know? You're not the CFO."

"Mitch, I couldn't ever do what you do." Ross waited a beat. "Nor could you do what I do."

Silence. "We'll see about that," Mitch said finally, and shut off.

Beyond his glass wall, Manhattan glittered like a Vegas slot machine. A million blazing windows, arc lights drowning the streets, thousands of headlights snaking in all directions, planes rising from Kennedy, Newark and La Guardia in an unending string of pearls.

All from crude.

So valuable that millions kill and die for it.

AS THE DELTA 737 DROPPED TOWARD BATON ROUGE, LILY calculated how likely it would crash. Dark cumulus at 10,000, buffeting winds, both pilots had looked young and inexperienced – a blonde woman with four bars and a slender black man with three – how many hours did they have? The plane felt worn – was it in bad shape? It was a 737, after all.

Sleet streaked the window. The plane shuddered as the wing flaps descended. Lily watched the first-class attendant tighten her skirt over her knees and scan anxiously out the window while the plane yawed and shook.

You could die now. Or on your flight home two days from now. Or your hundred and forty-fifth flight. Or your thousandth. Whenever it comes it will be awful.

The only way to beat it is not care if you die.

By the time she'd taken her backpack out of the overhead rack and led the other first-class passengers down the ramp, Lily had forgotten she'd been scared. Her mind was on Dale Robichaud.

Ian had wanted a profile on Robichaud that could help *Times* readers understand the CFTC, as well as the oil and gas industry, which whether they liked it or not powered the modern world.

This made her think of Rawhide's motto: *Energy is Life.* Was that true? She still wasn't sure what the CFTC actually did. Was it an impediment to free trade, an old boys' club, a government predator – what?

And how did the CFTC influence the energy industry? And what connection was there, she was beginning to wonder, between the U.S. energy industry and the Ukraine war?

"You need to get away," Ian had told her, *"from this Wuhan stuff you've wasted so much time on."*

"I'll get back on it as soon as I return," she'd answered.

"When you get back, we need to talk about that. We think you're headed up the wrong alley."

She didn't understand: what did *we* need to talk about? She was totally bilingual Chinese, she had studied the lab source for years, been five times to Wuhan, and ever since the virus first broke out 4Q 2019, she'd been trying to determine *Where did it come from? Was it accidental or planned? Is the truth being told?*

Was Ian now telling her to back off because she'd proven that the virus had come from the Wuhan lab? While despite all the recent evidence the *Times* was vigorously pretending it hadn't?

Why was the *Times* still trying to hide what was so obviously true?

How had things gotten that bad? Where you could only say the truth if the church agreed?

Your job as a journalist was to stay impartial and work like hell and hope the truth prevailed. That it might help someone understand something. Might help explain the world.

When she'd started out at the *Financial Times,* they'd said, *"Keep your opinions to yourself. Just give us the facts, the best independent analysis you can. Even if you have a dog in this fight, don't go there. If we find your opinions have snuck into your articles, we charge you ten bucks a word."*

Damn, she thought, as she headed downstairs to Hertz, ten bucks a word is still a lot of money.

But opinions seemed to be more and more what the *Times* wanted these days. As long as you had the right opinions. And the other Democratic Party media, the *Washington Post,* NPR, most cable news too . . .

Speaking of opinions, she still wasn't sure what she thought of Ross Bullock. Whatever it was, she'd keep it to herself.

"AN EXPLOSIVE DEVICE," TURK SAID, WHEN HE CALLED ROSS from Jakarta. "At fifty-four feet. We can send a robot to the bottom but don't need to."

Ross felt a rush of fury. "I *want* the bastards."

"Our pix are good," Turk said. "We even have blast evidence."

"What kind?"

"When the device went off, the outer wall of the steel pipe it was bolted to blew inward, right? And pieces of that outer steel wall, and the explosive behind it, should be implanted in the opposite wall, before that one blew outward."

"Should be implanted? So what?"

"I'm sending samples that we cut from those pipes to a lab in Belgium, best in the world at recovering traces of explosive, that kind of stuff."

"So it was a diver –"

"He had to have a mother ship, somewhere near. Or a sub."

"A sub?"

"Little one, two- or four-man."

"What's the range?"

"It could have a mother ship, too. So distance may not matter."

"Or?"

"Depends on the sub, with a small one, one-eighty to two-fifty nautical miles –"

"Out to our platform and back to Balikpapan –"

"– A larger sub like the MS200, could be over a thousand."

"Turk, we're going to kill these bastards."

"It won't be easy. Whoever they are, they're good."

DALE ROBICHAUD MET LILY AT THE DOOR AS IF SHE WERE A LONG-lost friend. She ducked away from his hug, trying not to slip on the travertine floor as she crossed the entry bigger than most homes and turned to face him. "Where shall we do this?"

He beamed down at her, larger than life in his ten-gallon mauve cowboy hat with its silver and jade band around it, the Navaho bollard tie, western shirt in red and green with pearl buttons, the stretch jeans over snakeskin cowboy boots – at least, she decided, they looked like snakeskin. Not that she'd know, she reminded herself, you don't see them a lot in Greenwich Village.

Was he larger than life for a reason? Was he trying to impress her, head her off, intimidate her? Did he actually think this was who he was?

He cocked his head, eying her quizzically. "The first time you've been to Bayou Country?"

"You mean Louisiana?"

"This part of it."

She felt attacked. "Never."

He nodded toward the river behind the estate grounds. "Let's head on down. I want to show you something."

"Mr. Robichaud, I've got lots of questions – can't we just sit down?"

He didn't answer, and unwillingly she followed him through the vast mansion, huge room after huge room hung with gilt and chandeliers, past the kitchen bigger than a fancy Manhattan restaurant's, across the rear porch of towering white pillars and stone terraces, down stone stairs and across a long flagstone pathway to the edge of a greenish brown river.

"Called the Vermilion," Robichaud said. "Used to be the most polluted river in America." Standing beside her, he waved a hand at the wide sinuous lake of dark-colored foam draining toward the sea. "Now, altogether, us citizens of Lafayette, the people of Layeasyanna, we cleaned it up."

"That's impressive," she said. "Now I'm sure you're very busy, Mr. Robichaud, and I don't want to take any more of your time than needed. Can we sit down somewhere and talk?"

He grinned at her. His teeth were enormous, like a beaver's. His ears hung down in great lobes. "I was going to suggest we go out in my boat." He nodded at the dock, where a long silver speedboat tugged at its moorings. "More secure that way."

She shook her head. "I've got only one recorder. We can turn it off any time you want."

He grinned again. "That's my girl."

She fought down disgust. *Record him and get out.*

She turned and headed back to the mansion. "Anywhere you like."

He chuckled, following her, his huge boots thumping the flagstones.

They sat in what he called a study. It was like a Loire chateau, all gold and silk and fake French landscape paintings. She set the recorder on the table between them. He smiled at her. "Ready when you are."

She had to get balanced. *He's trying to make you angry, disgust you. Why?* "Tell me a little," she said, taking out a notepad, "about the CFTC."

As he droned on, she watched his face: expressive, congenial, smart and flinty-eyed. He described the CFTC as the protector of the American investor. The rule of law. What would happen to international energy markets without the CFTC?

She stifled a yawn. "So there's only been one recent enforcement action by CFTC?"

"Rawhide Energy." Robichaud nodded. "A perfect example."

"Of what?"

"Of why the CFTC's so important. Without it to regulate markets, it would be like Russian roulette out there."

She bit her lip impatiently as he waxed on again about the CFTC, saying nothing about Rawhide. "But I've heard that the president of Rawhide –"

"You're not talking to *him*, are you?" Robichaud swung one snake-skin boot across the other knee. "He'll tell anybody anything, that guy." He grinned, leaned forward, and pointed a finger at her. "But don't you believe it."

This guy's used to pushing people, she reminded herself.

And they're used to obeying.

The powerful are only powerful because we allow it.

It was five-thirty when she refused a drink and dinner and drove her rented Malibu the 32 miles back to Baton Rouge airport. It had been drizzling and now was raining hard, cars both ways on Interstate 10 throwing up curving waves of spray. She had a steak and two vodka martinis at the Hilton Garden Inn Airport Hotel, but they made her feel no better.

Robichaud had danced around every question about Rawhide. Refused to even talk about the war. Why?

13

PERPS

DURVON ST. MILES had shorted two million barrels of Dukhan crude from Qatar, but that wouldn't cover the position on the damn Venezuelan Cerro Negro heavy crude he'd unwisely taken, with fucking Maduro and the Americans always at each other's throats, and because of the American sanctions the Texas refineries couldn't take it. So *now* what was he going to do?

He could fill two tankers and have them run into each other and sink and collect insurance on the loss, but there'd be environmental fuss and oily birds and dead fucking porpoises all over the place, and by the time he got his hands on the money he'd be dead too.

He could ship the crude to Nigeria and try to badge it out of there, but already there was too much Russian heavy crude in Europe despite the sanctions, and nobody wanted the damn stuff because it was harder to refine, and he'd been an idiot to take a position, had been told by that CIA guy Finnegan in Caracas he paid ten grand a month that the Americans and Maduro were going to kiss and make up, because the Americans needed the oil.

The damn trouble with heavy crude was its specific gravity and density number, as measured for every well by the API, the American Petroleum Institute. Any API number under 25 is rated "heavy," because it is harder to refine into gasoline and other products than the higher API crudes like Brent and WTI, which have 35-45 API numbers.

And the American sanctions on Venezuela were just like what they did on Iraq, Iran, Indonesia, Nigeria – you name it – whatever it took to make that country's government knuckle under and give American companies cheap crude at any environmental price. Nigeria . . . a comedy, what happened to Nigeria . . . Iraq, Iran, you name it.

Anyway, Maduro was a goddamn commie; somebody should break his balls. What Venezuela needed was a good revolution to put the military back on top. No doubt the Americans wanted to do it but now had their knickers in a knot with the mess they'd made in Ukraine, the Middle East and Taiwan, so overthrowing Maduro wasn't going to happen unless the Agency did it behind the president's back like it had ever since Kennedy in Cuba and all those podunk places in Africa – killing whoever needed to be killed, without first asking permission.

He paced his London townhouse, angry and alone. He was going to lose millions on the Dukhan crude, and maybe even more on the Venezuelan heavy crude. He needed to find a few billion bucks. Or a nice war with growth potential, a good place to sell his deadly toys, straighten things out.

"I CAN SEE A HUNDRED POSSIBLE PERPS." Isaiah King glared at them out of the video screen. "The hit on your platform timed for your speech against sanctions and nuclear war? If so, who was punishing you for that?"

"Obviously the White House," Ross said, "the whole pro-war crowd, the defense industries, politicians and Democratic media. Even before the speech, they knew it was coming."

Isaiah was a large broad-chested man with muscular arms and shoulders, a graying beard and disheveled curly hair. He leaned forward into the screen like a heavyweight confronting an opponent. "There's plenty of possible perps out there – organizations, companies, NGOs, whole countries, anyone making money on this war. And every major oil company that is now making billions off the president's sanctions. And every company and group and corporate media outlet that works for them. And the hundreds of thousands of companies around the world that work for *them* . . ." Isaiah shrugged his massive shoulders. "And the eight billion people on this planet, most of whom don't want to die in a nuclear war but depend on crude, one way or another, to get through their day."

"I told Ross," Mitch broke in, "not to fuck with the White House."

"They want these wars," Isaiah said, "and will do whatever they can to prolong them. So our question is, how do we outsmart them? Before this goes nuclear?"

"It's not just the White House," Victor broke in. "It's the Agency, NRA, Pentagon, our trillion-dollar weapons companies and all the politicians they elected, our several thousand secret intelligence groups, the corporate media. How do we bring them under control before they kill us?"

"Are your competitors trying to drive you out of business and raise prices at the same time? Or is this political against the whole US? Is it Iran or China?" The monitor screeched as Isaiah scratched his whiskers. "Or something ultraleft tied to North Korea, Zimbabwe or Venezuela? Organized crime, Italian, Chinese, Indonesian – they're the ones wanting their leases back . . . the list goes on and on."

LIZ TRIED TO DISLIKE TURK THE INSTANT SHE MET HIM. HE reeked of toxic masculinity – wiry, dark-tanned, dark-haired, a strong jaw and blue eyes, a relaxed muscular assurance and a bright smile – everything *Vogue* readers twittered over.

Not that she really believed in such silly ideas as toxic masculinity; she'd had too loving and strong a father. But maybe living in Indonesia's world of Muslim male control and intolerance had lessened her taste for men.

Though there was such a rough warmth in Turk's voice, a kindness in those beautiful blue eyes that it didn't really annoy her how good-looking he was.

He had just inspected the platform, had returned to Rawhide's Jakarta office, and wanted to see her right away. "You're sure it was a bomb?" she said when she got there.

In a conference room he pulled two chairs close to the table, punched some keys on his iPad and handed it to her. "That pipe's at fifty-four feet. You can see the blast patterns on the steel, the angle of curl on the torn steel."

Her stomach lurched with grief at this monstrous crime that had ended the lives of so many good people, some of them her friends. "Why?" She looked at him across the table, shaking her head. "Why?"

He shrugged. "Does it bother you, to talk about that night?"

She thought a moment. "You're the first person to ask me that."

He raised an eyebrow. "And?"

"Of course, it bothers me. But we have to."

He nodded sympathetically. "You were up on the third deck, right? The southwest corner?"

"Yes."

"Why?"

"I was watching the stars, the Southern Cross . . ."

"The only way a bomb could have been attached to that pipe is if a diver swam there from a boat. When you were up there did you see anything that could have been a boat, a wake of any kind, no matter how small?"

She tried to remember. The damp rail, the silvery rippling sea, the roiling current passing under the platform, a sky of many thousand diamonds. "No."

"Were you looking in all directions?"

"I couldn't see north, it was blocked by the tower."

"One of the choppers found some diving gear, chewed on by a shark."

"Where?"

"A mile north of the platform."

"Oh." She thought a moment. "So maybe the bastard didn't make it."

"I'm sending it to the lab where I sent the pipe samples, see if there's any residue on it."

"Residue?" she asked.

"These days the research is so advanced we can often find microscopic traces of high explosives like TNT and C-4 in the remnants of a bomb blast –"

"But in the water –"

"Even after a week or more. Even in salt water. Despite the explosive shock waves and heat over five thousand degrees Centigrade."

She huffed. "Impossible."

"We can even ID the specific explosive used, where it came from, maybe track it that way. Sometimes we can even find traces of DNA and fingerprints, they're called latent FPs."

She shook her head. "How can they? After the explosion, the heat, the salt water?"

"Obviously there won't be latent fingerprints on the exploded pipe because the diver would've worn gloves. But there might, just possibly, be latent FPs on the bomb fragments, or the tape, of whoever assembled the bomb."

"How do you know all this?"

"A friend in Belgium, a lab." He faced away, toward the window, tapping his pen on the table, then turned to her. "How'd you end up working on that platform?"

"Rocks."

"Rocks?"

"Ever since I was a kid I loved rocks." Her cheeks felt strange, and she realized she was smiling. "My parents didn't like to take me hiking because I made them carry home all the rocks I'd found. We'd go to the mountains, and all I'd want to do is figure out how they were made."

"And have you?"

Was he humoring her? "Of course not. The physical stuff, sure, but not the causality."

He nodded. "Like the explosion," she went on. "Easy to understand the physics, the engineering. But why?"

His eyes weren't just blue, she realized, but piercing violet as if light gleamed behind them. "There's many people out there . . . companies, governments, that could be behind this."

"Who?"

"We're working on that."

"I want to work on it too. I intend to *kill* these bastards."

ROSS LOVED RAWHIDE TOWER. STUNNINGLY BEAUTIFUL SIXTY-two stories in the heart of Wall Street, 125 people per floor, a working village of nearly eight thousand souls. Ross had leased out all but the top three floors, keeping most of his people in branch offices in Billings and Denver. He'd taken the top floor office facing where the World Trade Center had been, to remind himself that in becoming addicted to Middle East oil, America had made itself a victim of a feudal religious kleptocracy that had used America's trillions of dollars to bring Islamic fundamentalism back from the dark ages and enforce it on the world.

In the early days of the oil industry, American oil companies had been delighted, as had its politicians, to let a ruthless, backward Saudi desert tribe corner that country's oil reserves by killing everyone who got in their way. And who were more than happy to let Americans suck crude out of their deserts in return for dollars. Till the Bush family, that had helped create the CIA and numerous Latin American wars, bought two U.S. presidencies and was so indentured to the Saudis that after 9/11 the second Bush refused to blame them for what they had done, as did his successor, America's first black president, who however spoke often about truth and courage.

Crude, first from Pennsylvania and Texas, then as America's oil habit grew and domestic supplies became insufficient to feed the growing frenzy of cars and trucks and highways crawling across cities, farms and wildlands, the spiderwebs of power stations and factories. And so they went abroad, pillaging countries and overthrowing governments all over the world to keep the oil flowing cheaply. They bought American politicians for pocket change, killed the railroads and urban transit, poisoned the air, drove global temperatures higher, and turned the nation's placid streets and roads into roaring concrete death zones.

Though he'd told himself many times, we wouldn't be where we are today without oil. We'd still be stuck in the nineteenth century, lighting our homes with whale oil and taking six weeks to cross the Atlantic.

He punched at the pillow under his head. It was two a.m., and as usual he couldn't sleep. Thinking of every bad thing that had happened and what should he do.

The forces against him seemed overwhelming.

Now nuclear war.

All the lies from Washington that we can win a nuclear war. While everyone cowers in place, hoping our rulers let us survive.

But in a nuclear war, nothing survives.

TOM HOGAN'S BACK WAS KILLING HIM. HIS EYES STUNG. HE turned from his wall of computer screens and eased to his feet, rubbing his back and turning his head from side to side, making the bones crack. He hobbled from his computers to the window and stared at the swirling snow.

It was falling so thickly he couldn't even see the four guys he'd sent out to check the refinery's Unit 41, the Catalytic Cracker. What had worried him was that 41's numbers had suddenly taken a dive and though it was probably a computer issue, not a physical one, it could possibly indicate a pipe leak. Unlikely, but with this blizzard you couldn't see anything on the cameras. It bothered him that he wasn't out there with the four guys, but as night supervisor he had to stay here monitoring the other units, the data flow.

Two hours and forty-seven minutes till six a.m. when he could go home. And now this storm meant half an hour on icy Wyoming 287 and twenty minutes more on the gravel road to his forty acres. He'd miss the kids' breakfast, Wendy in her bathrobe, fresh coffee and pancakes from heaven, the whole double-wide trailer full of laughter and fun.

Acid rose from his stomach from the ham sandwiches Wendy had made. It wasn't that she used too much mustard; it was his drinking too much coffee to keep awake looking at these screens where nothing ever happened, making forty-one bucks an hour while big guys like Ross Bullock and his crew made forty-one *thousand* an hour.

He'd figured it out: with Ross's CEO salary of ten million a year plus stock appreciation, he was making at least forty-five million a year. Mitch Carter and Victor Minh, Betsy, all the top people. Who cared that Ross had been a tough guy himself on a wildcat crew, had driven plenty of his own wells, could run this refinery with his eyes closed? So could a lot of guys. Didn't matter he paid much better than any other refinery, with better benefits. So what?

The world was divided into the people who win out and the people who work for it, and don't forget, Ross had sure got a step up from Old Man Bullock.

Tom peered at the driving snow, nearly horizontal, fiercely attacking the windows, turning the world to ice.

But this crap we make here – he grinned – *it's the only thing keeps us warm. That takes me home to Wendy and the kids.*

He kneaded his neck. *Christ it hurts.* All the years bent over, peering down at numbers, charts, and gauges. How many billion gallons had poured through the screens in front of him?

Christ my neck.

White light flashed from Unit 41 and burst into an orange-red fireball, knocking him down in a crimson-white cloud as huge chunks of steel cavorted through the night and crashed down around him. A second explosion erased Unit 41, shattered the windows and slammed him across the room under a table that collapsed on him under a falling wall.

14

THE BLACK HAWK MOTEL

LIZ WAITED at the corner on Jakarta's Lemuri Avenue till the walk light turned green. As she started across, her phone throbbed, and she slowed to snatch it from her bag. A silver car roared at her from nowhere, whacking her leg as she dove for the sidewalk.

She stood swearing and rubbing torn knees, hobbled to the sidewalk, and answered the phone. "Yes? *Yes*, dammit!"

No one.

An old man with missing front teeth stood before her. Small and thin, in a faded T-shirt and trousers, barefoot. "They almost get you!" he whispered in Malay.

"You see it, the car?"

"BMW, everyone has one."

"License plate? Did you see it?"

"Not know," he shook his head, "how to write it."

"You remember? Tell me!"

"I remember, perhaps."

She glanced furiously up the street, but the car had vanished. "*Tell* me!"

"I am a poor man . . ."

"Here!" She fished in her bag and gave him ten thousand rupiahs.

"License was B 2129 POC –" He glanced at her bleeding knees. "You should be more careful."

OH MY CHRIST SO HOT. NO AIR . . . TOM HOGAN FORCED HIMSELF UP on one elbow, squirmed from under the table, and stumbled to the burning stairs. *Now or die.* He jumped down to the blazing landing and dove out the stairwell into the howling night, sucking in the icy air and crying out in terror and relief, rolling over and over in the soothing snow.

The others. The four guys who'd gone to check the crude line behind Unit 41. Had they set it off?

How?

Where were they?

Groaning, he staggered toward the blazing remains of Unit 41.

Have to find them.

SIX MINUTES LATER, ROSS GOT THE CALL FROM WYOMING.

By 8:15 he, Mitch, and Victor were on the Gulfstream climbing out of Newark toward Cheyenne.

"This is insane," Isaiah King said when Ross called.

"I *want* them. Whoever's behind this."

"You talk to the president?"

"He's still in Delaware. Not taking calls."

"What the hell!" Isaiah sighed. "How much you give him, last election?"

"Twenty."

"It wasn't enough. Plus you don't like his wars."

"I've got four more people dead, Isaiah. And another in the hospital. I've got to solve this."

Isaiah leaned into the screen. "We will."

"I'll see the surviving guy tomorrow morning, learn what I can. For now, I'm telling the media no comment till we know more."

"We'll send a forensics team to Wyoming asap," Isaiah said. "Let's see what they find."

"This is bigger than we thought. I don't know where it's going."

"I *told* you, don't fight the sanctions. Don't fight the president's damn nuclear war."

TOM HOGAN DIDN'T KNOW HE WAS ALIVE. THIS ETHEREAL SENSE of floating through clouds, this strange music, haunting and repetitive, this absence of touch or feeling, were all either the last synapses of his dying brain, or maybe there *was* something after you died.

The strange music slowly became voices and footsteps in the corridor, the swish of uniforms and a woman's voice calling doctors and nurses on a speaker. The clouds were disinfectant and detergent, chemicals and emptiness.

He lay there savoring this strange return to life. There was no pain. His arms and legs were wrapped in light gauze and suspended slightly above the bed by cables from the ceiling. As if he were trying, on his back, to fly.

Holy shit, the refinery. The cracker. The four guys.

People had been asking questions – who?

They better not blame him.

Just because he was refinery night supervisor didn't mean it was his fault.

"THE PRESIDENT'S VERY CONCERNED," NATHAN COLDMIRE SAID.

"You told me that already. I want to speak to him. Now."

"He's taking time off, right now."

"You tell him, goddammit, to lean on Keith and Wally in Jakarta! And now my refinery."

"Don't jump the gun, Ross. That could be accidental. Crackers blow all the time." The voice modifier whined as Coldmire changed his grip. "We're told the refinery's internal reports identified a leak on that cracker, for Chrissake, six *months* ago –"

"Not a chance. We'd have fixed it the same day. Who told you that?"

"And your platform – terrible shame."

"It was blown. I sent you the pix."

"We're getting pushback on that," Coldmire said.

"Who from?"

"Department of Energy engineers."

"How the fuck would *they* know?"

"And what we hear from President Widodo in Jakarta is that Rawhide never gave the Ministry the engineering drawings for those pipes. Nobody's even sure what they looked like."

"The hell we didn't! We have confirmed receipts of every document delivery to the Ministry. And we don't *ever* miss a safety review. And we're always watching every piece in that refinery, from the one million two hundred thousand nuts and bolts to the electronics and AI. We don't ever screw up. Ever."

"Well –" Coldmire drew out his answer. "It seems you have now."

"Our platform's destroyed with 131 people dead, our hydrocracker's blown with 4 dead and another in the hospital, our refinery's shut, the Indonesians are trying to steal our leases, the insurance pool's accusing us of negligence, the banks are pulling our loans, people are breaking off negotiations on our new deals, social media's screaming for boycotts, CNN and all those other assholes are spreading lies, everyone's selling us short in every market, and EastPac's trying to eat us alive. And you think it's accidental?"

"I don't follow you on the victim bit, Ross. From what I hear, it all sounds self-induced. Ignore maintenance, and some day it'll come back and bite you in the ass."

"It started the day I announced our opposition to your dirty, evil wars." Ross stared out the Perspex at the approaching lights of Sweetwater, the refinery glowing in the distance beyond the town. "No wars, remember? It's what you guys rode your white horse to the White House on – *remember?*"

"Ross, you made a big mistake. Or you're stupider than we

thought. You need to get behind our wars and stop knifing us in the back!"

"When you guys got to the White House, America wasn't in a Third World War. We weren't facing nuclear apocalypse, there was no inflation, no open border or illegal immigration, racism was at an all-time low . . . Now you not only have a war with Russia and another in the Middle East, both of which can kill us all, plus you're trying to start a war with China? Even with North Korea, for Chrissake! Don't you fuckers know?"

"This is a historical moment, Ross. I don't think you understand history."

"Who gave you the right to doom everyone?"

THE WHITE HOUSE IS GOING TO KILL US ON THIS," MITCH SAID AS the plane landed. "They're going to say there were no explosives on the platform pipes, and no trace of sabotage here at the refinery."

"We're going to need Isaiah and his investigators to make our case."

"It's just more expense, when we have no money."

"Don't fight me on this," Ross said tiredly.

"As CFO, it's my duty –"

"You don't give a damn about your duty. You're just afraid we might belly up and you'll lose your equity and be poor again."

Mitch flashed a sarcastic smile. "Like we all once were?"

"We're all risking our financial lives. But we can't just think of ourselves. There's 27,000 people who work with us. And millions more who invested in us because they *believe* in us, in our future. Who gave us money when we needed it. We're not letting them down."

Mitch huffed. "Thanks to your anti-war bullshit, we already have."

TV SCREENS IN THE SWEETWATER ARRIVALS LOUNGE FLITTED FROM relatives weeping in the glare of camera lights to chopper shots of the burning cracker and ground views of the smoke cloud rising from the debris. As Ross and the others walked past, it switched to interviews with firemen and with a short, hard-faced man in a beat-up white cowboy hat identified as Lyle Brant, sheriff of Sweetwater County.

"It was either accidental," Brant was saying, "or intentional. If it *was* accidental, we have to assume poor maintenance. Crackers don't explode if they're properly operated."

A wad of tobacco stuck in his lower lip gave him the petulant, aggressive look of a cocky rooster. He had a wide thin mouth, a narrow, pointed jaw, and high rugged cheekbones. "If it *was* intentional, we have to figure out who, now don't we?"

"An oil refinery," intoned the local NBC station, "is a *very* dangerous place. Millions of gallons of highly explosive liquids and gases, and sizzling with high-voltage electricity, catalytic crackers, vacuum distillation and other perilous systems, they are hyper-industrial cataclysms waiting to happen. With proper maintenance, however, accidents needn't happen. We're speaking tonight with Dr. Howard Batcheldor, Professor of Social Services at Yale University, who will tell us more –"

"An oil refinery is so dangerous," the professor with the gray hair and goatee said, *"that absolute fire precautions must be enforced. The tiniest mistake can lead to a flaming catastrophe . . . So they must adhere to strict safety and maintenance procedures. Which it appears the Rawhide refinery may not have done . . ."*

"Professor of *Social* Services?" Mitch snorted.

IT TOOK TWENTY MINUTES FOR THE BLACK CADILLAC SUV TO deliver them from the airport to the refinery, the road ahead clogged with fire trucks from Laramie and Casper, even Cheyenne, their crews standing in clumps chatting in the howling snowstorm, the cracker's glow haunting against the stacks and towers of the vacuum distillation, reformers and crude tanks.

In its veil of howling snow, the refinery looked alien, a space station, something from another planet, the steel towers like gigantic tentacles, the squat storage tanks deadly toads, the many thousands of overlapping pipes and cables like serpents throbbing with explosive peril, the thousands of fierce lights searing his eyes.

Ross had always loved the refinery smell, the crude, the stench of gas and many chemicals. But now all was danger and despair.

A figure in a white hat appeared out of the storm and stared up at him. "So you're the one," he said.

It was the sheriff on TV, Lyle Brant. "I'm the one what?" Ross said.

"Owns this horror show."

"I'm here to see the families of the missing people. And to talk to all the employees. And to help you in any investigations you need to do."

"Need to do? Hell, I need to know why that goddamn cracker blew. And who killed four people whom I'm supposed to protect. And injured another." He spit dark tobacco juice against the snow. "That's all I need to do."

"JUST BECAUSE THIS DIVER FRIEND OF YOURS SAYS THE PLATFORM was blown," Mitch growled, "that doesn't make it true!" In his under-shirt, a Coors bottle on his knee, leaning forward in a fake leather chair in Ross's room at Sweetwater's Black Hawk Motel he added, "I still think it was bad engineering."

Victor stood, his back to Mitch, staring out the picture window at the dancing snow. "Mitch, I'm getting tired of your goddamn aspersions!"

"Aspersions? Shit, you don't even know what that means."

Victor turned on him. "You making fun of my English? Why don't you try speaking Malay? C'mon, say something in Malay! Vietnamese? Say something in Vietnamese!"

"Okay, you two," Ross yelled. "Cut the shit!"

"You!" Mitch swung on him venomously. "You talk about shit? When *you* keep pushing this nuclear war danger? When all that matters is that it was poor engineering that blew the platform? I don't give a sweet goddamn what this diver says – some buddy of yours from North Dakota? Show me the goddamn ocean in North Dakota. What the fuck's he know? Maybe you told him to say this?"

"Turk was a Navy diver for eight years. His technical specialty was underwater demo."

"So maybe *he* blew the platform? And if it *was* a bomb" – Mitch faced Victor – "the insurance pays, because we have a terrorism rider. If it's bad maintenance, the insurance won't pay; it's stated in the contract. Same as this cracker explosion. Victor, you're the final guy in charge of maintenance and oversight on every asset we have, and when shit like this goes down – guess what – *you're* responsible!"

"Mitch," Ross said tiredly, "you're way over your head. Let's talk in the morning."

"In the morning my ass." Mitch yanked open the door. "In the morning, it'll be the same. Bad maintenance that blew the platform. And it was bad maintenance that just blew our cracker."

"You got to calm down, Mitch," Victor said. "Tomorrow we talk to the guy who survived the cracker explosion. Maybe he can tell us what happened."

"Yeah? Like Ross's friend the North Dakota diver? What bullshit!" Mitch slammed the door behind him.

"All this," Victor said morosely as Mitch's footsteps thudded away on the motel corridor, "is just going to drive our stock lower. So EastPac can start buying again."

"Maybe Mitch's right," Ross sighed. "We hit them with the shareholder buy option."

Victor shook his head. "Too late now. With this explosion coming right after the Mahakam platform, people are not going to be sucked in by low prices. Not when the price can fall even more."

"We're at what, forty-three?" Ross said.

"Forty-two twenty. And we're not going to be happy when Nasdaq opens."

"We can turn it around." Ross stood and straightened his aching back. "Let's see what we learn in the morning from the night supervisor."

"Amazing he survived."

"Get some rest, my friend. We have another horrible day tomorrow."

"Damn you, Ross. You always make things look better than they are."

"Because they're never as bad as you think." He squeezed Victor's arm. "But that's why we need you. Why we can't win without you."

Standing at the door, Ross watched Victor wander back down the corridor like an old man, as if partly blind, slightly crippled, an air of defeat.

Ross stepped back into his room and turned the bolt. He sat on the bed barefoot with the laptop on his knees, answering emails, an endless train of questions, suggestions, complaints, and attacks.

His ankle itched; he thought it might be a mosquito, but there were no mosquitoes here in October. As he leaned forward to scratch it, a thunderous crack and flying glass hailed past his head. As it roared again, he realized it was a bullet and hit the floor, scrambled from the room, dashed down the hall and pounded on Victor's door. "Get out! They're shooting at us!"

No one answered so Ross kicked in the door but Victor wasn't there. He raced along the corridor and pounded on Mitch's door.

Mitch wasn't there either.

15

DIE WELL

"HE FIRED from twenty feet outside your window," Lyle Brant said. "We dug two nine-millimeter slugs out of your wall. Can't believe he missed you."

It sounded almost a reproach. "I got out fast," Ross said.

Lyle wore beat-up cowboy boots, faded Wranglers, a Glock 22 in a quick draw holster on his right hip, and the battered white Stetson cocked back on streaks of thin gray hair. They sat with Lyle's deputy at a Formica table in the motel's breakfast room, the blinds shut.

Lyle took off his hat. "But when you got to Mr. Minh's room, he didn't answer the door?"

"Right."

"You kicked it in?" asked Lyle's deputy, a tall muscular broken-nosed black guy with a badge that said *Cassidy*.

"I thought he was in danger –"

"Did you, now?" Lyle said. "How long after you watched him walk down the corridor toward his room did the shots come through your window?"

"Twenty minutes, maybe."

"You were sitting on the bed barefoot, you said, when the shots came . . ." Cassidy added. "Did you put your shoes on before you left the room?"

"Hell, no. I was being shot at . . ."

"You were barefoot when you kicked in Mr. Minh's door?"

"It's not that hard."

"And when you got in, he was gone." Lyle watched Ross. "And you ran to Mr. Carter's door . . ."

"That's right."

"But he wasn't there either? You and him been having disagreements lately?"

"Of course not."

Lyle smiled. "The motel staff tells me you guys were yelling at each other just before he left your room, just a few minutes before someone shot at you at through your window."

"Mitch would never hurt anyone. And sure, we're disagreeing about stock purchases, things like that."

"What was he wearing?" Cassidy asked.

"Christ, I don't know, sweatpants, a T-shirt, slippers. He wasn't planning to go anywhere."

"We can't find any tracks of either of these guys leaving," Lyle said. "Not going to the parking lot, the lobby."

"Christ, look outside. It's snowing like mad."

"And neither of them had a car?"

"No, we were picked up at the airport by a company car."

"And after the shots were fired you ran to help Mr. Minh? And then Mr. Carter? You didn't care the shooter might still be out there? Or did you know he wasn't?"

"How could I?"

"What if it was you, Mr. Bullock, put those shots through your window?"

"That's nuts."

"And now Mr. Minh and Mr. Carter have disappeared," Cassidy said. "So we don't have their side of the story."

"What story?"

"Maybe Mr. Carter was so mad he went outside and shot at you?

Or maybe you were so mad you got rid of him and then put those two shots through your window so you'd seem the victim and not the perp?"

"Mr. Carter went to bed early. Mr. Minh stayed a few minutes more. We're all so exhausted . . ."

"We can find no tracks," Cassidy said. "Neither Mr. Minh or Mr. Carter took a vehicle, far as we can tell. We'll be checking every roadside camera between here and Cheyenne, but this is Wyoming, so there aren't many."

"There's several possibilities," Brant broke in. "*One,* Carter or Minh, or both of them, got picked up – or grabbed – and someone else shot at you, or *two,* one of them shot at you and then took off. Or *three,* Carter was mad because of your argument and walked out into the snowstorm, not realizing how dangerous it is."

"If so," Cassidy said, "his body's out there somewhere."

"In a blizzard like this," Lyle added, "impossible to find anything."

"And the four guys at the cracker?" Ross said.

"Vaporized."

Ross took a breath. "Do the families know?"

"Of course, the families know. They've always known, what the stakes are."

"I WAS SO PISSED OFF," Mitch said, still in his T-shirt, sweatpants, and slippers. He and Ross sat in one of the adjoining rooms on the second floor that the motel staff had given them, hopefully out of gunshot range. "I went outside, took a leak in this fucking snowstorm. Then when I tried to get back in, the door was locked. So I went around to the front, knocked on the door."

"I hammered on your door," Ross said.

"I wasn't there, for Chrissake. Like I said . . ."

"And you waited till the cops left, before you came back? How convenient."

Mitch slammed his arms on the table. "You suspecting me?"

"I don't trust anybody right now."

Mitch stood. "It's time to sell."

"In a pig's ass."

"You – you're *crazy!* I am coming to think you are *really* crazy. Victor's missing, somebody shot at you, we've lost a platform and a cracker and a lot of people and market value and good faith and every other damn thing that matters . . ."

"No, we haven't," Ross sighed. "We haven't lost what matters."

"Really? What's that?"

It made no sense but Ross said it anyway. "Our souls."

Mitch shook Ross's wrist. "Come back to earth. This isn't astrophysics anymore."

"It never was."

"When I look at it, no way we can survive. Market value, EastPac, canceled contracts, Indonesian leases, Sweetwater, our lenders, our insurers, the media –"

"The media? What the hell do they know?"

"Nothing. They just repeat the same shit."

"So? We start telling them a different story."

"We make shit up?"

"They do it all the time. Why can't we?"

"*DELAYED MAINTENANCE AND MISSING DOCUMENTS: A TROUBLING Pattern at Rawhide Energy, Investigators Say.*"

On his phone, the morning edition of the *Washington Post*, top of page three. For every investor to see.

Lies. Repeated till they become true. An indoctrination that sinks deep into the amygdala, the fight or flight response. Lies repeated till they engender an automatic hormonal response from the amygdala. The *amygdala hijack*, doctors call it. Lies that feel true.

"*Our sources reveal a pattern across a number of Rawhide assets, from the tragically lost Mahakam platform barely a week ago to this week's Sweetwater refinery catastrophe, to risky ventures in nuclear, when what the country needs is more renewable wind energy . . .*"

Oh Jesus. Ross paced the sordid, mildewed motel room trying to unwind, to stretch his muscles and breathe the electrically baked air. And for the thousandth time, as a fly batters at a window, tried to figure what had happened to Victor.

He was like a single Warsaw Jew, he thought, against a wall of German tanks:

If you're going to die, die well.

"**TELL ME**, old friend," Turk said, "has there been a vessel in and out of Balikpapan harbor, one that might have been a mother ship?"

The harbormaster sipped his greasy tea and wiped his mouth. "Yes, my old friend, there have been many small boats, sometimes twenty per day, who could have docked here and perhaps perpetrated this. But we have investigated all carefully. All of them have a perfectly innocent reason to be here."

There are no perfectly innocent reasons, Turk wanted to say, *for anything.* "Do you know of any small submarines that might take on fuel here?"

"None I would know." The harbormaster sat back, absently caressing his prayer beads. "How expensive," he said eventually, "is this problem you have?"

A FIST BANGING on Ross's door at 06:20 forced him awake after two hours' sleep. Covering himself in a towel he staggered to it and glanced through the peephole only to see Lyle Brant.

He opened the door. "Now what the fuck you want?"

"Stop running off at the mouth, Mr. Bullock." Lyle pushed past him and sat in the easy chair. "Come in. Relax." He glanced around the room, saw the coffee machine. "On second thought, brew me a cup of that plastic coffee. With two a them little creamers."

"You can shove those little creamers up your ass. What you want?"

Lyle leaned forward as if confiding good news. "The more we

learn about the deferred maintenance on that cracker, the more I plan to slap *your* ass in jail."

Ross snorted in derision. "You piece of shit . . ."

"If I decide that you or any of your flunkies are criminally responsible for this catastrophe . . ." Lyle grinned tobacco teeth up at Ross. "I'll bring you in."

16

BAD HEART

THE CLEANING LADY pushed the cart of sterilized mop pads, wipes, buckets, and cleaners down the hospital corridor, face hidden by a surgical mask and cap.

One of the cart's wheels wobbled and squeaked but there was nothing she could do about it now.

The day shift would come on in twenty minutes. But for now the corridor lights were still dim, and the intensive care desk at the end of the corridor was deserted.

When she reached Room 401, she backed the cart inside and softly shut the door. From his bed, his four limbs wrapped in white gauze and hung by cables from the ceiling, Tom Hogan smiled up at her.

"How you feeling?" she said behind her surgical mask.

"Better every day. Going to get out of here soon . . . My wife came this afternoon, said the docs think maybe in a week."

"You may be getting out even sooner." From a breast pocket she took a vial, uncapped it, inserted it in his wrist IV drip and pushed in the plunger.

"Hey, what's that?"

"Something to make you sleep."

"Sleep? I don't need . . ." His mouth opened, closed. He stared at her.

"Yes, sleep," she soothed. "A *long* time."

She held his wrist till the pulse stopped, then glanced out the door. At the end of the corridor a nurse sat typing on a computer but facing the other way.

She pushed the cart back to where she'd found it and softly stepped down the back stairs, only her eyes showing between her surgical cap and mask.

"**UNDER WYOMING LAW,**" Lyle Brant said on the phone, "I could arrest you right now."

"No, you can't," Ross said, stepping out of a grim meeting on stock price and bond ratings. "I'm not in Wyoming."

"It will be a federal warrant –"

"Why are you bothering me? Our explosion was a huge tragedy. We are all in sorrow. In the midst of this, I'm trying to help the families of our employees, trying to find who did this, who would intentionally blow up a place where so many people earned their livelihood."

"You don't give a damn about that –"

"How do you know what I give a damn about? And someone shot at me at the motel – do you care about that? Have you even investigated it? And Victor Minh, an engineering genius who helped build this company, is missing. Have you solved *that*? Are you even trying?"

"He wasn't much of an engineering genius if he built that refinery. Or that damn platform."

"Sheriff, stop this bullshit. Instead, please track down whoever attacked our refinery. They're the same ones who blew up the platform and are trying to kill us in the financial markets."

"That's not my department. Far's I'm concerned, you make the money, you pay the price."

"By attacking our company, you're harming your own fellow citizens, people who work there and don't want to lose their jobs. We can get the refinery back online in three months if you leave us alone!"

"As part of any action against you, we will require that you keep paying full salaries and benefits. No matter how long you're down." Lyle paused; Ross could hear the cold Wyoming wind in the background.

"We're already paying full salaries and benefits while we're down."

"You're going to be down one hell of a lot longer than three months. I'll see to that."

Ignorant and implacable, Lyle seemed beyond reach, following his own path regardless of reality.

"I MAY HAVE INFORMATION ON YOUR PROBLEM."

At first Turk didn't recognize the harbormaster's voice. "Which problem?"

"The very expensive one you call me about yesterday."

Turk stepped from the Jakarta sidewalk into a shop doorway, plugging his other ear to lessen the traffic noise, "Yes?"

"Would it help if a vessel like you described to me *has* been seen, one day at dawn, not far from here?"

"What kind of vessel?"

"You should come see me."

"HE CAN'T BE DEAD!" ROSS YELLED. "HE HAD NO SERIOUS INJURIES. What did you do to him?"

"Mr. Hogan apparently had a bad heart," Lyle said. "He'd had two stents already, had high cholesterol he wasn't treating – said statins made his bones hurt – his heart just got blocked, and he was gone before we knew it."

Ross stared out his office window unseeingly at the Wall Street skyscrapers. Now there was no witness to the refinery explosion. And the ruins were covered with five feet of blowing snow.

He reminded himself to breathe. The walls were closing in. As if in a Greek tragedy, predestined.

His right-hand partner had vanished and might be dead. His board of directors wanted him to sell, make everyone paupers overnight.

He put down the phone and stood thinking. Tom Hogan had been the only witness to the refinery explosion. Liz Chaplin had been the only witness to the platform explosion. How soon would the ones who just killed Tom Hogan find her?

"WHERE IS VICTOR MINH?" TRUMPETED SIMON WILT'S LEAD article in *Bloomberg*. As if *they* might know. "What might Ross Bullock be hiding about the Rawhide meltdown? How far will the stock drop?"

Ross called him. "Simon, what the fuck is with that headline? Who said we're in a meltdown?"

"Ross, for Chrissake calm down."

"*You* calm down! What are you doing, conniving to destroy me?"

"I'm on your side, Ross."

"But this is all made up! It's not true!"

"Just saying what I hear. And for what it's worth, I think Rawhide is toast."

THE HARBORMASTER PUT ASIDE HIS BEADS, OPENED HIS DESK drawer, took out an iPhone and placed it between them. "Mr. Holman – Mr. Turner K. Holman, is that right?"

"Yes."

"We are most grateful for your contribution of one hundred fifty million rupiahs to the Kalimantan Renewable Energy Fund. Please be assured that these moneys will go to the expansion of Kalimantan's wind energy program, which is scheduled to make Kalimantan ninety percent renewable by 2050."

It was hilarious, but Turk kept a straight face. That in this place where corruption governs and natural gas is nearly free – gets "flamed" from thousands of stacks – there'd be even a pretense of the wind energy scam. The 150 million rupiahs was not even eleven grand USD.

Be kind, Confucius said. *Everyone suffers.*

The harbormaster stood. "Perhaps we should meet again, once your most gracious contribution is received?"

Turk reached into his backpack. "It's here." He began to take stacks of hundred-dollar bills from his backpack. "So tell me, old friend, where was this vessel seen? And when?"

The harbormaster slid a photo from his drawer. "Ever see a little submarine, like this?"

It was Chinese, Aurora class, twelve meters. "I don't know it," Turk said. "Anyway, you say none like this have entered Balikpapan harbor?"

"This one may have been seen, however, nearby. Two days after your platform exploded."

"Where, nearby?"

"Take the Trans Kalimantan highway from Balikpapan to the Mahakam River." He gave Turk a sheet of paper with a hand-drawn map and phone number. "When you get to the river, you message this number, and it will tell you where to go."

"BUT WHY WOULD ANYONE DESTROY YOUR REFINERY," LYLE said, "if they wanted to take it over?"

"The oil business doesn't make sense." Ross stared out his office window at the miles of Manhattan traffic, realized his answer was obvious.

"Hell it don't," Lyle retorted. "It's *money money money* all up and down from the oil field wrangler to the hedge fund manager who gets rich and does nothing."

Ross smiled briefly. "You're absolutely right."

"So I don't think . . ." With his tongue Lyle readjusted the tobacco wad between his lower lip and gum. "I don't think it's these EastPac folks who tried to light up your refinery."

"And thanks to all your firefighters here in Sweetwater, it was stopped."

"And from Casper and Laramie. Christ, we even got a hook and ladder from Chugwater and two from Douglas." Lyle moved the wad to his left cheek. "Lemme tell you about Douglas."

"Sheriff," Ross snapped. "I've got to grab a plane."

"Well, before you grab your plane – and it's *your* plane, so you can grab it whenever you want. So way back over twenty years ago, that town, Douglas, had a busy and profitable house of ill repute, if you see what I mean –"

"Sheriff, my number two man and very good friend is missing. Someone tried to kill me. Someone tried to blow up my refinery and killed people I care about . . ."

"But the virtuous elders of Douglas, they were worried that harlotry is a sin against God, and everybody in the whole county might be cast down to hell."

"I can see that," Ross said wearily.

"So they voted to close down Mrs. Mercy."

"I can see that."

"Well, *that* was a mistake. After years in the world's oldest business, Mrs. Mercy had made a fair amount of money. And with some of it, she'd bought the town water company. So now she shut *it* down."

Despite himself Ross smiled.

"A week later, they killed that law, and the water flowed again." Lyle looked up at him. "Reason on that, Mr. Oilman. And try to understand Wyoming."

"I grew up in North Dakota. I think people from Wyoming are pussies."

THE ROAD TO THE MAHAKAM RIVER WAS A MICROCOSM OF the vast Indonesian tragedy – the raw pale bulldozed earth on both sides of the Trans Kalimantan Highway, the ravaged forests – once home to our cousin the orangutan so soon to go extinct – the shanty-towns, smoking factories, rusty metal roofs and wind-torn billboards, blistered fields, eroded muddy creeks and sedimented inlets, the squalid humid heat and howling insects. What the hell, Turk told himself. I don't give a damn.

His rented Nissan's right front wheel shimmied, the AC stank of mildew, and the radio kept turning on till he punched it so hard he had to lick blood off his knuckles. So sleepy he couldn't keep his eyes on the road, angry at himself for being here when his Bangkok bar could go under and Rawhide's prospects were barely better.

And this trip maybe a waste of time: who could say what anyone had really seen at dawn one morning on the Mahakam River? What if the harbormaster had been taking him for a ride? Or if there was someone waiting who didn't like him?

He settled his left bicep comfortably against his friendly little Walther in its underarm holster, and thought about cover and perimeters.

The problem with this business, he occasionally complained to himself, is that everything you do increases your overall risk. Every time you deal with something that needs to be dealt with, more people get pissed. And want to find you. You sleep with one eye open, as the saying goes. Never for a moment, ever, do you dare to feel safe.

A sub like the one in the photo could have hovered below the surface near the platform, sent out divers to attach the explosives, then headed for a dock somewhere on Kalimantan. But where did the mouthpiece and harness with the shark marks on it come from?

Bad as this was, it was the best lead he had.

Probably he was just tired of himself. It's fine to go beating about nasty places when a friend calls, but it raises hell with your home life.

Not that he had one.

The Mahakam River at the end of the road was a filthy chocolate torrent, a thirty-thousand square mile drainage of clearcuts, wildcat settlements, rape-and-run agriculture and illegal roads all pouring their billions of tons of fertile soils into the Makassar Strait, drowning the fish and coral in the process.

But you know what? He didn't give a damn. He was learning to live with how the world is.

That's what he told himself.

"**GO DOWN MAHAKAM RIVER** 7.4 km from Pertamina dock," said the new message on Turk's phone. "To a dirt road facing the island. Be there 19:35."

Pertamina. The Indonesian national oil company. They who would get Rawhide's leases if it went under. But why blow a platform that was grossing them ninety-two thousand dollars a day?

He stopped at 6.4 km and hid the car in a banana grove, jogged toward the river then south along its bank through low, wide trees, razor grass, rattan thorns, spiky ferns and straggling vines, the footing slippery, the river stench heavy on the wet air.

Where the dirt road faced the island, was a white pickup truck with someone standing beside it. Keeping his right hand near his Walther, Turk stepped into the clearing.

"Ah!" a woman said in English. "There you are."

Her eyes were black. The rest of her face was veiled. "We must be quick." She held out a gloved hand, a memory stick in her palm. "I took these pictures. When I was bringing the mule to the water, just before sunrise, and I see this boat coming upriver. Before dark I am standing in my field and I see him coming downriver. Now he was deeper in the water" – she held her palms downward – "so I am thinking he went upriver for fuel at Pertamina dock, and now he's headed off to do more evil."

He held the memory stick carefully. "How did you do these pictures?"

"I shot them with my iPhone, emailed them to my laptop and copied them to that stick. How else would I do it?"

Inadvertently he smiled. "I should pay you."

"Keep your money!" She turned away, back to him. "My husband died on that platform. You think I don't want vengeance?" She stepped into the white pickup and drove away, her headlights quickly swallowed by the jungle.

Four klicks out of Handil he pulled the Nissan into a Pertamina gas station, and brought the stick up on his laptop.

Twenty-four feet long, lean and ugly, an Aurora mini-sub. Can descend to a hundred feet, do twenty miles an hour, would burn most of a fuel tank from here to the platform and back.

Chinese, built in Wuhan.

SAFE HARBOR

"**H**E'S JUST VANISHED." Ross tried to keep the tension from his voice as he faced the screen of Rawhide board members.

"I've never seen a situation like this," said Jim Burleigh, the Texas oil engineer.

"Nor have we," Mitch added.

"Except in dictatorships," the McKinsey partner Deborah Quinn countered. "Places where people disappear in the night . . . Iran, Saudi . . . Not in Wyoming, for God's sake."

"I can't believe you just let Mitch and Victor walk out of that motel room," Burleigh said.

"I just went out to see the storm," Mitch said. "Couldn't get back in . . ."

"Let's sum things up," Asa Chomsky broke in. "We've lost a platform and a refinery and lots of good people, our stock's down forty-four percent, the Boston Group wants to pull our loans, Indonesia wants our leases, S&P and Moody's want to downgrade us, our insurers want to screw us, the media are eating us alive, EastPac's readying for the kill –"

"We have a way to deal with that."

"A safe harbor?" Burleigh snapped. "Not on my watch."

"– now Victor's missing," Chomsky continued. "Am I forgetting anything?"

"We have some good news," Ross said. "We've tracked down a sub that may have dropped off the diver."

"I thought he was dead," interjected Samsal Younane, the international financier. "Chewed up by a shark?"

Ross had a moment's fear that Samsal, a close friend, might turn against him. "That was a mouthpiece and harness. No way to know whose."

For a moment no one spoke. "To get down to business," Burleigh said.

"Yes," Deborah agreed.

"Yes," Mitch added.

"Ross," Burleigh added, "you've got to understand, at a time like this, the value of symbolic actions."

No one spoke. "Finding who's behind this," Ross said, "is a *real* action. It can save us. Not PR bullshit."

"What I'm talking about," Burleigh said, "is replacing the CEO."

"Remove me? From my own company? You're out of your mind."

"There's wisdom to it," Deborah countered.

"Not yet," Asa Chomsky said. "It makes us look scared. Pandering to the investment funds. The financial press."

"Who listens to them, for Chrissake?" Burleigh growled.

"The little guys do," Asa said. "The folks who don't know."

"Fuck them. What floats or sinks us –"

"I know, Jim," Deborah said, "what floats or sinks us is the big funds – if I hear you say that one more time I'm going to come down to Dallas and wring your neck."

"Please do. I'll have a bottle of rare bourbon and prime rib waiting for you."

"I've got a zoom with the Sweetwater sheriff," Ross said impatiently. "I'll keep you all posted, if anything of value shows up."

"Let's give it a few more days, Ross," Burleigh said. "But if things don't turn around fast, it's only reasonable to remove you. Not your fault, just how the market sees things."

"THE FBI IN FIVE STATES IS WORKING ON THIS," LYLE SAID. "I have four people on it full time. We've done hours of flyovers, three K-9 searches, talked to every rancher between here and Cheyenne, and alerted every federal, state, and local law office in the surrounding states. What else would you suggest I do?"

"With every hour," Ross said, "it's less likely we'll find him."

"Depends where he is."

"Or if he's dead."

"Why would he be dead? He's too valuable to kill."

Ross thought about this. "How's that?"

Lyle stared at him, exasperated. "A system can always be replaced. But a person, the knowledge how to run it –"

"Or how to take it down?"

"Precisely."

"He's a member of our Board. And even though he and I argued sometimes about strategy, he never would vote to fire me. But without his vote, the others can take me down."

"Humph," Lyle chewed. "Maybe that's a good reason to kill him."

"How's that?"

"What would change, if they got rid of you?"

"Maybe, like Mitch Carter's been arguing, we take in partners? Sell out?"

"If you sell out, who to?"

"EastPac's trying to grab us, that's mostly Chinese money . . ."

"Cassidy and me, we're trying to figure who shot at you in the motel. Was it Victor Minh?"

"Never."

"So who was it?"

IF THEY SOLD OUT TO EASTPAC, ROSS WOULD MAKE ABOUT A hundred million. Enough to live reasonably for the rest of his life. But would EastPac stop at that? The sale agreements would have clauses allowing them to sue him if he'd misrepresented anything – of course he wouldn't, but they'd accuse him of it anyway, make him spend millions on law firms and court fees. He might even end up paying most of their money back to them, simply because they were more powerful than he.

But if Rawhide didn't sell, they could lose it all. Right now.

On his way to Munich for a bank meeting, he sat back in his seat and looked out the plane window at the barren, snowy peaks of Greenland fleeting past. His every instinct, his prairie instinct said *Don't Sell*.

Mitch wanted to sell. He'd make about forty million, was young enough to turn it into more. He didn't think they could win this.

Victor hadn't wanted to sell. Though he'd have made forty million too, that his family would get now . . . There were others who'd get ten million or so each, and Board members like Burleigh and Deborah had locked in fourteen or more in sale bonuses.

Maybe it *was* time to let go. He could go back to JPL, the Jet Propulsion Lab, any time. Back to hunting outer space for other forms of life. For some meaning in the universe.

But what about the folks who'd bought shares above EastPac's price, who'd lose millions, some of them? The teachers' retirement funds, the firemen? The hundreds of thousands of people who'd put their savings into Rawhide because they had faith in the company? In him?

If he and the company survived, soon the stock would be back at seventy, and all these folks wouldn't have lost money. Sure, some who'd bailed out and didn't jump back in again. For them, the damage was already done.

Like us humans, who keep crashing forward through the damage we inflict on ourselves.

Millions of people are crushed every day, but humanity staggers on.

All those people who'd had faith. How could he betray them?

And what about Rawhide's twenty-seven thousand team members, the people who operated the dangerous drills and lived on the perilous platforms and worked in the refineries, drove the tanker trucks, and sat in the all-night gas stations fearing the next guy with a gun?

But if the deal went through, they might even come out worse. EastPac could cut their benefits and salaries and pillage their retirement and insurance funds. Takeover artists did it all the time, while the government looked the other way as long as they kept making campaign contributions.

If EastPac bought them, he'd give ninety percent of his hundred million to the employees. Ninety million divided by twenty-seven thousand people came out barely three grand apiece. Barely better than nothing.

With the remaining ten million he could start over. But not in the oil or banking business because of the non-compete clause.

Or with ten million he could live in Alaska and go fishing every day. Or go back to JPL and help find a way to get off this poor little planet.

The Rawhide team would be better with no EastPac deal. So would the stockholders.

That's all that mattered.

IT WAS TIME FOR ANOTHER VIRTUAL BOARD MEETING.

"I've thought about this long and hard," Ross told them. "I know you all have. On this decision rides not only our future but what we've done for many years, what we've built together. What my family has built over many years." He looked into the screen at them. "That's why we're not selling."

Shock struck Deborah's face. "Ross, we have no choice."

"You're throwing it all away," Jim Burleigh said. "My fourteen million, you're just throwing it away." He glared at Ross. "I won't let you."

"You don't need another lousy fourteen million –"

One after one they attacked him. He'd been naïve, he realized, to imagine that any supposed friendship might mitigate their anger.

"Ross," Burleigh stared at him derisively, "You're losing your mind."

That stung. He'd worried about it too. The attacks, the fear, the loneliness, having no one to talk to, were all eating him. Was he losing belief in himself, confidence in his ability, his strength, his likelihood of success?

He faced them one by one. "We're going to sit down now and work out a plan to save the company. To make us even stronger than before. And we aren't leaving till we're done."

"Ross," Mitch broke in, "we need to sell."

Asa Chomsky looked at his watch. "I've got a two-thirty."

"Cancel it. All of you, cancel the rest of today and tomorrow. We're going to get this done." As he faced the yellow pad in front of him, a cold tremor ran up his back, a fear that he was a fool to not even see how badly he would fail.

18
GLOCK 22

"**VICTOR MINH IS DEAD**," Lyle Brant said through his chaw.

Two thousand miles away, Ross took a breath and gathered his strength. "How?"

"Barefoot, froze in a snowbank. Snowplow near cut him in half."

"When?"

"When we found him was –"

"No. When he died."

"Same night he took those shots at you."

"Victor didn't do that –"

"We found a Glock 22 under his body. It matches the slugs we took out of your motel wall."

"**FOUR YEARS** I'VE WORKED FOR RAWHIDE," LIZ SAID. "AND ENJOYED every day. Till the explosion."

"What do you want to do now?" Turk glanced around the apartment that Rawhide had rented for her in the Eternity Tower, in the fanciest area in District 8, with its pools, saunas, gyms, hot tubs, and all the other crap no one needs. What did they think she was, a movie star?

It seemed artificial, the strange wooden sculptures and hammered metal wall hangings, the broad, shiny desk, the strange big-leaved plants, the bed in the next room with her underwear tossed across it.

"I want to help find the bastards that blew up my platform. Find them before anyone else does. And kill them."

"Other than that," Turk smiled, "you have any goals?"

"Find the bastard who tried to run me over. And kill him."

"Guess how many silver BMWs there are in Jakarta? About seven thousand."

"Maybe he was just a crazy fucker."

It shocked him, her language. *But she's seen it all,* he thought. "What about going home? Getting out of Indonesia?"

"At first I wanted to, but now I'm not leaving till I kill the bastards who blew my platform –"

He shook his head. "Look, Liz –"

"Don't you *'Look'* me! And I don't have a damn home. My folks are dead, and the loggers have destroyed the mountains where we lived, and it's a muddy awful mess and I can't get far enough away. Away from it all."

"Indonesia's no place for a Western woman."

"It's no place for any woman. Did you know, over eighty percent of Indonesian women have been genitally mutilated – the highest proportion in all the Muslim world? And most of them live like slaves. But I try not to think about it."

"Someday you'll leave?"

"Some day? Sure, some day I'd even like to get married and have kids. But I'm going to get these bastards first. And whoever's behind them."

"That shouldn't be a problem," he said sarcastically, thinking that fierce as she was, what guy would dare marry her?

"I WAS WRONG," LYLE SAID. "YOUR BUDDY VICTOR DIDN'T FREEZE himself to death."

Ross told himself he couldn't take any more. Yes, he could. "What?"

"The medical examiner had to thaw him out to look him over. And first thing she saw was his neck was broke."

Ross saw Victor, happy and alive, then with a broken neck. "Could've been when the snowplow –"

"Nah. He was strangled."

"Strangled." Ross found a chair in his living room, sat. "When's this going to stop?"

"Look, buddy, it's not my fault."

"I didn't say that."

"He was strangled and thrown in that snowdrift, that kept getting bigger 'cause the snow kept falling, till the snowplow finally come by."

Lyle was loving this, Ross realized, the tragic gory details. Was trying to make him pay. For what? "The gun you found –"

"Under his body?" Lyle said. "We're reassessing that."

"You mean you screwed up and jumped to conclusions that were the easy way out."

"I'm going to forget you said that."

"Who killed him, and who put the gun under his body in the snowdrift? The person who shot at me?"

"Maybe, maybe not. We will find out."

"Find out? You haven't found a damn thing."

"We're halfway there."

"There?"

"To solving this."

"No, you're not." Ross snapped. "And about Victor, the family wants his body home."

"Not yet. More forensic tests to come."

"For what?"

"See what he may have ingested prior to his death. Other tests I'm not at liberty to disclose." Lyle cleared his throat. "And Cassidy here's gone over the hospital camera film from the night Tom Hogan was killed –"

"And?"

"We can't identify an individual descending the stairs near the end of the night shift. Not someone on the hospital staff. So we're going to run an autopsy on poor old Tom Hogan, just in case."

Ross tossed the phone on a couch and stared through the vast glass wall and beyond the terrace at Manhattan's throbbing traffic and electric night. "So bright you can see it from the moon," he said, wandering through another living room and dining room and breakfast suite into the first kitchen but forgot why, and sat down to think. *If I hadn't asked Victor to go to Sweetwater, he'd still be alive. Did I really need him there? Or why did I want him to come? To keep my eyes on him, keep him and Mitch from starting a coup in my absence?*

There is an elemental gravity to things. You can fight something, but if it's going to win, it's going to win no matter what you do.

Never since the first years after Mary's death had he felt this alone. But we're always alone, suffer alone, die alone.

And maybe his ferocious drive and ambition and years of endless work had been only to stave off this reality of solitude and death?

Right now he didn't care. If he had to die to save Rawhide, he would.

"HAVE TO TELL YOU, CHIEF," NORM CASSIDY SAID, "CUT THIS man a break."

"Don't call me Chief."

Cassidy grinned. "I have to *say*, Sheriff –"

Lyle shifted his chaw from the left to the right, didn't like it there, and shifted it back. "The guy's running an oil company that just killed five of our people –"

"You think he doesn't care?"

"I don't *care* if he cares."

"Can't you tell he's all broke up? First, this horrible explosion in Indonesia. Hurts him so much he can barely talk about it."

"How you know?"

"You can see it in his face. How he talks. The man's alone in a sea of enemies."

Lyle gave Cassidy an exasperated grin. "What'd I ever do, without you, to be moral and all that?"

"You were always moral, Chief. That's why I wanted to work for you. You're a man of God."

Lyle shook his head. "Wish I could believe in God. Wish it was true."

"What if it *is*?" Cassidy leaned forward, creaking his chair. "You've been on Ross Bullock's ass from the beginning. But what if somebody did hit the refinery?"

"Yeah?"

"I've been talking to engineers. A prof at Colorado School of Mines, another in Houston. What happened wasn't a normal chemical reaction. Needs an explosive to make that cracker blow. What was the explosive?" Cassidy sat back, making his chair creak, and crossed one long leg over the other. "Far as I can tell, that Indonesian platform wasn't natural either, Chief."

"Don't call me that."

"Just keeping you on your toes."

Lyle smiled at Cassidy. He'd only been here six months, but what a difference he'd made. In a year, when Lyle retired, he was going to make sure Cassidy replaced him.

After retirement he was going to find an F150 three-quarter ton, rebuild the engine – *what fun to finally have the time to do what I love* – fix it all up, and put a camper on the back. He and Olivia could head for Grand Teton, Zion, Yellowstone, Canyonlands, so many other beautiful places in this beautiful country . . . remnants of a world that used to be.

THE PHONE RATTLED IN ROSS'S CHEST POCKET, DRIVING HIM awake. *Turk.*

"What time's it there?" Turk said.

"Hell, I don't know." Ross sat up, realizing he was on a living room couch. "Middle of the night."

"You alone?"

"Of course."

"I've tracked down the sub. Built in Wuhan in 2007, for nine years attached to the Chinese naval base outside Shanghai – mostly training missions, had some ventilation problems and a bent prop, so spent time in the Wuhan yard."

"Then?"

"Bought by an Indonesian oil prospecting group named Melindungi. It means Shield."

"Based where?" Ross said.

"You guessed it."

"Mahakam?"

"And Shield was bought last year by a Russian oil trader doing deals in Italy."

Ross felt his head spin. "Damn."

"The woman who gave me the stick, she lost her husband on the platform."

"What's her name?"

"Asmara Sudup. She didn't tell me that, but I asked your Jakarta office to crosscheck her address against the names of the dead."

"Send me the details."

"Do I cc Isaiah on this, or go through you?" Turk asked.

"Cc Isaiah on everything. This Russian oil trader, let's find him."

"He's got a villa in Sorrento. With a big dock. I'm thinking of heading down, have a look."

"From fucking Jakarta?"

"Qatar Airlines, one stop in Doha."

"Turk, we don't have time."

"Yes, we do. Time is on our side."

DESPITE HIS TEXAS CHARM AND BLUSTER, JIM BURLEIGH WAS A reactionary capitalist. He eschewed expansion, hated new ventures and acquisitions, and despised the financial press.

"That *New York Times* guy, won the Nobel economics prize? He's made me rich," Burleigh had said over his glass of Eagle Rare bourbon at a recent board meeting, "Whatever he says, I do the opposite."

"You were already rich," Ross had laughed. Burleigh was a good guy in his own way, the way we are all good in our own way, and Ross refused to categorize or dismiss him. Burleigh, in the final analysis, might be the guy you end up with in a foxhole. Who has your back.

But he was going to have to work on Burleigh. Keep him in the fold.

And the only way to do that was, as always, be honest.

"Christ, Ross," Burleigh had said when he called him. "When are you going to step down?"

"I'm not. You know that."

"We're going to carry your bloody body out of the Forum."

"No, you won't. Here's why –"

Ross said nothing. "I'm waiting," Burleigh said.

"We're tracking the people who hit our platform. It's a small sub, built in China, recently owned by a Russian oil trader. And we have a good lead in Wyoming."

"Wyoming? What lead?"

"The guy that died in the hospital, he got killed. And they have film of the killer."

Burleigh sighed. "None of this is good enough."

"For what?"

"To keep your neck out of the noose."

19

SHUT UP AND LISTEN

TURK NURSED A CAMPARI on the sunlit terrace of the Bella Paradisa Hotel in Sorrento and watched the cliffside villa below. The guards changed every hour – why? And the steel blinds they were shutting on the inland side – he'd already figured the windows were bulletproof, so what more did they want?

He tasted the Campari and almost spit it out. What were they thinking, the Italians, making *merda* like this? A comical sadism at the heart of the Italian soul. *We'll market something disgusting and teach you to love it.*

How was Liz doing, he wondered, alone in Jakarta?

Maybe he shouldn't have left her.

No. She can take care of herself.

The two crewcut guards patrolling the villa's gardens went inside and moments later reappeared on a wide-columned terrace to the left of the building overlooking the sea. Hands over their eyes, they scanned westward as if saluting the afternoon sun. A man and woman carrying what appeared to be PP 2000 submachine guns, plus three other men and two women, no doubt with handguns under their coats.

Beyond the villa the Mediterranean shimmered, blue and silver, too bright to stare at. The sun halfway down the west gleamed off Capri's massive limestone crest and threw crenelated shadows across the villa's rooftop terrace, where two other guards with what seemed to the latest version of the SR-2 Veresk, the one with the sound suppressor, stood chatting and smoking.

When a big blond guard glanced up at him, Turk pulled out his phone and began talking randomly. The guard trudged away on a flagstone path hedged with bougainvillea, his shadow elongated against the sunlit golden walls.

The sun slid lower. The fishing boats were coming home, tracing wide wakes across the glittering waves. The air stung with salt and sea; gulls cried as they eased past. The orange sun set the sea afire, the fishing boats vanished in its blaze, only to reappear minutes later closer to port.

He couldn't talk himself out of a vast unhappiness that almost precluded every action. Fear of failure, of being stupid, being fooled?

Here he was looking down on the cliffside estate of Nevgeny Lann, the Russian oil trader whose company paid 2.4 million Swiss Francs last year for the Aurora Class II submarine that had refueled at the Pertamina dock up the Mahakam River in Kalimantan after the Rawhide platform had blown.

The same year Lann had bought this place for thirty-five million Euros. Wide gardens on two sides, patrolled by a level of security Turk hadn't seen in a long time.

And no matter what type of listening device he locked on them, he got nothing but nasty snarls which his phone printed out in hilarious Cyrillic.

And trying to find the sub's present whereabouts had gone nowhere.

He couldn't take another Campari. He just couldn't.

Please Lord let something happen.

"**BAD THINGS** ARE BEING DONE TO YOU, IN THE MARKETS. IS WHY I call."

Ross didn't know the voice. A woman's, probably Russian. Silky but strong. Professional. Smart. Good English. How did she get through his call blocks?

Sitting at his desk, he switched to *Record*. "Who are you calling for?"

"*You*, of course! Who else should I call with this? Your CFO, Mitch Carter? The Securities and Exchange Commission? CFTC?"

"I'm sorry, I don't know what this is about –"

"Is about the future of your company. A lovely word, Rawhide."

"And who are you?"

"I simply pass on a warning," she said. "The CFTC is coming to get you."

"The Commodities Futures Trading Commission? Is *that* what you mean?"

"Of course is what I mean."

"And who the hell *are* you?"

"Shut up and listen: the CFTC is going to charge you with price manipulation of the Wyoming Basin crude market. And of conspiring with PEMEX directors to change refinery outputs . . . There is someone who is spreading this, what you call, fake news."

Ross felt the universe drop on his shoulders. The CFTC was the U.S. watchdog agency overseeing futures and options markets, specifically energy markets like crude. And they could shut him down any time they wanted. But who was this woman with the Moscow accent, and how did she know this? Or was it made up, to trap him?

"Why?" he said finally.

"Oil markets, such a dangerous place. I have seen companies devoured alive. But you are a good company. I see that conference you give, against the war? Very good. But the American weapons and oil companies, the Democrats, the media, they like this war. So they attack you. I want to help out."

"Why the CFTC?"

"Against you?" Her voice was rough yet soft. "One of them is doing *this*, in the markets, with the CFTC."

"*Who?*"

"Name is Robichaud."

The phone went silent. "Hey!" he snapped, but there was no answer. He checked his incoming calls. Country code 7, Russia; city code 495, Moscow. But there was no number.

He restrained the urge to throw the phone at the wall, instead punched in the cell number of Dale Robichaud, the Louisiana gas king, also an influential advisor to the Commodity Futures Trading Commission. As a member of the CFTC's Energy & Environmental Markets Advisory Committee, Robichaud was supposed to oversee trading in U.S. natural gas markets. But as a primary player in these markets, he had the power to tweak them to his own advantage.

Although he kept a mansion in DC and spent time at the White House, Robichaud could most often be found on his Louisiana riverfront estate.

The number rang four times then Robichaud answered. "Dale" – Ross held down his anger – "what is this bullshit I hear about CFTC and Rawhide?"

"We have no choice," Dale Robichaud intoned in his sleek Louisiana baritone, "but to treat this seriously. The information we received is highly creditable, from a very valid source – from several, in fact. Independently."

"Tell me who they are, Dale."

"You know I can't."

"What you *can* do is send me the data. Let's see how it compares with ours."

"We're using *your* data, Ross. That's the problem."

"That's nuts. I check the transactions of every company we own every day. So do my top accountants. There's no way we're messing with futures, buying up PEMEX execs. How could anyone be so stupid?"

"Alliance Energy tried it, remember?" Robichaud countered. "And Topaz Futures. Now you."

"This is an evil and destructive allegation; I will have a hundred lawyers on your ass the moment you move forward."

"You don't *have* a hundred lawyers, Ross. Not anymore."

"I have them any time I want them. Dale, why are you doing this? Who's got you by the balls?"

"That's a disgusting suggestion."

Ross shut off his phone, wandered into the kitchen, and checked the refrigerators for the sausage and rigatoni and salad that his housekeeper Carmen had left him, opened a twelve-year-old bottle of Barbera from the wine cellar and a bottle of Acqua Panna, carried them into the breakfast suite, and sat down to the first real dinner he'd had in a week.

Dale Robichaud, the Louisiana gas king. I'm going to take you down.

Behind Robichaud, who was doing this? *Cui bono,* as Mary used to say. It hurt his heart to think of anything she'd ever said. To think of *her.*

Cui bono, Cicero had explained, was how to find the perpetrators of a financial crime. You just had to ask *who benefits.*

As Isaiah King had noted, there were countless folks who'd benefit from Rawhide's crash. Most of all the war machine.

Who was this Moscow woman? Was she really Russian? Why call him?

The war?

How did she get through the blocks to his private phone?

Would she betray him, too?

"**DO YOU HAVE TIME,**" LILY HSIU ASKED, "FOR A FEW QUESTIONS?"

"Not over the phone," Ross said. "But we can meet at my place. Madison and 59th. I'll send a car."

"I can get there, thank you."

"I'm in town till noon tomorrow. What works for you?"

"I'll be there in half an hour."

LILY WASN'T WHAT ROSS HAD EXPECTED. IN THE ONE PRESS conference he'd seen her, she'd been businesslike, remote. Unlike most of the other journalists, she'd asked intelligent questions. Had even asked about astrophysics. Then on the phone she'd had a sharp no-bullshit attitude, like don't you dare treat me different because I'm a woman or because I'm Asian. Another symptom of the recent resurrections of racial hatreds in the name of political correctness, no doubt. Sergio the doorman buzzed, and Ross said send her up.

She was thirty something, tall, slender and light-footed, tight blue Levis and a pink silk blouse, a blue down vest, a laptop in one hand and a Starbucks latte in the other. "Sorry if I'm a little late, there's never a taxi when you want one . . ."

"I said I'd send a car."

She smiled, eye to eye. "Don't patronize me, Mr. Bullock."

He laughed. "Why would I do that?"

"You're on life support. I'm here to decide if we let you live."

"If you think that, you're an idiot and can get out."

She nipped her lower lip. "Your vitals are off the charts. You're not going to make it."

"You've been talking to Dale Robichaud."

She cocked her head. "Why would I?"

"Because he's one of the scumbags out to get me."

"Why?"

"If I knew, we wouldn't be here."

"But we are."

He nodded at the cardboard container in her hand. "At least let me make you a decent coffee."

She followed him into the first kitchen. "You could have a basketball game in here."

He shook his head. "Ceiling's too low."

"Do you know how most people live?"

"I know too well." He switched on the Pavoni and tossed some beans in the grinder.

"It's ancient, that thing."

"Made in Milan, nineteen fifty-one."

"Only thing in the room older than you?"

Damn, he'd made a mistake thinking she'd be human. "You want to talk, or not?"

She put her laptop on the quartzite countertop. "Ready when you are."

"Let me finish making your damn coffee."

"You offered it."

"Are you always this rude?"

"Only professionally."

He turned from steaming her milk. "Then let's be friends instead."

"I'm never friends with a victim." She glanced at her laptop. "I *have* been talking to Dale Robichaud . . . Apparently the CFTC is preparing an enforcement action against Rawhide, for illegal options transactions in natural gas futures?"

"That's silly. We don't do options trading in natgas futures."

"Much worse, they're investigating whether Rawhide paid bribes to executives in PEMEX, the Mexican oil company, for insider information on oil and derivatives trading, funneling those bribes through anonymous Caribbean bank accounts . . ." She read on, "rendering those markets less competitive . . . Rawhide then used that insider information to distort several Platts oil benchmarks –"

"I've heard this from Robichaud. It's laughable."

"– thereby impacting other swaps, futures, and other trades both physical and derivative . . . and thereby –"

"Enough." He felt overwhelmed by the meaningless of it, of how much time it wasted. "Lily – may I call you that?"

"If you wish."

"All this is untrue. Rawhide prides itself on honesty, on not cheating. That's how my parents built the company. Most energy companies cheat, every way they can. Most businesses do – look at the big tech and media companies – but we *don't*. It's part of our ethic, what makes our team, all twenty-seven thousand of us, happy to go to work in the morning . . ."

"So you say."

"But the problem is, once these lies are launched, this kind of false campaign, it takes many millions of dollars and months to defeat it. And in the interim it's believed, and it helps to bring us down. Particularly when Democratic media like the *Times*, WAPO,

MSNBC, NPR and all the others, plus big tech are pushing it. False as it is."

"Get a good lawyer."

"We have some of the best. And they're working overtime already. We're being besieged with lawsuits, insurance challenges, regulatory indictments, the banks are trying to pull our loans, the IRS and FBI are making up lies against us, Meta and others have closed us down, Indonesia's stealing our leases, the markets are short-selling the hell out of us, and on and on. And we haven't done a thing."

"Yes, you did." She thought a moment. "You blocked the sanctions. And you keep talking about nuclear war. Thereby pissing off the wrong people."

"Those are everyone who's making money on weapons for nuclear war. And all the lobbyists, lawyers and media, like your *Times*, who work for them."

"That's crap."

"And now the president is trying to take Rawhide down, via the EPA, for environmental infractions? And with the IRS, FBI, and Justice Department? It's a laugh." He said nothing, then, "And that you should believe this, it makes you part of the laugh too."

OUT OF THE BLAZING SILVER MEDITERRANEAN CAME A V WAKE like an arrowhead. A big motor yacht, sharp and fast. A woman on the foredeck in Kevlar with an AK over her shoulder.

With all these guns, Turk wondered, what were they so afraid of?

Trouble was, their fear interfered with his desire to place a listening device somewhere in their mansion, inside its digital shield.

The yacht came in on a great onrushing wake that splashed over the concrete pier at the bottom of the cliff. Men jumped from the yacht's deck and roped to the bollards. From midships they laid down a steel ramp, and an old man with a white cane limped down the ramp and turned left to walk to a door in the cliff. A minute later he came out the villa's glass doors onto the columned terrace.

It had taken forty-three seconds from the moment he'd disappeared into the cliff till he came out on the terrace. The elevator was fast.

Not that Turk planned to use it.

The old man limped across the terrace and sat under chestnut trees at a round glass table. People came up and kissed his cheek, one by one. Women from the kitchen in white frocks, guards with guns strapped to their hips. They brought him a bottle of red, a loaf of black bread, and a bowl of olives, and sat with him eating and talking.

This didn't fit any scenario Turk could figure out.

Why the intense security, then the old guy comes and it's like family day on the steppe?

Though the guards were still patrolling. What did they fear, in this ancient seaside town in Sorrento?

Every time he looked at his odds, they weren't good. A few problems:

The villa was insanely protected. Armed guards, electronics. How to get inside the barrier? Where to hide a listening device?

Chances were very good he'd get caught. Then tortured till he told them why he was there, then dumped off a fishing boat far out on the Med.

Or tossed off the two-hundred-foot cliff at the end of the terrace, and let the waves have their way with him?

Evasion and escape were a no-go. Narrow roads, tons of cars all the way back to the autostrada to Naples. The long Vico Equense tunnel, miles of traffic jams and poisonous gases. Even with his rented Ducati, he'd be a sitting duck.

A chopper was out of the question: he didn't have a setup, plus landing zones were few and well-guarded.

The only other way was by sea. He could find a boat, anchor off the cliffs a few hundred yards from the concrete pier, swim to it, and climb the cliff to the terrace.

That would be the easy way.

Sunset on the Amalfi Coast was barely lunchtime in DC. Turk punched in Isaiah King's number, and he answered right away. "What's up?"

"I've been watching Nevgeny Lann's place since yesterday," Turk said. "No change in the *golovorez* patrolling the place day and night."

"So?"

"Late afternoon, 16:37 Italy time, everyone goes out on the terrace to watch the ocean. Thirteen minutes later, this AB Swift comes in and docks, and an old guy gets out and takes the elevator up to the villa and goes out on the terrace. Everyone comes out and kisses him and they all sit down and drink wine and eat together."

"Send me the pix."

WHEN THE PIX CAME BACK FROM ISAIAH OF THE OWNER OF Nevgeny Lann's Sorrento villa, they were not what Turk expected.

Hale and hearty, Nevgeny Lann was a big-shouldered tall guy with a grin that crossed his entire face. In a beautiful suit in front of his massive Moscow mansion, holding the open door of a Maserati for a lovely blonde in her late thirties, well-dressed, high heels, the kind of dancer's elegance so many Moscow women have.

Turk stared out angrily at the night sea.

The white-haired old man who'd limped ashore from the AB Swift hadn't been the Russian oil tycoon Nevgeny Lann after all.

Or was he the real one, and the guy in the pix with the blonde and Maserati just a double, an expendable in case of assassination attempts?

DEFCON 3

"**E**ASTPAC UPPED THEIR HOLD," Mitch said, voice rough from too many phone calls, from not sleeping.

Ross bizarrely thought of Victor, how he would see this. *Do it,* Victor said from the grave. *Do it now.*

"We create thirty million more shares," Mitch said. "Give them a nice discount. That knocks EastPac back to five percent."

"They can buy them, too."

"We'll make it open only to investors of record as of a month before today."

Ross smiled. "SEC isn't going to like this."

"Fuck the SEC. We're on our own." Mitch cleared his voice. "You were right, Ross, when you didn't want to do this last week. If we had, they'd be all over us again by now. This way, you just bought us a week."

"In a week, you'll be surprised what we can do."

Ross shut off and went out to the edge of the terrace and stared down the dizzying fifty-seven stories to Mad Ave. The vertical concrete wall slid into the abyss, to a thread of sidewalk and tiny specks of humans, cars like flashing minnows in a sea of night.

So easy to just slide over the edge and end this. You could imagine wanting to do it, the horror so bad you can't take it anymore, tell yourself it's easier for everyone if you just step off this edge.

But nothing was worth doing that, no matter the convergence of horrors, because the horror of falling fifty-seven stories to smash into hamburger on the sidewalk was far more awful.

No matter what, he *was* dealing with this; they hadn't beaten him. He felt somehow unburdened, outside it, watching himself go through the actions.

Expecting worse to come, and ready to deal with that too.

TURK PADDLED AS CLOSE TO THE CLIFF AS HE DARED, LOOKING for a place to tie up, but there was nowhere the kayak would not be smashed against the rocks. The cliff dropped straight hundreds of feet from the villa to the sea, and straight down deep below the waves, with no place to tie up.

Like huge muscled animals, the waves crashed at the cliffs. Waves from all the way from the wild and cold Atlantic, rolling high and white-crested through Gibraltar across the Med to the Tyrrhenian Sea and past Sardinia to Capri to burst on this black rock.

From a curve of the cliff, the kayak bobbing up and down in the assault of the waves, he watched the pier, the cliff, and Nevgeny Lann's terrace wall far above it. No one moved on the pier but a single woman with a long blonde braid, an AK slung comfortably over her right shoulder.

The pier would be covered with cameras too. Motion detectors. He would not get through.

He turned and scanned the cliff to the left of the villa, toward Pompei. Sere and black in the starlight, flashing with the thunder of waves, the cliff was slippery and sharp, fatally unsafe.

He paddled back along the cliffs a half mile to the breakwater and a small boat harbor where he had liberated the kayak, tied it up against the rocks, took his mask, snorkel and flippers from his divepack and slipped into the waves.

He stopped at the curve in the cliff, treading water and watching for the AK woman on the pier or for a guard on the big yacht. The woman had patrolled to the end of the pier, done a perfect about-face, and started back toward him. The big yacht towered above him, no way to see a guard unless they leaned over the rail.

The swell had increased, hurling the waves higher up the cliff. He tugged off his divepack, shoved his flippers, mask, and snorkel inside it, and put on a thin pair of climbing shoes. He swam closer, waiting for a crest to drive him into the rocks, grabbed for an inch-wide ledge and held it as the waves battered him, swung up for another hold, then another.

The rock was slippery but good, hard Vesuvius basalt. Five meters up, he reached the ledge he'd seen from the kayak. It was wider than he'd thought – a good eight inches.

And even if he did fall, he'd land in water and not be killed.

He quietly tapped in a pin and hitched the divepack to it, traversed to the seam between two buttresses of lava, and worked his way up the cliff.

"THAT'S IGOR STEIN!" ROSS SAID TO ISAIAH AS HE SCANNED THE photo Turk had just sent them of the white-haired man off the yacht. "The Russian energy minister. What the hell was he doing there?"

"That's what I'm trying to find out," Isaiah snapped. "He landed in Naples yesterday at fifteen thirty-three on a private jet from Moscow, took an armored limo to the Naples yacht harbor, where this yacht was waiting. Then the yacht arrives at this villa, the old guy gets out, and everyone treats him like Father Christmas."

"So this Nevgeny Lann guy, how does he own the villa?"

"Via several intermediary corporations in Belgium and Luxembourg, and from there the link's to Gazprombank and an account we traced to him. But this Lann guy, we have good info on him, including some from GRU. They apparently dislike him."

GRU, the Main Intelligence Directorate of Russia's armed forces, was not someone you wanted to dislike you. Powerful, smart, ruthless, and dedicated, it was Russia's top intelligence and covert warfare group.

"What we don't know," Isaiah continued, is why was Igor Stein there? If you're the energy minister, every oil company in the world falls all over itself trying to offer you whatever they think you might want – magnificent girls, gold, fast cars, yachts, stock options, multi-million-dollar savings accounts . . . But why there?"

"What's with the yacht?"

"Registered in St. Martin, held by various companies that lead back to Nevgeny. It's all there in the report I'm sending you."

"Nevgeny owns the submarine we think delivered the diver to the Makassar platform. We need to have some one-on-one with him. What kind of security he have?"

"Too much to mess with."

"Why is he attacking Rawhide?"

"Or is it the oil minister? The Russians? Are *they* the ones trying to take you down?"

ON THE CLIFF TWO HUNDRED FEET ABOVE THE WATER, TURK reached another ledge wide enough to get his fingers into. Even better, a descending crack angled from it toward the villa. But now he could see what he couldn't before: a bank of cameras watching this part of the cliff, and there was no way to get closer without being seen.

Already he might have been seen. Quickly he backed away, lost his grip on a thumb-sized bump in the rock but grabbed another. *Slow down*, he thought. *Or, you stupid shit, you'll die.*

He took a careful breath, dangling in space, fingers aching from the strain. If he fell now, he might survive. Two hundred feet then hitting the water at two hundred miles an hour.

Keep going. Do not think. Do not look down. Do not breathe deeply or it will push you off the cliff.

He waited there, hanging in space, till his breathing slowed and his arms stopped trembling.

Easy now.

It's always easier to climb a cliff than go down. Because we're not like squirrels, we can't hang upside down to see where we're going.

Which is why a lot of people die going down. It's a horrible place to be and he tried not to think about it. This climb had been harder than it looked, much harder.

Or he was getting old and stupid?

"YOU SHOULD KNOW," Isaiah said.

"What now?" Ross stepped out of a finance meeting to an empty corner in the hall.

"It's worse than anything. These people are crazy."

"*What*, Isaiah? For Christ's sake, *what?*"

"They've gone to DEFCON 3."

Ross caught his breath. "He's going to kill us all."

DEFCON was the nuclear war alert system created by the Joint Chiefs and other U.S. war commands, showing five increasing levels of danger. FIVE was the least severe danger, and ONE meant nuclear war was imminent or had already begun.

"DEFCON 3 means we're sliding down a slippery slope with little chance to stop," Isaiah added. "In the old days, there was always contact between DC and Moscow, but these damn fools have cut it all off."

"I'll call him. But he's insane, the Prez." Ross cut off, stared out the sliding glass, imagining the magnificent universe above New York's toxic haze.

Two steps from nuclear war was how DEFCON 3 was defined by the war commands. A calculation in which the survival of humanity, of all life on earth, had no relevance.

Sick to his stomach, he sat on a couch, not knowing where he was. How could anyone want to kill everything? His gut wrenched.

No, you assholes. I can't let you do this.

He had the crazy idea to call Lily, suppressed it.

21

THE END

TURK CLIMBED DOWN the cliff, took his divepack off the pin he'd driven into the rock, slipped into the crashing waves and swam clear of the cliff. A hundred yards away, the AB Swift towered over the dark water, its cabin lights hazy in the mist. Along the pier behind it the blonde-haired guard trod steadily. Another guard would be on the yacht. At least one.

With his divepack over one shoulder, he swam closer till the Swift loomed far overhead, waves booming against the hull. He swam around the stern, staying close to the hull to avoid being seen from above, to where the hull lay beside the pier, separated only by the tractor tire bumpers strung along it.

From the bow and stern, mooring ropes descended to bollards on the pier. The metal ramp had been retracted, in any case too visible to use.

The only way up was a mooring rope. Preferably at the stern, farther from the villa and less visible from the deck. If he waited till the blonde sentry turned back toward the villa, he'd have time to get up that mooring rope.

If she didn't look back.

He swam into the oily darkness under the pier, where the waves roiled and crashed against the barnacled concrete pillars. He found a high niche to tie his divepack, swam to the stern mooring rope, waited for the blonde sentry to reach halfway back toward the cliff, checked that no one was looking down from the yacht, and climbed the rope. At the rail he swung hand over hand sideways till out of view of the pier, reached the port stern anchor hole and hung there, watching the rear deck and the cabin beyond it.

The yacht's rear deck was maybe a hundred feet long and sixty wide, with seating areas on both sides, a sunken dining table in the middle big enough for thirty of your closest friends, barbecues, parasols, a hot tub humming softly.

Forward of the rear deck was a small lounge, as he remembered from the plans he'd found on the internet. The lounge was lit, but no one seemed to be there. And forward of that was a conference room and beyond it a corridor with bedrooms down both sides.

He hung for another fifteen minutes on the rail, then slipped over it and along the port side to the shelter of the lounge wall beside the lit window where no one had appeared.

The blonde sentry had returned to this end of the pier and was watching out to sea toward the lights of Capri, rubbing the small of her back with her left hand, the AK shouldered on her right. She turned and marched back toward the yacht, then past it, on her way toward the cliff. Once her footsteps had faded, Turk listened a moment more, then crouched below the window to glance in.

It was a small, cheerful room of red leather sofas, expensive lamps and paintings, Persian rugs and a gleaming rosewood coffee table. He crouched, watching for five more minutes, went to the horizontal handle and pressed gently. As he'd expected, it was unlocked. Which made this easy, but also meant that people would be coming in and out.

He crossed the cabin and listened at the door to the conference room. Nothing.

It was an elegant room with a long hardwood table and easy chairs down both sides with screens for visual meetings. It was lit by tall stainless steel lamps along the sides and the ghoulish glow of five stock market screens in the far corner.

He slipped inside.

Three couches along each side, leather chairs between them, coffee tables with raised sections for laptops, a network printer crouching in the corner, a beverage cart stacked with clean glasses. A single door with a porthole-style window showing a half-lit corridor and closed doors on both sides.

The ceiling was acoustic panels set in white PVC frames – the best place for a bug. But too high to reach. Next best was the inside of a switch plate behind a couch, but that could be blocked. Or under a lamp, but if it was moved for cleaning wouldn't someone see? Or the underside of a coffee table? Or the AC screens on both walls, but when air rushed through them it would be hard to hear.

The ceiling was still best; with a chair to stand on, he could lift one of the PVC acoustic panels and clip the bug inside it. There would be perfect reception from anywhere in the room and even beyond.

As he reached for a chair, footsteps sounded in the lounge outside. He ducked behind a couch as two people came into the room.

One, angry, a woman's voice; the other a man's, more excusatory, both Russian. The woman was upbraiding the man over something Turk could not understand. Was it about him?

No way they could know he was here.

The man's voice grew reproachful as if falsely accused. Easy to understand, Turk realized, without knowing the words – the voice tones, the volume, the emotions packed into every instant.

The woman was not mollified. If anything, she grew harsher. The man was moving away, toward the corridor door, escaping her, the click of the doorknob, a higher ferocity in the woman's voice as she followed him out.

Maybe a waste of time but he'd recorded it all.

He had to place the damn bug and get off this boat. He listened at the padded door to the lounge but heard nothing. Beyond the other padded door to the corridor he could hear voices: the woman's, still strident, and another woman's, incredulous and concerned.

If they returned, he had two seconds to get out. He shoved a chair under an acoustic panel, clipped the bug against the frame and shut the panel as the sound of heavier, hard heels came down the aft stairway toward the lounge.

He shoved the chair against the table and as the hard heels came toward the conference room door he slipped through the other padded doors into the far corridor.

He was panting and tried to stop. What if the person who'd just entered the conference room came in here? He'd have to take him down.

Or if the two women at the end of this corridor came back this way? Came to meet whoever'd just come down the stairwell?

Did they know he was here?

Once in the corridor, he tried the first side door handle. Locked.

Crossed the corridor to the second. Locked.

The women were coming back. He would have to take them out. Or go back into the conference room and take that one out.

He tried the third door handle. Locked.

He was screwed. He tried the fourth. It eased open, and he slipped inside.

Dark. The two women passed in the corridor, talking shrilly. They went into the conference room and were met by a man's voice, loud and aggressive.

So that's the one with hard heels who came down from the deck. A captain?

Dark in here. He let out a breath. Took in a silent one. Breathed again. You could never get enough air . . .

He leaned back against the wall, breathing slowly and silently. Around him, all was not silent: a distant hum of reefers or freezers, the contentious voices in the conference room, the slight hustle of waves against the hull.

And something else.

Breathing.

Someone in the room was breathing. Slow and steady indraw of breath, then the soft sigh of exhalation, then moments of silence, then an indrawn breath again.

Four feet away. As his eyes adjusted, Turk could make out a bed with someone under a light sheet. A glow around the person's head that he realized was long blonde hair.

A guard, maybe, from another shift. She'd have a gun.

He had three choices:

One, stay here and risk her waking up.

Two, try to leave the same way he came in, where the two women and the man had just been.

Three, take the corridor the other way, into the bowels of the ship and hopefully up over the side.

For now, he could stay here. Unless she woke.

For a moment he let himself relax, his body wrecked by paddling and swimming and climbing cliffs and up the mooring rope of this yacht. Every part of him ached or trembled with fatigue, or both.

He relaxed into a crouch. The room was full of her breath, her odor, the smell of her clothes draped over a chair by the bed.

"*Kto ty!*" she said suddenly and pointed something shiny at him out of the darkness. "*Kto ty!*"

It sounded like *Don't move,* and the shiny thing looked like a handgun. He thought of answering *Da* but didn't.

"*Ty nikto.*" She pulled her arm back under the covers and turned on her right side away from him.

The handgun had been a bangle hanging from her wrist.

"**YOU DAMN FOOL,**" Ross said. "You've gone to DEFCON 3!"

"To hell with that," the president said. "I'm calling about money."

"*Money?*"

"My reelection is costing two billion. They tell me you have to give thirty million. Or the whole world comes down on you."

"*They* tell you?"

"They tell me everything. I trust them." The president paused. "But I don't trust you."

"I've given you lots of money, helped get you elected, back when you lost New Hampshire and were about to disappear. I helped keep you going, pumping the money in. But I was *wrong*. *Anybody* would have been better than you. Because now you're trying to kill us. *You're trying to kill us all!* And you don't even realize!"

"They said to tell you, remember. To remember . . . remember who your friends are."

"*Who* said?"

"Even back when I was a fighter pilot . . ."

"You never were a fighter pilot."

". . . it was very military, you see. Like now. When I drove that train . . ."

"You never drove a train – don't you realize? Who's running you? You don't even know what day it is . . ."

"Hey, I'm in charge here. Back when I beat up Corn Pop and his gang, *I* was in charge. Remember Iraq? I taught *them* a lesson! Didn't I!"

"You destroyed Iraq, you and Antony Blinken and Victoria Nuland and your other evil cronies. And Syria too and lots of other places. And now you've created a deadly war with Russia, but that's not enough; you've got a hot war going in the Middle East too, you're on the edge of war with China and North Korea, and now you've gone to DEFCON 3."

"They said –"

"*Who* said? Holy Christ, who said to do *what*? Don't you see how *dangerous* this is? And we're the only country in the world where one person – *you* – can push the nuclear button all by yourself!"

Ross took a breath and tried to back off. "When you took office, there was *no* escalating nuclear war, *no* World War Three in Ukraine, no Middle East war, *no* threat of war with China, *no* inflation, *no* bank failures, *no* open borders, *no* exploding national debt – How did you do so much damage so fast? Are you *trying* to destroy us?"

"I'll ask them." The president cleared his voice, as if thinking. "About that."

"*Who?* Who are you going to ask? Do you even *know* who *they* are?"

"Hey, I've been in politics longer than anybody. My grandfather was president too, did you know?"

"Do you really believe what you say?"

"They said to tell you." The president paused. "They said . . ."

"*Who* said?"

"You know the rules, they said. They *did* tell you, didn't they? The rules?"

"What rules?"

"You fuss with us and you go down? I think that's what they said. *No*, they said you *fuck* with us – that was *it!* But I didn't want to say the F-word," he chuckled. "I'm a good Catholic, you know . . ."

"Think of Christ, then! Think of peace! Before you kill us all!" Ross tried to calm down, to reach this man, somehow.

"Going to get a glass of water . . . Yes, that's what I need . . . A good glass of water."

"You brought this down on us. You and your friends!"

The connection whined. Ross listened a minute more, but there was nothing.

Final war was coming.

There was nothing he could do to stop it.

"I'VE BEEN WONDERING ABOUT YOU," LILY SAID WHEN ROSS called.

"And I about you," he said, caught himself.

"That's nice."

"I was going to ask you –" He hesitated.

I was going to ask you out, Lily bizarrely thought he'd say, though it made no sense.

"– was going to ask you, what happened to that interview we did, about nuclear war?"

"Oh. That one. I had trouble, getting it past my editor. He didn't like the angle."

"Happens all the time now. I give an interview and it comes out slanted, your peers cut my words to say something I never said. But when we complain, it gets stonewalled."

She laughed. "Maybe you should stop giving interviews."

Ross nodded, as if she could see him. "I've thought of it."

"But *I* want to *interview* you. As part of a story on the escalating nuclear missile race. I've been interviewing this Ohio congressman who says Russia, China, North Korea and Iran are all aiming thousands of nuclear missiles at us. He wants us to spend a lot more money developing better missiles to knock theirs down before they hit us."

He shook his head. "Hypersonics are too fast – we *can't* stop them. No matter what we do, at least sixty percent will get through. But even if only ten percent get through, we're cooked."

"That's what I wanted to ask you. Do you think this further endangers us, this constant nuclear missile escalation?"

"It makes nuclear war inevitable."

"Armageddon," she said, then nothing.

"In the New Testament that's the final battle between good and evil, before the Day of Judgment, when everyone who has ever lived is judged for their sins and condemned to heaven or hell."

"Funny thing about that congressman," she added. "I checked his political contributions. Most of them are from war contractors."

"They pretty much run Congress, the White House, the government, the intelligence and defense departments, the Democratic media..."

"Since your speech, I've been realizing they're not there for defense ... In the past, they were simply called the War Department."

He smiled. "That was before Doublethink."

"And ever since your speech," she went on, "I'm beginning to wonder, if we *are* risking nuclear war, how do we stop?"

"First of all, we keep revealing that a bunch of homicidal idiots are about to kill us all. Most people are already afraid of nuclear war. But our normal human response to great danger is to not think of it. Instead we show that we *must* think of it, that we *can* stop it, save ourselves. And save everything else."

"And then I ask myself is there's a reason why all these countries are arming themselves against us?"

"Because we first threatened them. Because we have an economy that lives on war, that's always seeking or creating enemies to keep the war funding going. That has put us in over forty wars in the last forty years. All which have done much harm."

"The answer is?"

"The answer is, we've gotten to the point where at any moment we can destroy the world. That we all have to work together to stop this insanity. I've worked many years with the Russians, the Chinese too, the Saudis, and even with the White House and Congress, and we're all the same. There's no reason to destroy the world because of any differences between us."

"And you really think it will destroy the world?"

"Once a nuclear war starts, every missile's going to be fired. Enough to kill everyone many times over. It's lethal we've let this happen, allowed these evil bastards the power to destroy our world. When they should all be in prison or insane asylums."

A sudden emotion warmed her. "Maybe you can reach enough people to stop it?"

"It doesn't matter. The war machine, they don't care what people want. *They're* in control; *we* don't matter at all, except in the number of dead people they plan for."

Lily shut off and stared downtown through the mullioned window of her top-story West Village apartment at the Wall Street towers in the rainy haze.

Could it be, that we really are facing the end?

How do we stop it?

Had she, bizarrely, almost *wanted* him to ask her out?

22
SINK OR SWIM

TURK listened to the woman's breathing and the voices of people in the corridors possibly hunting him. Soon they would look in here, or she would wake up.

For at least thirty seconds, there'd been no footsteps or voices outside the door. And in the last five minutes only one brief exchange in the conference room. Most of the movement was upstairs now, on the top deck.

His gut wanted to leave. He listened another few seconds, the urge to escape intensifying till he finally eased out the door and padded down the corridor away from the conference room to the twin doors leading to what on the ship's plans had been two small offices, one on each side, then the master suite and a second stairway to the top deck above and the crew quarters below.

If he could make it to the deck, he could get over the side. Fatal penetration distance of an AK bullet through water at close range was about four feet, so he'd have to swim deep. And not come up to breathe.

No sound beyond the twin doors. He pushed at the right and it didn't move. Nor did the left.

A man came through the conference room doors and Turk hit him in the belly with one fist and slammed his head against the wall with the other, yanked his pistol from his arm holster and eased him to the floor, crossed the conference room and rear deck, tossed the pistol over the side, slid down the mooring rope into the black water, dove under the dock, snatched his divepack, flippers, mask and snorkel, and swam under the dock to its far end two hundred yards beyond the Swift's stern, then out into the tall waves, glancing back over their frothing peaks to see a long silver speedboat flashing searchlights as it slid from the Swift's rear low deck, swung around and headed toward him.

He didn't think it had seen him but it was coming his way. He kicked down twenty feet and waited. The prop clatter slowed; now they were patrolling overhead.

A lightning flash darted through the black water. Bastards had a deepwater searchlight. Lungs pounding, Turk rose to the surface, his head tilted back, only his mouth and nose above water, sucking in air.

The prop pitch rose; it was coming. He dove fast to fifty feet and waited, pulse thudding in his brain. It passed overhead, slowed, hovered. Its light flicked down one side of its hull, around the stern and up its starboard side.

Hunger for air screaming in his lungs, Turk swam south, fifty feet below, away from the speedboat and back toward the dock. In the safety of its pilings he rose to the surface, gasping as he watched the speedboat quarter back and forth across the little bay, its searchlight stabbing at the night.

"HOW THE HELL YOU GET THIS NUMBER?" ROSS SNARLED, ANGRY AT being woken when he'd barely slept an hour.

"You are lucky I did."

The same Moscow woman. He twisted round to look at the clock. *04:11.* "It's what, noon in Moscow? You do realize we're not all in the same time zone?"

"I have maybe only two minutes to talk, every three-four days –"

"What is it this time?"

"I told you, last time I call, of the Commodities Futures Trading Commission? How they are coming for you?"

Damn Dale Robichaud, Ross swore. "So how are they coming for me?"

"Now they have taken it to the Securities and Exchange Commission –"

"The SEC? That's crazy – we're one of the most responsible companies out there –"

She scoffed. "You don't get it, do you?"

"Get *what*?" He desperately wanted to sleep, cut her off.

"It is because you are trying to stop the war. They will attack you till you are dead."

He sat up in bed. "Who *are* you?"

"A friend."

"I don't know you."

"Nine years ago, you were in Singapore. Just three days, May fifteen to eighteen. You were doing some long-term contracts with several buyers – Japan, South Korea, Vietnam. And a small Russian company called Navritok."

He scanned his memory. "Okay."

"You don't remember? You should."

He exhaled. "Why?"

"Because you could have taken advantage of Navritok. Some language buried in the MOU, the Memorandum of Understanding, that we had misunderstood. It was in English, of course, and the Russian translation was not good. You could have made many millions by forcing us to comply, maybe you could have taken us over. But you didn't. You understood that you could, but you didn't. Why was that?"

He sighed, almost a laugh. "I don't remember. Sorry, but I . . ."

"For us it was lifesaver. We learned to always hire American attorneys when dealing with American companies. And then we hire Russian and German attorneys to watch over them. So . . ." She hesitated. "Why did you do this?"

"Never kick people when they're down. We're all human, we all make mistakes."

"And that's why we are warning you. Of these things."

"Who is *we?*"

"*We* is Navritok. My brother and me. I am Anna. My brother's name you will know: Nevgeny Lann."

THE SPEEDBOAT QUARTERED BACK AND FORTH ACROSS THE OPEN bay for twenty minutes then sped north along the cliffs toward the small boat harbor where Turk had borrowed and returned the kayak.

It wasn't wise to stay under the dock, with the boots of the blonde guard thudding back and forth over his head. And when the speedboat came back, they'd scan beneath the dock with that searchlight, might even have a diver or two aboard. Would make sense, if they were somehow connected to the sub that blew Makassar.

When the guard had turned back toward the cliff, Turk swam to the far end and around the point to the south, away from the dock and bay and the small boat harbor. When he got to the stairs in the cliff that rose to the Bella Paradisa, he stuffed his flippers and other gear in his divepack, climbed the stairs to the main terrace, chimneyed up the two walls to the veranda of his room and popped the sliding glass door latch. He took a hot shower and called room service for two steaks, French fries, a double salad, two blackberry zabagliones, and bottles of gin, vermouth, and Barolo.

While waiting, he called Ross. "We are transmitting from their yacht."

"That's amazing. *You* are amazing."

"It's hitched to a satellite, so we can follow it anywhere. I've sent the connection to Isaiah, so his guys can monitor it."

"Astounding."

"Made in China. U.S. research, a U.S. patent, they just copied it. Put the U.S. company out of business."

"Guess what – this guy Nevgeny Lann?"

"Who owns the villa?" Turk said. "And the yacht?"

"I've been talking to his sister –"

"Holy shit! How is that?"

"Her name is Anna . . ." Even after Ross had given Turk a summary of the Moscow woman's calls, it still didn't make sense. And how did she know all this stuff, Dale Robichaud, the CFTC and SEC?

"You look them up?" Turk said. "Navritok?"

"Traders, medium-sized. Seem to be who they say."

"Hey, my dinner just arrived."

"It's what time there – two a.m.?"

"Don't matter. Hey, man, we're going to win this thing."

23

LUCKIER THAN YOU

F ROM HIS TERRACE Turk watched the silver speedboat go back and forth probing with its searchlight among the pilings of the dock, while guys with AKs watched from the prow and stern. Finally the speedboat circled up behind the Swift and was winched up the rear launch deck and stowed. There was a brief conversation on the deck between three people from the speedboat and those on the Swift, while the blonde guard patrolled up and down the dock as though none of this concerned her.

He finished his third gin and vermouth on ice, drank some Barolo and ate the steaks, salad and fries and thought about the blonde sleeper in the room he had snuck into. Why had she not wakened? Or had she?

If she'd been awake, she didn't set off any alarms. She'd let him go free. Why?

Or had she never wakened?

On the dock below a huge guard lumbered up to the blonde and gestured. She looked up at him and gestured back. She turned her back and strode quickly toward the villa. The guard unslung his rifle and took up the patrol toward the far end of the dock.

Turk finished the Barolo and the blackberry zabagliones and set his phone alarm for noon, which would be six a.m. in NY, when he could call Ross again.

Drifting asleep he remembered the blonde sleeper, heard her words in the darkness. *"Kto ty!"* she'd said, twice. A pause, then *"Ty nikto!"*

On his phone he hit a Russian-English translator. *"Who are you?"* it said, *"Who are you?"* Then came the answer: *"You are nothing."*

LYLE BRANT CLUTCHED HIS GUT TO QUELL THE DAMN PAIN. Damn thing hurt all the time now. Must have pulled it when he'd gone to Thermopolis Hot Springs with the grandkids. But damn that was fun. And afterwards, everyone chowing down on fries and deerburgers – how could he be so lucky to have this life?

He got out of his cruiser, hitched up his belt, and crossed the frozen parking lot into the Cowboy Cafe, breathed deeply the warm smells of sizzling meat, salty fries and coffee. He rippled his shoulders under the heavy jacket, letting in the warmth.

He got two Big Beasts with cheese and a black coffee and waited till Enoch Lightner, the manager, came over. "Tess says you want to see me?"

Lyle looked around and smiled. "First of all, to thank you for this bit of shelter in a snowstorm, and for these damn good burgers ..."

"Cut it, Lyle. What you want?"

Lyle chuckled. "Can't you sit down a minute?"

Enoch sat across from him, big belly jammed against the table.

"So when you worked at the refinery," Lyle said.

"Back then?"

"What was it like?"

Enoch pursed his lips. "Like any other job, you work good, you get ahead. They take care of you."

"Why'd you leave?"

"Did my twenty years, had my retirement. Wanted to buy this place. Rawhide gave me a big bonus when I left ... the president, that guy from North Dakota, he arranged it –"

"Ross Bullock?"

"He sent me a personal letter of thanks and best wishes, with a big check."

"Holy shit."

"Yeah, he did."

"How long ago you leave?" Lyle said, knowing already.

"Year and a half? Something like that. Was April something." Enoch started to count the months in his head.

"Where were they on maintenance?" Lyle said.

"They were *anal!* The minute any equipment, tiny or huge, got past its warranty date, it was gone. I worked at three other refineries before I came here, and they're all good on maintenance too, but nobody can touch these guys."

"Any idea why Tom Hogan got killed while he was in the hospital?"

"Killed?" Lightner's eyes widened. "I thought it was a heart attack."

"We did an autopsy. Turns out somebody came in and injected him with fentanyl. Causes cardiac arrest. We have pix of the person on the stairwell cameras, but the face is covered."

"Poor Tom –"

"We think it was a woman, the way the person walks, especially going downstairs. Went out the staff door and disappeared in the snowstorm."

"Jeez, might be someone who knows their way around the hospital."

"Or who even works there?"

Enoch leaned toward him. "Amazing how much I hear every day."

"You're the center of town." Lyle grinned. "The *real* mayor's office . . ."

"Let's see what I learn." Enoch eased from the booth. "Is it true, what they say, someone's pressing charges against Rawhide?"

Lyle shrugged. "Not my department."

"That'd be a crime," Enoch said and walked away.

Lyle got himself another coffee and watched the snowflakes twirling down the winter wind beyond the window, cloaking his parked cruiser in a white blanket.

Trouble was, everyone kept saying the same damn thing. The Rawhide refinery was the toughest on security, toughest on maintenance. Most refineries have frequent leaks, some have major spills. But Rawhide never.

Even worse, Cassidy had learned from the computer history that the gauges from the units surrounding the catalytic cracker had shown tight pipes with no leaks, as had all the data on the internal management system. What had happened had been an explosive surge, generated somehow or somewhere else. And therefore, damn it, if you took this to its logical conclusion, there'd been no failed maintenance.

So why had he been getting news it was bad maintenance? The first bulletins out of FEMA, other federal agencies, the FBI had all said that . . . Why?

What if he'd been beating up on this Bullock guy just because he inherited a company, while he, Lyle, had grown up in a trailer park with a drunk stepfather who liked to hit? Was he going to go that far?

Far as what?

Far as nailing a guy because he was luckier than you?

"YOUR REFINERY EXPLOSION?" Nathan Coldmire scoffed. "After evaluating all the evidence, we're going to decide it was caused by bad maintenance. Just like your damn platform."

"That's bullshit, Nathan." Ross wanted to reach through the screen and choke him. "And you know it."

"We, the government, are going to charge you with multiple massive crimes from criminal negligence to racism. You're going to lose your terrorism insurance coverage, and since it's now a pattern of bad maintenance, you'll be stuck in years of litigation without any payouts, and won't be able to cover the cash flow . . ." Coldmire chuckled. "We're going to take you down, Ross. Just so you know."

24

THE PEACE DIVIDEND

"**I F YOU GO DOWN?**" Lily looked at Ross across his quartzite countertop. "You want to make sure the president goes down with you – is that it?"

"Of course that's not it," Ross had answered, remembering Nathan Coldmire's call last night. "Anyway, Rawhide's not going down."

She'd called to ask could she come by with a few more questions, so he'd put aside this morning's 30-day projections for income, expenses, and stock price.

She smiled sarcastically. "After all these years of friendship –"

"My connection with the president was solely to advise him on climate issues."

"But you disagree over Russia. And Iran."

"The president loves wars," Ross answered. "He got seven deferments to avoid serving in Vietnam, but he's been in favor of killing people in every war he can find. As Chairman of the Senate Foreign Relations Committee, he was a major force behind the disastrous 2003 Iraq invasion, and lied repeatedly about the so-called Weapons of Mass Destruction. I fought in that war, and it was an evil, atrocious mistake. I lost many friends. We killed over a million Iraqi civilians and permanently destabilized the Middle East, leading to many years of war in Syria, Lebanon and other places, and nurturing many terrorist groups like ISIS and Al Qaeda. For years, this president has been trying to get us into a war with Russia, and now he has one that he's losing, plus more in the Middle East, and he's stupid as a rock and way over his head."

"The secretary of state, he's been traveling everywhere."

Ross smiled. "An old business adage: Never hire a fool to fix a mess he created. The secretary of state was in Kiev in 2014 organizing the coup. And he helped create the Iraq invasion too."

"How?"

"He was the clerk of the Senate Foreign Affairs Committee. Which our present president used to push the Iraq invasion through Congress."

"You don't approve of the president's stance in the Middle East?"

"He doesn't have a stance in the Middle East. He's funding Israel and Hamas and helping Iran get nukes. As did Obama. And the minute Iran has nukes, it's over."

"But," she argued, "he says he wants better relations with Iran."

"We lost Iran way back in fifty-four, when the CIA overthrew Mossadegh after he'd been popularly elected. We've done it many times since, in many countries all over the world . . . Like we did in Kiev in 2014."

"Iran, they were our ally, weren't they?"

"Till we let the Islamic fundamentalists run things. Now they have five missiles for every Israeli. And the president keeps giving them billions to buy more."

"And you're in favor of closer relations with Russia –"

Ross sighed. "It's too late now. All that's been ruined, for many decades to come, by this president and the war machine. Russia is not going to forgive us for their million losses. Nor, eventually, will the Ukrainians. But this is exactly what the war machine wants – decades more of the American people paying for weapons."

"But what about the Russians?"

"Their war budget is six percent of ours." He was quiet a moment, frustrated he couldn't reach her.

"At the *Times*, we never write about things like that."

"After the Soviet Union dissolved, the Russians were incredibly grateful for U.S. help, anxious to develop a Western-style economy, happy that the Cold War was over, and that we'd all been spared nuclear annihilation. The Peace Dividend was going to lower everyone's military budgets. The Doomsday Clock was backed up to the furthest we've been from nuclear war."

She cocked her head. "The Doomsday Clock?"

"It's a measure of our closeness to nuclear war. Created by Einstein, Oppenheimer, and other scientists after Hiroshima and Nagasaki . . ." He saw her flinch, and feared he'd hurt her, looked into her eyes . . . "It's updated every January by the Bulletin of Atomic Scientists, the people who actually design and build nuclear weapons."

She nodded, and he wondered if she'd understood.

"Our closeness to nuclear war," he added, "is shown by how far the Clock's hands are from midnight. The furthest distance was 17 minutes to midnight after the fall of the Berlin Wall, during *glasnost* and better relations between Russia and the West. Since then, the hands have moved steadily toward midnight, and in 2023 and 2024 were set at only 90 seconds away, the closest we've ever been to nuclear holocaust."

"So," she persisted, "you're saying that relations with Russia were better years ago?"

"Far better. After the Berlin Wall fell, cooperation grew quickly between Russia and the West; U.S. and European companies came to Russia by the thousands; income in Russia expanded across all economic levels. Russia dissolved the Warsaw Pact in return for U.S. promises not to expand NATO into Central and Eastern Europe. Russia requested to join NATO and the European Union . . ."

"*Nobody* talks about this."

"Bill Clinton turned them down."

"Turned them down? Why?"

"He was told to. By the one group that was terrified of peace."

She shook her head. "Who doesn't want peace?"

"The war machine. They're terrified of peace. The war contractors and all the politicians they own, their many thousands of lobbyists, lawyers, PR firms, retired generals, media hacks and other liars, the 'experts' the media drags out from the universities, think tanks, and NGOs, all trained to say the same thing in different ways. So while the Russians thought we were entering a new era of cooperation and peace, instead we've been surrounding them with missiles, armies, and bioweapons labs. We've broken every agreement we ever signed with them." He smiled. "Sorry, I've been living this too deeply."

Her heart went out to him. "You've talked about this before."

"I've worked all over Russia, all eleven time zones. Russians everywhere have been open and friendly, and the usual response has been, 'We love America!' followed by invitations for dinner, family visits, and friendship. This started to cool after our Ukraine coup in 2014 –"

"Coup?"

"Again, you should look up the history. In 2014, President Obama directed the CIA to overthrow the democratically elected president of Ukraine, Viktor Yanukovych, and his government, and replaced them with anti-Russian politicians. You can look it up."

She smiled. "You keep saying that."

"All directed by Victoria Nuland, previously Vice President Cheney's instigator of the disastrous Iraq invasion. But rather than being imprisoned or at least banished from government forever, she worked her way up the ladder till Obama picked her to organize his five-billion-dollar 2014 coup against the popularly elected Ukrainian government. She directed it, working with John McCain, Lindsey Graham, Vice President Biden, John Kerry, and a lot of other CIA and neocons. When Trump became president, he got rid of her immediately, but when Biden took over, he made her Under Secretary of State in charge of instigating this deadly US-Russian war in Ukraine."

"Elon Musk said that about her."

Ross nodded. "Elon's a wise man."

"Seems so."

"But when the president realized that his Ukraine war was collapsing and might cost him his reelection, he dumped her."

"And now, with this election almost here, he's in a very tight race, and you're saying when he was vice president, he got millions of dollars from these foreign companies in Ukraine and China?"

"*Many millions* of dollars, from shadow companies in Ukraine, China, Romania and other places, all funneled through twenty-two shell companies controlled by nine members of his family. The president then pressured the Ukrainian government to drop corruption charges against one of their shadow companies called Burisma, and pay him and put his son on their board of directors. That's just the tip of the iceberg. And it's a major reason for this war that may kill us all."

He put a memory stick on the quartzite counter between them. "It's all here. The president's fake companies, the hidden entities, the dark money behind many of the transactions. And his foreign interventions they all paid for. Like Ukraine."

She picked up the stick delicately, as if it might explode. "How'd you get this?"

"The CIA works closely with the oil industry. So anyone high up in the oil industry has deep access inside the agency. And many agency people believe this war is leading to nuclear holocaust, so they want to stop it."

"Did this information, what's on this stick, make you decide to challenge the sanctions and create all this fuss about nuclear war?"

"I've known for years about our government's continuing encirclement of Russia. Several times I've briefed administrations on Russian concerns about this. Anyone at top levels of government or industry knows all this. Many former U.S. diplomats from Henry Kissinger and Robert Gates to secretaries of defense, ambassadors to Russia and retired generals, have been warning that this continuing encroachment on Russia is wrong and will lead to nuclear war."

"Wow." She sat back, thinking. "At the *Times* I don't think we've ever covered this. I looked in our files, the other day, about Ukraine. We backed the 2014 coup."

"That's what you were told to do."

Lily had a flash of stunned awareness. If what Ross was saying was true? And to have this story first . . . But would the *Times* even take it?

"Also on that stick," Ross added, "are spreadsheets of political contributions he's received from the war machine. And all the billions he's brokered for them in return."

She watched him. "You really mean this?"

"Of course."

"Why me?"

"Because you're tough. You're fair. You're honest."

She shook her head. "We've hardly met."

"I've read a lot of things you've written."

She took a deep breath and sat back. "You really are naïve."

He gave a half-shrug. "Lots of people have thought that. Over the years."

She rose and crossed the kitchen to the glass living room wall and its stunning view down Mad Ave to lower Manhattan. She turned to him. "With all *this*, are you happy?"

He glanced at the glass wall. "Don't have time to think about it."

"Some people, no matter how hard they try, they're never happy. Other people don't even try, they're just happy."

"Which are you?"

"Oh, I'm completely happy. Sure, I care about the world, war, hunger, sorrow, all that, and try to change them. But I'm a very happy person."

She seemed to him charming, almost innocent, very smart and a bit devious. "And I believe," she added, "that you are too."

He thought of Mary, as he instantly did whenever the idea of happiness occurred to him. *Have I been happy?* he wondered. *Not lately.*

Yet this young woman infected him with a moment's pleasure, for whatever it was worth.

"THAT RUSSIAN YACHT JUST PULLED OUT OF SORRENTO," ISAIAH told Ross. "And we're already getting good stuff."

"From the energy minister?"

"Igor Stein? There's definitely a gruff older guy on board who everyone kowtows to, but who they really seem to love. Most of the staff is basically security."

"That's what Turk said."

"Soon as we're done translating, we send it to you. At least once a day. If it's urgent we call you."

"This could be a gold mine."

"IRS CHARGES RAWHIDE WITH FRAUD AND TAX EVASION*"* WAS THE bold headline atop the first page of the *Times*:

The Internal Revenue Service announced today it is charging Rawhide Energy with seven counts of wire fraud, two counts of mail fraud, and three counts of tax evasion. The company, the IRS states, has been utilizing a Ponzi scheme to cheat its investors by illegally transferring capital expenditures to profits, as well as by illegal operations to boost production on its poorly-maintained gas platform and refinery.

The company then attempted to hide these actions by falsifying corporate tax returns over the last two years, the IRS additionally charged, with even further charges expected. "Rawhide has been running an illegal crap game with other peoples' money," said Acting Deputy Assistant Attorney General Barbara Keta-Jarman of the Justice Department's Tax Division, "and it's time they face the consequences."

IRS-Criminal Investigation, the Department of Justice, and the FBI are also investigating the case, he/she added.

"If this is true," Jim Burleigh exhaled, "I will be truly ashamed. To be associated with such a criminal enterprise."

"If you repeat a lie often enough," Deborah Quinn said, "it becomes the truth."

"What's astounding" – Isaiah leaned into the camera – "is it came out of nowhere. No prior investigation, no information requests, nothing. Out of nowhere."

"Can we fight it?" Mitch said bleakly.

"We can fight anything. But it will cost millions. And then we'll lose."

AS RAWHIDE'S FATE DARKENED, ROSS REALIZED THE JOURNALISTS at his press briefings had grown far more confrontational. Just weeks ago, they had been puppies quivering for tidbits, jealous of each other's access and glowingly quoting from company handouts. Now they'd become scavengers trying to take down a wounded prey and feast on its entrails.

Rawhide's demise would be journalistic gold for weeks, and for years would show up in learned business publications, business courses, and other foolish places.

Another reason to make sure it didn't happen.

He stared out at the room of journalists, some trying to look attentive, others sitting back in a cynical, knowing pose, the TV cameras, the *clik-clik* of stills, the air of stilted waiting – his fifth press conference since the world had gone upside down a mere two weeks ago. And for the first time, he realized he didn't need them anymore.

They'd done all the damage they could.

It was time to turn the tables. "Yes," he answered a question, "all Rawhide people remain on full salary and benefits even in this downturn. Even though some of them can't work."

"At less pay than you –"

He looked at the NPR reporter. Late twenties, overweight, a nose ring and pink pugnacious face, thick saggy arms. "Rawhide pays better than any other energy company –"

"So who is funding this? Are you reaching out to banks? Are you . . ."

He let her thunder on, displaying her total lack of knowledge, till finally he said, "*I'm* the one who's funding it."

She halted. "Is that because you have so much money? Because Rawhide is a gold mine you inherited from Daddy?"

"My father started with nothing. He worked day and night seven days a week, and my mother too, to build this company. He could have chosen to waste his weekends listening to NPR or going to the mall. Mom could have done a million other things. But they both worked and worked and worked to create this thing they loved, Rawhide Energy. Which I inherited and have built from a four-million dollar company to one of America's fastest-growing and most solid international corporations."

"But given the level of recent mismanagement . . ."

He tuned her out. Why were these questions not aimed at learning a truth they could convey to their listeners or readers? No, it was all "gotcha" – catching you off guard, hoping you might say something they could use against you, to make them look good. It wasn't about information any more, it was about ego. Their ego. Each one wanted to be the one to strike the fatal blow. But why? For whom?

He tuned back into her harangue. "Not just this platform disaster," she was saying, "which the authorities say is due to poor maintenance –"

"Can you explain what you mean by poor maintenance?"

"Well . . . it was in the pipes, they say."

"Who says?"

She shrugged. "The *authorities* say."

"Which authorities? What pipes?"

"I don't know, you tell me."

"You don't have faintest idea what you're talking about, do you?"

"I'm a journalist, I ask questions –"

"Shouldn't you know something about what you're asking? Otherwise you're just parroting someone else."

"Well, if you refuse to answer . . ."

"Are you threatening me with retaliatory coverage? You're already giving me retaliatory coverage. Don't forget, your salary is paid by the American taxpayer. Don't you owe them at least a little honesty?"

Ross ignored the grumbling and waving hands in the room, focused on her. "Go ahead," he said. "Write another snotty piece about what we've done wrong. What's your experience running an international company? How would you like to be personally responsible for the livelihood of twenty-seven thousand families, for providing energy to the world so it can function?" He broke off, disgusted with her, and turned to the room. "Does any of you have a real question?"

For a moment they were silent, then a hand went up, then more. "Yes," he called to the first.

An earnest, crewcut young man: *Fox News.* "Do you think, Mr. Bullock, the poison pill strategy you've employed to undercut EastPac will be sufficient in the long term?"

"Good question, thank you. Yes, I think it will be sufficient, at least for a while. And we have plenty of other tactics we can also use, if need be. I don't think EastPac has the resources for a long fight, one they're sure to lose in the end."

"How can you be so confident," the NPR woman called, "when you have catastrophic losses, your insurers are trying to drop you, your leases are being cancelled, EastPac has you by the throat, you've got problems with the Commodities Futures Trading Commission, the IRS, the FBI, you've tanked in all the markets – do you really think you can fix this?"

He smiled at her. "Isn't that what I get paid for?"

CENTRAL PARK

E VERY NIGHT before going to sleep, Ross checked his messages and voicemails one last time. In the last hour, there were a hundred and forty-nine new messages and two hundred eleven calls which he deleted one by one after checking them, till he got to a breathy voice message from the engineer who'd survived the platform explosion – Liz something... He couldn't remember.

"*Please call me!* Turk's not here ... someone's tried to kill me."

He hit Call Back. It rang, on and on. No one answered.

He called Turk. "How fast can you get back to Jakarta?"

Turk shook himself awake and glanced at his phone. "Dammit, Ross, I just got to sleep!"

"How fast?"

Turk sat up, took a breath. His head spun. Too much gin or salt water. Or both. "What the fuck for?"

"Liz Chaplin's missing."

"Oh shit." Turk leaped out of bed and checked the time. "If the tunnel's not jammed, I can be in Naples by one-thirty. If the traffic around the airport's not bad ... But there won't be flights out."

"I'll have a Lear pick you up in Naples, drop you Jakarta."

Turk thought of the Russian energy minister who'd flown into

Naples yesterday and what had happened since. He headed for the shower. "I'll get there fast as I can."

"The plane's in Rome. It'll be in Naples in half an hour."

"She better not be dead."

Ross called the CIA Jakarta station for Keith.

"He's in conference," a young woman said.

"Get him out!"

"It's high-level. I can't interrupt."

"I don't care what kind of level! Get him out. Now!"

Perplexed, the young woman wavered, then said, "I will check."

"Don't check. Get him out. There's an American about to die."

The phone cut to twanging Balinese music and the thunk of drums. Ross paced, pulse thudding in his brain.

"What the hell, Ross!" Keith rumbled. "This better be good, or I never speak to you again."

"Our employee, Liz Chaplin, the one you didn't want to put a detail on, she's vanished."

"Ross, we're not a dating service. We don't follow single young women around –"

"Can't you get it through your fucking head there's more to your job than eavesdropping on Muslims and communists and having dinner at Kahyangan?"

"You don't know the half of what goes on."

"Neither do you. Or you're part of it."

"Fuck you, Ross."

"This isn't politics. She's American. Find her." Ross shut off, stared out at the glittering, uncaring city.

Was she already dead?

"I KNOW IT'S LATE," Ross said, "but figured you were up."

"Hardly sleep anymore," Senator Sidney Hollit said. "Just lie there and worry."

"What the point of that? We're all dead soon. You can worry then."

"Where are you? New York?"

"Yeah, but I'd rather be fishing with you up on the Madison, catching rainbows, feeding mosquitoes and ducking grizzlies."

Hollit chuckled. "Christ, we had some good times, back then."

"There was a pool, about eleven miles downriver, where you dumped the canoe."

"Wasn't me. You never could paddle worth shit."

"The Prez says I should sell for what I can, get the hell back to North Dakota."

"What do the banks say?"

"They're waiting for the right moment to cut my throat. When they can make it look like a mercy killing."

"This EastPac thing," Hollit said. "Can you beat it?"

"For the next few days, at least."

"*Barron's* still being nice."

"That won't last."

"You going to fight your way through?"

"I think so. Still figuring it out."

"What can I do?" Hollit asked.

"How well you know Edith?"

"I pushed her appointment for director of national intelligence through the Senate. She wouldn't be there without me."

"I know the Agency's against us. But there's an American woman missing, the only survivor of the platform. A brilliant geologist, may be kidnapped. In danger of being killed."

"The Agency is the president," Hollit said. "You know that."

"But Edith can kick their ass, if she wants to."

"Well, the president nominated her, so she's very pro-war. But now he's so out of it, she's worried he's going to push the button."

"Because we're the only country in the world where just one person can all by himself push the button?"

"That's what she's afraid of. If he wants to, no one can stop him. And she's also afraid he won't be re-elected, and we might get someone who opposes these wars. So she says get rid of him. And if she can use you, use Rawhide, somehow . . ."

"Sidney, *we can have a nuclear war before* the election! Killing your grandchildren, *all the children*, everything!"

"The folks running the president, they're not afraid of nuclear war. Think they can win it."

"They're homicidally insane."

"Who blew your platform? Blew your refinery? Do you know? What about the Chinese, or the Russians, radical Sunnis, the Iranians? A banking cabal, or just some wiseguy investors selling you short?"

"The Jakarta station chief doesn't see it that way. Says we blew it on purpose, or it was bad maintenance."

"Keith? You know where his balls are."

"My platform gets blown up on his watch and he tells me fuck off. Now Liz Chaplin, who survived the platform, has vanished right after she calls me saying she was in danger. Keith doesn't care. Wally doesn't care. They won't even look at it."

"Keith was with EXXON, how many years?"

"Can't remember. Many."

"I wonder if he's still vested," Hollit said. "You get taken down, three years later he gets an extra ten million, who's to know?"

"I go down, he gets more than ten million."

"I'll call Edith right now."

"Christ, it's late."

"She's in Canberra. The Five."

This was the international intelligence group composed of the US, UK, Canada, Australia and New Zealand. "Tell her," Ross said, "that Liz is in great danger."

"Maybe she's already dead?"

"I'm afraid."

"Is that why Keith's ducking you?"

LYLE BRANT WAITED TILL THE BLUE MUSTANG LOWRIDER AND several more cars had passed and then pulled out behind them. The Mustang took Main Street, then Powell and North Avenue till the houses thinned out. The other cars had turned off; the blue Mustang, ass-down, headed for the Interstate.

Before the truck pulloff, Lyle accelerated up behind him and hit the flashers. The Mustang braked, saw the pulloff, hit his right turn signal, and rolled to a stop.

"You, Pedro!" Lyle called over the loudspeaker. "Get out with your hands *way* up."

A tall, gangly man with a pockmarked face and short patchy hair crawled out of the driver's seat and flashed the finger as he raised his hands.

"Anyone else in that car, get out now. NOW!"

"Just me," Pedro called. "What you stoppin me for?"

His palm on his gun, Lyle walked up to him. "Hands behind your back."

"What *for*, man?"

"If I have to tell you one more time . . ."

Pedro thrust his hands behind his back, and Lyle clicked his cuffs. "You're gonna pay for this," Pedro said. "I wasn't doing nothing."

"You're never doing nothing, shithead." Lyle gave the cuffs a nice wrench. "My bet is you're on the way to Denver to do some shopping – right? A little fentanyl, a little meth, some oxy, all kinds of good stuff. Right?"

"Sheriff, you're hurting me."

Lyle twisted a little tighter. "I can call the mobile lab right now, and we'll find so much crap in that junker of yours that you'll be back in Rawlins tonight."

"Sheriff, it ain't me. I been straight. I love to drive around at night, is all."

"You think we don't know what you do? We're just waiting for the right time to pull you in, so you never get out."

Pedro's head dropped. "So," Lyle added, "I'll make you a deal. We don't call the mobile lab and have them vacuum your car. I uncuff you and you get to finish your drive around at night, long as you don't bring anything back."

Pedro shook his head. "What for?"

"What for?"

"What you want?"

"I want whoever broke that Chinese guy's neck and shoved him in the snowbank for the plow to cut in two." Lyle gave the cuffs another twist. "You know every dirty, twisted evil little thing that goes on here, so I want *you* to tell me."

"I'm not part of this, Sheriff. You know me better'n that."

"I'm listening."

"Go see Coyote Jim."

"THE DEVICE TURK PUT ON THE YACHT," Isaiah said, "it's perfect. I've just wired you the recording of a discussion off the coast of Italy between the Russian energy minister, Igor Stein, and his Saudi counterpart, Abdulaziz al-Biltin al Saoud."

"Where the hell did Al Saoud come from?" Ross asked.

"Flew into Rome with a bunch of aides, choppered to the yacht when it was out in the Med where they thought they were beyond discovery. The translations from Arabic and Russian are theirs, but checked by us."

Ross split the screen to read the attachment. The first pages recorded the chatter in the yacht's conference room as two women brought vodka and caviar and the men joked till the women left. Then it got interesting:

SAUDI ENERGY MINISTER: "It's a good idea, if we do this right."

RUSSIAN ENERGY MINISTER: "Now, because of this damn war with the Americans, it's a good option."

SAUDI: "How many times have they betrayed you, the Americans? Us, too, they have betrayed. But now they're afraid to lose us –"

RUSSIAN (laughs): "Iran –"

SAUDI: "We thank you for your help there."

RUSSIAN: "They did this to themselves, the Americans. Why can't we all live in peace and be happy?"

SAUDI: "You guys going to shoot first? You going to kill us all?"

RUSSIAN: "Never will we shoot first. We love our country. We love the world, our families, life. Who wants to destroy all that?"

SAUDI : "The Americans, still thinking they run the world."

RUSSIAN: "But as we've said, if crude isn't priced in dollars . . ."

SAUDI: "Together, you and us, we're the world's biggest crude producer. A quarter of the world market. Then *we* decide how crude is priced –"

RUSSIAN (chuckles): "But all these damn sanctions and embargoes –"

SAUDI: "They haven't hurt you one bit. Your crude exports are at an all-time high, the ruble too, so stop complaining."

This was true, Ross knew. Before the Ukraine War, Russia exported nearly half its crude and refined products to the European Union. After sanctions, EU sales decreased but Russia simply redirected its supply to the rest of the world.

Though sanctions had almost no impact on Russian oil sales, they had very negative impacts on the EU, and huge benefits for the U.S. oil industry. Hilariously, the US/EU price caps were set well above current market prices, guaranteeing that Russia could continue to make good profits despite them.

SAUDI, continuing: "Anyway, you're who chose this stupid war."

RUSSIAN: "What would you have done? What if, like in the old days, when you and Iran were enemies? And if after they promised peace, they put hypersonic nuclear missiles all around your borders? Then built twelve bioweapons labs all upwind of your capital, your whole beautiful country?"

SAUDI: "If we'd had nukes, we'd've blown them all to hell."

RUSSIAN [chuckles]: "And the rest of us, too."

SAUDI: "What we can't understand, is why the Americans can't see the reality. What if you Russians put your missiles along the U.S. borders in Canada and Mexico? Like they've put their missiles along yours? After they promised not to?"

RUSSIAN: "Look, those guys, how many wars have they started? Since their war in Vietnam?"

SAUDI: "Since then? I would guess, what, more than forty?"

RUSSIAN: "And how many civilians they have killed?"

SAUDI: "In their wars? Maybe ten million? They don't talk about this."

SAUDI: "You Russians, like us desert Arabs, we have the tradition of honoring our word. Of not betraying our partners."

RUSSIAN: "True."

SAUDI: "But the Americans, like the Chinese, sometimes do not honor their agreements. [LAUGHS]. But on to business. This agreement our ministers have prepared, we sign it?"

RUSSIAN: "On our end, there are still concerns."

SAUDI: "Back in 2020, together we cut worldwide prices thirty percent. Flooded the markets and drove down the crude benchmarks . . ."

RUSSIAN: "You can survive that easier than we."

SAUDI: "So now, we cut production they will shit themselves. When they can't enforce the sanctions any longer, because crude suddenly costs too much?"

SAUDI: "It is not our fault, this stupid war."

RUSSIAN [sighs]: "It is everybody's fault, this stupid war."

SAUDI: "So which way we go? Up or down?"

RUSSIAN: "So if we cut, the price goes up, it fucks their sanctions. *And* their economy."

SAUDI: "And everybody else's. Except yours and ours. And some of our friends."

RUSSIAN: "And if we increase production?"

SAUDI: "They will also shit themselves."

For the next hour they argued while the yacht cruised the Tyrrhenian Sea toward Naples. The best part came at the end.

SAUDI: "My dear friend, it's good to work together on this."

RUSSIAN: "But as I have said, this is just one option."

SAUDI: "You have been the Americans' punching bag for years. Us too."

RUSSIAN: "Bullshit. They make you rich. You guys used to live in tents in the desert."

SAUDI [laughs] "They used to need us, so they were nice, as long as we gave them back half our profits by buying their weapons."

RUSSIAN: "It's their game, weapons."

SAUDI: "That and oil. Because of fracking they're now producing more crude than even they can use. For us, and for you, this has three bad consequences: *One*, it drives down the barrel price, cutting our revenue. *Two*, it steals part of one of my country's biggest markets, the fat cow of America. And *three*, selling *their* damn surplus to the rest of the world drives down *our* total market share. Not so?"

RUSSIAN: "Is true. So do we cut production and drive up the price? Or increase it and blow them all out of the water?"

SAUDI: "Last February, we cut our Asia price two dollars. Look what happened."

RUSSIAN: "It is what we must decide. At the last moment."

SAUDI: "As we have discussed, at a price below thirty-seven fifty for West Pennsylvania crude, their fracking completely dies. Even out west, where they are getting it almost free from the government. But it will take time for all this to come together. Can you afford it?"

RUSSIAN: "You do not know Russia."

SAUDI: "What about this guy, Rawhide? Is he really on your side?"

RUSSIAN: "Bullock? He is a good guy. But he's not on anybody's side."

SAUDI: "I hear they are really coming for him."

RUSSIAN: "We hear this too. We don't think he can make it."

SAUDI: "We are staying completely out of it."

RUSSIAN: "We too. They already have their own billionaires buying and selling their elections."

SAUDI: "If *we* don't run the world, Igor, who will?"

RUSSIAN: "We are afraid, though, this might hurt the president's re-election."

SAUDI: "Your friends in Beijing, too, they also want to keep him safe."

RUSSIAN: "He is making them much money."

SAUDI [laughs]: "Works every time."

RUSSIAN: "The question is you and me, do we do this deal now?"

SAUDI: "If we wait, will that hurt him in November?"

RUSSIAN: "For many reasons, if we do this, we do it soon."

SAUDI: "With no announcement. We hit the markets cold. Agreed?"

RUSSIAN: "As soon as I get to Naples, I'm flying back to Moscow. I'll have a brief discussion there, then we sign."

SAUDI: "How is he doing?"

RUSSIAN: "Christ, he's fine. His stomach hurts. He broods at night over every soldier's death."

SAUDI: "That's crazy. Death is death. PAUSE, THEN ADDS: "My helicopter's on the way."

RUSSIAN: "Have a good trip back to the desert."

SAUDI: "Take care. You too, stay safe."

[SOUND OF PEOPLE MOVING, CHAIRS SLIDING BACK]

SAUDI: "We are about to change the world. And it doesn't even know what's coming."

IF THEY WERE ABOUT TO CHANGE THE WORLD, WHICH WAY would it be? Ross reread and reread the transcript.

"Up or down?" they had discussed but not decided.

If Ross could figure it out, could it help stop the war?

If crude went up, it would hurt everyone. Except the producers.

If it went down, it would hammer U.S. production.

Which way? If he could figure out what the Russians and Saudis were going to decide, he could go long or short.

Maybe save Rawhide.

Maybe even help the world avoid what was coming.

BALLS

"SHE'S ALIVE," Keith said.

"Where?" Turk leaped to his feet and almost lunged across Keith's desk to throttle him. "You bastard, why didn't you tell me?"

"Calm *down*! Not like she's your girlfriend or anything."

Turk stepped around Keith's desk, gripped his shoulder, and leaned into his face. "Where *is* she?"

Keith pointed at the ceiling, pushed Turk away, stood, and pulled on his jacket. "C'mon, you're buying me lunch."

The sun outside was glaring hot, too bright. Turk was shaking with fury that Keith wouldn't tell him, but feared pissing him off so he might not tell him out of spite. *Then I'll kill him*, Turk thought. *If anything happens to her, I'll kill him.*

They took an inside table at Ah Whu Take-Out & World Cuisine. "We don't know why they've taken her." Keith leaned forward, elbows on the table, hands clasped. "Don't know *who* they are. Have to be working for somebody."

"Keith, where the fuck *is* she?"

Keith's fingers clenched. "Basement of a shopping center. About a mile from here."

Turk stood, spilling tea. "Why aren't we *there*?"

Keith patted the table. "Sit down. We're covering the place, waiting for the right time." He cocked his head eastward. "Central Park Shopping Center. We have the blueprints, have cameras and watchers on it. There's shops in the lower level, and storage rooms. There's even a porn film studio down there, with a black steel door."

"Porn studio? The government'd kill them."

"That's where she is."

"Who's got her?"

"Three people. Rotate on a four-hour basis."

"Jesus, Keith, who *are* they?"

"Wish we knew. They're armed and know what they're doing. One of them may have been part of the FPI, the Islamic Defenders Front."

"Jesus," Turk repeated. "Why them?"

"Maybe they want something from her?"

"How'd you get this?"

Keith grinned. "Broke a few bones."

"Since when are you back in the business of breaking bones?"

"We have lots of nasty intel on top government folks, so when we hold something over their heads, *they're* the ones who break the bones." Keith smirked, palms upraised. "Don't blame me."

"After days of telling us to fuck off, why the sudden love?"

Keith gave a soft shrug, as if his tailored white silk jacket didn't quite fit. "Got the word."

"From where?"

Keith raised his palms as if in surprised adoration. "Above."

"Every fucked-up thing that hits you comes from above? What about BIN – Badan Intelijen Negara? Or Budi, Teddy, all those guys? Where were you when this shit was being planned? You were out at the Royale Jakarta Golf Club, on one of those twenty-seven holes with your dark money friends? Or in the clubhouse? Those gin and tonics are going to be the death of you, Keith. So don't tell me" – Turk leaned forward – "that it was from above."

Keith sipped his tea. "You're very lucky, and you don't even know."

"Really? Why is that?"

"Because now I'm on your side."

"You'll never be on our side, Keith." Turk shoved the table back and stood. "Either you guys and I are going to Central Park right now, or I go there myself and kill them all."

Keith grinned up at him. "Fine, you can do that. But you two will be the first ones to die."

"I REMEMBER WHEN ROSS WAS FIFTEEN." NASH O'MALLEY PEERED at Lily through the Skype screen. "He'd jump into the pit with the rest of us. Tough as heck even then. Saved a man's life, that first summer, in Mandan."

"Wow, how'd that happen?"

"Guy got his arm caught in the casing head. Was spinning around, woulda been yanked down the hole. Crushed alive. Ross leaped in and got him free. Just as he was about to go down."

Lily tried to imagine this. "The guy was okay?"

"Got his arm chewed up, that's all." A smile crinkled Nash's cragged sun-worn face. "Nineteen years ago, maybe. I would've been fifty-six, and now I'm seventy-five."

"Though his parents owned the company, he started at the bottom?"

"It was a small company back then. Ross worked summers and vacations ever since junior high, as a laborer, then I think he was a refinery pipe-fitter, and learned to be a boiler mechanic, and while he was in high school he helped program the Sweetwater refinery's software, then he left to go to college in Montana."

"Why Montana?"

"To play football. Didn't want to play at the University of North Dakota – can you imagine?" Nash moved out of the camera, came back. "Sorry, just checking my dog. She was looking like she wanted to chase the cat."

"The cat okay?"

"Heck yes. Every time the dog goes after her she rips a new hole in his face. He just doesn't seem to get it."

Lily smiled despite herself. "What kind of dog?"

"Red setter. Dumb as the rock he was born under."

"Well, thank you for discussing Rawhide with me. I'm sure you've seen some amazing changes – what was the company revenue back then?"

"Heck knows." Nash shrugged. "Three-four million, maybe."

"And now thirty billion. And seventy billion in total assets . . ."

"A fine kid, Ross. *Really* smart. Tough as steel pipe. Friendly and kind, never acted like it was his family's company. Trusted us, liked us. And we liked and trusted him. Still do."

"What do you think about what's happening now?"

"These war bastards, trying to ruin him, destroy the company."

"I'd heard the problems were mostly from poor maintenance –"

"With Ross? Never. He's a fanatic. Even I used to tell him, after he took over the company, you're overspending." Nash raised his hands in deprecation. "Fell on deaf ears."

"So why are they trying to destroy him?"

"Follow the money." Thumbs tucked into the suspenders of his worn blue coveralls, Nash glanced down. "There's a lot of money in killing people. But Ross is a tough one." He faced up at her and smiled. "Don't count him out."

Maybe, she thought. Maybe not.

TO MAKE MONEY, Ross knew, you have to know ahead of time what's going to happen.

If this Saudi-Russian agreement increased production, thus lowering crude prices, much of the world would be happy. By flooding the market, it would reduce the energy burden of billions of people. Until it wiped out every oil company that couldn't produce below thirty-five a barrel. When they were all gone, the big guys would cut production, and before you knew it we'd be at ninety a barrel again. Then a hundred and fifty. Like when the Bush presidents twice invaded Iraq to drive up the crude price, to make the Saudis and all their other friends richer.

During GW Bush's presidency, the crude price quadrupled, and at one point even sextupled, which very much pleased the international oil companies he was working for.

This deal would work, too.

But if instead of increasing production, what if the Saudis and Russians cut it? Crude and product prices would take off like a rocket, causing even more inflation and driving a stake through the bond market and the president's chances of re-election.

An aging, befuddled president, senile and unable to speak intelligibly without a teleprompter, ducking journalists and way down in the polls, could easily be beaten.

It might be the only way to stop his wars.

Which would hurt him more, a price increase or cut? But why would the Russians and Saudis want to keep him in office? And the Chinese, too?

Would the U.S. war machine even allow him to be defeated?

If Ross could figure which way the Saudi-Russian deal was going to move, he could go long or short on billions of barrels. And with resulting billions in profits, he could do a stock buyback and get Rawhide back on top.

He wondered if Turk had met up with Keith. If Liz was still alive.

And if Turk could find her.

CRITICAL DEFENSE

TURK HATED Central Park Mall like he hated all the big Jakarta shopping malls and all malls everywhere – why create a monstrous thing simply to take people's money for stuff they don't need?

It was all lights and glitter, flickering greens and blues and reds and purples enticing people into its cathedral of consumption, its sparkling false joys. Hard to imagine fifty years ago this place had been jungles and fields.

And Liz was somewhere inside it. In a downstairs porn studio with a black steel door.

He bought a shirt in Lacoste and put it in a plastic Lacoste bag. In Giordano he purchased two silk scarves and put them in a Giordano bag, went into Estée Lauder and found nothing, then to Krispy Kreme where he bought a big box of doughnuts and put them in another bag.

With the bags in both hands, he took an elevator to the bottom floor and followed past Socialla, the women's beauty product store, past a "Ladies and Men" coiffeur, till the corridor narrowed and he reached a black metal door set in a steel frame. It was locked. Beside it was an unlocked broom closet of mops and rags that smelled of Lysol.

Footsteps neared around the corner. He walked back past the coiffeur and Socialla, climbed a stairway to the main floor, and waited to see if the person behind him had followed. He hadn't.

After thirty seconds Turk dropped back down the staircase, returned to the locked back door and listened. Inside all was silent.

He returned to the "Ladies and Men" coiffeur, where a beautiful girl in a full headscarf gave him a number. "Fifteen minutes," she said.

He pointed to three empty chairs, a table with a stack of magazines. "I will wait."

He sat flicking through magazines in Malay with photos of fancy pomaded young men and shyly smiling young women, scanning the text as if he could read it.

When a coiffeur's chair was available, he didn't take it because it was in the back and he couldn't see the locked door. "I want this person," he said, indicating a tall, spare, veiled woman who worked the first chair.

Twenty minutes later she was free; she brushed the previous woman's hair from the chair and said something in Malay. He pointed to a magazine photo of a scowling young man with short hair. "Like that," he said in English.

She scanned him, surprised, then with an open hand invited him to sit. He spun the chair so he could sit watching the locked door. She hissed a rebuke but did not turn the chair.

After she had cut one side and was beginning the other Turk saw a tall, skinny man stop at the locked door and take out a set of keys. He shoved some rupiahs into the woman's hand, grabbed his shopping bags and walked from the door down the corridor toward the man.

As the man opened the door, Turk slammed a fist into his chin, his jaw shattering like glass. Turk dragged him into the broom closet, lashed one of the two Giordano scarfs over his face and tied his wrists to his ankles with the other scarf. He grabbed the man's keys and opened the locked door.

Tied to a chair, blindfolded, her mouth taped, Liz turned toward him.

He yanked the tape from her mouth. "God!" she mumbled. "How'd you get here?"

He cut the ropes binding her to the chair and pulled her to her feet. "Can you walk?"

"Of course!" She hobbled to the door.

"Quick!" Holding his packages in one hand, his other arm round her waist, he led her to the elevator and up to the mall exit. No one seemed to notice.

"Goddamn drugs they gave me," she coughed. "Hardly see straight."

"You're okay." He wanted to hug her, protect her. "We're going to move you to a new place."

They took a quick taxi ride to the Ritz Carlton to pick up her things, then another to the Shangri-La, where with a Dutch passport and KLM credit card in the name of Daan van der Rijk, he rented a suite with a kitchen, bedroom and a separate study with a foldout couch. They sat at the kitchen table while he took notes and recorded her story.

"THE DAY AFTER THAT GUY IN THAT BMW NEARLY RAN ME OVER," she said, "I went into the Department of Motor Vehicles in Jakarta Barat, waited two hours, paid a twenty-thousand-rupiah bribe, gave them the BMW's license number . . . with that plate number, it had to be in Pondok Indah, a really nice suburb of South Jakarta –"

"Damn it, you should've told me. Before you did this –"

"I was fine on my own! I don't need you."

"You're a dumb bitch."

She rolled her eyes. "They told me to wait." She glanced out the window at the blazing Jakarta dusk. "I'm so drugged. Give me more coffee."

He poured her another cup. "Get back on track. Before you fall asleep and I don't get another word out of you."

"At the Division of Drivers Licenses they told me to wait in a room, then four guys came in, grabbed me and had my mouth taped in seconds, wrists too, punched me with a needle, and I woke up where you found me."

"A porn studio."

She recoiled, then laughed. "How funny is that?"

"Can you ID them?"

"They had a hood over my face. I never saw them. That place had a bed and a TV and a bathroom. When they brought me food or came to give me a shot, they told me first to put the hood back on."

"You heard them?"

"They spoke English to me. But I could hear them talking together sometimes. They didn't know I understand Malay. Not a native, mind you. But when I got transferred here, I learned it in six weeks. It's not a hard language. While they had me, I listened to everything they said. Even when they thought I was sleeping."

"What did they say?" Turk asked. "To each other?"

"They argued whether to kill me then or later."

There was no reason, he wanted to tell her, why they didn't kill her right away. Or was there? Was there a connection between these guys who'd grabbed her and the Sorrento villa and the Russian energy minister? The Russian yacht with its armed guards, the Russian oilman who owned the yacht? The Chinese sub whose diver had blown up the platform?

"What else do you remember about these guys?"

"Not much. Those injections kept me out of it. See, my arm's all bruised."

He was surprised when he touched her arm how connected he felt, how angered, as if her flesh were his. *Damn fool woman.*

She was the only witness to the platform explosion, so of course they were going to kill her.

If he hadn't found her, they would have.

Why hadn't they killed her right away?

Using her to bait him? Were they that good?

What had she seen, or could have seen on the platform that made her so dangerous? What about this driver who'd tried to kill her?

"We have to keep you under cover."

She nodded wearily. "I don't care . . . I'm so tired . . ."

He could talk to the Embassy, ask Keith to put a detail on her. Or get her out. But would that put her even more at risk? "We're going to fly you out of here," he said. "Somewhere safe."

"Balls you are." She gave him a clear, hard look. "I'm staying till I find them."

"**DON'T MIND KEITH**," Senator Hollit told Ross. "He's an asshole, but he's mostly our asshole."

"He gave me the tip that got Liz out –"

"Liz?"

"Woman works for us, got kidnapped."

"You rescued her? Good for you." Hollit was calling from Kansas, an overnight trip, he'd said, for his re-election campaign, and Ross was in New York, but to Ross it seemed as always they were in the same room.

"Thought I'd let you know," Hollit said. "Brushing you off – Keith had to do it."

"Why?"

"Came down from State."

"Since when does State tell the Agency what to do?"

"From all the way to the top. Goddamn CDD."

"CDD?" Ross said.

"Critical Defense Decision. Part of Presidential Decision Directive 63, the Department of Defense Critical Infrastructure Protection Plan, or 'CIP.' To protect critical infrastructure from disruption by acts of terrorism and information warfare. Another Beltway goatfuck."

Ross tried to digest this. "The president can declare I'm a national defense threat?"

"You know how things work these days: you're guilty till they decide otherwise."

"This is insane . . ."

"And you're giving aid and comfort to the enemy," Hollit went on.

"Fraudulent and dangerous operations in various locations that could negatively impact our energy reserves and infrastructure. And thus our own energy operations and our economic and therefore political relations with our allies."

"Then why's Keith come around?"

"Edith."

"You got to her?"

"She and I had a good talk. About Senate budgeting of nonexistent programs. I'm on Appropriations –"

"I know."

"She told State to back off, this was her baby."

"So who's after me with this Critical Defense thing?"

"Don't know," Hollit said. "But I'll find out."

Ross shut off the phone and stood at the window staring at the bright Manhattan night. Senator Hollit had reached Edith. And she had leaned on the Agency. The president was owned by the Agency because of all the inside dirt they had on him. But Edith and the president were no longer friends, because she'd decided he couldn't get re-elected, creating the danger that someone might win who'd stop the wars.

And if the CIA was trying to kill Rawhide, maybe Edith would help him. Or maybe it would reverse, and she'd be the one to bring him down.

He stared at his worn reflection in the window. Could he keep doing this?

Just keep on. Keeping on.

EVERY TIME LIZ FELL ASLEEP AT THE TABLE AT THE SHANGRI-LA, Turk nudged her awake. "C'mon, we're almost done," till she finally stood and stripped to her bra and panties and climbed into the bed.

"Look, sweetheart," she yawned, "you can ask all the questions you want, but I'm going to be sleeping."

She had a gap between her front teeth that he found insanely attractive, and this annoyed him even more. He stood, gasping in the sudden pain of brutalized muscles, oft-broken bones, exhaustion, and no sleep. Of having flown halfway around the earth to rescue her.

For hours he'd been looking forward to that bed.

He went into the study and lay down on the couch. It was too soft and too short and squeaked when he moved. A large spring poked him in the back. Swearing silently, he returned to the bedroom, lay down opposite her with his clothes on, and fell instantly asleep.

NO NUCLEAR WAR

"**I**T'S ME AGAIN," Anna said.

Ross shook himself awake. "Now what?"

"Where are you?"

"New York. Asleep. You?"

"Moscow. I am always in Moscow. I never sleep."

He rubbed his unshaven face. "What are we talking about this time?"

"A tip for you. About trouble coming."

"What do I have to do, for this tip?"

"Shut up and listen."

Ross thought of cutting her off but didn't. She'd been right twice already – warning him about the CFTC and Dale Robichaud, then about the SEC. "Okay."

"First, the Romanians are going to suspend your dividends from the Kamitz pipeline, which you own 33.72 percent, until the Mahakam platform report is done."

The Kamitz line was feeder pipe from the Urals fields to the Druzhba main pipeline supplying Eastern and Central Europe with heavy crude. "They can't do that."

"They will," she said. "Tomorrow."

"It's just a way to duck payments."

"I think the White House told them do this."

"How do you know?"

"Shut up and listen. That is *first* thing happening tomorrow, in Romania. *Second* thing is what is to happen four hours later on the Footsie, your utility, Kent Power in the UK –"

He tried to focus, saying nothing.

"LSE:KEC is yours, yes?"

He nodded, then realized she couldn't see him. "Yes."

"Is coming a ratepayer challenge filed by the Consumer Advocate. It will kill Kent's stock price. At a time when you were depending on it to help you ride this storm, no? And will cause an enforcement by the UK Financial Conduct Authority, unfortunately . . . Which makes you *a priori* guilty, no?"

Kent Power, thanks to careful power purchases, superb teamwork, and excellent client and investor relations, had accumulated a huge bank balance that Ross needed to do a multimillion crude short.

He was numb to it, he realized. Like a man being lapidated, who barely feels the latest stone.

"How do you know all this?" he said, but she was gone.

"**YOU SLIMY PIECE** OF PIGEON SHIT," LYLE EXHALED. "TELL ME what I want to know."

"Jesus, Sheriff, you're breakin my arms."

Lyle laughed and slammed Coyote Jim again against the jail's concrete wall. "You know what resistin arrest means? You know how many years *that* can get you?" He spun him around. "So who was it?" He shook him hard. "*Who* was it?"

Coyote Jim nodded. Snot was running from his nose and drool from his mouth and blood from where his forehead had hit the concrete. "But I *didn't* resist arrest, Sheriff. "You got no *reason* arrestin me."

Lyle slammed him against the wall again.

"They weren't from here," Coyote Jim moaned.

"Okay, where?"

"Listen, Sheriff, you'll get me killed –"

"I may kill you now. But if you're lucky I'll just arrest you on first degree in the death of Victor Minh, that poor little old Chinese guy with glasses."

"He weren't Chinese, Sheriff. He were Venta-meese."

ANNA WATCHED THE SNOW FALL BEYOND HER LEADED GLASS window of red, blue, and yellow flowers wreathed around unicorns' necks, and behind them towering forests and magic mountains. The afternoon sun through the falling snow cast these colors across the floor of old oak, gleamed across the paintings on the walls, and glowed like coals in the vast granite fireplace.

It made her sentimental to think of this house's many lives – built on a field above the river Moskva in 1849, three generations of a family whose greatest sin was to make money and share it with others, then its takeover by Lenin's troops who pillaged then left it to crowds of homeless displaced by the German 1914 invasion. The years after of total dilapidation, when beautiful places like this were dying everywhere. Then the atrocious German invasion of 1941 that killed one in every seven Russians and destroyed the entire western half of the country, including Ukraine. Then the tragic, slow rebuilding until *glasnost*, the fall of the Soviet Union, followed by years of starvation, then the rise of Putin and the economic and spiritual rebirth of Russia.

Long may it live.

Inspired by the USA, we wanted to learn capitalism. Which we did, very well. Till they turned on us, planning to attack us while proclaiming peace. Could we ever get back together with them the way we were – business and scientific partners, almost allies and friends? Was that great chance of world peace gone forever?

Now instead of cooperation we were enemies again. Why? Russia's war spending, though still only six percent of that of the U.S., had more than doubled since the Ukraine war began. The Americans, too, were increasing their already enormous war budget – hypersonic missiles, tanks, drones, robots, deadly bacteria and other killing tools, plus six hundred billion more in new nuclear warheads for submarines, long-range bombers, and intercontinental missiles. And everyone was making the missiles faster and faster, invulnerable to defense.

The outside window was a triple-paned 8 R rating, from the US/Russian window factory south of St. Petersburg, that is now closed. Best windows in the world.

What good we could have done together.

Together there would have been no nuclear war. And some day, no nuclear weapons.

"IT *WEREN'T* ME, SHERIFF – YOU *DO* KNOW THAT?" IN A YELLOW jail suit and shackles, Coyote Jim looked up pleadingly. *"Don't you?"*

"You're a sniveling snot of snail shit. That's all I know about you." This was a lie; Lyle had arrested Coyote Jim seventeen times and knew a lot about him. Specifically that Pedro, the lowriding fentanyl dealer with the blue Mustang, had fingered him for the death of Victor Minh.

"I'm trying to be honest. Sir," Coyote Jim added hopefully.

"You wouldn't know honest if you fell over it in a septic tank."

"You be sad if you don't believe me. What you say, put me in a septic tank?"

"I didn't mean that. But it's not a bad idea."

"You're just making fun at me, Sheriff."

"If you insist – against all evidence – if you *insist* it wasn't you who killed this Chinese guy –"

"Venta-meese, sir."

"I'll Venta-fucking-meese *you*, ass*hole* – if it wasn't you who killed him, and *I* think it was – who the fuck *was* it?"

"Four guys. Chinese. Came up from Colorado."

Lyle turned to Cassidy. "Book him. Murder one. Let the whimpering piece of weasel shit try to find a lawyer."

"It's true!" Coyote Jim wailed. "I even got their plate number."

"How's that?"

"I was comin' out of the Gas'n Jug with a bottle, and this shiny SUV burns the red light at Wadsworth, so I think maybe I can get his plate as he comes by, and if I give it to you, maybe you guys'll go easier on me next time . . ."

"Spit it."

Coyote Jim looked up coyly. "It's on my phone."

"Where's your phone? This better be good."

Coyote Jim smiled meekly. "Under Wyoming law, if I tell you what I know – not taken part of, mind you – if tell you what I know, I don't have to be charged – now do I?"

"I'm no lawyer, but that may be true."

"And I wouldn't even necessary be arrested."

"Depends. Where's your damn phone?"

"Well, if I wasn't arrested, I could go back to my trailer and get it, couldn't I?"

"Cassidy'll take you."

Lyle leaned back in his chair with his feet up on the desk and watched a single star shimmer beyond the window. How far away it was, how far away any life, in this whole endless universe? If we're the only ones? And some of us are scum like Coyote Jim and Pedro and these Chinese guys from Denver and whoever brought humans to this once-lovely earth in the first place.

He was nearly asleep when Cassidy came back. His feet were numb from being up on the desk. His belly hurt from worrying about the refinery and that poor little Chinese guy with glasses, and why would that Chinese gang from Denver come all the way up here to kill him? And kill Tom Hogan?

"I ran the plate," Cassidy said, stamping snow off his boots as he came in. "Silver Yukon, three years old, stolen in Denver. Reported missing only yesterday, after the owners came back from Maui and found it gone."

"But these guys were driving it when Coyote Jim took that picture."

"Dated two days before the refinery explosion."

Lyle stood and reached for his coat. "I'm beginning to think, more and more, it weren't no accident."

What he disliked most about Coyote Jim, Lyle thought as he drove home, was he was on county welfare as an Indian, while maybe he was twenty percent Crow though he called it Cheyenne. Whereas Lyle had a Lakota grandmom married to his German grandad, and a Blackfoot grandad married to his Irish Catholic grandmom. Which if you did the numbers, made him fifty percent Sioux.

Lyle had never taken a free thing in his life. And didn't like people who did.

"And that's why *I'm* the sheriff," he told Olivia, his wife of thirty-six years and mother of their five beloved children, as he peeled off his uniform in the bedroom at two-fifteen a.m. "And *they're* not."

She patted the bed covers. "Shut your face and get your skinny ass in here."

29

DON'T FUCK WITH WYOMING

TURK BECAME AWARE of a loud noise. A machine gun, but steadier. Or a propeller underwater. *Wake up*, his brain screamed. *Danger!*

He sat up. Remembered.

There she was, short brown hair, a gentle face, the lips a little too large, the nose too, the wide eyes shut under long lashes. Bare shoulder under the bra strap, supple muscles, strong bones.

"Holy *shit*," he said softly.

Her eyes flicked open. "So?"

"Jesus, you snore."

She sat up, lovely breasts in the filigree bra. "I do *not!*"

"I should have recorded you."

She fixed him with fierce brown eyes. "I've had lots of boyfriends, and none of them ever said I snored."

"Jesus, they were all deaf."

She dove under the covers. "Call room service. I want three cappuccinos and five pastries. *French* pastries."

"Coming, Your Highness." Turk checked his phone. *06:13*. They'd had almost six hours' sleep. Scratching his chin he shambled to the hotel phone and hit nine for room service. "What you got for break-fast, bro?'

It was a long list. "You got French pastries?"

"Not at the moment, sir."

"You got cappuccinos?"

"We have many cappuccinos. Vanilla, chocolate, peppermint . . ."

"Please, just espresso and steamed milk. You got scrambled eggs?"

"With mushrooms, tomatoes, peppers –"

"You got just scrambled eggs?"

"Of course, sir."

"You got ham?" One had to be careful; this was a Muslim country.

"We have many hams, sir."

"We'll have seven cappuccinos and five orders of scrambled eggs with Canadian ham and a bottle of Piper-Heidsieck."

"Very fine. On the champagne, sir, what year?"

"I WOULDA TOLD YOU ANYWAYS," ENOCH LIGHTNER SAID TO Lyle, "about Mama Gaia. She's not the kinda thing you keep under wraps."

Lyle nodded encouragingly. "Right."

"Soul Fitness Retreat, that place in the mountains, north of here . . ."

Lyle shook his head. "Stop shitting me, Enoch."

"Apparently four Chinese guys came to town two days before the explosion. They left two days after the explosion. Before Tom Hogan was killed."

"What's this got to do with Mama Gaia?"

"She runs Soul Fitness Retreat, right? They stayed there, the four guys."

"Who says?"

"Gladys Higgins. She works there, drives into town twice a week to do the shopping, always stops here for a burger. She said these Chinese guys were strange."

"She say what they were driving?"

Enoch thought a moment. "Nope."

Lyle thought of telling Enoch about the stolen silver Yukon. But no, first he and Cassidy would talk to Gladys.

Enoch bent closer. "What if those Chinese guys blew up the refinery? And it wasn't bad maintenance at all? Who would profit from that? And who'd go under?"

Lyle stood painfully, batted his hat against his knee to shake off the melted snow. "We're just a little ranching community in the middle of nowhere. And I'm just a small-town sheriff. No way we can figure all that out."

"WHAT HAPPENED TO YOUR HAIR?" LIZ ASKED TURK.

"I was getting it cut in Central Park, the coiffeur down the hall from your porn studio, when this guy comes along, starts to open your door . . ."

"Where is he now?"

"Maybe still in his broom closet."

"You kill him?"

"Probably not."

"You should have."

Turk scowled at the wreckage of breakfast spread across the king-size bed, empty plates, egg and ham dishes, papaya and tangerine skins, cappuccino cups, an empty bottle of Piper Heidsieck, and two empty glasses. "You eat like a horse."

"Champagne makes me hungry."

"Question is, do we order another one?"

"It'd be a crime not to."

The thought of crime unnerved him. For these few hours he'd been human, not caught up in pain and destruction. He called the order down, picked up all the breakfast trays from the bed, and put them outside. "After this," he said, "let's go over what you told me last night. We have to figure out exactly who grabbed you and who they're working for. Before we do anything else, we have to get this down."

When she smiled, the gap in her front teeth was entrancing. "We haven't *done* anything else."

"I forgot, I'm living with a porn star." He pulled off his clothes and slid into bed beside her.

THE QUESTION WAS COULD ROSS RAISE SEVEN HUNDRED FORTY million to short Arab Light? As an initial margin at thirty percent cover, it could give him access to enough funds to do a stock buyback that would raise Rawhide's value enough to save it. And all he risked was the seven hundred forty million, which anyone should be willing to lose in case of a mistake.

But if the Russian/Saudi deal wasn't to raise production, but to cut it? He could lose most of the seven hundred forty million in a selloff and margin calls.

Standing at the bathroom mirror brushing his teeth, he ran through his mind the assets he could put in play. Assets with low leverages; if he could pool several, he might raise that amount.

Ever since he was a kid, he'd worried about every penny.

"Now I know why you're rich," one of his refinery managers had once said.

"Why's that?" Ross had answered, shrugging it off.

"Because when we walk across a parking lot, you pick up pennies when you see them."

"It's an old family thing. Never waste anything. My grandmother, who grew up in a sod hut in the ferocious North Dakota winters, used to talk about money too good to use. I know what she meant."

But the problem was if he lost this seven hundred forty million, he'd be totally broke, couldn't fight anymore. So maybe he should put up less margin, like five hundred million, but that wouldn't give him enough cash to do a buyback and keep Rawhide on its feet.

But could he trust this information? He'd asked Isaiah to verify the voices on the yacht – he'd already known both voices were correct – and yes, they both came back as the Russian and Saudi oil ministers. And this wasn't the first time they'd done a secret deal: back in March

2020, Saudi Arabia, an original OPEC member and its largest exporter, was secretly negotiating with Russia, a non-member, about cutting oil production to keep prices up.

But when they couldn't agree, the Saudis backed out and lowered production substantially to drive up prices, but this was when the Wuhan COVID pandemic started cutting worldwide oil demand, so crude prices dropped, contrary to what the Saudis had hoped.

If the negotiations between the Russians and Saudis fell through again, would the same thing happen?

He caught himself in the mirror, ragged-faced, half-shaven, weary and nearly beaten.

Either you risk the seven hundred forty million or you take the safer path of wait and see.

He grinned at himself in the mirror. *Don't be stupid. Go for it.*

Long or short? Up or down?

IT FLASHED ACROSS THE LIVING ROOM AND SMASHED INTO THE glass door to the balcony. Turk leaped from the bed and knelt down to the tiny pile of fluff.

"Oh shit," Liz said, coming up behind him. "I hate it when they do this."

"Not their fault. They can't see the glass." With the bird warm in his palm, Turk elbowed the terrace doors open, went out and sat by the glass table in the shade of the potted banyans. "Can you get me a glass of cold water? With ice cubes if we have them?"

The bird twitched then shivered and lay still. Liz came out with ice water and he trickled a little on its head. After a few minutes he did it again. It opened its eyes, closed them. When he did it again the bird stood unevenly in his palm and suddenly flew away, a flash of blue and gold among the glistening high-rises.

"We need to get going," Liz said, stepping into her underpants. "That bird was a message."

"That it hit the wall?"

"We all hit the wall sometimes. That it survived."

It made him leery to say this: "We will too."

LYLE HAD LEARNED SO MUCH SO FAST HE WAS HAVING TROUBLE understanding it. He scowled at his morning coffee and tried to remember what he'd figured out during the night.

By catching Pedro on his weekly buying trip to Denver he had scared the shit out of him and learned that Coyote Jim might know something about who killed Victor Minh.

Coyote Jim, coward that he was, had coughed up the license plate of the stolen Yukon that had driven into Sweetwater two days before the refinery explosion. After that, somebody shot at Ross Bullock, Victor Minh went missing, Tom Hogan was killed in the hospital, and surely more bad stuff was going to go down. It was just a matter of time.

Then Enoch Lightner had said four Chinese guys had stayed at Soul Fitness but left before Tom Hogan was killed in the hospital.

The Yukon had vanished. At the refinery, the heat of the catalytic cracker explosion had been so hot that no clues remained. The possibility of an explosive signature was being denied by the FBI. The bullets taken out of the walls of the Black Eagle Motel matched the Glock 22 found under Victor Minh's body, but it was a ghost gun, no serial number, untraceable, like nearly half the guns that cops were dealing with these days.

The FBI had been helpful at first but then had gone cold on the whole investigation. Did they think there was nothing to it? Why else would they stop calling back, stop analyzing the blast data?

The person who killed Tom Hogan had not left a trace, DNA or otherwise. And if these Chinese guys had already gone before he was killed, it was probably somebody local who did it. Question was, who?

The number two goal was to find the Yukon. But these guys were too good. If it did appear eventually, it would have been wiped clean and burnt to a crisp. No clues.

Number three was to re-scan all the refinery cameras. If there had been a bomb, whoever set it had to show up someplace. Again, these guys were so good, they'd probably never show up.

Denver detectives had dusted all the entries to the property where the Yukon was stolen, but had found no new fingerprints. They were going on the thesis that whoever stole the Yukon knew that the owners would be gone in Maui. And maybe they were right, but that was not his department. Since the president opened the border and Denver decided to be a sanctuary city, they had so much crime down there he didn't know how they kept up.

Answer was, they didn't keep up. No one could.

The whole damn thing gave him a pain in his gut. That kept getting worse.

But if they'd come up from Denver in the Yukon, there might be camera footage of them on the way, maybe Exit 254 near Fort Collins, the Johnson's Corners truck stop, the Colorado border cameras – he listed them all in his head.

He finished his coffee and called Cassidy. "You there yet?"

"On my way."

"You're lyin."

"*Almost* on my way."

"Let's call the Denver cops and see what camera action they can pick up for that Yukon. Between Denver and here. Since two days before the explosion."

"I got it half done already."

It bothered Lyle that these guys who stole the Yukon thought they could come up from Denver to Wyoming and commit any crimes they wanted. Blowing up a perfectly good refinery, killing five people with deep roots in the community.

These guys from Denver just didn't realize, don't fuck with Wyoming.

It will come back and get you.

30
SOUL FITNESS

L YLE AND CASSIDY drove north out of town into the hills and canyons of pinyon pines and juniper, toothed with limestone crests and little cliffs, blue sky and white clouds soaring above.

"What I like most about this job," Cassidy said, "is the unexpected."

"Gets less and less, over time."

"Better than LA, where all that happens is you arrest really bad-ass guys, and twenty minutes later they're out again, no bail. And they do another horrible crime and get released again. We called it the Soros syndrome. But today, driving into these beautiful hills under a bright October sky . . ."

Lyle grinned. "You're just hot to see the Soul Fitness Retreat."

Cassidy adjusted himself in the driver's seat. "Sounds like some Nineties show."

Lyle shifted his chaw. "History does repeat itself. But each time it gets worse."

Cassidy swung the cruiser into the Retreat parking lot and took the only empty space. "We got a used-car lot going here." Cassidy got out and adjusted his holster. "So how do they know our four perps? And why?"

"We go ask." Lyle put on his hat. "Isn't that the polite thing to do?"

MAMA GAIA WAS A LARGE WOMAN IN HER LATE FIFTIES WITH A GRAY crewcut, hanging jowls, a hexagonal purple crystal flashing from her wrinkled neck, and an odor which Lyle thought might be patchouli but also cats and sweat. In a super-size kimono, she lounged across a pink leather sofa, a large mastiff at her side. Pine fires crackled in the two living room fireplaces, Led Zep howled miserably from speakers on the walls, and a cigar smoldered in a yellow Mexican ashtray on the glass coffee table before her.

"Why am I so favored?" she said, after a young woman had ushered them in.

"Just checking," Lyle said, "on your recent out-of-town guests."

"Oh, those four boys. So deep, tranquil – unusual for young men."

"Tell me more," Lyle said. "When did they arrive?"

"It was October seven. I remember so well because it was Kismet's birthday."

"Kismet?"

"The Siamese there, with the flat face. That's she."

"Really?" Cassidy said. "And when did these guys leave?"

"Oh, four days later it was. They came, they meditated with us, and they left."

"What kind of car did they have?"

"Oh, a great big silver one. We don't pay much attention to cars. We're into deeper things here."

"When they were here," Lyle said, "did they spend time with anyone?"

"With Rudi, yes they did. Helped him meditate right out of his depression."

"Where's Rudi now?" Cassidy put in.

"He's over there –" She pointed a saggy forearm. "The orange and tan kitty. He's my little boy."

Without asking, Lyle sat on an ottoman. "Let's try to get down exactly when they came and left . . ."

"They aren't suspected of anything, are they? No, they couldn't be . . ."

"No?"

"Four of the deepest young men we've met. So polite . . . that's Asian, you know. To be polite."

"They speak good English?" Cassidy said.

She shook her head. "Sadly, only one spoke a little English. He did the translation thing on his cell phone."

"They have a lot of baggage?"

"They each had a big black duffel. With heavy things inside, that clunked. Weights, they told me. For exercise."

"How'd they pay?" Cassidy asked. "Credit card?"

She shook her head. "Strange as it may seem, they paid cash. Two thousand four hundred twenty dollars even."

"You still have the dollar bills?"

Again she shook her head. "Glad took them to the bank yesterday. We try not to keep cash on the property."

"How many people here," Cassidy said, "saw or met them?"

"Well there's me, of course, don't forget me."

"We won't."

"Then there's Glad."

"What does she do?" Lyle said.

"Gladys is the cleaning lady. And there's Trim. She's the one who showed you in. She leads the meditation sessions. Sometimes she does sex therapy too. She's good at that."

"Anybody else?"

"Just us chickens," she chortled, hugging the mastiff. "And Caesar."

"Caesar?" Cassidy asked.

She hugged the mastiff tighter. "This little guy."

"We'd like to talk to Gladys and Trim," Lyle said.

"Go ahead, but you're wasting your time. Those four boys are special. You can tell from their aura." The sofa squealed as she rolled to a sitting position. "No one can fake an aura."

"What do their auras say about them?" Cassidy asked.

"That they're on the good side of changing the world."

"Really?" Cassidy said. "Who's on the bad side?"

"You." She glared at him. "Cops." She nodded at Lyle. "Him too."

"LILY –" Ian Hamilton leaned across his desk, confidentially. "Dale Robichaud's a big political donor. He –"

"You're saying I can't touch him? Even with the truth?"

"As you've learned, nothing's true till the *Times* says it is. And we're specifically *not* going to say this."

"I tracked down every single allegation Robichaud made against Rawhide. There was no substance to any of them. There were no PEMEX payments, the Caribbean bank accounts don't even exist, there were no fluctuations in oil benchmarks . . . The SEC has dropped the whole investigation!"

He took a breath. "I shouldn't tell you, but there's a list of people we don't cover, and a list of people we do cover, but only in a certain way. Mr. Robichaud's on that second list."

"Yes, he's close to the president. I mentioned that, page three." She was leaning forward in her chair, she realized, as if ready to attack. Ian looked small behind his big, wide desk, in his Princeton blue-striped dress shirt and red bowtie. She told herself to back off before she strangled him.

"This is not covered fairly."

"Fairly? Jesus, Ian!" She forced herself to sit back. "Since when have you covered Rawhide fairly? It's as if you have a third list, people you must always attack!"

He smiled. "Of course."

"It doesn't matter that everything Robichaud alleged was false? Like the Vermilion River – he boasted how it had been cleaned up, but it's worse, and he's its major polluter? Aren't you ashamed?" she asked him finally. "Ian! Aren't you ashamed?"

He huffed. "Let's talk about what we do with this."

She shook her head. "I'm not writing you a puff piece!"

"We're going to deep-six it. It never happened."

"Imagine, if you *had* published Robichaud's CFTC story without my final-checking it? It would have destroyed Rawhide's stock price. As if we're working for their enemies!"

"That's the fourth list. The people we obey."

"Who were you obeying when you refused my piece on nuclear

war? My Wuhan COVID story? When you guys fired our wonderful editorial page editor, Jim Bennet, because he accepted an op-ed by a Republican Senator?"

"The same people, of course."

She stood. "I'll take this to the *Journal*."

He picked up his phone. "I'm calling Becky right now, asking her not to take it."

GLAD WAS THE LEAST GLAD PERSON CASSIDY HAD EVER MET. HE and Lyle had separated her and Trim into two rooms and interviewed them separately.

There is a fate in names, Cassidy believed, and sometimes in interrogations you can get inside a person's head by thinking about their name.

Though her name meant *princess* and *sword*, according to the internet, Glad was certainly neither.

She sat hunched on the steel chair with head bowed and hands clasped. At first he was mean, but he saw how quickly she collapsed, and that there was nothing there. Like what Hippocrates said about medicine, never do unnecessary harm – the cop's first oath.

"You really mean you had no contact with these guys?"

She faced him with her dark-rimmed, smoker's eyes. "They never wanted me to even clean their rooms. Never spoke a word to me." She looked down, as if ashamed.

"Did that bother you?"

She shook her head. How pretty her hair is, Cassidy thought. "Not at all," she said. "It was easier that way."

"Did you ever tell anyone about these guys?"

She flinched and glanced up at him. "Why would I?"

TRIM WAS TRICKY, LYLE QUICKLY REALIZED. SHE EMANATED A FEAR of discovery that meant there was something to discover. But she was obdurate, wouldn't disclose it.

In a leopard leotard stretched tight over a young athletic body, that of a long-distance runner, a yoga coach. Scarlet hair cascading down lithe shoulders. Nipples and pubis outlined under the thin fabric.

Lyle shifted his chaw to the east, toward Nebraska. "Why the name *Trim?*"

She flicked him a comic glance, as if he were a fool but out of kindness she'd answer. "My folks ran a marijuana farm, up in Humboldt County."

"Nevada?"

"Northern California. Redwood country. Weed capital of the West. Everywhere the loggers trashed the redwoods, we planted marijuana. My folks got rich."

He grinned. "And happy?"

She stood, twisting her body as she did. "They were always happy."

"So why the name?"

"From trimming the marijuana plants. Even as a little girl, I could always tell where in the branch to cut, how to thicken the plant – a good marijuana plant is really a small tree – how to get the plant focused on producing THC, the sticky sex hormone that gets us all miraculously high . . ."

"You admit you smoke marijuana?"

"All the time."

He smiled. "That's against Wyoming law."

"Shame on me!"

"What we really want to know is about the four guys who stayed here."

She turned stretching the snaky leopard leotard. "I only knew two. That I slept with and exchanged vibes."

"What vibes you get?"

"Kwan's more forthright; Zhen hardly talks at all. Kwan said they're looking at a large ranch in the back country for a buyer willing to pay up to five hundred million."

Lyle thought a moment. "There's no ranch that big in Wyoming. Nor in Montana, or Idaho or the Dakotas. He was bullshitting you."

She grinned at him, bright teeth in a luminous smile. "Of course not. He was buying it from the government."

"No way."

"I figured it out. It's 145 million acres of Bureau of Land Management holdings in eastern Wyoming. Owned by the American people. BLM owns over ten percent of all the land in our entire country, originally stolen from the Native Americans and now belonging to American citizens. But it is consistently and horribly ravaged and mismanaged by the so-called government agencies that allow it to be raped and pillaged by the logging, mining, cattle, and off-road industries." She gave them a grin. "The world the way it really is, huh?"

"True." Lyle nodded.

"Everything I know about these guys is that Kwan is a quick, ferocious fuck and Zhen's more patient and resourceful."

"Did they blow up the Sweetwater refinery?"

"Of course not. Four of the most tranquil souls I've ever met."

"Why'd you only do sex therapy with two?"

She smiled. "The other two were into each other."

Unfortunately, both Glad and Trim had alibis for when someone had gone into the Sweetwater Hospital ICU and killed Tom Hogan. After the four guys left the Soul Fitness Retreat in the stolen Yukon, Glad had gone to her sister's in Nebraska, Trim to a high school girlfriend's in Boise. Both were confirmed by the sister and high school friend, by credit card data, and by a number of surveillance cameras in both locations.

Glad had given them nothing, knew nothing. But Trim had given them, in a way, a bit more.

"You think," Lyle said, "she'd be fun in bed?"

"Holy Jesus," Cassidy exhaled. "Don't go there."

They drove out of the Retreat onto the one-lane dirt road back toward Sweetwater. "Missed dinner again," Cassidy grunted.

Lyle switched his chaw to the right side. "Does Shirley get mad when you're late?"

"Most of the time she's pretty good about it. But if I miss one of the kids' birthdays or a night we were supposed to go out, she can get real mean . . . Like last week, that head-on collision up on State 120, and I came home at four-ten a.m. after eight hours trying to saw dead children out of a Dodge Caravan . . . It was my son Patrick's birthday. The same age as one of the kids we took out in pieces. All the time I was doing it there were tears in my eyes . . . Every cop on the site was crying."

"Yeah." Lyle sighed, took a breath. "Olivia's like Shirley. Gets mad sometimes, even when I can't help being late."

"You been married what, thirty-six years? You guys are doing okay."

"Sometimes I wish we never been married. For her sake."

"You're both so cantankerous neither'd be happy without the other." Cassidy flicked on the windshield sprayer to clear off the prairie dust. "And you, without her? You'd be even more insufferable."

Lyle smiled. "Good to know."

"Glad and Trim. What a pair."

"Not that they gave us much."

"Same old story. These four guys in the Yukon are quiet, polite, bow to you and say something unintelligible. They go out mostly at night. The night the cracker blew, they came back late. The night Victor Minh got kidnapped and Ross Bullock got shot at, they never came back at all."

"But the problem," Lyle said, "is they left Sweetwater before Tom Hogan was killed."

"My bet is it was Trim. Who went in and killed Tom."

"But why? What's she get out of it?"

Cassidy was silent, his eyes on the thin road snaking ahead of them down the mountain. A doe and two fawns darted across, a bobcat eyed them balefully from the shoulder, and the lovely frozen night hissed through the vents. "You think," he said, "most folks agree with that woman, that us cops are evil?"

Lyle grinned and shifted his chaw. "Not in Wyoming."

31
NOT TO WORRY

L YLE HATED AIRPLANES. Particularly these tiny ones, which were all he could get from the State of Wyoming – bouncing around in the windy, wintry skies while he and Cassidy scanned the frozen landscape for a silver Yukon in the middle of nowhere.

If it was in the middle of nowhere, it was nowhere to be found.

There was, however, lots of snow. White-covered rolling hills and canyonlands to the far horizons, worn limestone ridges of juniper and pinyon pine, a piercing blue sky cluttered with white clouds, a herd of antelope scattering, their sunrise shadows darting ahead of them across the white crust.

"My tanks are getting low," the pilot yelled.

"Keep going till we have to turn back," Lyle said.

"I already have."

They landed in clouds of blowing snow. The pilot slid open his side window and spit tobacco on the runway. "How you going to find a silver car in all this snow?"

"Tell me what I don't know," Lyle grunted.

"But it's your old instinct at work again, isn't it?"

Lyle shook his head. "Don't have any clues."

"I get sent out sometimes twice a day, all over the place, I'll keep an eye out."

They headed for the office, Cassidy driving, Lyle feeling angry and crochety and worn down. "We're not getting anywhere."

"Every case," Cassidy said, "starts like this. You don't know much. Then you learn something. Then a little more. Things start to fall into place, clues match up . . ."

"Yeah, that's when you know you're wrong."

"True," Cassidy said as he slowed behind a school bus.

"Pass them," Lyle said.

Cassidy grinned. "For an instant I was afraid you meant it."

"I do." Lyle rubbed the back of his neck where it hurt most. "This case is wearing me down. There's no resolution. We're not learning anything new . . ." His phone rang and he moved to shut it off, saw it was the Denver detective, and answered.

"Just finished an aerial," Lyle said. "Saw nothing. If it's out there, within thirty miles of Sweetwater, it's invisible."

"Maybe you're looking in the wrong place," the Denver detective said.

Oh shit, Lyle thought. "Where do you suggest?"

"You were right about checking freeway cameras –"

Lyle sat up. "Norm Cassidy's idea."

"Good for him. Because we now have IDs on two of the four guys in that stolen Yukon."

"Holy shit!" Lyle turned to Cassidy. "They have IDs!"

"They pulled up at Johnson's Corner," the Denver detective continued, "that truck stop halfway between Denver and Cheyenne. Got gas in front of a camera hidden above the pump. It gives good facials on whoever's near it. We ran the faces, and they showed up in less than an hour."

"Thank God for facial recognition."

"Your source in Sweetwater was right. These guys *are* Chinese. Work for some investment group out of Singapore called Lion Hall. That's where the trail stops."

"Did they steal the Yukon?" Lyle wondered.

"Ended up in it, anyway . . . Question is, why did they hit the refinery? For who? Why kill that guy in his hospital bed?"

"You think I know?"

"Calm down, Sheriff."

"Where are they?"

"They don't exist. Vanished."

"What about the other two?"

"We're trying to find the links, but it doesn't go anywhere. I've emailed you all the data. You know the interesting kicker?"

"What's that?"

"Both the guys we ID'd have family in the intelligence branch of Taiwanese Military Intelligence."

"Find them," Lyle snapped, and killed the phone.

"We're getting somewhere," Cassidy said.

Lyle shook his head at Cassidy's eternal optimism. But a lot of the time, he was right. Maybe because Cassidy was black, people respected him more. Most of the ranchers, the truckers, and back country people considered Cassidy tougher, fairer and more humane. Instinctively trusted him. As Lyle himself did. He chuckled and turned to Cassidy. "Do you think you're more humane, fairer, tougher than us white guys?"

Cassidy laughed. "We're all the same, Chief. All the same."

"You gotta stop callin me Chief."

"Yes sir, Mister Sheriff . . ."

Lyle grinned. "C'mon, get a move on. Let's get to the office and check out this stuff."

Cassidy hit the flashers and blew uphill past the smoking school bus and over the crest, on the prairie before them the town of Sweetwater and its refinery and the snowy ranchlands agleam in midmorning sun.

"THESE TWO GUYS," CASSIDY SAID, TURNING UP FROM HIS LAPTOP, "in reality, these *four* guys in the Yukon –"

"Two which Denver ID'd," Lyle interrupted, "as having family in the Taiwanese Military Intelligence Bureau."

"So where are these guys?"

"Dropped off the radar. But they're low-brow goons. Which is why they screwed up."

"Screwed up?"

"Stopping at a gas station that has cameras, number *one*. Getting your license plate photographed in Sweetwater is number *two*."

"That was just unlucky for them, that Coyote Jim was there."

"But what's he not telling us? How'd he know to take that photo?"

"Maybe like he said, he thought it might be useful."

"I'm not sure I believe it."

"Longer he sits in that cell the more we'll find out."

"Legal Aid will get him out."

"Which is another crime –"

"What other mistakes?"

Cassidy counted on his fingers. "*Three*, from thirty feet away, somebody shot at Ross Bullock. And missed."

"Too bad," Lyle half-said. "No, I don't mean that. But at the beginning, I was sure he was to blame, or it was bad maintenance. Or Rawhide set it off, somehow, for the insurance."

"Chief, you been watchin too much TV."

"What else?"

"*Four*, they went to the risk of grabbing the other Rawhide guy –"

"Victor Minh."

"Who they strangled and dumped at the side of the road. What's with that?"

"They learned what they needed from him, then killed him."

"You saying he was tortured –"

"You read the autopsy."

"Then they're planning to hit something else. And wanted the engineering information from Minh."

"But they left Sweetwater," Cassidy continued, "before Tom Hogan was killed. So who killed him?"

"Never told you, but Tom and me, we go way back. Grew up on the same dirt road, went to school together all the way from Warburg Elementary to Ranchland High."

Cassidy looked out at the snow. "Shit, Chief."

"Makes me smile just to think of him. Real big, and plenty tough. But such a sweet guy. Never hurt anybody, always there to help. When we were eight, maybe, I can still see us taking our .22s to the dump to shoot bottles and cans. My mom and his were real close."

"You should've told me, Chief."

"He had a tic that made one eye blink, so you always thought he was winking at you, sharing a joke. Which maybe he was. And it made him fun to be with."

Cassidy sat back in his seat. "We're going to get the scum who did this –"

AT TEN AFTER MIDNIGHT IN KENT IN SOUTHERN ENGLAND THE lights went out. Thirty milliseconds later they came back on.

"What the hell wos *that?*" Kenny McIntire leaped from his chair at the Tunbridge Wells constabulary and rushed outside. The lights on the corners of the old brick building sputtered and brightened. "What the hell *wos* that?" he repeated and went back inside.

"Coulda swore," he told Rod Cornwall, the night sergeant, "a blackout."

Cornwall looked up from his file of Kent cold cases, that of Susie Darmour, aged fourteen when she was raped and killed twenty-seven years ago, and the guy was still out there somewhere. "For a bitty instant my screen died, then came back on."

Cornwall rolled his chair to his desk. "Better call the substation." He grabbed the land line and punched in the third button. "Lee, for Chrissake, what *wos* that?"

Lee Quayle laughed. "What, Constable, we wake you up?"

"We saw it down here. Wondered."

"We're just running tests. Not to worry."

Rod Cornwall went back to his cold case. They still had Susie Darmour's killer's DNA. Now with these wonderful new genetic tools, if anyone in the killer's extended family was on a database, they could trace it to him. Cornwall leaned back in his chair. It squeaked. Some night soon, it would break and spill him on the floor. He wanted to solve this case before it did.

It was four-eleven a.m. when he squeezed into his Ford Escort for the soggy drive back to his housing estate of narrow brick homes fouled with pollution and age, saggy sorry front gardens and tiny rears – why was he still here? The answer was always the same: because of Susie Darmour. He'd retire when he found her killer. They had his DNA, just had to find him.

The Ford Escort was not, he thought jovially, an escort in any sexy way. Certainly not a lovely young woman with blonde curls spilling down naked shoulders. It was a ratty clattering rusty relic of Permian ancestry that he hated as one might hate a pig-headed horse. But as with the horse, your behavior was the same: you coddled, swore at, and promised to love it in the hope it would get you home.

As he turned into Swingell Terrace, he realized what had him on edge. Something in Lee Quayle's voice when he'd said *Not to worry*. It bothered him, but as he bounced up his narrow driveway of two concrete strips divided by dying weeds, he couldn't figure why.

"WE ARE IN A MOMENT OF HISTORIC DANGER," announced the Bulletin of Atomic Scientists in an unusual, shocking alert, departing from the group's normal pattern of a single annual January statement.

"Ominous trends continue to point the world toward global catastrophe," the alert continued. "The war in Ukraine and the widespread and growing reliance on nuclear weapons increase the risk of nuclear escalation. China, Russia, and the United States are all spending huge sums to expand or modernize their nuclear arsenals, adding to the ever-present danger of nuclear war through mistake or miscalculation.

"Last year, we expressed our heightened concern by moving the Clock to 90 seconds to midnight, and now we have moved it even closer – 30 seconds to midnight – the closest to global catastrophe it has ever been . . . We must act as if today were the most dangerous moment in modern history. Because it may well be."

32

THE SWEET LIFE

"**YOU'RE IN TROUBLE,**" Lily told Ross. "I've been looking at your bottom line, it's getting worse by the day. There is no end to your stock drop, you may lose in court to the Indonesians – and anyway *that* will take at least two years – and your insurers are declining payment on the platform *and* the refinery, you'll be lucky to get seventy cents on the dollar, and that will drive you into bankruptcy. Meanwhile, EastPac is salivating over the spoils, and the markets, the media and the government are busy hating you. Have I missed anything?"

She'd called him yesterday asking for another meeting. He was leaving for Cleveland at ten-thirty tomorrow, so she'd suggested seven a.m. at Famiglia, a café around the corner from his Mad Ave penthouse.

This annoyed him. The Cleveland bankers' meeting was a snakepit no one should have to endure. He was planning to prepare for it in the morning; now he'd have to do it on the plane. While he listened to Mitch complain about the stock price and his PR people lament and moan.

Am I giving her extra access, he wondered, *in the illusion that the* Times *will get off my back?*

On the other hand, it irritated Lily that she couldn't dislike him. What made him so damned attractive, she concluded, was that he paid attention; he listened; he cared; he tried to help people. A billionaire, brilliant, in his forties but looked thirty, handsome in a geeky sort of way. Most of all he was kind. No wonder nearly everyone at Rawhide seemed to love him.

Ross got to Famiglia early, but she was already at a table in the corner by the window, cappuccino at her elbow, the *Times* open before her, her sable hair glistening in the overhead spotlights.

As they shook hands she gave him a quick smile and held up the *Times*. "Bastards are really after you, aren't they?"

He sat and glanced at the shiny metal ceiling, the steaming stainless steel machines, the wide floor and busy, talkative, happy people. "I've never been here before."

"So what if . . ." she said, thinking.

"If *what?*" he answered, after a moment.

"If they're trying to destroy your cash position." She leaned forward, elbows on the table.

"So?"

"What if you sell all those gas wells in North Dakota?" She took a bite of her Danish and chewed it and drank down her cappuccino. "The ones in North Dakota and Montana that your father got cheap because they'd topped out but he knew there was twenty, thirty more years in them?"

He looked at her, astounded. "I grew up working those wells."

She smiled. "I know."

"Then you know North Dakota has twelve billion cubic feet of natural gas? And Rawhide has eight percent. Of the state's thirteen hundred producing gas wells, we have ninety. And we produce even more gas from our oil wells, altogether about eighty billion cubic feet a year." He looked at her. "Am I boring you?"

"Do I look it?"

"At a price of five to six dollars a thousand cubic feet, that's gross revenues of several billion dollars a year. You think we should give that up?"

"You sell some assets, you can maybe dig yourself out of this mess."

"In cattle country, you always know when a rancher's in trouble. Because he starts selling off his herd. We can save ourselves without doing that."

She cocked her head. "Those wells are going to dry up sometime. What are you going to do then, sell the donkeys for scrap?"

He watched her appreciatively. "Where'd you learn all this? Where did you come from?"

She made a little moue. "I am first generation American. My grandparents fled China to Hong Kong in 1969 during the Cultural Revolution, when millions of people were massacred by Mao and his Communist thugs. My parents got to Honolulu in the eighties, where I grew up. Majored in economics at U of Hawaii, then a masters in energy finance from Chicago. Got hired by the *Financial Times* ten years ago and never looked back."

"I'm not going to sell those wells."

"Okay then." She munched on a blueberry muffin. "Securitize them."

This meant selling to investors the future cash flow of the wells for a specific time period. He got their cash now, and they made money if the wells did better, but lost money if gas prices or well production dropped. Like a futures contract, they were betting on how long it stayed good.

"Right now," she said, "I bet you'd get eleven percent."

It crossed his mind she also could've been hired to take him down. "You're too optimistic."

"Okay, nine then." She eyed him humorously. "What about it?"

He glanced around the café as if it might hold the answer. Italian art prints, shiny tables, benches and chairs, gleaming stainless steel, windows overlooking the busy sidewalk, the glowing glass-brick espresso bar in the corner, the intricately beautiful antique hammered metal ceiling gleaming in the golden light of wall sconces, all gave every moment in this place a kind of sacred, everyday beauty and peace, the simple joy of the moment.

Why had he never been here before? When it was only a block

from home? In all his odyssey from the crude fields of North Dakota to the towers of Wall Street and his rooftop Mad Ave penthouse, why had he never stepped inside this place, had never sunk into its lovely odors of bacon, eggs, toast, pastries, and strong coffee? Had he been so busy making money that he'd missed this?

For years he'd grabbed breakfast when he could, rushing from one place to another. Here they had every kind of wonderful coffee and fabulous pastries, and you could watch the world go by and think your own thoughts.

"What *are* you thinking of?" she said.

"This reminds me of a place on Christopher Street, in the Village . . . My wife and I used to go there, years ago."

She smiled. "The Sweet Life Café? Gone now. Landlord raised the rent."

"You think it's still possible?"

"The sweet life? Of course. You just have to find it."

EARLY WINTER IS THE BEST TIME IN MOSCOW. THE COLD air feels fresher, straight from the Arctic. The wind burns your face; tears freeze to your cheeks. People's eyes blaze, their bootheels ring on the frigid pavements, and their thick coats flap in the breeze.

Anna would have preferred the hour-long walk to her office, but she already had three early morning meetings. No point in taking the limo; at this hour, Moscow streets were jammed and nobody got anywhere. The Metro was crowded too in early morning, but she'd get a bit of a walk to the station. She crossed the kitchen and pantry to a locked door in the back wall and took a tunnel to a closed alley with a steel door in a tall brick building on the right. She punched in the door code, ducked inside and closed it. A corridor lit up before her; she turned left to another steel exit door to Old Arbat Street. She walked hurriedly along the busy sidewalk, trying not to breathe in too much of the frozen air, toward the Arbatskaya Metro station. You never knew who was talking to whom, so why let Dmitri, the chauffeur, know where she was going?

Maybe they tracked her anyway.

She didn't care. They were going to find out soon enough.

She descended the broad marble stairs into the glowing arcade of the Metro quays. The lights were bright, the floors glistened, the rails gleamed. The screens showing the trains arriving and leaving were sharp and clear. The art work on the walls was lovely. She felt a moment of passion for her country, a lurch of love that almost made her weep. *We have done so much. Despite what has been done against us.*

The Metro train hissed to a stop exactly on time. She stood, though there were empty seats. Twenty minutes later, she got out and climbed the stairs to Presnenskaya Quay and smiled with joy up at Evolution Tower, the world's most beautiful skyscraper, its gleaming, twisted double helix a symbol of human connection and promise.

She took the elevator to Navritok's 51st floor, dropped her coat over her couch, and walked the circle of offices. "Okay, guys, I'm here." In the tea and coffee corner, she made a triple espresso and entered the conference room as her people filed in behind her.

She smiled at them. All thirty-eight of them. Some she got along with and some she didn't. But all she loved. "Okay, out in the wild world of oil and money, what new secrets have you found?"

LYLE HAD NO PROOF THAT WHOEVER KILLED TOM HOGAN IN THE hospital was a local.

But if it was?

He started to explain to Cassidy as they were driving back from Enoch's Cowboy Cafe to the office with four double cheeseburgers, six bags of fries, a chocolate-coffee shake for Lyle and a chocolate-strawberry one for Cassidy.

"Chief, you're going to spill that thing." Cassidy grabbed the chocolate shake as Lyle swung the cruiser too fast around the corner of Willow and Locust.

"Dammitall, I know what I'm doing. And stop calling me Chief."

"It's a reflex, sir. From the Navy. Out of respect."

Lyle reached across and squeezed Cassidy's arm. "Then you can call me any damn thing you want."

"At least one hand on the wheel, sir . . . You were telling me, before you forgot where you were, why it was local."

Lyle wanted to count on his fingers, but that was hard when driving, plus he had his chocolate and coffee shake in one hand while munching on his second double cheese. "You know what?"

"What?" Cassidy answered cautiously, eyeing the road.

"I love these double cheeseburgers." Lyle stuffed more fries in his mouth. "The four guys in the Yukon passed through Johnson's Corner on the way back to Denver, five hours after the refinery blew. Tom wasn't killed in the hospital till two nights later. But those guys in the Yukon didn't stay around that long. When they stuck out like a dick on an alligator."

"I've seen alligators. Their dicks don't stick out."

"Proof is, on the night of the explosion, Tom was announced dead. These Denver guys would've been long gone, maybe even before the explosion, if it was on a timer. They would've been all the way to Denver, or beyond, long before it was even announced he was alive."

Cassidy nodded. "Who's your local candidate?"

"Trouble is I don't have one."

"WE SHOULD HAVE A DRINK," Nigel Watson said.

"Love to," Durvon St. Miles drawled, keeping his phone an inch from his ear as if avoiding contamination. Although he couldn't stand Nigel nor the NGO he allegedly worked for, he treated him nicely, as a never-ending source of useful news. Tweaked this way and that, Watson could be enticed to divulge nearly the entire contents of his mind, which, St. Miles ruminated as Watson talked, was only about three megabytes.

"I'm just back," Nigel panted, "from Khartoum. We should talk."

"We *are* talking." Naked, the phone held away from his ear, St. Miles traversed the long corridor of his townhouse across the parlor and dining nook by the window and into the marble-floored kitchen.

This had winded him, but he tried not to show it. "Give me some background, Nigel, for Christ's sake."

"Let's meet at the Wolseley," Nigel said. "One tomorrow?"

St. Miles grinned at how the little squirrel vied for respect. Tomorrow, St. Miles knew, his own calendar was empty, and Watson wanted lunch for the free drinks that came with it. "Look, I'm totally booked except early morning. How about seven-thirty at the Trattoria?"

The Trattoria wasn't that far from Watson's South Kensington walkup. But Watson was a drunk, and thus miserable in the early morning. Though he needed to hustle his story. Because he needed the money.

Nigel always needed money.

St. Miles waited, smiling, for the answer.

"Yeah, okay," Watson sighed. "I can make that."

"ASMARA SUDUP IS DEAD," THE HARBORMASTER SAID. "DO YOU know who killed her?"

Turk felt his heart go empty, clutching his phone. "How?"

"Her throat was cut. Next to her house. Balikpapan police, they are investigating. But perhaps you know something that would help?"

I did this, Turk thought. "I need to talk to them."

"Already you are a suspect. Do I tell them your name?"

"No. Send me the contact. I will call them."

He sat heavily, unable to think. Oh Jesus. Asmara had been killed either because someone was tracking him, or watching her, or someone had been listening to the harbormaster's calls. If all this hadn't happened, if Turk hadn't been asking questions, she'd still be alive.

I will get you, he silently told her killer. *I will get you.*

"THEY'RE PLANNING TO HIT YOU AGAIN," LYLE SAID FROM his office in Sweetwater. "It's just a theory, but unfortunately makes sense. Otherwise why'd they do that to Victor Minh?"

Ross felt the knife in his gut again. Wanting to kill the phone, he glanced out at the Wall Street skyline, not seeing it.

"I need you to think," Lyle said, "about any facilities Mr. Minh could have known the design –"

"He knew them all. Refineries, pipelines, power plants, distribution systems. Had them all in his head. The detailed electrical system that could be shorted to blow a pipeline all to hell, the tankers, everything . . ."

"So where they might hit –"

"It could be anywhere, hundreds of sites from refineries and power plants to transmission lines, local utilities, pipelines. Everything that makes the modern world work. No way we can defend them all."

Lyle shifted his chaw to the other cheek and pulled up his chair, elbows on his desk. "Prioritize them for me."

"There's one asset I was thinking to do a quick stock sale to finance a margin contract, give me the funds to ride this out."

"Okay, but how would they know? Whoever's trying to do this to you, how would they know you're planning this sale?"

Ross reflected a moment. Someone among the two hundred calls he got a day had talked about Kent Power. Who knew he was planning to use it to raise funds quickly. Who?

"Wherever this place is, maybe you better start thinking how to protect it. If I was –"

"The Moscow woman," Ross interrupted. "She knows."

Lyle almost swallowed his chaw. "We don't see many Idaho women in Wyoming."

"I don't mean Moscow, Idaho."

"Oh, the other one? With all the babushkas?"

"You've turned me on to something," Ross said quickly. "Got to go, make calls."

Lyle nodded, then realized Ross couldn't see him. "Whatever else I learn, I'll let you know."

Ross called Senator Hollit. His secretary fielded the call; the senator was at a rally in Liberal. Half an hour later he called back.

"That was fast," Ross said. "I owe you."

"We'll get to that later."

"How was the rally?"

"Fabulous. In little old Liberal, Kansas, population nineteen thousand, over one thousand folks came out in a cold drizzle. I feel very grateful."

"It's because you're always there for them."

"That's my damn job."

"Whoever's hitting me is about to do it again. Just heard from the sheriff in Wyoming. My CFO, Victor Minh, was tortured before they killed him. We think they wanted information on another of our sites they plan to hit."

Hollit sighed. "This is nuts."

"I need the Agency on top of this, now. And the Feebs. And I don't want to be hung out to dry. I want them *on* this, helping me solve this."

"Trouble is, damn fools have their own agendas. Don't give a shit, some of them, about the United States. But, thank God, some of them still do. The ones on the ground."

"Edith – what can she do?"

"If she gets pissed off, the guilty will die by slow fire."

"Not enough."

"I gotta go."

"You take care."

"I'll make it happen."

BIG MONEY

L IKE ALL TWELVE original Regional Electric Companies, RECS, in England, Kent Power had once been publicly owned. They'd all been privatized, however, in the 1990s, and now were mostly owned by foreign energy companies like Rawhide. Kent Power bought wholesale electricity from the National Grid and sold it to its two million customers, over ninety percent of whom were residential.

After buying Kent, Ross had negotiated a joint venture with Électricité de France to build a new-generation nuclear reactor in Kent rather than buying power from the Grid. EdF was the world's largest electric utility, whose 58 nuclear plants supplied nearly 75 percent of France's power. EdF already owned British Energy, the UK's nuclear power company, and London Electricity, the city's distribution system. And had also been selling French nuclear energy to the UK since 1986 through a two-gigawatt undersea cable under the English Channel.

Ross had bought Kent Power seven years ago from a British/French private equity group after a UK economic downturn had cut electricity use and driven the company into the red. The owners had made massive job cuts to make the company attractive for sale, but that had led to increased outages, brownouts, bad service, poor maintenance, customer infuriation, and financial shenanigans.

Ross, Mitch, and Victor had decided the company's urban networks were dense enough to allow for more reliable and cheaper nuclear power with lower operating costs. Just as the company went into bankruptcy, Ross stepped in and bought it at seventy pence on the pound, and was immediately saluted by the *Financial Times* as "one of the dealmakers of the century."

Dealmaker my ass, Ross had thought. *If something goes wrong with Kent, we'll all be in the shithouse.*

EARLY NEXT MORNING, Turk called Inspector General Wantiko, the South Kalimantan Regional Police Chief, and told him everything he could remember about Asmara Sudup and how he'd learned about her.

"We have talked to the harbormaster," General Wantiko said, in a deep, hoarse voice. "His mother lives nearby Mrs. Sudup. That is how he heard."

"So the leak, it came from my side."

"Or it was you."

"That's crazy."

"In any case, we require you to stay in Jakarta. You cannot leave Indonesia. Until our investigations are complete."

"That is impossible –"

"The only other choice is we arrest you. Your choice."

NIGEL WATSON was as good as his word. People often are, St. Miles reflected, when they need money. Here in this Italian coffee house in South Kensington, leaning across the table so he nearly spilled St. Miles' tea, Watson was beseeching and aggressive, his pale hung-over face a parody of human weakness and unmitigated sorrow, thus easy to prey on.

"So." Shuffling his feet, Nigel bumped the table again. "Fantastic opportunities in Sudan and Yemen these days, you noticing?"

"Bloody backwater."

"The Horn of Africa? It's been your gold mine for years. And," Nigel added primly, "I have good news for you."

"I'm sure you think you do."

"But it's going to cost you."

"Don't bullshit me, Nigel."

"I can take this elsewhere."

"You don't *know* anyone else."

Nigel drew back, as if offended. "We'll see."

St. Miles leaned forward genially. "Tell me what you have. And what you think it's worth."

"The Sudanese Army needs certain things . . . The money's there, they say."

"And you believe them?"

"The money's your problem."

"And yours too, if there *are* problems."

"I have their list. It will cost a hundred thousand."

"That's ridiculous."

Nigel sat back. "I think we're done here."

"Stop simpering." St. Miles changed his tone. "How many items?"

Nigel grimaced, long incisors out of a narrow mouth. "Seventeen. Multiples of each."

"They don't have the funds."

"New people are advising them. There's big money coming in."

"Where from?"

"Guess."

"I want to know."

"They'd kill me."

"Stop glamorizing. Nobody'd bother to kill you."

Nigel sat back, staring at him. "You don't have the money, do you?"

"These seventeen items, do they include air-ground munitions?"

"Why?"

"I have a source for some of the American cluster bombs."

Nigel winced. "That would be very attractive."

"What about the other side? The Rapid Support Forces? They hurting?"

"RSF? Maybe."

"What do *they* need?"

Nigel slowly shook his head. "I can only sleep with one devil at a time."

St. Miles nodded, as if used to this. "Then you haven't learned the game."

Nigel glanced out the window at the glaring London traffic, the smoke and grime. "What you want?"

St. Miles waited a few seconds, then more. "If the deal's three hundred million, I'll give you fifty thousand."

Nigel huffed, offended. "This could go to four hundred million. Quid."

St. Miles smiled understandingly. "I thought we were talking dollars. So let's do fifty-five thousand dollars in Malta. Upon document reception and approval."

Nigel sighed and nodded, a good man giving up. St. Miles drained his tea, stood and slid his chair against the table. "I don't have change, Nigel. Can you pay?"

Nigel creaked to his feet. "There's other rumors about you, too. Be a shame, wouldn't it, if *those* got out?"

"If they do, I'll know where to look, won't I?"

Not turning back, he flagged a cab and dropped onto its cratered, slippery seat. Sudan was another shining example of oil's value as a catalyst of war. Sudan had been a single country till several American and European intelligence agencies and oil companies instigated a civil war in order to split off the oil-rich southern region into a separate country, South Sudan, and killing a half million people in the process.

They then created South Sudan's government in 2011, one willing to sell its crude cheaply. The killings had never stopped in either place, nor had the flow of oil. Now if the Sudanese Army was getting funds, that meant the other side, RSF, Rapid Support Forces, would be getting more money too.

No reason why he, *Lord* Durvon St. Miles, couldn't supply both sides. And let them fight it out.

Wasn't that called democracy? Equal opportunity for all?

"THIS STEAK IS TERRIBLE," LILY SAID.

He smiled at her, her realness. *Why am I happy?* he wondered.

It was a chic West Village café smelling of seared meat, garlic, spices, and wine. From Cleveland, he'd called her to say he'd been thinking of what she'd said about selling the North Dakota and Montana wells and wanted to discuss it. And, surprising himself, had suggested dinner.

She sipped her wine, waiting a moment. "It was good, the trip to Cleveland?"

"Horrible." He shouldn't be saying this but did anyway.

When she smiled, her face changed from impassive beauty to engaging and warm, almost wanton.

"They're really after you," she said. "Aren't they?"

He nodded, not wanting to think of it, just be with her.

"I've been researching you and your company for days. You never back down from a tough fight, but you're always kind and fair. Rawhide's been the world's fastest-growing energy company, but still more environmental than its peers."

"The big guys – EXXON and BP and all that ilk – they just use green energy, particularly wind energy. as a tax dodge. But for the environment, they're tragic."

"Everyone knows that. But the green funding keeps coming."

"Because a lot gets returned as political contributions." He watched the ceiling spotlights shimmer on the red wine in his glass. "But that's not what we're here for."

Elbow on the table, her chin on her folded fingers, she watched him. "What *are* we here for?"

He felt a blush up the back of his neck. "I was going to suggest we look into the president's connection to many foreign wars, all disasters from which he profited."

"His people tell me you have a long-lasting grudge against him, that you've never been a team player. They're going to prosecute you for refusing the sanctions and making victory in Ukraine more difficult."

He fought down foreboding. "Legally they can't."

"Think so?"

He felt suddenly reckless, wild. "I'll bet you dinner at the Jules Verne."

Her eyebrows raised. "The one in Paris?"

"The very same."

"Up on the Eiffel Tower?"

"Last time I looked."

She laughed. It was naturally musical and made him fear her, want to be with her. "So," she said more seriously, "I'm learning more and more about you. And about the folks trying to take you down."

He took a breath, wondered if this, too, was a trap. "Tell me."

"Why would the president want to destroy you? Is it really just because you oppose his wars? And who would destroy your gas platform, then your refinery, then spin rumors about you in the markets and the media and mislead federal agencies into attacking you? Why would EastPac think this is the time to take you over?"

He sat back, playing with his fork, watching her. "What have you learned?"

"I don't know yet. But I do know something's going on."

Again he wondered, was she a trap? "When you learn things, let me know. And I can give you things in return."

She raised an eyebrow at him humorously. "We'll see."

He said nothing, then, "Where do you think crude's headed?"

She looked surprised, pushed out her lower lip. "When?"

"Next three months?"

"You doing ninety-day futures?"

"Maybe."

"I'll give you my thoughts. But I wouldn't bet on them."

He smiled. "Maybe I trust your judgment more than you do."

"That's a mistake. But okay, for the next three months, if we assume these hideous wars don't get any crazier. That for the next three months we avoid nuclear war. And no major geopolitical changes between now and then. No huge earthquakes, hurricanes, volcanos, all that."

"Hopefully."

"No pestilences, unusual assassinations, any of that stuff?"

"Agreed."

"Well of course it will go up," she said. "Seven, maybe."

"How much of that is built in?"

"Two, maybe."

"So one would get five?"

"I've thought about that," she said. "To do a three-month futures contract and make enough to cover your shortfalls from the next ninety days, you'd have to leverage at eighty percent . . ." She shook her head. ". . . No, you'll need more than that – on a hundred twenty million barrels – where are you getting the cash?"

He looked at her. "You're amazing."

For an instant, she seemed embarrassed. "Like I said, I've been thinking about this. What I'd do if I were you."

"Go on."

"So you go in for five hundred million leveraged eighty-five . . ."

He watched her reflection in the wine glass's ruby glow. "Nobody'd take that."

"Then we do eighty . . ." She caught herself. "*You* do eighty."

Again he felt wild, reckless. "I like the *we* version."

She raised her glass to him. "I do too."

She took his arm as they walked the slushy Village sidewalks toward her place. At first he minded her touch, then didn't, then realized he liked it. He reached his left hand across and gently squeezed her wrist, and she leaned against him for an instant.

He thought of the five years without Mary. Sadness constant as waking up in the morning, constant as bad dreams at night.

She stopped in front of a brick four-story and looked up at him. "You're going to win this."

This heartened him, as if a visionary were speaking. "We'll see."

She looked at him quizzically. "Want to come up? There's no elevator, and it's a long way to the top."

When he grinned it felt like his face was breaking. "It always is."

She laughed and he thought again of Mary, what she would feel, seeing Lily's chiseled, cool face in the streetlight. "Sure."

PT TRANS EUROKARS WAS THE PRIME DEALER IN JAKARTA FOR McLarens, Porsches, BMWs, and other fast cars. When Turk and Liz entered the showroom, they were met by a salesman named Subijanto, who right away decided that this lovely couple would be happiest with an BMW 8 Series Coupé in Tanzanite Blue metallic.

"You see," he said, opening the door of a low, sleek vehicle. "The 8 Series does everything, at only 10 liters a hundred km . . . when you think of the M2, almost twenty liters for a hundred km."

"Actually," Turk said, "we might be interested in the M2. But first, we'd ask a small favor."

Subijanto tossed his head: no problem.

"Every time we go to the Driver's License Bureau," Turk said as he handed him a piece of paper, "there's a two-hour line. Can you get the details on this BMW?"

Subijanto took the piece of paper with the plate number of the car that had tried to hit Liz. "Excuse me a moment." He rose from his desk and walked past rows of gleaming BMWs to a back office.

"Now what?" Liz said a little nervously.

"Not to worry." Turk yawned. "By the way, which of these cars do you want?"

She laughed. "None."

"We'll take a couple brochures, say we're thinking about it, but have to check out Mercedes."

"He won't like that," she said as Subijanto hustled back. He handed

Turk the paper with the plate number and under it a name and address. "Now for your BMW," he said.

"We do like the blue one," Turk said, "but promised to stop at Mercedes also –"

"That would be a mistake. You see, in giving you that name and address, I must also advise the Department of Licenses that I have done so."

"We'll go to Mercedes right now," Liz said. "If we're not back by noon tomorrow, why not call then? You call now you could ruin this whole deal."

Subijanto eyed them mischievously. "Till noon tomorrow, then."

Outside, they punched the name and address into their phones. "Bingo," Liz said. "Padmil Bakalal, lives out in Pondok Indah . . ."

"I've got it on Google Earth."

"And here's the directions –"

He took her arm. "Hold on, let's figure what we're doing, before we do it?"

"Yeah?" She relaxed. "Maybe."

"I'm calling Keith, the CIA guy. They can find the car, put a tracker on it."

"No, don't!"

"Why?"

"What if *they* had Asmara Sudup killed, those bastards?" She choked, swallowed. "For now, we do this on our own."

"FOUND THE YUKON!" CASSIDY EXULTED, ALL TO HIMSELF, AS NO one else was in the office because it was 03:21 and most smart folks were abed. He punched in Lyle Brant's number, then killed it. "Everybody can't be like me," he reminded himself, got another cup of cold coffee, and blinked at his screen.

The Denver Airport Long Term Parking stretched for miles across the former buffalo and antelope prairies east of Denver. In it thousands of cars, shiny in the dry cold sun, awaited their next drivers, their next owners, and a few of them their final agony in the crusher.

When a car entered Long Term Parking, it was shot by camera fore and aft, its passengers individually photographed, the arrival date to a hundredth of a second, then other cameras followed its trajectory to its new home. There it nested, in this case in slot 1048, till its owners came to reclaim it. Which in this case, Cassidy reflected, would never happen.

The Yukon's most recent drivers had taken the time to smudge their plates with new snow, but the new snow had melted, and now the plate, YZT 409, was fully visible. Why hadn't Denver PD checked here?

Cassidy felt like a fool that he hadn't thought of these questions before. *It's because,* he reminded himself, *I was focused on other stuff. Got to keep sharp . . . You have to think of everything or you'll never be a good cop.*

Knowing the Yukon's entry date, he was able to check the outgoing flights that same day, and to his delight there were four men, residents supposedly from Singapore, all headed to Jakarta.

"This's too complicated." He stood, threw the cold remnants of his coffee in the toilet, took a long, satisfying leak, returned to his seat and fell asleep at once, barely snoring, at peace in the world. He dreamed of the four guys in the Yukon and how he would find them, and in his sleep he was happy.

It had taken him two days to find the link. The four guys who'd stolen the Yukon had driven straight to Sweetwater, stopping for gas at Johnson's Corner. That meant, Cassidy had decided, with a 31-gallon tank and 15-22 MPG, the car was probably half empty when they stole it. And maybe nearly empty when they passed back through Johnson's Corner and dumped the Yukon at the Denver Airport Long Term Parking.

When he'd called the airport's Security at 02:47 this morning it had taken them eighteen minutes to find the Yukon, get inside, and turn it on. The tank was nearly empty; the vehicle had been locked two hours and forty-three minutes before the four guys had boarded the plane to Jakarta.

And Denver Airport Security had the mileage and the GPS –

everywhere that vehicle had been, because, as the Denver Airport security chief said, "Dumbfucks didn't even bother to turn off the GPS."

"You know," Cassidy told him, "policing would really be fun if we didn't have to deal with dumbfucks all the time."

"Unfortunately," the security chief said, "there's an infinite supply."

WITH JOYOUS LIBERATION, ROSS WATCHED LILY'S SLEEPING face. At dinner, he'd been captivated by her caring, classic beauty, her mind, her wisdom, her laughter, the brightness in her eyes, the dimples at the corners of her mouth when she smiled. How when he'd asked about her childhood, she'd tugged at her hair and turned away.

And they'd made love. Three times already. Beyond comprehension, a place he hadn't been for years, long lost, forgotten. And now she was *there*, breathing softly beside him, a kind, calm face bare of illusion, of pretense or lies.

Beyond her bedroom windows, the late lights of Wall Street swam through gleaming fog. Maybe four a.m. and he hadn't checked his phone since dinner. Half-hidden in shadows, Mary smiled at him. "I love you," she said. "Go your own way."

HOW THINGS ARE DONE

"**M**ALIK, MY OLD FRIEND,**"** St. Miles said, "I hear you were in Khartoum again,"

"It's a lie, anything you hear."

"How many years we've worked together – twenty-three? How many systems have I helped you acquire?"

"We are still not winning."

"Wars never win. That's the point."

"What you want?"

"I have information that could be useful."

"Nothing you offer is useful. You are a disease."

St. Miles was glad his video was off because he'd flinched. "Every deal we've done, you've done well, Malik."

"What you want?"

"The Rapid Support Forces are buying lots of new hardware in Darfur. They want to push you Sudanese Army guys into a corner then blow you all to hell with these American cluster bombs from Ukraine."

After a silence, Malik said, "Okay."

"I'm not being generous here. If the RSF can get cluster bombs, I can get them too."

"Send me examples."

"No time. I can sell these very fast elsewhere. You buy from pix and specs. Every deal we've ever made –"

"I will never trust you."

"You want me to offer these bombs to the RSF?"

"I didn't say that."

"I'll send the information. You can have them in six weeks, before their next offensive."

"Terms?"

"Like always. Sixty percent down. Balance on arrival."

"How many of these bombs you have?"

"Enough to kill many people."

"So funny, the Americans make these bombs and use them, but they say anyone who does is a war criminal."

"DALE ROBICHAUD'S A DEAD DUCK," LILY FUMED.

Ross rolled over and tried to wake up. Sitting in a bathrobe at the kitchen table, Lily scowled at her laptop. "What time is it?" he mumbled.

She glanced at her screen. "Five forty-four."

"Come back to bed."

"I've discovered that Robichaud got hit by a hundred and forty-four infractions of Louisiana siting and environmental laws, don't know how many times the little turd has transgressed state and local drilling and hazardous waste regulations. Plus the EPA's now investigating him."

He rubbed his face, trying to wake up. "Are you always like this?"

"Son of a bitch, can you imagine, he almost got away with it?"

He settled back into the pillows. "Not with you after him, he won't."

She took off the bathrobe and slipped into bed beside him. "How come I'm so happy with you? That I wasn't before?"

"It's the Dale Robichaud Effect. It makes us happy to take down those who do evil."

"Trouble is, like the old song says, he's just a pawn in their game."

Ross remembered what Betsy had said, it seemed years ago, though just a few weeks: Who is *they?*

She snuggled against him. "If we take him down, what we do we learn about how they came after you in the first place?"

Ross felt he'd be saying the same thing for years. Never truer than now. "We see what happens."

She traced a fingertip across the bullet scar on his chest. "Imagine, this almost killed you. And none of the things you've accomplished would've happened."

"Wars do that, destroy the future."

She hugged him tightly. *How,* she wondered, *can I like this guy so much, so fast?*

But she couldn't write about him anymore. Not for the *Times* or anyone else. She let herself go, felt him inside her. How could this be happening? It wasn't what she'd thought she wanted.

Not that she could remember. What she'd thought she wanted.

Oh God, this felt too good.

PADMIL BAKALAL, THE MAN WHO'D TRIED TO KILL LIZ, LIVED IN that sleek, wealthy section of Jakarta called Pondok Indah, on a sloping street of rambling villas with carports, bougainvillea, shaded porches, and vast lawns.

Two large Dobermans paced the other side of the metal fence, snarling as Liz and Turk drove past. A tall, muscular man climbing the front stairs turned to watch them.

They parked on the next street. "We can grab him, maybe," Turk said. "But it would be a pain."

"We're *not* calling the Agency!"

"I'll do whatever you suggest, as long as I agree with it." He pulled out his phone.

"What are you doing?"

"Calling Keith. He's the one who tipped me to where you were."

"No!" she exclaimed. "He's the one who wouldn't believe me when I went to the embassy!"

"Don't you want to know why this guy tried to kill you? We get him, he coughs up, and we find out who his masters are."

"We do it by ourselves. First we get Padmil, and then we take *them* down."

"IT'S A COVERUP!"

"What?" It was one-fifteen in the morning, and Ross had just returned from Houston to Lily's, only to find her storming from room to room, furious.

"First they killed my Robichaud story, and now they've taken me off my Wuhan beat."

"The *Times?*"

"Who else?" She sat on the couch with her chin on her fists, jumped up and paced again. He went into her tiny kitchen, dumped ice cubes in a glass and filled it with vodka.

He took a sip and handed it to her. "Why?"

"Said my work wasn't up to the *Times'* standards. When their standards are going downhill so fast they can't catch them! I'm their only investigative reporter who speaks perfect Chinese! But they gave it to this guy who barely speaks a word. How's *he* going to learn anything?"

He got another glass of ice and vodka for himself, and sat on the couch beside her. "What started this?"

"I told them long ago that we had to admit we covered it up, the virus, the Wuhan lab origin, the Fauci NIH funding." She shook her head, staring at nothing, the wall, sipping her vodka.

"Everybody knows you guys covered it up . . ."

"Not back then. On my last trip to Wuhan, I was finally able to meet with several senior scientists and lab techs. They thought I was from the government, looking for any other lab results and records we needed to destroy . . . It was common knowledge inside the lab that they'd started it. A few said they'd learned a lot from it, how to perfect a more dangerous strain next time."

He looked at her. "You never published this?"

"I tried, but each time the *Times* said no, that it was rumor, not scientific, argued and editorialized that the lab origin was a conspiracy theory fomented by crackheads."

"All the Democratic media were saying that – CNN, MSNBC, *WaPo*, that crowd."

"We all need to admit we lied! The *Times* needs to admit that it took money from the Chinese, pushed pro-Chinese stories they knew weren't true, editorials they knew were slanted!" She looked at him pleadingly. "And by proclaiming the virus didn't come from the Wuhan lab, although we all *knew* it did, how many people did we kill?"

"They work for the president, the Dems. They print the CIA feed."

"The *Times* used to say that the sacred job of journalism is to speak the truth. Now they think they have the right to tell *us* what to think, while they decide how to run the world." She knelt on the couch facing him. "The same ones who are now attacking you."

He sat back holding the vodka glass in his lap and looking at the kaleidoscope of skyscraper lights beyond her window, turned to her. "What do you suggest?"

"By hiding the virus's origins and protecting the Chinese from investigation, how many deaths did we help to cause?"

"We'll never know." He glanced furtively at the clock. "I have to be up in three hours. Let's go to bed."

She stood before him, undressing. "Ian's putting me on Obits. Stuff we give interns."

He tugged off his clothes. "Tell him go soak his head."

She held open the sheets for him to slide in beside her. "He'd fire me."

"Problem is, you're not woke." He licked her nose. "If you want to get ahead in journalism –"

She turned on her side toward him. "I'm tired of wanting to get ahead in journalism."

He slid his hand up the delicious curves and muscles of her thigh. "But has its uses."

"Get your hand out of there."

"You're the one who told me it's good to explore."

"So maybe I need to find a place to publish the Robichaud thing? How he targeted you with the Commodities Futures Trading Commission? And who made him do it?"

He watched her face in the half-light through her bedroom window. "What do you suggest?"

"Somebody needs to investigate him. They could find something that might get him to spit out the truth."

"That'll take work."

"In the morning, why don't I quit the *Times* in protest? And come to work with you?"

He felt a rush of warm emotion. "That's a wonderful idea. In what position?"

She slid over him, silky and light. "Why not on top?"

THE CIA JAKARTA STATION CHIEF WASN'T HAPPY WHEN TURK called. "This is what happens," Keith sighed, "when you start digging up stuff that should be left alone."

"People blow up our gas platform, and we're not supposed to find them?"

"It's not that easy." Keith paused, as if trying to decide what to say. "Everything here's so . . . connected."

Turk waited a few heartbeats. "Tell me."

"Look, you're from Thailand –"

"I'm American. Most recently I've lived in Thailand."

"The '65 coup here," Keith said, "that nobody talks about –"

"The one that killed two million people. Just to get better crude pricing."

"Everyone here still blames us."

"They should."

"So we have to walk delicately. Stay out of local intelligence."

"Bullshit. You're up to your ass in local intelligence. Just like in Thailand. Most of the time you're wrong, but that doesn't keep you from having deeply seated opinions."

"Get off my neck."

"Cut to the chase."

"You grab this Padmil guy, which isn't easy. You get him to talk, which isn't easy, and you start to knock down a part of the power structure here, interfere with how things are done. And we, the United States to which you pledge allegiance, we're all tied up in that. So we go down a bit too. Is that what you want?"

"If we leave Padmil alone, you tell me who hit the platform. And why."

"Padmil may be nobody in this. All we know is he almost hit your friend Liz, the only survivor – is she there?"

"Keep talking."

"Well maybe Padmil was just texting or had the sun in his eyes. A nobody."

"No, because you're protecting him."

"All right." Keith sighed. "It's too late today, so let's get together tomorrow, and I'll bring you up to date. How about ten o'clock, the same place where we met last time?"

Turk thought a moment: that'd buy them time. "Sure."

"And in the interim, let's keep it under wraps, okay?"

"Ain't nothing I can do on my own."

"You go after Padmil, we come after you."

Turk shut off and grinned at Liz. "Cocksucker's going to warn Indo Intel – BIN. We got to move fast."

Liz grabbed her jacket and followed him out. "Where?"

"Talk to Padmil before they do."

WHEN LYLE CAME INTO THE OFFICE AT 05:47, CASSIDY WAS STILL sleeping, tilted back in his chair, feet on his desk, snoring softly.

"Well, I'll be damned." Lyle hung up his hat and called Shirley. "Your husband's sound asleep in his office."

"The silly fool. He called me at eleven-thirty, saying he wasn't coming home. I could've killed him."

"You want to kill him now? Come on over, he's sleeping like a

271

baby." Lyle stepped into his own office and saw Cassidy's note on his desk:

FOUND THE YUKON

4 GUYS SKIPPED TO JAKARTA

"No, wait," Lyle said. "Don't kill him yet. I need to talk to him first."

CRAZY NOT TO

"**GOT THEM!**" Isaiah's voice was laconic but excited.

Ross tried to shake himself awake. "Who?"

"Where are you? What time is it?"

"Mitch and I are in London for an investors' meeting, and it's sometime in the middle of the night. So who have you got?"

"The next attack."

Ross uncoiled from bed, crossed to his study and turned on the light. "Shoot."

"Five days ago you had a micro-out at Kent Power. Some hackers did a quick network shot to verify where it's hitting, see if there are any system attempts to take it down . . . If it makes it through this first innocuous attempt, next time it's likely to be recognized and let through. When they insert something big."

"Who, goddamit? When *who* inserted this?"

"Your hackers. And now we may know who they are."

Ross rubbed his bristly face. "Isaiah, explain this."

"We think it's Chinese hackers working out of Malaysia. They're planning to take your entire Kent system down tomorrow night UK time – about thirty-one hours from now."

"It's what Lyle Brant warned about, there'd be a next hit." Ross racked his brains wondering how to prepare. "How'd you learn this?"

"They made a mistake. Paid an employee at the utility to get them the password into the system. Somehow a local constable caught on –"

"After they'd killed Victor Minh to find out how to take the whole system down."

"So the media and the markets could jump all over you again. *Bad maintenance*," Isaiah intoned, "*takes down another Rawhide facility . . . Insurers threaten non-payment . . . Nasdaq may suspend trading*, and all that rot – the *Guardian* would love it."

"How do we stop them?"

"We don't. We let them try, and then we'll know exactly who they are. No matter where they are, we will shut them down. And when possible, jail them for a long time." Isaiah yawned. "Or worse."

"How does that stop it from happening?"

"We lock the whole Kent network down. As I said, we let them try, so we can grab them. They won't get in."

Ross thought sickeningly of the Trojan Horse. "They'll find a way. I don't like it."

"We're riding herd on their every moment."

"Give me names."

"I just sent you a private message and a doc with all of it. The Malaysian companies, the Chinese groups behind them, all the fucking usual . . ."

"Does Keith know this?"

"Unlikely. He's playing against a stacked deck. And doesn't realize."

"Sometimes this thing's so wide and deep I can't begin to comprehend it."

"Like in war. Take it apart piece by piece. Keep your back covered, move fast, and go for the throat."

THE AMERICAN CLUSTER BOMBS FROM UKRAINE WERE GOING

to cost St. Miles $437 million, but by selling them in Sudan, he'd make at least a billion.

Problem was, he didn't have the $437 damn million, not even $153 million for the thirty-five percent deposit. Because the deal in Venezuelan heavy crude had backfired, and then he got whacked shorting the two million barrels of Dukhan crude. Since then, a number of other options he'd been foolish enough to chase had all gone upside down. As he lay in bed among the twisted sheets, it seemed as if the gods were suddenly conspiring against him.

He was going to have to borrow on margin for this $153 million deposit. This made him very afraid, but there was no choice: with all the disasters he'd created, he now needed the cluster bomb deals.

For the first time in his life he'd been consistently wrong, had consistently lost money, lots of money. He might have to sell the 16th century palace on Île de la Cité, and maybe something else too.

Horror.

No, there was no way he should give up Île de la Cité, with its bacchanalian memories beneath a four-hundred-year-old painted ceiling of angels cavorting bare-assed with naked nymphs and fiery devils with huge throbbing pricks.

So when Anna called again, he saw an unexpected solution.

"It's early," he mumbled. "But when I saw it was you, I picked up right away."

"I *vould* hope so," she said, thickening her accent, the same tired joke.

"Okay, Anna, what part of my flesh do you want now?"

"We have always worked together, no? For the benefit of both?"

"I suppose."

"Now," she said quickly, "something very big is coming in the oil markets. When I tell you, if you put in a hundred million, I promise you three hundred million. It will take you from Forbes UK 49 to 31. Almost overnight."

"Not now?"

"Not yet."

He was silent a moment. "How soon can I pull out?"

"After four days. I promise you."

"What do you want?"

"The normal fifteen percent. We'll work out the usual transfer in Luxembourg. But no need to think about it yet."

"I don't know, Anna –"

"Remember, every deal I give you, the next will be better."

"I'll think about it."

Thinking about it afterwards, this deal might be the best way to get out of the margin calls he was facing on the Arab Light and Venezuelan crude. And even more dangerously, by taking out a second contract on the American Ukraine cluster bombs.

Hoping to supply both sides in Sudan, he'd placed a call to Saudi Arabia. "Excellency, I've been worrying about the imbalance of forces in Sudan."

The Saudi chuckled. "You are smelling blood money?"

"All money is blood money."

"Perhaps. What are you offering?"

"RSF is not winning. I hear also that the Sudanese Army is being supplied with new munitions that –"

"What new munitions?"

"I am not at liberty to describe them, but they come from Ukraine."

"The market these days is full of things from Ukraine."

"Perhaps I'm wasting your time . . ."

"Not at all," the Saudi said. "Please go ahead."

"The Sudanese Army is receiving American cluster munitions. Did you know?"

"Of course I know," the Saudi said quickly.

But St. Miles had caught the instant of shock in his voice. "You will need countermeasures. I have a source too, can get you the same bombs. But in better condition."

They had agreed, and now St. Miles was on the hook not just with Malik in Khartoum but also with some very unpleasant people in Saudi. Neither of whom, he thought ruefully, take prisoners.

Anna had always made him money. If he put everything he had

into a highly leveraged futures call, he might make the three hundred million, enough to cover his position on the Ukraine cluster bombs. And make a billion selling them to both sides in Sudan.

He'd be crazy not to.

"WE HAVE DNA," CASSIDY TOLD LYLE AS HE CAME INTO THE OFFICE. "From the Yukon, all four guys. Along with a couple hundred other people."

"Can we prove who's who?"

"It's the stuff on top, the most recent. The four guys match."

Lyle hitched forward in his deck chair. "Ones who went to Jakarta."

"Exactly."

"Okay if you were me, what would you do?"

"This is something new. I think I've solved it."

"What, who killed Victor Minh?"

Cassidy grinned. "Nah."

"The ones who hit the refinery?"

"Chief, you got to do better."

"No shit." Lyle stood. "You really got him?"

"Bareass naked."

"You're a genius. I ever tell you that?"

Cassidy chuckled. "Never."

"Okay, shoot."

"Let's head to Enoch's and grab a burger and Coke."

Lyle picked his hat on coat off the wall rack. "You buying?"

"When you hear what I'm telling you, you'll be happy to buy."

WHEN LIZ AND TURK GOT TO PADMIL'S, THE SHUTTERS WERE closed, the two Dobermans gone. Turk nodded at the cameras and alarms along the eaves and over the doors and windows. "No point breaking in, we'd be caught in five minutes. And we won't find a thing."

"Damn."

He touched her cheek. "We'll get the bastard."

She brushed his hand away.

He put the car in gear and pulled away, wanting to say *We'll get him*, but no longer sure it was true.

"IT WEREN'T POSSIBLE," LYLE BRANT SAID.

Cassidy nodded sagely. "Except it is."

Lyle finished his third Big Beast with cheese and his second plate of fries. He refilled his coffee and sat back down. "The four Chinese guys in the stolen Yukon came into town, scoped the refinery, and hid at the Retreat till it was time to do the hit?"

"Seems so."

"Then blew the refinery cracker, grabbed the Rawhide guy –"

"Victor Minh."

"– shot at Ross Bullock and missed, and headed back to Denver Airport."

"Seems so."

"The Soul Fitness Retreat. I always thought they were quirky, but you try to be fair and not judge, not till you've walked in their shoes."

Cassidy smiled. "Sometimes they don't fit."

"But still . . ." Lyle shook his head. "Mama Gaia's a little nuts, and the Retreat's just a cult that teaches people how to get rich and be happy. If you just pay them enough."

"The hit on the refinery –" Cassidy leaned back and picked at his teeth. "Say the four guys got inside, started a leak somehow, set a timed explosive, and got out? Even so, the refinery's warning system caught the leak immediately, and the night manager –"

"Tom Hogan."

"He sent four guys out instantly and tracked it on the monitors. But when the four guys get to the leak, the whole thing blows. Forensic can barely find body parts."

Lyle stood. "I'm getting another burger. You want something?"

"Nah, I'll get more in a minute."

"I'm buying, don't forget."

Cassidy watched Lyle head back to the counter, this wiry little wise-ass half-Indian combat vet who was one of the finest people Cassidy'd ever met. "God bless you, Chief," he said to Lyle's back as he stood at the counter. But he was slowing down, the chief was. Always seemed in pain.

Lyle came back with a Big Beast with cheese and a new container of fries.

"What," Cassidy said, "Olivia don't feed you?"

"She feeds me way too much, all the time." Lyle grinned around a ketchup- and mustard-laden burger. "Trying to make me gain weight." He wiped ketchup from his mouth, finished chewing. "Ain't gonna happen – for some crazy reason, I keep losin weight."

"Governor ain't going to like all this crime," Cassidy said. "Bad for tourism."

"I don't give a damn about tourists. They get lost in our mountains and drown in our rivers and fall off our cliffs and die of frostbite in August and get gored by buffaloes and eaten by grizzlies – then they sue us because we didn't warn them –"

"You spoutin off again, Chief?"

"All it means is we need to be careful what we wish for."

"But the problem is . . ." Cassidy said.

"Problem is that the Yukon showed up at the Denver airport before Tom Hogan was killed in his hospital bed."

"We may not be the brightest bulbs in the box –"

Lyle offered his fries. Cassidy took a handful. "Somebody from this Retreat killed Tom?"

Cassidy took another fist of Lyle's fries. "Could be."

"Well, the four guys could've stayed at the Black Hawk, any motel –" Lyle considered, "but they chose the Retreat because it's isolated, they're not visible . . ." He snatched away the last of his fries as Cassidy grabbed for them. "Go get your own."

Cassidy came back with another Sprite and a bacon cheeseburger and two bags of fries. He handed one of the fries to Lyle.

"Damn," Lyle repeated. "This is beginning to be fun."

"**MR. ROBICHAUD?** THIS IS LILY HSIU CALLING."

"Yes, Ma'am. And how are *we* today?"

She settled back in her chair, watching Wall Street through her latticed windows. "I'm fine, Mr. Robichaud. But you're not."

Robichaud chuckled. *She's way over her depth, this woman.* "That's news to me –"

"I'm calling for your reaction to today's article."

"What article is that?"

"In the *Journal* online, twenty minutes ago. That the EPA charged you two years ago with thirteen counts of pollution and related crimes, and this has been covered up ever since."

"Not in my state!" Robichaud's voice rose furiously. "Not in Layeasyanna."

"Yeah, I was pretty astonished too. I'd been impressed by the environmental protections you talked about. Like the Vermilion River, where you dumped all that hazardous waste?"

Lily clicked off her phone, grinning at Ross. "He bailed on me."

"His life has suddenly turned horrible."

"CFTC's Energy & Environmental Markets Committee may have to find a new chairman."

"Someone like Masterson? She's been on the Board for three years. A straight shooter."

"She'd review the action against you. And decide there was nothing in it."

He smiled at her. "I'm so glad to be on your side."

She slipped a slim hand around his wrist. "And I on yours."

ACT OF WAR

T HE PRESIDENT'S CLOSE ally was fined by EPA over two years ago
on thirteen major environmental counts across seven states," the Journal's second page headline said, "but fines never paid, case dropped.

Dale Robichaud, 56, owner of vast gas and oil leases across public lands
from Wyoming to Arkansas, was fined $147 million by the EPA for hiding
evidence of environmental damage on multiple leases.

Although these charges were filed by the EPA over two years ago, the fines
were never paid and were mysteriously removed from the books last year.

When asked what had happened to the unpaid fines, neither the EPA nor
the president's office returned our calls.

In one of the thirteen counts, EPA fined one of Robichaud's companies for
a massive crude oil discharge into Louisiana's Vermilion River. EPA investigators found that the company waited for a heavy rainstorm to release
"bottom of the barrel" crude residue into the river.

Another of his companies was charged with dumping toxic wastes into
local groundwaters, where it polluted the drinking wells of two Iowa counties.

Known as a "bagman" – or "money bundler" for the president, Robichaud
is rumored to have raised over a hundred million dollars for the latter's
previous campaign. Thereafter appointed by the president to the Commodity
Futures Trading Commission, Robichaud has long alluded to their close ties.

But when asked earlier today about his relationship with Robichaud, the president, who has previously called Robichaud "one of my closest friends and advisors," said, "In presidential campaigns you meet lots of people. I'm not sure I remember Mr. Robichaud personally."

Ross closed his laptop and went down to *Famiglia* for coffee and pastries, thinking of Lily while standing in line watching another Ukraine war scene on the TV over the counter. Why in war coverage is there always plenty of ammo? Stacks of artillery shells waiting to shatter lives, cartridges spewing from barrels like dandelion seeds in the wind. But where did all these weapons come from? Who are they killing? Who sold them? To whom? Why?

As he put five bucks in the tip can, it suddenly seemed he'd crossed a line, was living more deeply. Had the escalation toward nuclear war, plus these constant attacks and dangers, sharpened his awareness?

Was it Lily?

Was he beginning to think he could win this? Maybe even help stop nuclear war?

"WE HIT THEM EARLY." ISAIAH FILLED THE SCREEN, HUNCHED OVER his desk with a coffee cup at his elbow. "We'd planned to wait till the last minute, be sure we got them. Then we had a breakthrough decoding their first entry, back when they took Kent out for what, a few microseconds –"

"Thirty milliseconds," Ross said. "I checked it, right after you told me."

"We backtracked them from that . . . All the way – can you imagine, where we can go, these days?"

"Who and where?"

"Rogue Chinese company out of Malaysia. We're going to have them by the balls."

"I want who hired them," Ross said.

"The instant we ID them, we take them down. In public. In one hour, we can destroy them. The penalty for ever hacking again will be so severe they never do. And the best ones come to work for us."

"That's convenient."

"Keeps God on our side –"

"Right now I need to do a buyback."

Isaiah eyes widened. "With what money?"

"Mitch and I have a deal going. Off-balance sheet."

"Do I have a right to know?"

"For your own protection, no. But I'll keep you posted."

"IT'S TIME," J IM B URLEIGH SAID AT THE NEXT VISUAL BOARD MEETING. "They're offering a good price. We'll come out looking like kings. Like we set this up."

"Not a chance," Mitch snapped.

"Christ, you guys wait any longer you're going to have a snake up your ass. You *can't* ride this out."

"I'm watching EastPac every hour," Mitch said. "I'm watching our stock. We're up from yesterday."

"And down from Wednesday."

"Jim, do you care more about your money," Ross said, "or the company?"

Burleigh chuckled. "Both."

"Go ahead, then, sell us short. And we'll drive up our numbers and wipe you out."

"Hey, hey, no need to get testy."

"You have to find the balls to do this," Ross said. "We are going to fight EastPac and win."

"You're dreamers. You're going under and taking us all with you."

Ross turned to Deborah Quinn. As another Board member she had the same power, almost, as Burleigh did as chairman. With her McKinsey background, three decades in high finance, she should see the light. Burleigh really was just an oil engineer, wily, devious, charming, and relatively crooked. He didn't understand the numbers.

No, Ross reminded himself. Burleigh probably understood the numbers best of all.

"Damn," Deborah said, "these are crazy times."

"I don't agree with Jim on this."

"He's the chairman, Ross."

Ross turned to Asa Chomsky. "What do you think?"

"Our stock's in the basement," Burleigh interrupted, "the FBI and IRS are on our ass, Boston Group just knifed us in the back –"

"There's no way," Asa said, "that a banking pool can contravene the financing structure they agreed to."

Burleigh shook his head. "That's not going to keep EastPac off our throat."

"I'M GONNA HAVE YOU CHAINSAWED AND FED TO THE HOGS," Dale Robichaud said. "You put that woman on me, didn't you? That reporter?"

"You went to the dark side," Ross said as he shut his limo window. "You did this to yourself."

"I got pressure," Robichaud sighed. "You'd have done the same."

"I don't screw my friends."

"I didn't know you had this much weight," Robichaud said sarcastically. "Or I might not have done it."

"CFTC will be much more honest with Emily Masterson at the top."

"Thirteen counts. You had to bring that up, when it was under the rug, you bastard? That's much worse than what you think I did to you."

"I don't *think* it." Ross smiled at the traffic going by. "I know it."

"Okay okay. If I dig my way out of this, you're dead."

"You're not going to dig your way out of it. You may not go to jail, not in Louisiana. But you're going to lose your mansions and be broke for the rest of your life. Even your lawyers are going to hate you. And lots of other people."

"Ross, maybe we can deal here."

"You can start by telling me who leaned on you to sink me."

"Jesus, I do that and everything goes to hell."

"It'll be private," Ross said. "Just you and me. And when I take them down, they'll never know it came from you."

"You don't quit, do you?"

"When I was a kid, the son of the company's owner, and I was working oil rigs in North Dakota, a lot of bigger guys thought they could knock me around. Like you, Dale, they learned that when somebody hits me, I'm going to hit them back so hard they'll never be the same."

"You want to know who told me to take you down? The president of the United States. You really think you're going to hit him back?"

"WE AND THE SAUDIS," ANNA SAID, "ARE DOING A DEAL TO CUT production."

Ross had a moment's shock that she knew what he had learned from Turk's listening device on the yacht that belonged to her brother. He tried to sound disinterested. "That's crazy."

"In Russia we would like higher prices. We are not worried by the sanctions."

"I am against the sanctions too."

"Is why I keeping calling you."

"Thank you for what you've told me, about CFTC, the SEC, Kent Power. So what is this Saudi deal?"

"Very few people know, soon to be announced. A production cut, at least twenty percent. Prices will go very high. It will break the sanctions, which are not working anyway."

"When," he said casually, "is this supposed to happen?"

"Very soon. I can call you before. You would like?"

"Why not? It will be good to know."

In her earlier calls about the CFTC, SEC and Kent Power, he'd wondered if she'd really been working for the other side, feeding him bits of truth till she could trap him with something big. But then she'd told him about a time in Singapore when he could have financially destroyed Navritok but hadn't. He'd had this checked, and yes, in Singapore nine years ago, May fifteen to eighteen, he'd been there.

And now she'd confirmed what he already knew: the Russia/Saudi deal. And that they were going to cut production.

And drive up the price.

And break the sanctions.

In the oil markets, an act of war.

3 7

TURANDOT

"I F THE WUHAN SUB refueled at the Pertamina dock," Turk said, "somebody knows."

"Mrs. Sudup did," Liz said.

He bit his lip. "Whoever did the refuel."

"After that, where did it go?"

"There are eighteen thousand islands in Indonesia. Many thousands of unknown inlets. And the north side of Kalimantan is Borneo, and across the strait the rest of Malaysia. Not to speak of the countless thousands of miles of coastline of Thailand, Cambodia, Vietnam, all across the South China Sea . . ."

"If it refueled in Kalimantan," she said, "could it reach Vietnam?"

Turk thought a bit. "Yes. And from there it could get to China. If they didn't have the diver, it'd be even lighter . . . You suppose they intentionally abandoned him?"

"Gets rid of a witness." Liz turned off the tub's faucets, unsnapped her watch and tossed it on the bathroom counter. "Like Asmara Sudup."

"I'm thinking the shark got him before he got back."

She sat down on the creaky bathroom chair and pulled off her clothes. "There had to be more than one guy."

He sat on the tub edge. "We need to get you out of here before you get killed."

"You too." She slipped into the tub and sighed. "The trouble with getting killed is that afterwards, when your enemies get killed you don't know."

"That sucks."

She grinned up at him as he pulled off his clothes. "We need a back door."

"I'm working on one. You leave first, to trick these bastards, then I nail them while they're dicking around –"

"You are *not* getting away with that. Not with me you're not."

He smiled as he sat in the tub facing her, their legs entwined, seeing deeply her face, her eyes, her smile, and even before they made love feeling perfectly connected to her.

"THIS MOSCOW WOMAN IS ALMOST INVISIBLE," ISAIAH told Ross. "We've studied every data base we can access, and all that comes up is Navritok. She and her brother Nevgeny. The parents started the company years ago, and when they died, she and Nevgeny took it over, and have made it one of the best in Europe."

"It's what people I trust have said."

"Interestingly, Igor Stein was on the Navritok board until he was appointed oil minister. His nephew, Peter Mikhailov, went to university with Anna. And Igor met with the Saudi energy minister on Anna's brother's yacht. Make of all that what you will."

"The question is, do I trust her? Everything she's told me so far has been true at every level. If there's going to be a Russia-Saudi deal, and I now believe there will be, will she tell me the truth now?"

"Holy fuck, how do I know? I'm just your advisor."

THE TROUBLE WITH MOSCOW RESTAURANTS IS USUALLY THEY'RE so busy you have to reserve three weeks ahead. But Anna got a table for two at Turandot for 21:00 tonight. One could argue forever about the many great Moscow restaurants, but to eat the magical cuisine of Russia's great heartland, a table for the Czars, that would be Turandot.

Then she called Peter Mikhaillov. "I have to see you."

"Bless you, Anna. To what do I owe this sudden attention?"

"Something's come up. Can I see you tonight?"

"What do I get out of it?"

"I'm still not going to sleep with you. But I can make you even richer."

"Maybe you'll make me so rich you'll marry me to get half my estate?"

"Even if I do, I might not sleep with you."

The most interesting thing about her, Peter reflected as he killed the phone, turned up Dire Straights on the speakers, and settled deliciously back into the throbbing jets of his jacuzzi, *is she's so smart.* The brightest of the math PhDs at Moscow's high-tech Lomonosov University. And with a big streak of Russian kindness, an instinctive gentleness, a woman whose father had loved her well. Her mama too.

He thought of his own mama with her chubby elbows, youthful smile and white hair, Papa with his mustache, silver front tooth, their enormous strength and love.

Love is all it takes to have a good life.

Happy parents make happy children.

After all these years, could she really not love him?

When they'd been kids together at their Black Sea summer homes, she'd been fresh, alive, exuberantly gamboling along the beaches and forest paths, laughing and tickling him when they crouched in a cave in the rain. He'd been two years older, but she'd been already far smarter than he, and he'd loved her for it.

Then on teenage snowboarding trips in Ukraine she'd been friendly but reserved, more interested in getting down the mountain fast, as if training for the Olympics. "Life is short," she'd once quoted Turgenev to him. "And to waste even a minute of it is unforgivable."

As undergrads at St. Petersburg, she'd kept to an arbitrary line: we're colleagues and friends. Since then, he'd had many lovers, always delightful but none he'd wanted to spend a life with. And her lovers? Hard to know. Maybe in that clandestine side of her life.

Where she kept what she could never tell.

This also made him love her.

She'd made tons of money predicting the markets. A true insider. But did she now know too much? Made too much?

He imagined making love with her, her lovely body spread across the bed, her legs tight around his back, her nipples hard and breasts firm against his chest as he thrust deeper and deeper inside her . . . her sighs and moans, her passionate face tangled in golden hair.

But Anna never called without a deeper reason. What was it now?

An Isaac Levitan painting appeared on the multimedia screen over his jacuzzi, *Above the Eternal Peace*. One of the 19th century's greatest landscapes, a green point of land, ancient church, and graveyard amid a wide blue lake under the vast Russian sky.

When there was no danger of nuclear war.

Eternity, Levitan had once said. *What a horror, what fear.*

IT BOTHERED LYLE EXCESSIVELY THAT HE HAD NOT CAUGHT whoever had snuck into Tom Hogan's hospital room and killed him. Usually within days of a case, he had it going in the right direction and soon got it solved. And since Cassidy'd arrived six months ago, their solved rate was a hundred percent. Except for who killed Tom Hogan. And who blew up the damn cracker.

He'd die soon and didn't want this failure on his rap sheet. When he stood before God. To ask forgiveness, as we all should, for all he'd done.

One of the great things about Wyoming is there aren't many potential perps to select from. The best choice was Jamal Curtaine. Squat, broad-shouldered, a truculent stare in his hooded angry eyes telling you that no matter what you did he might kill you. If he felt like it.

And nothing you could do or say would make a difference.

It wasn't that complicated. Perps like Jamal, they'd sometimes knife somebody then go home and pass out on the couch watching ESPN, the bloody knife on the floor beside them. Or they'd shoot someone and hide the gun in the glove box of their Dodge Ram.

So he dropped in on Judge Levene for a search warrant. "There's shit in that trailer of his," Lyle said, "we need to see."

"You think he killed Tom Hogan?"

Lyle sensed thin ice here. "That's what I'm trying to find out."

"Okay, I'll give you a limited one. Don't you override it now."

"Never, your Honor. Absolutely never."

"BEST CAVIAR IN MOSCOW." ANNA BIT INTO A RYE CRACKER TOPPED with sturgeon roe.

"There are many best things," Peter said. "One of them is seeing you. But why so sudden?"

"I need to make sure –" A lock of hair tucked under her chin, she questioned him with her wide blue eyes. "Up or down?"

"That whore of a Saudi prince, he may be setting us up."

Her guts froze. This was new. "That's old news," she said.

"This big production cut that Igor's been negotiating with them? What if at the last minute the Saudis don't cut? What if they pump like crazy, drive the price down, put us underwater, and grab more of the market? We'll be stuck with our hats full of shit, and Arab Light will eat us alive. And the Americans will be laughing all the way to the bank."

"It hurts them too."

"They don't care. All they want to do is kill us."

"A shame." She shook her head. "We were becoming friends."

"America doesn't want friends. It's bought plenty of friends. What it wants is enemies."

"And we fill the bill." She looked down; for a moment, everything meant nothing. "The Saudis, is there good intel on this?"

"Of course."

"It could really hurt us."

"Not if we plan for it."

She leaned forward, ruby bracelet flashing. "How?"

"Don't worry, Igor's dealing with the big picture."

"What about me? I take a chance and go short? How far could it go down?"

"Enough to make or lose several hundred million."

She looked away, then back at him. "Too risky."

"The Saudis are America's butt-hole buddies –"

"It astounds me, they planned the World Trade Center attack, yet the Americans still won't admit it."

"2001 is already ancient, Anna. Victims are abandoned, rulers rewrite the past. In five years, there may not even be a real record of it."

She thought a bit. "The Saudis? We can get them for this –"

"Maybe later." He watched her lovely, unbreakable face. You could tell her things, but would she listen? Too damn smart. And stubborn as a Siberian mule.

For a moment's distraction, he scanned the palatial, gleaming restaurant. Turandot was a princess, he remembered, in some Italian opera, Puccini maybe. So beautiful that many men pursued her, but so cold that any suitor who could not solve her three incomprehensible riddles would be killed. One by one her suitors died, till one answered all three riddles and won her heart.

Peter already knew the answer to the first riddle: *What is like ice yet burns?*

Anna herself, cold yet burning with desire. Frozen fire and lust.

And the other two riddles?

How to outwit this Saudi threat?

How to stop this war before it turned nuclear?

If he solved them, would she warm to him? *Dammit, I don't care. In Moscow so many thousands of smart, fascinating women.* "How's your brother?" he said.

"Nevgeny? He's so busy with his yachts and mansions that he's not managing the refinery group – he's supposed to do that side, refining, and I do the crude and product side."

"Interesting that Igor and the Saudi minister met on Nevgeny's yacht, somewhere in the Med."

"We're back in the Middle Ages." She twirled her wine glass, swirling ruby reflections of Satrapezo. "Was the wine this good, back then?"

"Georgian wines have been good for eight thousand years. Archaeologists have found pruning knives and amphorae even older . . ." He leaned forward. "My grandfather used to tell me that in Viking times, our warriors wove grapevines into their chest armor, so if they were killed, a grapevine would grow from their hearts."

Because Russia grows from our hearts. She glanced at the magnificent restaurant, its fabulous odors, superb wines and vodkas, flickering candles all like doorways to a deeper world. Food so good it induces prayer. "So" – she smiled over her wine glass – "what do we do?"

"Do we believe the Saudis will betray us? If we're right, we'll make hundreds of millions."

"And if we don't believe?"

"We might lose everything."

She flinched. "Nothing's worth that." She watched his muscular hands flex and relax. Tough, these Cossacks. Millennia of war. Never accepted Lenin, Stalin, Beria, all the others who sent millions to their deaths. "There's a guy in London."

This intrigued him. "Who cares about London?"

"And a guy in New York. I'm going to destroy one and save the other."

"Why?"

"Getting even."

Peter wasn't sure what she meant but was comforted that she was going to destroy at least one of them.

"This could make or break us," she said softly.

He nodded. "Forever."

She turned her large blue eyes on him. "So the moment you know –"

He squeezed her hand. "You will also."

IN AN ASTOUNDING INDICTMENT GUARANTEED TO IMPACT *November elections, the president has been charged with a wide network of bribery and pay-for-play schemes involving many millions of dollars from several foreign countries. Most significantly, the money trail leading from Ukraine to the president, beginning when he was a vice president, indicates what may be his real reason for dragging us to the brink of nuclear war.*

Published today by the Congressional Oversight Committee as part of its ongoing investigation of the president for "international influence peddling schemes," the report is already causing a firestorm in Congress, with the president's opponents calling for immediate impeachment while the Democrats scramble for a last-minute replacement.

"We now face the real risk of nuclear war," the report concludes, "because the president has been manipulated, since his years as vice president, by powerful interests in Ukraine which first arranged many of his illegal deals, then threatened to reveal them, which would inevitably lead to his impeachment."

Central to the indictment's findings was that the president, when he was vice president, forced the firing of Ukraine's prosecutor general, due to the latter's prosecution of a corrupt Ukrainian energy company named Burisma. According to the indictment, the president, when he was vice president, held up billions of dollars in funds to Ukraine until the prosecutor was fired. Once the prosecutor was fired, the investigation ceased, the president's family received payoffs, and the president's son was appointed to Burisma's board of directors at a high salary, although he had no experience in energy or much of anything else, and was a seriously compromised drug addict.

The indictment identifies the president's manipulation by the Ukrainians as a standard intelligence setup, a "Kompromat" in Ukrainian: "First the target is enticed to take a bribe, then another, and soon they are under your complete control simply because you can at any time reveal it."

The indictment references recent testimony by six of the largest U.S. banks, including Bank of America, JP Morgan, and Wells Fargo, that they had sent over 170 Suspicious Activity Reports (SARs) to the Treasury Department about the president's family banking transactions.

"For most companies," the indictment notes, "a single SAR is enough for

all your accounts to be closed. Several indictments would doom a company. A total of 170 is completely unheard of."

The indictment additionally reveals some of the president's pseudonyms used in arranging these hidden payoffs, itself a potentially impeachable offense.

Ross scrolled farther down the front page of Lily's *Journal* article, some of which seemed sourced from the memory stick he had given her. *"According to former presidential confidant Ross Bullock, CEO of Rawhide Energy, the president's income from these schemes may exceed seventy million dollars. Making this, if true, the largest political corruption scandal in U.S. history."*

"The president never talked to his son about business," White House press secretary Mildred Fossy said when asked about the indictments. "Mr. Bullock is a conspiracy theorist at the end of his tether. His whole corporate structure is being revealed as a shoddy and dangerous Ponzi scheme, he's struggling frantically to save a fraudulent empire, and he's knifing in the back a man who has always been his friend."

But it was the last paragraph that got him:

This reporter has interviewed Mr. Bullock several times. His story has remained consistent and is backed up by careful examination of Congressionally-subpoenaed banking records from several nations, including many in the US, as well as thousands of email messages, White House recordings, and other sources revealed by the House Subcommittee.

A related question is why have most of the media, whose responsibility is to inform us of the truth, so consistently covered it up?

"LET'S GO," PETER SAID TO ALEX, HIS DRIVER, THEN REALIZED HE hadn't meant to be sharp, and said more softly, "I'm pissed off. Let's go home."

"Whatever works," Alex said, goading him a bit.

"She frustrates me."

Alex turned the Panamera onto Tverskoy Boulevard toward the Moskva River. "It isn't me suggested you should have dinner with her."

"Would you stop acting so superior!"

"Of course, your Honor."

Peter chuckled. "How come she treats me like this?"

"She doesn't always. She usually ignores you."

"Thanks."

"I would too, in her case."

Peter scanned the busy Moscow streets flitting past the tinted glass. "Why?"

"Because sometimes you're an asshole. That's why."

Peter sat back and thought about this. Alex never said anything that he didn't believe. "So," he said, "tell me how to do better."

"Shit, boss, I love you as you are. Just remember, nobody's always right."

"Do I trust her? With a billion-dollar bet?"

"Who else you going to trust? You aren't exactly popular right now."

He asked Alex to drop him off at the walkway along the Moskva River. It was flowing fast, half-frozen, white-capped and dark, raging southeast toward the frozen reaches of the Volga and the Caspian Sea. He stopped at the slight bend below the Kremlin, wondering if this was where 1,400 years ago the Vikings had built their first trading post, and soon the 800-year Viking government of Russia had begun. That lasted in relative harmony and power till Ivan the Terrible, and it made Peter feel good that his blood was theirs. *We are the Vikings who gave us the name Rus. We are the warriors who never give up.*

We who love life too much to allow defeat.

38

ALMOST OVERNIGHT

"**YOU'RE GOING TO DIE**," Doc McGuire said. "Soon."

Lyle felt the chill slink down his spine but tried to grin. "*How* soon?"

"A month, maybe."

Lyle's mind shifted to Olivia, then to all the news about nuclear war. Now he might die before it happened . . . "That sucks."

McGuire sat on the stool opposite him. "Forty-one years I've been a doctor. Most of it right here in Sweetwater. Telling you this is about the hardest thing I've ever done."

Lyle felt damp under his collar. "How many thousand lives have you saved?"

McGuire shrugged. "To save even one life is wonderful." He sat forward and tucked up a trouser crease. "I've looked through every case like yours I can find, but no, we can't buy our way out of this. No matter what clinic we send you to, it won't change the outcome."

Lyle swallowed. "So how long can I be active?"

"Already with these terrible pains that brought you here, if you're lucky, a couple weeks. But you, you're made of old elk hide, Lyle."

Lyle nodded, taking it in. "I got a case I have to finish, can't do it in two weeks."

"My advice, you who've been my good friend since Miss Lander's class –"

Lyle smiled. "That two-room schoolhouse in Cody? Amazing how many good people it's turned out." For a moment, Lyle realized, McGuire had distracted him from the shock of dying by recalling him to time and eternity. His heart plunged.

"– my advice is finish the case. No matter the cost." McGuire leaned forward, his hand on Lyle's knee. "You're going to live a long time, in all the good you've done."

"This's going to kill Olivia."

McGuire nodded. "Up here, the women mostly outlive the men. How many widows in their nineties go to bed every night still missing a man who died twenty years ago?"

Lyle shook Doc's hand and listened mechanically as his old friend told him how to live out his last days. How to ease his wife into it.

And solve his last case.

WHAT IF THE WUHAN COVID RELEASE *HAD* BEEN intentional?

What was plaguing Lily was the difference in COVID mortality rates between the U.S. and China. While China had lost only four people per million to the virus, the U.S. had lost 3,500 people per million. And China's economy had barely stumbled while the rest of the world's fell apart.

The world's first COVID victims were Ben Hu, Ping Yu, and Yan Zhu – all three scientists working on Anthony Fauci's Gain-of-Function research at the Wuhan Bioweapons Lab.

Who had wanted this truth repressed? Why had the media, particularly her former home, the *Times*, tried every way they could to deny it? Even ridiculed, maligned and demonized those who said it?

How could an unseen force be so strong, so absolute? How to reveal it?

A carved wooden sculpture of the Three Monkeys had hung above the television on the living room wall of her Honolulu childhood home: *See no evil. Hear no evil. Speak no evil.*

In the Confucian sense, this had once meant to refuse to see, hear, or repeat bad rumors. But it had changed into a cultural mindset: Pretend all is good no matter how bad it is. Because we fear it and don't know how to deal with it.

What could she do about it? What could we all do?

Speak truth to power, and power may not win?

Fat chance.

IT WAS 02:17 A.M. IN MOSCOW WHEN ANNA CALLED ROSS.

"I've just found out" – she sounded hurried, almost breathless – "the Saudis may back out."

"Oh shit," he said inadvertently as he stepped out of a late budget meeting. *This could screw everything.* He'd been planning a series of futures transactions that he'd do just before they announced the cut. Now there might not be a cut, and he'd be out hundreds of millions.

"Sorry," she said. "I'll keep you posted."

She was gone. *Damn,* he told himself, *what do we do now?*

FOR TWO DAYS LYLE RODE AROUND IN HIS SHERIFF'S CAR WITH Cassidy and never said a word. Went home to Olivia and watched her face thinking *how much I love her,* and said nothing. Sought every moment of their lives in her face, her words, what she did. The thought she'd soon be alone drove a stake through his heart. That in a few weeks he'd no longer wake to see her face in golden-gray sleep-tangled hair or hear her voice in the kitchen talking on the phone to their kids and grandkids, feel her warm palm in his. "Death sucks," he wanted to say to Cassidy. But didn't.

They did a drive-through through the Sweetwater High School parking lot. Lyle had done it several times a day ever since Columbine and all the other school massacres that followed. And every time, he reviewed the training they'd done if there was a shooter there. "What the hell's gone wrong with our world?" he said.

Cassidy pulled up beside the gym, nodding at the far rolling prairies all sheeted in snow. "Looks pretty good to me."

Lyle snatched the toothpick from his mouth. "You can be a real pain in the ass. You know that?"

Cassidy smiled at him. "I've been told that, many times."

"By Shirley?"

"Exactly."

"Don't believe her," Lyle said.

"She's right."

"You're a great cop. I'm recommending you for the next county sheriff."

"Chief, you don't have to think about that now."

"Yeah. I do. These pains I've been having? It's cancer. Real bad. Have a couple weeks, maybe a month."

Cassidy crimped his lips, his face going hard. He glanced away at the endless cold prairie. "I been worrying."

"For a while I've had these pains. Down the side of my gut. Finally went to see Doc."

"Should've gone earlier."

"Nah. I'm just like you."

Cassidy wiped at his cheek. "Damn it, Chief."

"I talked to the county commissioners. You got a unanimous vote."

Cassidy turned away. "I don't care about that, Chief."

Lyle swallowed, and waited till he could speak. "You're going to be a great sheriff."

"Not like you."

"Fuck you won't." Lyle unbuckled his seat belt. "Let's go see if one of these little turds has put a bomb in the locker rooms."

IT WAS 5 A.M. IN JAKARTA, BUT STILL EARLY EVENING THE previous day in New York, when Turk called Ross. "I just heard from the South Kalimantan police chief, Wantiko."

"The one who doesn't want you to leave Jakarta?"

"He just emailed me a file. The woman who was killed, who took pictures of that Chinese sub from Wuhan? Her house had a motion camera under the eaves. It recorded the guy who killed her."

Ross put down his sandwich. "And?"

"Not a local. *Orang kulit putih.*"

"What's that?"

"Indonesian for white man. And guess what? Her camera had sound."

"So?"

"He said something. In Russian."

"DON'T YOU *DARE* PUT THOSE BOOTS ON THE BEDROOM RUG," Olivia said.

Lyle took his boots out to the kitchen and put them by the snow room door. Though they were only a little bit muddy.

"Who'd you arrest today?" she said.

"Tommy Gordon's cousin. The one with the moustache? Tried to pass a fake twenty."

"Vince? He doesn't learn from experience."

"And Paula Moore again. Eighty in a thirty zone. Hammered on pills."

"What you do?"

"Locked her up. Two weeks, Judge Levene says."

"Who's going to take the kids?"

"Sonja Perkins. She's done it before."

"Those kids are headed to the slammer too."

He sat on her side of the bed and took her hand. "Honey, I got to tell you something."

39

SUNSET

T HE GUY WHO SPOKE RUSSIAN and had killed Mrs. Sudup shouldn't be hard to find, Turk told himself. How many Russians, after all, showed up in Mahakam? Though for sure it was a contract killer who'd come through Jakarta, but no one stood out in the passenger lists he'd wangled from airport security. And it might have been a private plane into Balikpapan, its passengers impossible to trace.

"Ready Rentals." Liz looked up from her computer. "Their database two days before she died shows a guy named Kulug flying in from Ulan Bator, Ukrainian passport –"

"Lots of nasty people have Ukrainian passports."

"– rented a KIA for three days."

KIA. Killed In Action – how could they name a car that?

But it was annoying how she grasped at straws, saw clues where there were none. These people were too careful. They didn't leave clues.

She ignored him, busy with her databases. He finished his bitter coffee, looking out at the palm trees tossing in the rainy wind. True, she was amazing; he'd never met anyone like her. But damn it all, she was too quick to jump to conclusions.

"So who is he?"

"Can't get into those files. Just that he rented it."

And she'd been the only one to survive the platform. Fierce, determined, and relentless ever since he'd met her two days after the explosion. She wouldn't stop till she found who did it and killed them.

Or they killed her first.

Because she was the only survivor, of course they'd keep trying to kill her. Even worse, she'd pissed them off by escaping when they thought they had her.

And now she was tracking *them* down, closer every day.

Even *more* reason to kill her.

Why hadn't they killed her in that Central Park basement? Had they hoped to catch *him* when he came to save her?

He leaned over her and kissed her fragrant hair, the line in the middle where the skin showed through.

Every day, in every way, he had to protect her.

LILY FOUND IT UNSURPRISING THAT HER FORMER HOME, THE *Times*, had chosen to dismiss the Congressional Oversight Committee report on the president's Ukraine activities. "It's just like what it did on the Durham report," she said when she called Ian Hamilton, "that revealed the FBI lied repeatedly to the previous president . . . And now the *Times* is saying again, there are 'no startling revelations,' as if everyone already knew what was in the Oversight Committee report – basically that the president used his connections to make millions in foreign countries, and that the Ukrainians had used this to trap him – what's the word? *Kompromat* – to trap us into this endless, deadly war? As though the *Times* is saying, *it's okay to be a crook. Because everybody is?* It's for this that the world may end?"

"Quiet down, Lily," Ian cautioned.

"And the *Times* did again after the Justice Department report said the president was too senile to stand trial? What's going on here?"

"*Shush*, Lily! For Christ's sake, we're being recorded –"

"Since when?"

"Since recently. For legal reasons. To protect us, they say."

IT HAD BEEN THREE DAYS SINCE LYLE WAS TOLD HE HAD TWO weeks to live. Enough to track down Tom Hogan's killer. Often sleeplessly in bed at night, he'd remember Tom, wondered how two kids could know each other's lives but still not understand life. It was as if finally, after Tom's death and just before his own, they were becoming brothers. Or recognizing they always had been.

Now, as he tapped his thumbs on the top of the cruiser's steering wheel, he tried to sum up the case against Jamal. He'd gone missing the day before the blast, and surfaced the day after Tom Hogan was killed. He had no alibi at all for that time, other than, "I been drinking real hard, Sheriff, the way I do sometimes." Jamal straightened up, tucked at his collar. "I met this girl, we went to her trailer . . . she had some meth . . ."

"Even a meth whore wouldn't spend four days with you. You're a worthless piece of shit."

Jamal ran skinny fingers through his blond-dyed Afro, nodded.

"But the sad thing is," Cassidy said, "in your heart you're a good guy. You take care of your friends. You'd even help *me*, if I was hurt or something. And I got to be *last* on your list."

Jamal nodded, not looking up.

"You can change who you are in one simple act: tell us who got you into this."

Jamal looked up, straight into Cassidy's eyes. "I didn't do it. I was sitting in a cabin way up in middle of the Little Sweetwater Wilderness. Staying off booze and meth, praying on my knees. To become a better person."

ROSS WATCHED THE LIGHT ON THE PINE TRUNKS AS THE SUN SET among the Montana peaks in the silence that came with dusk, shook himself awake. He was here in Manhattan where there was neither sunset nor sunrise, nor mountains nor forests, nor fresh air. And never silence. Was truth as equally absent here as it was present in Montana?

Rawhide had grown far beyond what he could have imagined. His parents' brilliant, hard-working years had been the dawn of a world-wide company. Like the universe, the more we know, the more it keeps expanding.

"You love this astrophysics so much," Dad had said one night, golden brandy in their glasses as they sat by the pine fire in the log house above Red Lodge, "you don't need to run Rawhide. We can go public, let some Wall Street crook run it."

Ross scoffed and put down his glass. "I love Mary too, far more than I love astrophysics. But I don't have to give her up to run the company. Nor astrophysics either."

Dad sat back, creaking his leather armchair. "Just figure out where the hell the carbon atom came from. That's good enough for me."

Dad was long dead, but Ross kept bouncing ideas off him. And Dad always answered.

Would Rawhide be destroyed? Would he be defeated, financially ruined? Looking back at this years later, what would he see?

"For Chrissake, kid," Dad said. "Tough it out."

Who would destroy the platform at the moment when Rawhide was trying to stop nuclear war? The American War Machine, as they called it? Some invisible and nearly absolute power running the government, dooming us all? Over which we the people had no knowledge, no control?

"For Chrissake," Dad repeated. "That's your job for the rest of your life. Destroy the bastards."

Why was Victor Minh tortured, killed, and dumped in a Wyoming snowbank?

Why attack the refinery? Could he trust Lyle, the sly Wyoming sheriff who first seemed against him and now supposedly believed him?

Why had the journalists turned like jackals against him?

And old acquaintances piling untrue accusations on him? Sensing him weakened, had attacked him?

Or because someone, some force, had enticed them to do so?

"Jesus Christ," Dad added, "you know the answer to all that."

Not everyone had turned against him. Not Turk. Not Liz, that woman from the platform. It was Turk who found the Wuhan two-person sub up the Mahakam River – had *it* attacked the platform? And the woman now dead who'd told Turk about the sub. Who had killed *her*? Were they tied to the ones who killed Victor in Wyoming?

Who was wearing the diving gear that got torn up by a shark?

Who? How did they know so much?

Anna, the woman on the phone from Moscow, what did she really want? Who was she working for? Or was she just giving him a small truth here, a bigger one next, till she drove home the knife?

Now Lily.

Was *she* the same? Draw you in till she can kill you. Who could *she* be working for?

So often in his long nights studying the stars and galaxies and the dark space between them – the infinite, never-ending cold darkness – he'd felt vastly alone. Out there in cold dark infinity, alone, *alone*. But when she was sitting across from him, why did he no longer feel alone?

Dark endless space was still everywhere around them. But in that magic moment, it didn't matter.

And if it doesn't matter, it's energy. That lives forever.

With Lily's help, he'd begun to pick apart the motives of those against him, like Robichaud the Louisiana gas king who trashed the environment, or the president pretending to be a man of peace as he stumbled us into nuclear war?

Ross had learned to see energy for what it was: the world's lifeblood that was however permanently altering it. And the wars it caused that would soon kill us all.

In history, every strong nation eventually loses its power to something wilder, less principled, more ruthless and ignorant.

Every great nation dies of suicide, Toynbee said, not murder.

LILY LIKED TO GET UP EARLY. But it was still dark outside, and the cold wind came through the cracks in the old windows and chilled her coffee before she had time to drink it.

Ross was in Los Angeles for a petrochemicals meeting, and she couldn't stop thinking about him, instead of what she was supposed to do. Frustrated that she couldn't think, she blew on her cold fingers, tugged the yellow pad closer, and tried to organize her thoughts.

1. Ross had called the president's bluff, refused to follow the Russia sanctions, and warned of nuclear war. Then somebody blew up Rawhide's platform and then the Wyoming refinery, then tried to shut down Kent Power. Who?
2. Somebody had unleashed the media on Rawhide. This was her profession, and it made her angry. How to track down the source? Start with Ian Hamilton.
3. Isaiah King had said the Kent Power hackers were Chinese, working out of Malaysia – how to find them was Isaiah's job.
4. Who was behind the concerted attacks on Rawhide's stock, media presence, and debt position? Could the war machine really control the media, the markets, the banks?
5. If the banks called all Rawhide's loans, could it survive? She made a note to call Goldman and a few others and get the latest inside talk.
6. Who had killed Victor Minh? And all these other deaths – the refinery guy in the Sweetwater hospital, the Indonesian woman who'd ID'd the Chinese sub?
7. Who was the diver was whose mouthpiece and harness got chewed up by the shark?
8. Who were all these people willing to risk nuclear war? What had they to gain if everyone on the planet died? Did they think it wouldn't happen?

Early sun streamed through her mullioned windows. There are

times in life when every instant feels worthwhile . . . every moment tantalizing and deep.

The effervescence of life, so brief. She wanted it. More of it.

She went and lay down on the bed, stretching her back muscles. *I need a new bed. This one's too soft. But the bed in Ross's penthouse is nice and hard, just the way I like it.* She grinned at the double entendre. *You never knew you wanted a harder one till you met him.*

"CHIEF, YOU DON'T HAVE A BRAIN," CASSIDY SAID AS THEY SAT at a window booth at the Cowboy Cafe.

"I know that," Lyle snapped. "So what?"

"I don't have one either." Cassidy unwrapped his Big Beast and glowered at Lyle. "You're getting thinner and thinner, Chief. This work, it's killing you."

"*Cancer* is killing me."

"You're dying even faster, 'cause of this."

"Stop bugging me. Let's get this done."

Cassidy popped another Big Beast in his mouth and washed it down. "Neither one of us looked into to somebody's work history . . ."

"Whose?"

Cassidy finished chewing. "Trim was a night nurse at the hospital. Quit five months ago."

IT HURT LYLE TO RIDE IN THE PATROL CAR BUT HE WOULDN'T GIVE IT up. Cassidy wouldn't let him drive, fussed at him all the time. Now it was late night again, and they were headed in the patrol car to wake up Trim at Mama Gaia's Soul Fitness Retreat.

It was midnight when they got there. Needless to say, she wasn't expecting them. Took her ten minutes to let them in and go back to her room for a bathrobe and slippers.

She leaned forward in a red leather armchair in the living room, the silk bathrobe open at her breasts. "I'd call my damn lawyer," she sniffed. "If I had one."

She went to the fireplace and jostled the coals, the slim robe tight over her ass. "We need you to tell us the damn truth," Cassidy said. "You worked for the hospital till five months ago, so you knew just how to get in and find Tom Hogan . . ."

She glared at him. "You're absolutely nuts."

She pulled a movie maneuver, crossing her legs. Lyle felt offended, belittled. "We can save you the death sentence. Maybe get you only ten years. Y'ever been down to Lusk, the Women's Prison?"

She looked up again, startled. "Why would I?"

Lyle filed this away, the pretense. "We'll take you down there for a look. We'll even show you the women's death row. Soon as we bring you in."

40

CLUSTER BOMBS

READY RENTALS didn't look ready at all. In fact, Liz decided as she crossed the parking lot littered with transmissions, engine blocks, tires and junkers, it looked as unready as possible.

The office was a little blue hut roofed with asphalt shingles bedecked with dead palm fronds. The single window was open, the air conditioning on. There were no cars in the parking lot. She squeaked open the door and went in.

The A/C was roaring, but the air was hot and humid. A little man in a blue short-sleeve shirt looked up at her, surprised. He stood and moved back from his desk. "How can I help you?"

"I was looking," she said, glancing around the room, "for a rental."

"A car?"

"Of course. What else do you rent?"

He made a submissive sideways gesture. "Of course."

He'd gotten over the shock of her sudden appearance, and of her speaking Indonesian. But both had made him suspicious. "We are closed today."

"I don't want it for today."

"No, I mean office. Office closed."

"The door was open."

"Mistake. Should be closed."

She tugged Turk's camera off her shoulder and showed it to the man. "A guy I met, he left this in my apartment."

The man's eyes widened; he reached to fondle the camera. "Is very nice."

"Is worth a lot of money."

He looked at her openly. "Why you bring it here?"

"The guy's name is Nachin Kulug. I want to give him back his camera, but I don't have his address."

He clutched the camera. "I can send it to him."

She shook her head. "Not a chance. You give me his address, *I* send it."

"Cannot give addresses."

"I'm sending it along with a pair of my underpants . . . Like these." She lifted her skirt to show a panty edge. "I don't think he wants *your* underpants . . ."

He tried to smile, disconcerted, excited.

"With you, he spoke English?" she said.

"Yes." The man nodded. "Yes, good."

She took a fifty-dollar bill from her purse, leaned across the counter showing her breasts, and tucked it in his shirt pocket. "I need to see your receipts from when Nachin rented that KIA. So I can send him his camera." She smiled. "And the other stuff."

He patted his shirt pocket. The money crinkled. "Just wait."

He went into the closet and came out with a cardboard box, pawed through it, and showed her a folder. "This, it is him."

She reached for it. "Good."

"No." He pulled it away. "I give you this, I can lose job. Jobs not many now, take months for new one. Job pays eleven million rupiahs a month. Need six months' pay."

Eleven million rupiahs was almost nine hundred bucks a month, times six months was more than five thousand USD. She laughed at him, stepped back from the counter, and held up her phone. "It's all in here, what you just said. I send this to your bosses in Sikharam Road, you lose your job today."

She watched him think about coming around the counter to attack her. "And I have a friend parked outside, who hears this all too . . . Isn't that right, baby?"

"That's right." Turk's voice came over her phone speaker from the car parked outside. "But I'm not your baby."

She turned to the man. "You're going to take those fifty dollars. And be grateful for it. And no one, ever, is going to know."

He went to a rusting Xerox machine in the corner and made her a copy.

"Ah, Nachin," she sighed, turned to the man. "He's going to be so happy when I show up in Ulan Bator to give him his camera."

"That is a long way, costs much. You would do that?"

"I'm a stewardess. The flight's free. And the look on Nachin's face will make it all worthwhile. Especially in front of his wife."

LILY WENT TO THE *TIMES* OFFICE TO PICK UP HER LAST FILES AND LEFT at six-forty. She decided to take the IRT Seventh Avenue train from Times Square to the Christopher Street station in the Village. At this hour, the Manhattan streets were still jammed with cars; even if she found a taxi, it would be a long, slow drive downtown. The subway would only take ten minutes, and Ross was coming at eight.

She pushed through the turnstile and downstairs to the platform still crowded with commuters on their way from their offices to their apartments – from one box to another, she thought ruefully, and had a moment's longing for green grass, fresh air, and sun.

She moved to the platform edge to look down the tunnel for the lights of an approaching train. There was a quick step behind her, and two hard fists slammed her down onto the tracks. She yelled and grabbed at the platform edge to climb out, but a ragged-coated man kept stamping on her fingers and kicking at her face.

"Filthy China bitch!" He towered over her, his spiky afro haloed in the ceiling lights. "Spread China disease!"

"Help!" she yelled. "Stop him!" The rails creaked as a train roared out of the tunnel.

In an instant's horror she saw it was an express, wouldn't even slow for this station, *couldn't* stop fast enough. She'd be crushed, ripped apart.

"China bitch!" the man raged, stamping on her hands.

Everyone on the platform seemed frozen, as in a nightmare. Then an old man ran forward, knocked her attacker aside, and yanked her up as the train, steel wheels screeching, thundered past.

"You be okay, lady?" the old man panted.

She leaned over to catch her breath, gasping, "Oh God, thank you!" She looked for her attacker, who was wandering farther down the platform, waving his arms in the air and yelling, "No China disease!"

People gathered round her sympathetically. *They didn't help me*, she thought, *when it happened.*

"You be okay?" the old man repeated. "Okay, lady?"

Her knee hurt terribly. Blood was running down her torn tights into her shoe.

Some people were staring at her as if what had happened was her fault.

Her files were spread all over the greasy black gravel between the tracks. She thought of climbing down to get them, but that was crazy. *It's okay,* she decided. *The* Times *is truly gone.*

Her rescuer was gone, too, and her attacker. *They'll have him on camera,* she told herself. Painfully she limped to the stairs and up to the exit, dizzy and sick to her stomach.

It was snowing, big fat flakes melting on the cindery sidewalk. Cars blocked Seventh Avenue, headlights hazy in the falling snow. She pulled out her phone and almost dropped it, shivering so hard she could barely speak. "Ross, I've got to cancel . . ."

"Lily, *what happened?* Where *are* you?"

She feared breaking down from the warmth and worry in his voice.

"Tell me where you are! Lily!"

In minutes he was there, shirt half-buttoned, no coat. She hugged him tight, not wanting to let go.

It was then, seeing the worry on his face, the fierce strength, she realized how much she loved him.

FOR A HOLDING CELL, IT WAS PRETTY NICE. THE BUNK WAS LONG enough, the toilet didn't stink. The yellow concrete walls were clean, the bars not too rusty. There was a vague smell of vomit, but you could get used to it.

Trim sat on the bunk, her hands gripping the edge so hard that she seemed ready to leap at Lyle. "I didn't do it." She ran fingers through her tangled hair. "Can you get me a cup of coffee?"

"Just tell me why you did it," he answered, "and you can have all the coffee you want. And you'll get off easier than if you hold out on us."

Trim pulled down a lock of hair and let it go. "I worked in the hospital, sure. Lots of people did. Or do. That doesn't mean any of us would've killed that poor man."

"Did you know him?"

She frowned. "Never heard of him. We're kind of isolated, up at the Retreat."

"So why are you there?"

She looked at him, surprised. "It's peaceful in the wilderness. And the people who come to us, we really help them. But it's the place that does it, not us. We just send them in the right direction, are there to talk whenever they want . . ." She glanced down. "I've never hurt anybody." She looked up at him. "Please, let me go. I didn't do anything. Not anything at all."

Lyle stood, pain shooting through his gut. "I can't let you go, but I'll get you that coffee."

Carefully he walked down the corridor toward his office, bent over to hold in the pain.

If Trim didn't do it, who did?

If she was in the sack with a couple of the perps, how much *did* she know?

And what about the old broad, Mother Nature herself – the Gaia woman?

I'll never finish this case before I die.

FOR THE AMERICAN CLUSTER BOMBS FROM UKRAINE, ST. Miles had put quick high-interest loans on all of his real estate, raising $31M that he then leveraged to make the deposit of $153M and hold the bombs for delivery. He'd hoped for better terms, but the bombs were in demand in many other conflicts including the Myanmar war and ongoing wars in Ethiopia, Colombia, Afghanistan-Pakistan, and thirty-one other countries. And it wasn't like the old days, when suppliers were fewer and buy/sell connections more established. Now with the worldwide explosion of human hatreds, it was a seller's market.

But in Sudan, Malik kept postponing his down payment, saying the funds were being held up by "some damn bank, but don't worry."

All St. Miles did was worry. And now he was getting squeezed on the margin accounts for his borrowed $153 million, and risking some nasty new enemies.

THE STREAKS OF RAIN DOWN THE GLASS WALLS OF HIS MAD AVE living room made Ross miss Montana winters, when the snow blew so hard you couldn't see fifty yards from the house to the horse barn. You were enclosed, sheltered. Safe.

If Anna was correct that the Saudis might pull out of this secret deal at the last moment, it would be a kick in the balls for the Russians. In a Siberian early winter, a reduction in crude production can't be reversed quickly. And if at the same time the Saudis raised production, thus lowering prices, it would push down Russian, U.S. and worldwide crude prices too. So if Rawhide could take short futures contracts on crude plus ninety-day agreements with a few airlines and crude refiners, it could profit both ways if the Saudis did raise production.

But on the other hand, if the Russians and Saudis both stuck to their agreement, cut their runs and raised prices, OPEC would have to follow. And Rawhide, just a medium-sized fish in this big sea of avarice and discontent, could put twenty-seven million barrels of crude on the market. And make a few billion in the process.

Which would drive up Rawhide's stock by at least seventeen percent.

Either way, if the Saudi-Russian deal went through or not, he had to be ready.

He called Chuck Rasmussen, the CEO of Midwest Fill'n Go. They had 1,149 service stations across the Midwest, just a drop in the bucket compared to the almost 170,000 stations nationwide, but they were a high-volume reliable market. They had no refineries and no crude. They usually bought their refinery products from Saudi Aramco. It was time they started buying from Rawhide.

41

DARK WEB

WHY, Lily couldn't decide, *were most of the media still attacking Rawhide? Who was rewarding them, with what?*

Why was her old home, the *Times,* the worst? Sometimes three negative articles a day – one on the business page (*Rawhide stock faces potential new historic drop*), another in the political section (*Will Rawhide's history of poor maintenance embitter relations with our allies?*), and even the society page (*Troubled Rawhide CEO shuns NY charity events*). Every day, nasty articles quoting unnamed sources, heavy with sarcasm and contempt.

Why the similar rants against Rawhide by CNN, MSNBC, WAPO, all that bunch? Why weren't they worried about nuclear war? Who was telling them what to say? Why were the only sane voices in the conservative press?

What was the link between the *Times* and the president? Why were they protecting him? Couldn't they see the danger the world was facing by refusing to reveal the war machine that was generating the horror in Ukraine and the Middle East? Did they not care?

The moment people stop speaking the truth, everything falls apart.

She'd waited till eight-thirty to call Ian Hamilton. By then he'd have had two double martinis, plus a bottle of Margaux or

Chateauneuf with dinner. As usual, he'd seem stone-cold sober, watching the angles. But he wouldn't lie, not to her.

A former colleague had let it slip that Ian had lost his post as news editor, though it wasn't going to be announced till the end of the quarter. Lily felt sorry for him. For all his genuflections to the higher-ups, he was still one of the best journalists she'd ever worked for. Perhaps resentment, if not gin, would loosen his tongue.

At eight-thirty it still didn't feel right to call, so she waited till eight-forty-seven and hit his number.

"Lily!" he said, light-voiced. "How nice. I'm making dinner –"

"What are you having?"

"Copper River salmon, French fries from my *friteuse*, a Greek salad with kalamatas and feta just in from Heraklion . . ."

"I heard the news. What happened?"

"They've taken my contributor status, special reports. Moved me downstairs, inside office."

"That's crazy! Why?"

"God knows. I've been with them twenty-eight years. Risked my *life* for them, how many times? How many war zones did they send me to? And I've been covering race issues since I started . . . Then the other day I did a nice piece on Iceland. They sent it back. Not racially diverse enough."

"*Ice*land? They're all Vikings. They don't *have* any racial issues!"

"If the *Times* says so, they have to!" Ian countered sarcastically. "Didn't you listen to anything I told you when you were working here?"

"Diversity's the buzzword these days. And when they've forgotten it, nothing will have changed."

"I told them we can't just make things up, then say they're true because we say so."

"Those four lists at the *Times* you told me about?"

"Yeah," he sighed.

"The first list was the people we don't cover, the second was the people we cover only in a certain way. Like Dale Robichaud?"

"That was a good piece, darling. A shame we couldn't run it."

"There were two other lists, right?"

"Yeah, the people we're always supposed to attack."

"Like Rawhide?" she said. "And the fourth list is the people you obey."

"Yeah, and they're the ones who axed me."

"They say why?"

"Somewhere I've gone astray, Lily. Don't know how. It's like that Kafka book where a guy's arrested, imprisoned, brought to trial, convicted and executed, without ever knowing what the charges were against him."

"The Trial."

"Yeah. Of course."

"And you told me," she added, "that the *Times* is on a vendetta against Rawhide, and their CEO – what's his name – Ross Bullock? Because he's on the third list?"

"Those are the kinds of questions that got you fired."

"I wasn't fired. I quit."

"That's not what they say."

"Ian, you know who *they* are."

"Look, I've got to get to my fish . . ."

The liquor's hitting him, she decided. "So where's the president in all this?"

"Lily, the president doesn't even know where he is, most of the time. He –"

"We all know this, but –"

"It's the people who run him who are making these wars, making them bigger. They want to break Russia into republics they can control, get the crude. It's all about crude, darling."

"Oh my God. Nobody can destroy Russia." She realized she was shaking.

"And these people who run the president, they're angry and *determined* to crush Rawhide for not playing by their rules. Just like they want to crush Russia." He cleared his throat. "You can't fight them, Lily. Keep your distance."

"No worries."

Ian took a swallow; she assumed it was gin. "This Bullock guy is an American success story," he added. "But he's hurting the Prez on Ukraine. Worrying people about nuclear war, for Christ's sake. Nobody wants to hear about that. The people who run the Prez want everybody happy for his re-election. And they want to expand the war, because it's hard to unseat an incumbent in wartime."

"They're risking nuclear war to get him *reelected*?"

"Of course. Think of Nixon, an evil manipulator if ever there was one. Got re-elected by escalating a war in Vietnam that nobody wanted, and killed a million more people. This guy, Bullock, he keeps saying the Prez is going to kill us all. But the Prez, he's got to do what he's told. Not much time before the elections, and his polls aren't good. So he needs a lot of last-minute advertising. Needs to keep the money pouring in."

"It's such a horror show. So many innocent dead."

"Face it, Lily, there's no such thing as reality anymore; reality's whatever we're told it is, until we're told something else. Me, I'm just trying to keep my head above water for two more years so I can retire."

"You don't even have a byline anymore."

"It's happened so fast . . . Ten years ago, we still stood for something."

"I'M GOING TO OWE YOU BIG FOR THIS ONE," TURK SAID, ON HIS cellphone from Jakarta.

"You already owe me," Yuri Ivanov said, glancing out his office window at the tankers anchored in Vladivostok harbor.

"A dickhead named Nachin Kulug killed a woman in Kalimantan –"

"That's not my territory –"

"Then flew back to Ulan."

"So what you want?"

"Find him."

"What do I get?"

"The names of six guys in Shali planning to blow up the post office."

Yuri sighed. "Fucking Chechens."

"Islam drives them crazy."

"I'll find what I can."

"I need to know where he is in Ulan. And I need pix."

"Be back to you."

"I just sent you info on the six guys."

"I just met a new girl. I'm in love."

"You've never been in love with anybody, Yuri. Except yourself."

"This one's different."

"Jesus, I hope so. May the good Lord love and protect you."

"I'll be back to you."

"Tonight."

"That's what I just said."

Liz watched Turk from across the kitchen table. "How'd you know about those Chechen guys?"

"Friend in DC."

"And this Russian guy you were talking to?"

"A few years ago, I helped the Russians recover a submersible in the Baltic. Back when our two countries were still friends . . . That's where I met him."

"You've got friends everywhere."

"That way I'm never lonely." This jarred in his head. "Actually, it's only since I met you I haven't been lonely."

"Don't depend on me." She grimaced. "To keep you alive."

"Only I can keep me alive. Maybe even I can't."

She held up her phone. "In Mongolian, the word Nachin means Falcon. And Kulug means Hero, a very brave man."

"Brave men don't kill women."

"People don't always live up to their names." She reached across the table and squeezed his arm. "Do we?"

"Why do you have to be so hard?"

She gripped his arm harder. "Ever been the sole survivor of an exploding gas platform?"

MAMA GAIA WAS LOUD, LARGE, VISCOUS, AND UNAPPEALING. LYLE didn't even want to be near her. She repulsed him, yes, that was the word. Then how come she'd had so many grateful students? People who loved her and came back to see her?

I don't want to be in this world, he thought. *Not anymore.*

Then remembered he wasn't going to be.

Ever since he'd released Trim for lack of evidence – it wasn't even that; he'd known in his gut that she hadn't killed Tom Hogan. She was too kind, too simple. Too openly affectionate. But Mama Gaia was another story: under all that cheery opiniated mass of pink, sweaty flesh, he sensed evil.

But portly as she was, she was definitely not the masked figure who'd descended the hospital stairwell in the security footage.

But did she know who it was?

"Did you ever discuss your hospital work with anyone?" he'd asked Trim when he and Cassidy had dropped her back at the Retreat.

She looked annoyed. "Sometimes."

"Like who?"

Lyle waited, watching and not watching the wide, log-walled room at Soul Fitness Retreat, the white lace curtains, the Russell Indian prints on the walls, the wide soft leather couches, the braided rugs.

"Gardiner," she said.

"Gardiner?"

"My husband back then."

"Where's he now?" Cassidy asked.

"Sweetwater graveyard. Car wreck. Four years ago." She watched them with steady, steely eyes.

"I'm truly sorry." Lyle answered.

"Ever talk to anyone else?" Cassidy asked softly.

"Well, of course Mama." Trim sat tightly, knees locked together, facing ahead, her exuberant sexuality gone. "After Gardiner died, I totally lost it. We'd been together fifteen years . . ." She glared at them. "Don't ever love."

"It's all we've got," Cassidy said.

"Those lonely nights I'd come home from the hospital – sometimes a patient had died, another nurse had broken down – and you knew you were skating on the edge of insanity – Mama'd listen, she kept me going . . ."

"THIS IS WHAT WE'RE GOING TO DO," LILY TOLD ROSS. WHEN SHE was done, he sat thinking a long time. The risk was enormous. An article in the *Times*, fallacious as it might be, could trigger a cascade of copycat negative news that could kill Rawhide.

It made no difference that it was false. Particularly if it came from the *Times*. And because it was false it might even win them another Pulitzer.

If he agreed, she would get back to Ian Hamilton. A relic, she'd called him. "From back when we had a real newspaper."

"You still say *we*."

"It still hurts." Lily shrugged. "That after all those years I gave them every bit of genius and hard work I had, loved them, loved what we did . . ."

Ross watched her face, impassive, though she was close to tears. "Nothing lasts forever."

"BACK TO YOU," YURI IVANOV SAID.

"You see my message, the six guys?"

"Three of them we know already. Two others are relatives. The sixth is a lone wolf. We'll find him."

"I'm sure you will."

"I sent you three photos of Nachin Kulug," Yuri said. "When he's in Ulan Bator, he stays at the Blue Sky, always the same room on the thirty-third floor, goes to the lounge every night to pick up a girl, or later at the Vegas Club downstairs. He's supposedly a mining engineer for the strip mines of coal being sent to China. But he's really just a small-time operator behind the scenes for the Chinese takeover of Mongolia. We Russians already have a 4,200-kilometer border with China. We don't want the Chinese taking over Mongolia and adding another 3,500 kilometers of border we have to worry about. So we don't like this guy."

"So why is Nachin doing this? If he's Mongolian?"

"Half Mongolian. Other half Chinese." Yuri paused. "He even has a daughter in university in China."

"Where?"

"Wuhan. You should go see this guy. You might learn a lot. But do it invisibly . . ."

"I'm always invisible, Yuri."

"*Дерьма* – bullshit. We most always know where you are."

"Your new girlfriend, she's a Chinese agent."

Yuri laughed. "It's always fun to talk, you and me."

"I can't believe how horrible, this war."

"Your senators saying you can win a nuclear war? What kind of crazy is that?"

"We all have to stop, turn back." Turk said.

"Turn back? After the Wall came down, *glasnost* and Gorbachev and all that . . . Our generals toured each other's missile sites, we shared strategic information, were open to each other . . . And all we wanted, us dumb Slavs, was to learn capitalism. Instead you guys stole everything you could."

"I'm as unhappy about it as you are."

"And we're at each other's throats again."

Turk nodded, as though Yuri could see. "Our war machines."

"But yours is twelve times bigger than ours."

"Funny thing," Turk added, "you guys are the most like us of any country I know."

"We don't want war. But this president of yours, he's always wanted wars. Maybe soon, he be gone?"

Another voice came on the line, in Russian. *"Da,"* Yuri said. "Turk, I got to go."

"Thank you both," Turk said. "May we all become friends again."

"*Дерьма*," the voice said. *Bullshit.*

LYLE DROVE TO THE TOP OF THE HILL, PARKED, AND LOOKED OUT over the prairie where dead grass stood bent and broken above the crusted snow, the sunset air crystalline, only the sun's coppery glow on the distant peaks. Funny to think this was his evening too, with night coming fast.

A week now he had, Doc said. Already sometimes he didn't know where he was, the pain was so atrocious. He tried to avoid the codeine they gave him because it made him even more fuzzy-headed. Because he was about to die, everything seemed crazy.

Growing up in Sweetwater there was a natural law: Do harm, and harm will be done to you. So nearly everyone avoided doing harm. Most people even avoided it out of natural goodness.

And the few perps would have done harm anyway. Most of them spent their entire lives seeking punishment. To fill their empty hearts.

But no matter how hard he tried, he hadn't found who killed Tom Hogan. He saw Tom now as he'd known him, a dirty kid with skinned knees and a big smile.

And some bastard killed him.

A week to live.

42

TOO CLOSE

THE VAST MONGOLIAN desert spread beyond the plane's wing to the far edges of the wind-scarred, empty earth.

"What are we going to do?" Liz said. "If we find him?"

"Nachin? Find out who paid him to kill Mrs. Sudup."

"You think he's going to tell?"

Ulan Bator rose before them out of the desert dusk. The windows of new skyscrapers gleamed in the fading sun. Beyond the new downtown, the miles of huts crouched over dirt streets under the bitter wind, and beyond them the tan and forested hills and endless steppes of central Asia.

The outside temperature was thirty-four below, according to a display in the arrivals hall. "For Ulan Bator this is a warm spell," Turk noted, to Liz's irritation.

He'd reserved them a suite at the Blue Sky Hotel, a tall skyscraper curved like a scimitar, a Mongolian sword. It had a huge bedroom and an adjoining living room so he could work while she slept – she'd given up worrying about his lack of sleep. Most nights she completely wore him out, so if he couldn't sleep after *that*, it wasn't her fault.

The window of the suite overlooked Sukhbaatar Square, and far beyond the vast ragged city, the dusty frozen outback of Ulan Bator.

Turk glanced at his watch. "We're not eating here."

She gave him a puzzled look. "Who talked about eating?"

"The food's okay here, but we're eating French."

"We came here to get Nachin. Not eat dinner."

"I'm hungry. We've been eleven hours in airplanes. We have a few hours free, so we're going to the Bistro Français. Food to feed the soul. Then back here for Nachin. According to Yuri, by then he'll be at the Blue Sky Lounge on the 23rd floor. And about ten p.m. he'll head down to the Vegas Club."

"According to Yuri?" she said.

"You're hungry too. Let's go."

It was a ten-minute walk across Peace Avenue and up Ikh Surguuli Street from the Blue Sky to the Bistro Français. "Almost like Paris," Turk exhaled. "They get their cheese and wine every week brought in by the French ambassador's plane."

It annoyed her, his innate awareness, natural self-assurance, ability to always make things work. "That's called corruption, isn't it?"

"Yeah, it's pretty cheesy." He grinned happily at her. "Though you haven't had the cheese yet . . ."

This infuriated her. "I looked at the online menu."

"You did not." He squeezed her hand. "But anyway, you may be right."

This annoyed her even more, the ease with which he'd agree, which dismissed her. "I don't think you're right, that this is how to do Nachin."

"Show me a better way."

She retreated, still angry. "There must . . ."

"Show me."

I hate you, she told him silently. *But damnit I love you too.*

IN THE PHOTOS Yuri had sent, Nachin was medium-height, slender, about forty-five, short-haired, an angular face and narrow mouth. He was easy to recognize when Liz and Turk got to the Blue Sky Lounge, ensconced in a lounge chair by the window, two cocktail glasses on the table beside him. He wore a wrinkled blue suit in the former Soviet style and had an unlit cigar in his mouth. He waved at a beautiful young waitress who silently took his order, and as she turned away, he slapped her ass.

A band was playing soft rock, fronted by a woman vocalist in a red dress. Liz and Turk took a table not far from Nachin and ordered Indian Tonics with cherries and ice. Beyond the window, Ulan Bator gleamed like a sea of diamonds. Headlights by the thousands slid like serpents through the streets; thousands of windows glared at the stars.

"Half of all Mongolians now live here," Turk said.

She shivered, and turned from watching Nachin to glance out the window. "It's so cold."

"In the old days, they lived in villages and pastured their herds in the mountains in summer, then brought them back to the village for the winter. Butchered half the herds each winter and lived off the meat, took the young ones back out to the mountains when the grass began to grow . . . Often a family had three hundred animals, a hundred horses . . . It's why the mountains are bare, so overgrazed . . ."

AFTER MIDNIGHT, Nachin followed the band downstairs to the Vegas Club. From a corner of the bar, Liz and Turk watched him while pretending to play cards and drinking more Indian Tonics with cherries and ice. Nachin ordered Mai Tais one after the other, ogled the women, and motioned to several, but they passed him by. He lit a cigar, put it out when asked, then relit it.

"He's not getting laid tonight," Liz said.

"Hey, there's always hope."

Liz scowled, took the elevator upstairs, and waited in the ice machine alcove twenty yards down the carpeted corridor from Nachin's room.

Turk played solitaire and drank another Indian Tonic till Nachin stumbled toward the elevators. "Coming up," Turk messaged Liz, and stepped after Nachin into the elevator.

It felt evil to stand in this shiny elevator with the bastard who'd killed Asmara Sudup, but Turk pretended to be half-asleep. The elevator stopped and Nachin stumbled out, halted to blow cigar smoke at the *No Smoking* sign, and weaved down the corridor.

Twenty feet behind, Turk followed him toward his room, astonished he wasn't watching his back. As Nachin pulled his keycard from his shirt pocket and slid it into the slot, Turk slipped up behind him, coshed him lightly on the right temple, and lifted him into the room and Liz shut the door behind them.

"Too easy," she whispered.

"Drunk. Doesn't expect danger here." Turk flex-cuffed and gagged Nachin and turned on his phone recorder. "Not a pro."

Nachin came awake, looking up at them in shock. "How's your head?" Turk said.

Nachin said nothing, surprise turning to fury in his eyes. He wrenched at his cuffs, twisted his body, and lay still.

"We're going to play a game," Turk said. "We're going to play that you're Asmara Sudup, and we're going to kill you."

Again the look of wide-eyed surprise. Nachin shook his head and tried to talk through his gag.

"You want to talk? We can do that. You have to promise not to call out, yell, anything."

Nachin nodded eagerly.

"Just to make sure," Turk added, "this lady here is Mrs. Sudup's best friend. She's going to hold this very sharp knife right over your pretty little prick, and if you talk too loud, she's going to cut it off. Then we let you bleed out. Understood?"

Nachin nodded, muttering through the gag.

Turk untied it. "Who paid you to kill Asmara Sudup?"

Nachin shook his head. "No English."

Turk smiled down at him. "Don't even try that. Or we'll do a little dick surgery, right now."

"What Asmara?"

"The lady you killed in her back yard on the Mahakam River. Unfortunately for you, there was a motion camera to see if a mongoose came to kill her chickens. Instead the camera got you. Who paid you?"

Nachin shook his head again. "Not know this lady."

"Go ahead," Turk said to Liz. "Cut his dick part way through. Get a towel first, for the blood."

"Wait!" Nachin panted. "Somebody called me. Told me. Five thousand dollars at start. Twenty more when done."

"That's too cheap, Nachin. You could face life – for twenty-five grand?"

"Because of Moonlight. They will kill her."

"Moonlight?"

"My daughter, Sarangerel. Name means Moonlight, in Mongolian."

"She's here?"

"Wuhan. The university . . ."

"Wuhan? Why?"

"They gave her free studies. Travel, apartment, money." Nachin swallowed. "Economics and languages. She speaks Mongolian, Mandarin, Russian, and English. She wants to make a lot of money."

Studying economics is not a good way to make money, Turk thought but didn't say.

"But," Nachin said, "they took away her social credits."

"Social credits?"

"What you get for being Party member. What she gets if she is good student, someone they can send back to Mongolia to promote friendship with China. Someone who understands international finance, can negotiate good deals for China – the Mongolian desert is full of coal and special metal for cellphones and solar cells. China wants it."

He said nothing, then, "Now they take away her travel permit, so she cannot even leave Wuhan." He tried to sit up, but laid back. "They said they would kill her."

"And that's why you killed Asmara Sudup?"

Nachin shook his head. "I know who did this. My job was, set it up."

Turk turned to Liz. "Cut it a bit, just across the top. So it bleeds . . ."

"No!" Nachin writhed and tried to sit up again. "I did."

"That's the last time, Nachin. Next time you lie, she cuts it off. *Your whole dick.* Then we wait a while for you to bleed out, or I cut your throat. Maybe I'll let you decide. And in the morning, the cleaning lady will find you. But no one will ever find us. Okay?"

Nachin sighed. "How you find me?"

"By your smell. You stink, Nachin. And you have ten seconds to tell us the whole thing. From beginning to end. If you want to save your prick."

"After you do what? To me?"

"After, we let you go. We could turn you in, but you've probably already paid off the law here in Ulan Bator, so you have nothing to fear from us. And the Indonesians were told to not give a damn about Mrs. Sudup. It's just," Turk said, nodding at Liz, "like I said –"

"Best friend?"

"And we want to know *why*. And *who*."

He watched Nachin think about this, try to decide if they were going to kill him anyway. If they were, there was no point in talking. If he told them everything, there was a better chance they'd let him go. If he didn't talk, there was a much greater chance they'd cut his throat. Particularly if this woman holding that sharp knife over his dick – which was smaller now, from being so scared – had indeed been Mrs. Sudup's best friend . . . but how could she be? She clearly wasn't Indonesian.

"They call me," Nachin said, "but no number to call back. In my mailbox, send directions. To this lady's house, when to go." He was quiet, then said, "I tried to do it fast."

"She choked on her own blood. You didn't do it fast."

"No. Not true. I watch her die."

"How many people you killed, in your life?"

"She only one. Ever."

"Who else you work for?" Liz said.

"Only this voice."

"How do you get paid?"

"Bitcoin, of course."

"Where you from, Nachin?"

"I am born in the mountains, near China. But grow up here."

"And it's always this voice. No one else?"

Nachin shook his head energetically.

"Where does he send you?"

"China, sometimes. But most in Myanmar or Mongolia."

"Always the same voice?" Turk repeated.

"Always. Can I go now?"

"Soon as you tell us your daughter's address."

"Moonlight? I not know. They have her –"

Turk turned to Liz. "Cut it off."

"No!" Nachin wailed. "Is real, what I say. Please not hurt her –"

"How do we find her, Nachin? Maybe we can help her . . ."

"You would promise?"

Turk thought about it.

"Yes," Liz said. "We will help her. Otherwise we cut off your dick. Then we kill you."

Again Turk watched Nachin try to decide. "I have no choice," he said finally.

"We will help her," Turk said.

"She lives in the student quarters at the university, Building Five, floor nine, room one thousand seven-two. She with three other girls. But you must not go there, you must meet her invisibly. Every day she must come back from her work, from China Construction Bank, by Bayi Road and Guangba Road."

"How do we recognize her?"

"In my wallet is her photo."

"What should we tell her?" Liz said.

"That I am sending you to help her. Tell her the name I call her –"

"What name is that?"

"*Roo*. For *roo caixan*: Beauty." Nachin licked dry lips. "Moonlight is not like me. She is a good person . . ."

Turk tied up Nachin's gag again and flex-cuffed one of his already-cuffed wrists to the metal bedframe. From his pocket, he unfolded a one-page *Wanted* sheet in English he had downloaded from the Kalimantan Police, showing Nachin in the motion camera as he turned away from Asmara Sudup's body, knife still in his hand.

Back in their own room, Turk called Inspector General Wantiko, the South Kalimantan Regional Police Chief who had told him to stay in Jakarta after Asmara Sudup had been killed. "Sorry it's a little late," he said.

"Where are you? I ordered you not to leave!"

"I'm in Ulan Bator. I have Asmara Sudup's killer. He's named Nachin Kulug, and he's cuffed to a bedframe in Ulan Bator. Room 3309 of the Blue Sky Hotel. Next, I'm calling the Deputy Commissioner of the Criminal Police here in Ulan Bator. He will have Nachin in custody in about twenty minutes. I'm sure he'll be happy to extradite him, providing you agree that Nachin goes to jail for a long time. In the morning, I'll email you all the background plus a recording of my interrogation of Mr. Kulug . . ."

"How did you do this?"

"There are still many unanswered questions. Mr. Kulug was hired by someone but he doesn't know who. He has a daughter studying at Wuhan University. They were going to kill her if he refused the job –"

"Wuhan?"

"– the Mahakam platform . . ."

"Yes?" Wantiko's voice deepened.

"Mrs. Sudup got killed because she saw the Wuhan sub refuel at the Pertamina dock. After it blew up the Mahakam platform."

"So a connection is possible?"

"Very."

"Then, my friend," Wantiko said, "you are on to something big."

"You have your ways to question Mr. Kulug. I think you can learn a lot. Please let me know."

"Are you watching your back?"

"Always." As he shut off, Turk wondered if General Wantiko was just warning him, or threatening him?

"Do me a favor?" he said to Liz.

"Maybe."

"Find us the next flight to Wuhan."

"Jesus, when are you going to stop being digitally impaired?"

"Maybe never."

"It's because of Moonlight? You want to go to Wuhan, talk to her?"

"We're going to drop in on her unannounced. Then there's a sub base I want to visit."

43

MOONLIGHT

HER FACE in Nachin's scratched wallet photo was absolutely beautiful in that easy Mongolian way. Oval face, high cheekbones, black hair, black eyebrows, black eyes, a wide full mouth with smile lines on both sides. So beautiful that Liz felt sorry for her, for the sorrow her beauty could bring her.

Liz recognized her easily as she walked quickly along Bayi Road in Wuhan, and followed her into the Wise Happiness teashop. Moonlight wore a faded down jacket over a tan cotton shirt and pants and black running shoes. She was blowing on the top of her teacup while using it to warm her hands.

"Sarangarel," Liz said as she sat opposite her.

The girl glanced up, wide-eyed, and sat back. "*Wǒ bù míngbái.*"

"Your father Nachin says to call you *Roo* . . . Don't jump up, don't look around. Smile, like I'm an old friend."

"*Tīng bù dǒng!*"

"Don't give me that. You speak English."

"Here too many people." Moonlight glanced around nervously. "Who you are?" She was, Liz thought, just like her name: flashing dark eyes and black hair against a golden face, the moon shining through bare trees.

Liz squeezed her hand, amazed at how slim and strong it felt. "Nachin wants me to get you out of Wuhan."

The girl's eyes widened. "I am so afraid. They have cameras everywhere. Know everyone's face. Follow everyone."

Liz had a sudden image of human-size cameras wandering the city and hunting people down. "I'll wait outside, forty meters left along the sidewalk toward Guangba Road. Count to sixty, then follow me. We turn left at the corner. In seventy meters by the curb is a red Qoros sedan. A man is sitting in front. He is my partner; you can trust him. You and I get in back. Then we can talk."

"No."

"There's no surveillance –"

"There is always surveillance."

"We checked. No cameras." Liz stood. "If you want to get out of Wuhan, wait a minute, then follow me."

Moonlight's black eyes blazed, her face pinched and watchful. "You will not steal me, drive away?"

"Of course not."

When Liz turned left at the corner, the girl was still behind her, pretending to gaze in a dress shop window. Liz opened the Qoros' curbside back door and went to the other side. The girl dropped in beside her but shrank back in fear when she saw Turk in front.

"Hi, Sarangeral," he said. "We're going to get you out."

"Cannot."

"Why not go home to Mongolia?" Liz said. "Teach economics at the University of Science and Technology? Work in the Ministry of Finance?"

Moonlight looked at her, surprised. "They will come for me."

"Who?"

"Who do you think?"

"Not in Ulan Bator . . ."

"They not let me leave China."

Liz thought of Mrs. Sudup. "Have they asked you about Indonesia?"

"What about Indonesia?"

"The submarine?"

Moonlight glanced out the window. "What submarine?"

"C'mon, Sarangarel – you know *what* submarine."

The girl faced down, fingers fidgeting in her lap. "My father, he asked me . . ."

"Asked you what?"

"If anyone here ask me about a submarine."

"Did they?"

The girl was clearly scared, fingers twisting, lips trembling. "I do not know these things." She looked up at Liz. "You want them to kill me?"

"Who?"

"Same."

"The ones who told your father to go there?"

"Maybe . . . same."

"Your father's been arrested," Liz said.

Moonlight shivered. "Where?"

"Ulan Bator."

"Can you . . ?"

"Can we what?"

"I can perhaps help him . . . I am too afraid here."

Liz felt the heaviness of the moment, a refusal to lie. "We can."

"We will," Turk said.

"But they watch the airports, the border. Check everyone."

"Meet us at the train station, the Jining line, at ten tonight. I'll have your ticket."

"Jining only? That is not the border."

"I'll tell you more when we get there."

"Now tell us about the sub," Liz said. "It's your last chance, or we leave here without you."

The girl nodded, deep in thought, long black hair like a curtain down both sides of her high-boned face, a quick breathing of her small-breasted chest, her writhing hands. "My father asked me."

"Asked you what?"

"If a sub come back to Wuhan."

"And when was that?" Turk said.

"Some days ago."

"You told your father?"

"He call me twice. Said he had to know. So I check and tell him." Moonlight looked down, then up at Turk. "Can I still go, with you?"

"Of course." Liz smiled.

"I will take my backpack. Like I am going to class."

"You have to leave everything else."

Moonlight shrugged. "Better in Mongolia with nothing than here with much."

"IT'S ME," Anna said.

St. Miles rolled over in his silk sheets and peered at the clock: 04:37. So barely six-thirty a.m. in Moscow. "Don't you ever sleep?"

"Not when there is fun going on," she said, plying on the accent.

"What fun?"

"Send the boy, or boys, out of the room: it's almost time to pull the trigger."

He glanced around the room. "There are no *boys*."

"Good for you. Time to think sharp. You watching crude?"

He peered at one of his bedroom screens. "Brent is $86.23."

"Good for you. When we make our move, we don't want to alert the markets. So you must get into as many different markets as possible. Then once I know for sure which way to go – up or down – throw every penny you have at it, high a margin as possible. When the news hits the markets, crude will take off or drop like a stone. And you'll be even richer, no? When I'll call you, be ready to go."

"Call me? *No!* I want to know *now*," he said, but she'd shut down.

He slammed the phone onto the Persian rug beside the bed and lay back among his silky pillows. *She's cock-teasing me.*

He felt a spasm of fear. *Maybe I shouldn't do this deal.*

A **COLD DRIZZLE** COATED TURK'S CHEEKBONES WITH A GREASY mist. The Yangtze River was a vast, fast current of smoky wavelets that stank of burnt rubber, sulfur, diesel, and sewage. Arc lights of the Wuhan Naval Shipyard on the far shore glittered across its oily, roiling surface. The city's roar and clatter sounded faraway, muted.

The *huáchuán*, a little sampan he'd liberated from its rope tether on the south bank of the Yangtze, was infernally difficult to manage because he had to face forward using the single wooden paddle instead of facing backwards and using two oars to pull.

He thought of the kayak he'd borrowed days ago on the Sorrento coast, when he'd paddled to the Russian yacht, climbed aboard, and almost got caught.

But this was harder. To recon the Naval Shipyard, find the sub, and take some pix. Probably impossible.

Thinking of the kayak in Italy, he slid the wooden oar from the oarlock and paddled, two strokes to one side, then two to the other. The *huáchuán* moved faster, rustling a thin wake across the pale-flecked, swirling water.

Asmara Sudup had taken photos of the sub at the Pertamina dock on the Mahakam River, put them on a memory stick, and given them to him. When Nachin's employer – whoever it was – found out, they had Nachin kill her before she could tell anyone else. And now Nachin was in jail in Ulan, and he and Liz had found Moonlight. She who couldn't get out of China.

He reached the first docks of the Naval Shipyard and waited in the shadow of a moored ship till two barges passed, diesels thrumming, their wakes rocking his *huáchuán*, their bow and stern lights fading into the fog.

And *there* it was, the little sub, just as Moonlight had said, tethered in a drydock halfway down the left-hand wharf. Above it, a single arc light flickered through the mists. Either the sub had traveled from the Mahakam along Vietnam from port to port all the way to Shanghai and up the Yangtze to here, the Wuhan Naval Shipyard, or a mother ship had picked it up and brought it. And there was plenty of Chinese shipping along the coast – they *owned* that narrow sea where one-third of the world's maritime shipping passed through.

It was astonishing he'd found it in plain sight. If he had used this sub to blow the platform, Turk reflected, he'd have cut it up and melted it down long ago. Or sunk it somewhere deep in the South China Sea. Did they think no one would come here looking, eventually, for answers?

He paddled closer, wavelets slapping his hull. No one seemed to be patrolling this part of the drydock or on guard near the sub. He sidled the *huáchuán* toward the drydock's pitted concrete wall, the current sloshing along it.

He took a few pix and paddled closer. It worried him that no one seemed on guard. A trap? But if the sub was unlocked, he might get inside.

Even if no one was guarding, there'd be cameras. The little Wi-Fi's – China produced millions a month, sold them all over the world. He'd have a quick look anyway, then make a break for the far shore where Liz waited in the rental car. He tied the *huáchuán* to a rusty O-ring and stepped onto the dock.

Pebbly concrete, wet and slippery underfoot. The sub looked too low in the water, the gangplank tilting down, as if it were sinking. Or perhaps there were people waiting inside. He took a few photos of the deck and hull, and checked his perimeters.

Still no one.

He descended the gangplank and eased open the hatch. A light flickered on inside: tarnished steel, a tiny cockpit, a yellow instrument panel, and the central shaft to a lower exit hatch. It exhaled a warm, fetid air against the oily downriver wind.

He climbed in, closed the top hatch, and switched on his head-lamp. Keeping carefully to the sides of the cockpit, he took a forensic fingerprint kit from his backpack and began methodically to apply the magnetic applicator to the locations in the sub most likely to have retained prints, particularly the tiny crew quarters and the edges of the lower exit hatch. As the fingerprints began to show, he took a photo of each, then lifted it with print tape, put a plastic strip over the tape, and stored it in the waterproof case.

From another case he removed several forensic DNA swabs and began to pull samples from the most likely locations – the tiny toilet, instrument panel, edges of the two cockpit seats, and any other areas where human skin might have touched. He opened several other swabs and set them out to collect e-DNA, the background DNA that could be used to identify people almost as well as a direct sample.

He then shot photos of the instrument panel and interior and eased open the hatch. No one in sight. He climbed out, shut the hatch, recrossed the river, and tied the *huáchuán* where he'd found it.

"Too easy," he said to Liz as he dropped into the passenger seat.

She drove back across the Yangtze Bridge. "Stop here," Turk told her, at a brightly lit Sinopec station and convenience store. She pulled in and filled the tank while he sent the pix of the fingerprints and sub interior to Ross, then called him. "You get them?"

"Coming through now. What you want me to do with them?"

"Keep them safe. I'll be getting them analyzed, but if you don't hear from me . . ."

"I better –" Ross snapped.

"I've got swabs too but don't dare send them. I'll keep them till I can get them analyzed."

"Imagine, if we can prove this."

"I'm beginning to think we can." Turk shut off, eased back in his seat, and clicked the belt. "Let's go meet Moonlight. And grab our train."

As they drove away from the river back into the throbbing city, he had the sudden fear that someone had seen what he'd done, the cameras that followed everyone. That someone was waiting for the perfect time to strike.

"I USED THE N-WORD," Ian Hamilton rasped. "So they're sacking me."

"For what?" Lily put the phone on speaker. "Why?"

"Article I wrote eighteen years ago. I interviewed a black power guy who used it all the time. I didn't think anything of it. None of us did. I quoted what he said. It was common, back then. All those rappers . . ."

"Even now, guys like Kendrick Lamar, they say it all the time –"

"The *Times* kindergarten has gone off the deep edge, Lily. It's horrifying to watch. I call friends who've been there for years, and they're just trying to keep their heads down, plus all the reporters and editors who've gone elsewhere, and they all say, 'Oh my God.'"

She thought a moment. "So you'll lose your retirement?"

"A good part of it."

"You want to get them back?"

"Sure." He sighed. "There's no way . . ."

"What about this: a negative report, intended to move the market against a company? Give it to the *Times*, let them run it and drive down that company's stock, then it's proven wrong and they have to do a retraction."

"The *Times* doesn't *do* retractions, you know that. Not real ones."

"This time they'll have to," she said. "They'll have egg all over their face."

"What if other people pick it up, run with it? Too much could cause damage . . ."

He was right, she realized. Too much damage *was* the danger. If the *Times* did run with it, could its impact be limited to a quick stock dip? Just enough to freak Rawhide's enemies into going short and start the whole downward cascade till Ross dove in with a stock buyback and announced new supply contracts with major distributors?

THE TRAIN CHUGGED SLOWLY OUT OF WUHAN'S INDUSTRIAL wasteland, then swung north toward Jining, laying down a blanket of coal smoke behind it.

Turk stared at the huge buildings flickering past, millions of families crammed into concrete towers. "Amazing, that just a couple miles from here's the bio warfare lab that killed millions of people and ruined the economies of many countries."

"And got away with it," Liz snapped.

"And isn't it amazing," he added ironically, "they had so few deaths? China with its massively polluted cities where nearly a billion people live crammed into tiny apartments, often three generations of one family . . . And their economy took off while most of the world went under?"

"They made that virus on purpose," Moonlight said. "To kill people."

"Who said?" Liz asked.

"People here who know, they say it."

"Who?"

"The ones who made it. I speak good Mandarin. But when I'm in a meeting about Mongolia with Chinese officials, the moment something important comes up, they shift to a dialect they think I can't follow. But I can . . . That was when I understand they are saying the truth to each other. And they are just using me. As a way, how you say, *khyamd zarna*, to sell Mongolia down the river?"

"Down the Tula," Turk said.

"It is full of sewage now, the Tula."

"The sacred Tula, whose waters fill Lake Baikal?"

"Sometimes people don't know I understand them. And when I look at the economic impacts of this Wuhan virus on Mongolia, I realize the scientists, some of them, they knew this virus was created here in Wuhan, not by accident, but to kill people. They know the Americans – you people – paid partly to make this virus, but did not expect it would be used against you . . ."

"To the Chinese, if you're not Chinese, what's the word they use?"

"*Yěmán rén.*"

"Barbarians."

The train's "First Class" compartment was tiny and stank of mold, grease, and other even less appealing substances. The single bathroom at the end of the car was filthy. The toilet had no seat, was stained with feces, and the trap door at the bottom hung open, the wooden ties flitting beneath.

Turk watched the eroded countryside pass by. "From Wuhan to Jining South Station is eight hours. We have a wait there, then it's six more hours to the Mongolian border. But there's a stop at Erlian, about twelve kilometers before the border. We'll get out there and go overland."

"Overland?" Moonlight gasped. "Impossible. It is desert with electric fences. They watch from satellites."

"There'll be someone," Turk said, "to take us across."

"You know this person?"

"No. But I'll find him."

IT WAS DARK WHEN THE TRAIN CROSSED THE ENDLESS CONCRETE suburbs of Jining and pulled into South Station. Turk bought three tickets to Erlian, leaving at 1:07 a.m., reaching Erlian at 6:50.

It was another dank "First Class" compartment. Turk took a top bunk. It was skinny and too short, and smelled of old sheepskins. Liz and Moonlight took the bottom two.

"You and I can get through the border, no problem," Liz said to Turk. "But for Moonlight, she could climb up there." She pointed to the metal ceiling panels. "Before the soldiers come through to check the compartments."

"Oh no!" Moonlight said quickly. "They open them. Check every ceiling."

At dawn they left the train in Erlian. It was bitterly cold and windy, the red desert frozen in the sunrise. In the distance, toward the border, lines of gigantic windmills stood in lines, their blades not turning. Dust danced in pirouettes down the sullen streets and swirled around the stolid concrete buildings. When you looked north you could see Mongolia, but it seemed impossible to get there.

"We must go back," Moonlight whispered, hugging her coat to her chest.

"Nah," Turk said. "We're cool."

"It is not cool here, is very cold. Is that what you say?"

Turk smiled down at her. Already she seemed like a little sister. "Tonight we'll be in Ulan."

"You will know how?"

"He always does," Liz said.

On a side street they found a run-down café with a dusty parking lot filled with trucks. Dust devils spun around them like dervishes; the wind cut to the bone.

They pushed open the double glass doors and went inside. The air was thick with wet cooking smells and cigarette smoke. Truck drivers in leather and canvas coats hunched over tables of tea and rice, their dark Mongol faces tanned even darker by sun and wind.

They sat at a table in the back and ordered lamb stew, rice, and tea. After a few moments of silence when the truck drivers at the other tables watched these three strangers, the conversations recommenced in a mix of languages.

Turk checked them out for a while, then went to one table and leaned down. "Speak English?"

The man glanced up. "Little bit," he said with a thick accent.

"I am looking for someone from Mongolia. Going to UB."

"Not we. We south."

"Is someone here," Turk asked him, "going to UB?"

The man nodded his chin at another table, of three men in bulky tan coats with gnarled dark hands and tough faces. "May I ask a question?" Turk said to them.

They watched him, silent. "English," one said, older than the others.

"You from Mongolia?"

They watched him. The older one nodded.

Turk looked back at Liz and Moonlight, then at the man. "We want to get across."

The man grinned. "Take the train."

"That woman, black hair, is Mongolian. She needs to get home."

"Chinese want to keep her?" The man watched Moonlight for a while, then turned back to Turk. "Expensive."

"In your truck, what are you carrying?"

"Chinese tools. Sadly, Mongolia does not make our own."

"China wants to steal Mongolia."

The man shrugged.

"In your truck, is room?"

"Perhaps."

Turk took out five hundred-yuan notes. "That is for the border guard, if you need it." He took out five more. "And this will be for you, after we cross over."

The man looked at him through the smoke of the cigarette he held between a thumb and forefinger. He waved the smoke away. "Not enough."

Turk stood. "I'll find someone else . . ."

"It's not good to advertise that you are looking."

Turk nodded, pretending to realize his error. "So?"

"For me, one thousand yuan. But it must look as if you hide on truck, and I not know." He took a pinched puff of cigarette, squinting against the smoke. "In case you get caught."

44

HIDEOUT

HIDDEN AMONG hundreds of larger coal trucks at the back of the parking lot, the man's old red Dongfeng had rusty fenders, broken mirrors, and worn tires. It smelled of cold grease, diesel, metal fatigue, and frozen dust.

The man unlocked the rear door, glanced around quickly, and nodded with his chin. "Go in!"

Inside smelled of coal dust and a sweet revolting odor that might have been rotten meat. Large cardboard crates labeled in Chinese and Mongolian Cyrillic were stacked to the ceiling, a crawl space between them.

"Money now," the man said.

"Not till Mongolia," Turk said.

Moonlight said something rapid in Mongolian. The man inclined his head, as if reconsidering.

"I asked him how we know you not turn us in," Moonlight said.

"Money now," the man repeated.

"Tell him," Turk told her, "then we'll turn *him* in." He held up his phone and replayed what he had recorded in the café, of Turk negotiating with him. "Tell him, he keeps us safe, we keep him safe." He yanked the wad of yuan from his pocket. "This will all be yours," he said to the man, "once we reach Dzlilyn Ude."

The man gave Turk a black look. "Takes long time, the border. You will be very cold."

"Then you better go fast," Turk answered, turning to Moonlight to translate. "Tell him you are needed by the Mongolian government. That you must return."

The man listened, then glared at them savagely. "After the border is Dzlilyn Ude. Train station. I leave you there." He hopped down and slammed the back doors.

"Okay," Turk said, "let's make ourselves comfortable."

"Maybe," Moonlight hissed, "they will shoot us."

"Nah." Turk grinned. "Bullets are expensive."

Squeezing through the crawl space between the piled crates, they squirmed to the front. "We'll build a wall," Turk said.

"One of the other men called him Chuluu," Moonlight said. "That is not good."

"Why?" Turk smiled, trying to be upbeat.

"Means Stone. Not a good name."

Liz felt the stone on her heart. *Why are we doing this?*

"Not too late," Moonlight added, "go back to Wuhan. Be safe."

"It *is* too late," Liz said.

"We open truck, walk to railroad station, very quick."

Turk took the wad of yuans from his pocket and held out a handful. "Go back, if you want. But you will never be safe."

"No matter where, I will never be safe."

"You will be safe in Mongolia." Turk began shoving aside the huge crates. "We're going to be like kids, build a hideout. Where the frontier guards won't find us."

"Unless Chuluu. He tells them."

Rust pinholes in the walls let in a feeble light. In the far end behind the cab was a pile of sheepskins that had recently been stripped of meat. Chunks of black rotting flesh stuck to them and stank with the same sweet odor. Gobi wind shook the truck and hailed it with sand, and wailed through holes in the floor, freezing their feet.

"If we get hungry," Turk said, "we can always chew these skins."

"Not funny!" Liz snapped.

"Not to worry."

"I always worry. That's why I'm still alive."

"Me also," Moonlight said. "Always worry."

"Let's make ourselves at home." Turk spread out the sheepskins and dragged crates to block off the front. "It's going to be a long day."

HOW MANY TIMES HAD DURVON ST. MILES TOLD HIMSELF HE'D BE crazy to spend another rainy October in London? Anywhere else – St. Lucia, Virgin Gorda, even St. Barts – he'd only be four hours later than London. The London markets opened at eight, four a.m. British Virgin Islands time. No problem.

But here he still was, in London.

In London the rain came down sideways, sometimes almost horizontal. Like that Beatles song about getting a tan standing in the English rain. But there was a reason why he stayed. Boys will be boys.

Just not enough in the tropics. Hard to find more than one at a time. Pretty soon you're churning up the same dead fish. See them once, never again: only way to do it.

Anna would be calling. With a tip that could make him even richer. So he could do this Ukraine cluster bomb deal in Sudan. Before someone else did.

When you thought about it, he'd told his pug Winston, humans love war far more than peace. To which Winston had sniffled and looked at St. Miles' pocket for a treat. "Only thing people love more than love is killing."

If people wanted to kill each other, who was he to stand in their way?

But he had to stay in London to jump on Anna's deal instantly. Not waiting for the clouds to clear over some volcano in BVI.

He wasn't going to admit he was getting a little annoyed with her. Three days since she'd promised to call. To go short or long and maybe make a billion. But if he bet wrong, it would take everything he had.

Why was she doing this? She saw angles in the futures market, didn't have the money to make the full bets herself, turned him on to it, and took her fifteen percent.

Soon she'd have enough money she wouldn't need him anymore.

If he felt annoyed, that meant she was slighting him. And that made him annoyed at himself, that he'd allowed anyone to slight him. Just because he needed money to reverse the losses he'd had and be able to close the cluster bomb deal.

You put in a hundred million and I'll make you three hundred million. In less than a week.

That's what she'd said. And she was going to let him know which way. Up or down.

Amazing that he could make more in a day of trading than ten thousand people made in their lives. Why he'd soon be *Lord* Durvon St. Miles. And a lot of people on both sides in Sudan who didn't have cluster bombs would soon have them. Straight from Ukraine. All the latest American tools of death.

Wasn't that democracy? Equal opportunity?

"YOU'RE STABBING AN OLD FRIEND IN THE BACK," SAID THE president's man, Nathan Coldmire.

Ross almost laughed but held it. Whatever Coldmire wanted, it could be dangerous. "Really, Nathan, how is that?"

"The president's gone out on a limb for you. The Agency, the markets, your lenders. And you keep pushing this conspiracy theory about him and nuclear war . . ."

"The Agency? He told them to get me."

"Look, this is complicated. But we think there's a way out. We need to talk."

"Talk? You guys have done so many evil things against us. You turned your media against us, the markets, pressured our insurers to drop us, sent the FBI and IRS after me and the company, hit us with

SEC charges – *fraudulent* federal charges specifically to drive our stock down, screw us with the banks, told all the social media zombies to target us. And you want to *talk?*"

"You're taking too much at face value –"

"Why'd you guys do it, Nathan?"

"Do *what?*"

"Try to take me down. What was *he* getting out of it?"

"You're hallucinating. Because of your bullshit, our polls are going to hell – why'd you leak that report?"

"You've destroyed Ukraine, and peace among nations. Ever lived through a nuclear war? No one ever will, even with your White House bomb shelter. Not that they'd let you in."

"So what else you going to do to us?" Coldmire said.

Sometimes you could make an opponent even more fearful, defeat him more easily, by a relaxed threat. "I don't need to *do* anything. You've done it to yourselves. And to all the rest of us."

SEEN THROUGH THE RUST HOLES IN THE TRUCK'S SIDES, THE Gobi Desert expanded forever, flat, frozen, arid, and empty. The air inside their truck hideout stank frigidly of dead sheep. In the cardboard crates, the power tools rattled and clanked in tune with the bumps in the road.

The truck slowed, tires wailing, muffler clattering. Turk peered out a pinhole. "The border."

Liz's feet were freezing, her ankles numb. *I should never have fallen for this*, she thought. *A Chinese jail is no place to grow old.*

"Lots of traffic ahead," Turk added. "Empty coal trucks headed home. It's how China's fighting global warming – they reduce domestic coal mining and are strip-mining Mongolia."

To Liz the whole world seemed confusing and dangerous, and she cursed herself for being here. She scowled at Turk: *because of him.*

But no, that wasn't true. How many times had she told him, *I will find the bastards that blew up the platform*. He'd rescued her from the Central Park kidnappers. She could've been killed, *would've* been, but

Turk had saved her, when the Jakarta Police and CIA were doing nothing. She needed to remember, have confidence in Turk, stop disbelieving.

She'd survived the exploding platform and the Jakarta Police, the damn Agency, the hit-and-run driver, even Central Park. And now, getting Moonlight home was part of finding the bastards.

So she should stop complaining.

For hours, the truck eased forward, braked, and shut off. A few minutes later it would start up, edge forward, and shut down again. Then it halted, engine idling, Chinese voices in the cab and around them. "They're here," Moonlight whispered.

The back doors squealed open. Sharp Chinese voices, Chuluu arguing back. The voices climbed into the truck, a light flashing down the crawl space.

"What are they saying?" Liz whispered.

"Border guards. Want Chuluu to take everything out."

More argument echoed from the back of the truck. Finally just two voices, Chuluu and one guard. "Chuluu telling him too much trouble to take everything out. Guard says then he must pay fine . . ." After a moment she added, "He is paying him."

The guard and Chuluu stepped down from the rear of the truck. The doors groaned shut. A few minutes later the truck revved and jerked forward, ran in low gear for a few hundred yards and stopped again.

More voices, now in Mongolian.

"Home!" Moonlight whispered. "You saved me!"

FROM DZLILYN UDE, THE TRAIN TOOK ELEVEN HOURS TO ULAN Bator, the endless sparse brown landscape flitting past the dusty window. It had been a day and night since they'd met Chuluu, and now it was day again. The compartment was warm and welcoming and they soon climbed into their bunks.

As Turk watched the desert roll past, he tried to understand the wider meanings of what he was learning. If this sub in Wuhan *had* blown up the platform, was China also behind attempts to kill Liz? Could the Chinese somehow abduct Moonlight from Mongolia?

When the Mongols attacked a city, the city had two choices: One, open the gates and hope the damage would be limited to raping, stealing, and taking men for more war. Or two, fight back and eventually lose – because the Mongols always won – and everyone would be killed, most of the women and girls, even the little ones, first raped, many times.

Every country at war is the same.

This was bad shit, but you had to think about it. If you wanted to make a better world.

BEFORE THEY REACHED UB, Turk turned on his phone and had Moonlight repeat what she knew about the Wuhan sub. "It will make a difference in your father's arrest," he told her, "if you tell us everything." When she hesitated, he added, "If you don't, you put him in danger under Mongolian and Indonesian law – you know that."

"It makes him look like he was part of it. He was not."

"That's why you have to tell the truth."

"My father was sent to Indonesia not to kill the woman. He was sent before that, to wait for the submarine to come upriver to the Pertamina dock, then call a number in Wuhan, leave a message."

"But he killed her." Turk said.

"That was after. When they learn she gave you a picture. They had to get the phone, erase it."

"How did they know she'd given it to me?"

"Didn't say."

"Are they Chinese? If the Chinese wanted to track the sub, why not use their own navy?"

"My father is Mongolian, and Chinese. If he is arrested, Chinese will be invisible. They have no risk . . . But like my father say, if he not kill that woman, I will be taken."

"For how long?" Liz said.

"Forever. Because I am killed." She gave them a smile one gives the uninitiated, the naïve and credulous. "If you have daughter, wouldn't *you* kill to save her life?"

"So tell us more," Liz said, "about the virus."

The girl stiffened. "I already did."

"It will make a difference for your father," Turk said.

"I only know that some of the officials said this, that the P4 laboratory was the one who made the virus. That is only four kilometers from where I have been living. These Chinese scientists are proud of these words, *gain of function* – working with the Americans to make the virus better at killing people." She swallowed. "Is true. Is no doubt, China makes this on purpose. In Mongolia, two thousand people die. In the world, how many?"

They took a taxi from the train station to Sukhbaatar Square and the Blue Sky Hotel. Turk rented two adjoining rooms and propped a chair against Moonlight's corridor door. It was good to be out of the truck, but no matter how many showers they took, they couldn't wash off the dead sheep smell.

"Tonight we're going to eat French food," Turk said. "And tomorrow I'll call the Deputy Commissioner of the Criminal Police. They will come and decide how to protect you."

"My family," Moonlight said, "I must call them."

"Not till tomorrow. Till you're safe with the police."

The deputy commissioner and his staff arrived at 08:00 next morning. "You will be a good witness to have," he told Moonlight as she slung her backpack over one shoulder, hugged Liz and Turk, and followed him to the elevators.

"I kind of worry," Liz said after she left, "what will happen."

Turk took her in his arms, happy they were alone again. "The commissioner will be delighted with what she tells him about the Wuhan sub, and about the Chinese framing her father and not letting her leave. In Mongolia they worry about China. The commissioner can gain power just by what he reveals, or chooses not to."

"What would you do," Liz said, "if you had to kill someone or else your daughter would be killed?"

"I don't have a daughter."

"If you did?"

"Either way, it's horrible."

"YOUR KENT POWER HACKERS," ISAIAH SAID, HIS WORDS delayed by the secure connection, "we shut them down. Tracked them, as I told you, to a rogue Chinese company working out of Malaysia."

"I remember."

"But when we moved against them, they weren't there, never existed except digitally. But we managed to follow that trail to Cyprus, then . . ." Isaiah sighed. "Hell, it's not who you think."

"Who I *think?*"

"We stayed with them till we got to the States. Then we ran into a wall we couldn't get through. They vanished."

"The States?" Ross jumped out of his chair. "That's nuts! What's the connection?"

"That's what we're going to find out."

DEFCON 2

C HECKING OUT of the Blue Sky the next morning, Turk was shocked to see Moonlight's photo on the front page of *Onoodor* on the counter. "Who is that?" he asked the clerk.

The clerk glanced at the newspaper headline, "That is a Mongolian woman just back from China. About how they imprison her. How China want to take over Mongolia just like they did Inner Mongolia, just like Tibet. Very brave, this young woman."

"Is she in danger?"

The clerk puffed out his chest. "Not in Mongolia. China wants to own us, but they afraid war. War make them look bad."

"I never thought we'd get her out," Liz said as they sat in UB's Chinggis Khaan Airport waiting for the seven-hour MIAT flight to Frankfurt.

"We said we would."

"A promise is a promise?"

"Even to a killer."

"IT'S NOT TOO LATE," NATHAN COLDMIRE SAID, "TO MAKE A DEAL."

Ross wanted to hurl the phone against his office wall. "What you got in mind?"

"You think we've been part of this move to take you down –"

"I *know* you have, Nathan. You and the president and the people he works for."

"That's a false narrative. You should drop it. Look –"

"I've got five calls waiting, Nathan. What you want?"

Coldmire sighed. "We can tell people to back off. And there's billions of Ukraine money we can use to get you reparations . . ."

"You're going to bring my dead people back to life?"

"People die all the time, get over it. And maybe your platform *was* at fault."

"You know it wasn't," Ross snapped.

A short silence. "Okay, we can also offer interest-free debt relief, and maybe a back-door buy of your stock to drive it up. All that crude you were going to refine in Wyoming –"

"Before somebody blew up our cracker –"

"– we'll buy it for the National Petroleum Reserve –"

"You want to tell that to the families of the dead?"

"Stop dramatizing," Coldmire said. "We're thinking globally here. Who knows *who's* at fault? But you're an American company, lots of Americans own your stock. We're not going to stand by while you go down, and take the jobs and savings of hundreds of thousand Americans with you."

"You were happy to, before our report came out."

"Ross, get off your high horse. You shut up about this nuclear war crap, and we'll put Rawhide back on top. No more Congressional investigations, no more SEC inquests, no more FBI and IRS, no more ranting and raving in the media. We can tell Meta, Microsoft, Google, TikTok, all the big platforms, to reinstate you."

"You saying you can tell them what to do?"

"We threaten them with Section 230, take away their immunity from legal action, and you know there'll be a landslide of suits against them for defamation, censorship, all kinds of crap."

"They made him president; they can unmake him. He knows that."

"We took the White House together, we and them," Coldmire declared. "We work *with* them."

"What about the Indonesians stealing our leases?"

"I was getting to that. We've talked to President Widodo. The maintenance data on the platform is open to question. Those Ministry letters could have been written later, after it happened. Truth is very fluid, these days."

"And the Agency?" Ross said.

"Keith's been looking into things. He's deciding that some of your concerns seem relevant. He's going to discuss it with the ambassador."

"Wally? They were both in that meeting in Jakarta. Telling me to fuck off."

"Look," Coldmire stated, "we're willing to meet you halfway. But you've got to give us something in return." Coldmire cleared his voice, a purposeful pause. "No more criticizing the president's war in Ukraine. And you need to change your tune about nuclear war –"

"Nathan, he's going to kill us all!"

For a moment Coldmire was silent. "I was getting to that." Again he paused, as if cogitating. "We do need your help, Ross." He cleared his throat. "The situation's gone up a notch."

"What situation?"

"DEFCON 2," Coldmire whispered.

"DEFCON 2? You crazy bastard, we're at 3!"

"Not anymore. The president decides the DEFCON level. Him and the Joint Chiefs, and they want 2. Putting the Russians on notice."

DEFCON 2 meant *the final step to nuclear war.* It had been reached only once before, in the 1962 Cuban Missile Crisis, and then only partially.

"Nathan, are you saying that the president has gone to DEFCON 2 to *threaten* the Russians? When they have far more and far better nukes than we do? Are you fucking nuts?"

"We need to learn where they're at. All the lines of communication between us and them are down –"

"That's your fault."

"With the goatfuck in Ukraine, and since the Iran Hamas thing, we appear weak for destroying peace initiatives in Ukraine and then giving Iran all those billions. And then giving them advanced missile technology. So we have to look tough, go to DEFCON 2."

"You can't *win* a nuclear war, Nathan. You can't even intercept most incoming nukes; everyone will be killed twenty times over."

Coldmire's voice softened. "I know that. We all know that. So now we've made our point, we can back up a bit, find our way out of this. That's why we need you to stop attacking us. Say you're confident we're doing the right thing, that you don't think nuclear war's a danger anymore –"

"But you just took us to DEFCON 2! So it *is* about to happen! And you want me to say it's not?"

"If you say things are getting better, then we've made our threat and can seem to back off."

"These things have momentum. You can't just back off."

"Unfortunately, the Russians – we didn't expect this – they've gone from Elevated to Military Danger, their last step before full-on nuclear war." Coldmire sighed. "We thought they'd back down . . ."

"You're fools. Insane fools." Ross sat on the couch, an icy awareness of universal death sliding up his spine. "You've done this to all of us, you bastards. To everyone. You're going to end the world."

"Maybe not if, you'll help us out of this."

"I can't pretend the world is safer when you're about to end it. We're all going down, Nathan. Thanks to you, there's now no way to stop it."

Ross shut off and went out on his office terrace into the cold Manhattan October wind. The city was alive with energy and light, skyscrapers to the horizon, throbbing streets full of people. Then in a flash it was gone, a desert to the horizons of blazing radioactive cinders.

"EVER BEEN TO LEUVEN?" TURK SAID.

They were in Frankfurt Airport drinking Paulaners and waiting for a flight to Belgium.

"Where's that?" Liz yawned, tired after the long trip from Ulan Bator.

"Twenty minutes from Brussels Airport."

"What's there?"

"The Belgian Federal Police labs at Leuven University. Their forensic pathology researchers are among the world's best at identifying traces of fingerprints and DNA on explosives. It's where I sent the pipe samples and the shark-bitten dive gear. They'll analyze the swabs and fingerprints I've brought from the Wuhan sub."

On a ticket folder, he sketched a fingerprint. "In making a bomb, microscopic traces of fingerprint ridges end up on the sticky side of the electrical tape used in the explosives. We can stick these tiny bits of tape to transparent foil so the fingerprint traces can be visualized on the foil with what's called white wet powder or similar FP diagnostic tools. Okay so far?"

"Maybe."

"The microscopic ridge details in these traces, called latent fingerprints or FPs, can be detected using CA, cyanoacrylate, then enhanced with a fluorescent dye called basic yellow 40, or BY40. Still with me?"

"But this was fifty-four feet underwater –"

"We can still find traces on underwater explosives for a week to ten days, longer in fresh water than salt. And when the bomb tied to that pipe blew, it forced microscopic traces of the explosive into the shredded pipe . . . so when we cut off that piece and sent it to the lab, they were still able to identify the explosive, that it was C-4 and not trinitrotoluene."

"What's that?"

"TNT. But we didn't expect prints, and that's where we were astoundingly lucky, because on the adhesive sides of tiny shreds of duct tape embedded in the shredded pipe, there were latent FPs – microscopic traces of fingerprints that this lab, amazingly, can amplify to the point that part of the entire fingerprint can be compared to others on file to find a match . . ."

"So if any of the latent fingerprints from inside the sub match the ones from the exploded pipe or the dive gear that got chewed by a shark, then we have proof that the diver came from the sub? And that he didn't make it back?"

"But if the lab finds that the DNA in the swabs from that sub, even the e-DNA, matches the DNA from the dive gear, then –"

"And if these fingerprint traces on the explosives match those on the dive gear . . . If they match any fingerprints you found in the sub . . ."

"Exactly."

"Then if we can compare them with fingerprint files, Interpol or something."

He nodded. "If the latent FPs match any prints in the sub, then we know our bomb-makers are Chinese. And the Chinese government keeps a detailed file on every citizen – fingerprints, facial scan, DNA, voice recognition, iris scan, medical data, social and personal history, internet and social media use – all that stuff. And we can access that."

"Then we can ID the bastard," she exclaimed.

"And the Leuven lab can analyze the DNA swabs from the sub, using what's called a DNA IQ casework pro kit and identify what's called short tandem repeat – STR – sequences, and can get a full DNA profile. Even if it's just a couple of cells –"

"And if the DNA in the sub matches what they found on the bomb? And the dive gear?"

Turk exhaled. Rather than being excited, he felt exhausted. If all of this was true, then there had been a Chinese mission to destroy the platform. How to prove it?

What then?

He took her hand. "When we're done in Leuven, where shall we go?"

She sat back, letting the weariness of the last weeks sink through her. "I don't want to go back to Jakarta. Ever."

"We're not going to."

Her eyes glistened. "I couldn't have made it through all this without you."

"Nor I without you."

"Yes, you could. You're indomitable."

"No one is."

"Every night, still, I'm on that exploding platform –"

"It will get easier."

She tried to imagine all the explosions and catastrophes he must have lived through but never spoke about. "So maybe we *can* get the people who blew up the platform."

He glanced at the Departures screen and stood. "Let's see what the DNA and latent prints say. If they find any."

THE PARANOID EVIL MINDS OF THE WAR MACHINE – AND THEIR thousands of government, media, and industry allies – were gambling with our lives. How had we allowed this? Given them the option to destroy everything?

Every magical day and blue sky, every moment of happiness, every child, every bird and deer, every fish in the sea, the entire biological masterpiece of life, its billions of years of evolution – the very number of living things on the planet – the very life of the planet itself – to destroy forever?

Ross could not comprehend how we had reached this point. Where physicists worked to increase the number of times we kill each Russian from thirty-two to forty. And biologists created more and more deadly plagues for us to use on each other.

One could blame the lethal corporations behind it – not only Lockheed Martin, Northrop Grumman, Raytheon, Honeywell, General Dynamics, and Boeing, but also the thousands of smaller barracudas in the "defense" industry. And the shareholders and mutual funds all reaping their harvest of death –and all their Congressional lackeys, lobbyists and media – weren't they all part of it too?

What right did these evil fanatics, these terrorists, have to gamble with our lives?

To threaten all life, not just human, but every living thing on earth, now and forever, was the greatest evil in history. And those responsible the worst terrorists of all time.

Could we stop them before they killed us all?

If he didn't stop thinking about this, he'd go crazy.

Maybe he was already crazy.

Trying to find a way to stop what couldn't be stopped.

"ANATOMY OF A CORPORATE DISASTER," TRUMPETED THE *TIMES* in its early morning print and online editions. *"Rarely in recent history has a major company broken so many rules in its precipitate race to the bottom . . . Investors beware: Rawhide's catastrophic stock drop is but a prelude of worse to come . . ."*

As the lead story in the financial section of both editions, the article had instantaneous impact. Major fund managers who were already worried about Rawhide threw in their chips and sold, sold, sold. Half a million small investors who watched the morning financial news frantically called their brokers or bailed out online. Rawhide's stock took a punishing drop, from $39 to $32 in less than fifteen minutes. Ross steeled himself for a further drop, but the stock held steady in the $30-33 range: the *Times* hit piece had done its job.

"IT'S TIME," ANNA SAID.

St. Miles felt a cold terror in his breast. This was the moment . . . She'd always been right, made him lots of money. Had to trust her. But he was so afraid he feared his heart might break.

How had he made so many mistakes? Not just the Venezuelan heavy crude, but all the other screwups he'd recently stumbled into. And now the US-Ukrainian cluster bombs around his neck – where was Malik's deposit, anyway? "It's so much money . . ."

"You'll make so much *more* money," she husked. "You've never been so rich as you're about to be."

"You're right, I just have to steel myself."

"Take every penny you have and short Arab Light."

"**TAKE EVERY PENNY** YOU HAVE," ANNA TOLD ROSS, "AND GO LONG on Arab Light."

"When?" Ross said.

"Now. The announcement's tomorrow morning, 10 a.m. Moscow and Riyadh time."

"A twenty percent production cut? It's going to blow the market apart."

"Just as I told you."

"If this works, I'm going to owe you."

"Keep trying to stop this war. On our side, we are trying too."

"You think we can?" he said, but she was gone.

A joint twenty percent cut would inflame prices, so if he went long on Arab Light, he could make a few billion. Enough for a stock buyback to fight off EastPac and get Rawhide on its feet.

In the UK for a Kent Power stockholders meeting that would soon announce a major profit increase, Ross sat at the Italian glass kitchen table of his London townhouse running the numbers again and again until the table was littered with scribbled yellow pages. Till he was sure of the amount that crude prices would rise after the Russian/Saudi deal was announced. A production cut that would piss off the EU and most of the world's non-producing countries. Now that the U.S. had driven three major producers – Saudi, Iran, and Russia – into each other's arms, and with their supply chains to China, India and two thirds of the rest of the world, it could be a crippling blow to the US, causing an even greater inflationary spiral, and would further undercut the dollar as the world's dominant currency.

Russia and Saudi together produced one quarter of the world's crude, so a twenty percent cut would cause a huge price spike. And if

Iran joined them, that would push prices even higher. It might last two to three months, but to be safe, he'd get in and out early.

An hour before the announcement, Ross placed heavily leveraged long orders through seven different futures brokers for both Arab Light and Russian heavy crude. He caught them both in a slight dip, but as his big orders started hitting the market, the price stabilized then slowly began to climb.

It was five to one in the morning when he finished. Drugged with fatigue, he staggered into the kitchen, poured a glass of gin on ice, and opened a bag of chocolate chip cookies. When the gin and cookies were gone, he poured another gin and ate another bag of cookies, and called Lily in New York. "What you up to?"

"You're still up? You're crazy."

"Just threw away seven hundred and forty million."

"You'll get it back." So as not hex it, she chuckled, "Maybe."

"Otherwise I can't make it."

"Then let EastPac buy you and ride into the sunset."

"You want that?"

"Why not? Life's too short."

He thought about this. "So if everything goes upside down?"

"Things are not going to go upside down. But if they do . . ."

He watched the screen for Arab Light as the line started a sudden sharp climb and a green *BUY* icon flashed. The other screens followed its lead, flashing BUY then *BUY!!!* in green neon as their curves shot up almost vertically. On another screen, the Saudi and Russian oil ministers stood side by side announcing the agreement to cut their joint production; twenty-two percent; another screen showed panicked Singapore oil brokers screaming into their phones.

"Fantastic," she said. "I'm seeing it too."

"Not sure how high to ride it."

"It's not going to last."

"Yeah, how long do they want to torpedo their own production to make a point? Particularly Russia?"

"A three-dollar margin at ninety million barrels a day and thirty-two a barrel, or a nine-dollar margin at sixty-five million barrels a day? They'll be the last man standing."

"I plan to cut out at ninety-one."

"That's way too low. Leaving half a billion on the table."

"When the party's over, it'll drop like a rock. With no stops."

"How long can you stay awake?"

"A week if I have to."

"I'll stay up with you."

He felt a flush of gratitude. "You in New York and me in London. Phone sex about oil and money . . ."

"They *are* sexy. And there'll be time for the other when you get back."

"I think about it way too much."

"We can put you on injured reserve. If you wish."

He laughed, shocked at himself for laughing, and changed the subject. "Kent Power, we still can't find the hackers. Isaiah traced them from Malaysia to Cyprus to Florida but then hit a wall."

"Florida? That's where the U.S. Central Command is. In Tampa."

"They run the wars in the Middle East," he said. "Not in Ukraine."

"But that's where the divers came from who blew up Nordstream."

"It's disgusting we did that . . . One of the worst environmental disasters in history . . . What a bunch of evil fools . . . The good news is Kent's doing fine. And making lots of money."

"I just checked out the site. It's brilliant –"

"Thank you."

"– you can calculate their power production by the second. It's been right on the norms. Nothing's gone wrong . . ."

"You're a genius."

She laughed. "We both are."

"Arab Light just hit eighty."

"I'm there right beside you. Let's ride it as long as we can."

When finally they shut down and her image retreated from the screen, he sat back in a timeless state. Since Mary's death, he'd avoided women. Almost fearful. Hadn't slept with a woman in more than five years. He'd been so alone and hadn't known.

Lily'd changed this. Changed everything.

For some reason he remembered one of his father's comments, a November night in hunting camp high in the Wind River Mountains:

Never continue a fight past when it's beneficial.

When is a fight no longer beneficial?

What if, after this, he got rid of it all and lived a normal life?

And now, DEFCON 2.

How could he worry about his life, his company's, even Lily, amid what might be our last weeks, or even days, on earth?

46

NO PRISONERS

"WE JUST MADE FOUR BILLION?" Jim Burleigh roared. "Holy shit! How'd you *do* it?"

"Got to believe in God." Ross turned from the screen, thinking of Anna.

"Jesus, I don't have the balls."

That's why I run this company, Ross wanted to say, *and not you.* But Burleigh already knew it.

"There's going to be some bad press coming," Ross added. "But not to worry."

"Bad press?" Burleigh grew cautious. "What kind?"

"It'll temporarily drive down our stock price, but that's okay."

"Jesus, you got me worried now."

"We're going to win this, Jim."

"I hope. That's what we're here for."

You coward, Ross thought as he shut the screen and stared out the streaked window at the rainy London night. He ached with weariness, decided he'd give almost anything for all of it to go away.

Wondered if somehow Burleigh might be still trying to take him down.

Power corrupts; absolute power corrupts absolutely.

Oh Jesus, when can this be over?

But isn't this what we're here for, we humans? To do deals?

He thought of Lily. *Not me. Not anymore.*

Wow, imagine even saying that.

A TALL ELEGANT WOMAN STEPPED INTO THE LEUVEN University visitors' lounge, kissed Turk on both cheeks, and hugged him tight. "It's been too long," she said in English.

Turk introduced her as Elodie. Liz smiled and shook hands, instantly hating her.

"Liz and I have been doing a little work," Turk said.

Elodie took them down a busy corridor to a windowless office smelling of chemicals and stale coffee. She locked the door, gave Turk a quiet smile. "Those pipe samples you sent? We found TNT."

"TNT?" He felt a surge of joy. "That's fantastic. Can you trace it?"

"Working on it."

"I never thought we'd find it. What a gift –"

"It's not a gift," she said. "You worked for it."

"Hey, I brought some swabs and FP pix we'd like to check."

"I'll have to enter them –"

"It's better you don't."

She looked at him curiously, then at Liz. "I see."

Turk gave her the case of swabs. "This is off-radar. I'll pay for it."

"It might be just a test run, like we do sometimes. No need to pay."

"I'll owe you."

She smiled at him sweetly, at Liz. "You already do."

"Who is she?" Liz said as they took another taxi back to their Brussels airport hotel.

"Elodie? She's an old friend, helped me with stuff in the past."

"I'm sure she did."

"No need to get mad."

"I'm not!"

"Yes, you are."

"I'm just pissed off. That she treated you like that."

"Like what?"

Liz stared at the flat, industrialized landscape unrolling beyond the freeway. "Like she owns you."

"Time to go home."

"Home? Where's that?"

"Wherever we're together."

She scanned him an instant, a passing car's headlights brightening her eyes. "That could be anywhere."

"Yeah, that's what I said."

"Ask Ross. Maybe they need us." She glanced at the taxi driver.

"He'll drop us off at the hotel," he said, understanding her perfectly. "We'll take another cab wherever we go."

"EVERY AMERICAN HAS BEEN SHOCKED," THE PRESIDENT OF the United States read from his teleprompter, "by the fraudulent conspiracy theory involving my alleged reception of illegal foreign funds."

Back in Manhattan, and at their favorite spot at the kitchen countertop, Ross tilted his phone so Lily could watch the press conference. "I can assure you . . ." The president glanced again at the teleprompter ". . . that I can assure you . . . it won't happen again . . . I mean, we'll put a stop to it." He looked up. "We'll make *them* put a stop to it." He nodded forcefully. "Whoever they are."

"They've swallowed it." Ross had a shiver of fear that this could have gone so wrong.

"Yes," Lily whispered. "I never imagined –"

"Hush! I want to hear this."

"And we've been the target . . ." The president checked his screen. ". . . Of some fake news recently, and I'm happy to tell you that the perpetrators have 'fessed up.'" He gave the camera a wide, white grin. "Ross Bullock," he read, "the departing CEO of Rawhide Energy, has admitted his claims against us are bogus." He looked around blankly, then back to the screen. "We understand that some of the company's Indo . . . into Egypt . . . Andalusia . . . No, *Indonesia* . . . leases will be taken over by the Chinese national oil company Cinderpeck . . . No, Sinopec."

The president then read the last line on the teleprompter. "Turn right and leave the room. Do not answer questions."

Ross took a deep breath. "The United States is the sole country where one person all by himself can push the nuclear button. And he doesn't even know where he is."

"His speech should drive Rawhide down enough," Lily said, "to make another four billion."

"Once the new price contracts hit the news."

She turned to watch the stock screen. "Twenty-nine fifty."

"Unimaginable six weeks ago." He called Mitch Carter. "What you think?"

"In this range," Mitch said, "it's all gravy."

"Want to wait?"

"Christ, I don't know. How much lower can it go?"

"Well, the *Times* did its kill piece, and now the Prez has just tried to finish us off. High tech and most of the media are slavering for our blood. There's some big money in Hong Kong doing a heavy short. And probably EastPac's about to try for another five percent."

"This could be it."

"Let's announce the new contracts."

Seventeen minutes later, Mitch called back. "Press release hitting the media. It's already online at the *Journal*; looks like the *Times* is trying to cover its ass."

"They never retract," Lily laughed. "Let's see what they do now."

Yes, Ross thought, *they've published an article about our false demise, they swallowed all the bullshit, because it matched their narrative, what they've been told to say. And in the space of a few hours, they'll have to eat crow. Not only did Rawhide not go under as the* Times *and the president predicted, we announced multiple new contracts with substantial margins, enough to buy us six months. And our stock price will prove it: Not only are we fighting back, we are starting to kill.*

It took less than an hour. As if Rawhide were some precious relic suddenly salvaged from the grave, the markets, those supposed arbiters of value and truth, bounced it from $29.45 to $34.40. And minutes later to $41.

"It's working better than I thought," Ross said.

"It's working." Lily smiled. "Just like I thought."

"It just hit $42.30."

"It'll float there," she said. "Give it a day."

"In a totally unexpected reversal," the *Investor's Business Daily* was streaming across the screen, "Rawhide has not only come back from the dead – it's taking no prisoners. Investors betting on its demise are scrambling to cover their short positions. Including some very big money in Hong Kong."

Exhausted, he rubbed his face. "I can't think. I am completely gone."

TWO HOURS LATER, ROSS STEPPED THROUGH THE SWINGING leather doors into Rawhide's Wall Street conference room. It quieted, a hundred journalists clustered on plastic chairs before the dais that raised him like a god above the penitent.

He stepped down among them. "You who aren't close," he called, "gather round. I have some news."

They rustled closer, curious.

"As you know, we just announced that the Saudi-Russian production cut gave us the opportunity to sign eleven new supply deals worth five-point-seven billion dollars." He smiled at the *NPR* woman who so recently had been trumpeting his demise. "And today we're using some of those funds for a stock buyback, which will have historic benefits for our market valuation, stave off any hopeless takeover schemes, strengthen our investors' portfolios, and have a host of other positive effects."

He turned to Mitch. "And you all know Mitch Carter, our unstoppable CFO, who will tell you more about the buyback and where we're going from here . . ."

He watched the room of milling journalists calling their editors, some racing for the door. "$43.21," Lily called. "No, $43.44 . . . No,

$43.69 . . ."

That evening they sat in his kitchen, at the countertop where a month ago Lily had first interviewed him for the *Times*, eating the sausage and rigatoni and salad that Carmen, his housekeeper, had left in the refrigerator for them. He held her hand a moment, amazed by the current between them, the feeling of strength, a sudden hunger for the future.

"**YOU ARE VERY LUCKY,**" ELODIE SAID WHEN SHE CALLED TURK, who was asleep on the recliner of their room at the Brussels Airport Hilton.

"The swabs from the sub," he said quickly, "what'd you get?"

"Good news. But why you're lucky, you don't know?"

"What'd you find?"

"You're lucky with this woman, Liz, yes?"

He glanced at the door. Liz was in the next room. "Yes."

"She will be good for you. She doesn't take prisoners."

"Neither do you."

"Yes, but I'm married, remember?"

"*Fuck it,* Elodie, what about the swabs!"

She waited a moment. He imagined the smile in her hazel eyes, the grin on her wide mouth. "The swabs from the Wuhan submarine contain the same explosive footprint as the pipe samples you sent before."

His heart surged. "Holy Jesus!"

"And get this – we even picked up a trace of DNA from the pipe samples. And it matches the DNA on the mouthpiece and harness."

His head swam. He repeated what Liz had said two days before: "We have our man."

"And we have the country," she said. "But it's not who you think."

LYLE SAT ON THE EDGE OF THE BED AND DROPPED HIS BOOTS ON THE floor. He couldn't go a step further. Couldn't put them away. Just bending down would kill him.

He smiled at the boots. Funny when you're dying, everything is sacred. These old Red Wings, scarred by years of horseshoes, blizzards and barbed wire . . . You don't want fancy boots if you're a cop, you need something functional and safe.

Like you're supposed to be.

"You okay, sweetie?" Olivia reached from under the sheets and took his hand. Hers felt warm, life throbbing through it. *How cold is the grave?* "We ID'd the guy who did Tom."

She sat up in bed. "Who?"

"Some Mexican gang guy, come up from El Paso. Just to kill Tom." Lyle pinched his nose to stop the tears.

"You shoot him?"

He shook his head sorrowfully. "Can't."

She sat up straighter. "What do you *mean*, you *can't?* You take the bastard out in a field. A drop gun, a slug in the back of his neck. Gives his filthy brain time to think."

He caressed her shoulder. "Now, darling . . ."

She touched his face, his mouth, his chin. "I love you, sweetie."

He lay down beside her. "I love you so much. For thirty-six years I've loved you." He kissed her hand. "Ever since the night we met."

"You had tobacco juice on your teeth –"

"I'd never seen anyone like you. Never heard a voice like yours. Your eyes, your beautiful smile . . ."

He was quiet, and soon she realized he'd stopped breathing. She cried and cried, holding his cooling hand to her heart.

47

DAGGER IN A SMILE

"**Y**OU GUYS DO THIS ONE," Ross said.

"These journalists out there," Mitch said, "they want to see *you*."

Ross glanced at Lily for support. "I'm tired of being seen."

Lily grinned. "Just do it."

Again he stepped through the swinging leather doors into the auditorium. This time, all the journalists snapped to attention. The difference, he realized, between when they think you're going down and when they think you're winning.

"I wanted to give you more good news," he said. "The Indonesian government . . ." The room grew silent, a sea of cell phones aimed at him ". . . has dropped its attempt to take over our leases. They state that, quote, *after detailed study there is no evidence of maintenance deficiencies. It now appears likely that this most regrettable and criminal explosion was due to subsurface sabotage,* and they are now assisting us in tracking down the killers."

Again the rapid cellphone calls, journalists rushing for the exits.

Once again, strangely, his word had been enough.

"WHAT'S HAPPENING?" SCREAMED DURVON ST. MILES, DARTING from one screen to another as crude kept climbing. Why had Anna told him to short it? Did she know it was going long?

Beyond his windows it was another grim London rain. He was already underwater five hundred million and if the stock kept climbing, he'd have to cover his positions – but with what? "Oh Lord help me," he wailed as the little digital number continued to flitter upward.

"Ah!" he sighed, a moment's relief as it dropped from $44.27 to $44.19. "Keep going down," he begged. But it was a moment's dip, probably as another foolish short seller took his losses and bailed before the losses got worse. Or another long seller taking his profit and readying to dive back in again?

"You bitch," he screamed at Anna, but she wasn't there, didn't answer her phone no matter how many furious messages he left.

"I will get you!" he promised, stomping around his vast office, grabbing antique Royal Dalton figurines from the shelves and smashing them into the fireplace. "I will get you!"

But how?

ANNA ANSWERED ST. MILES ON HIS PRIVATE PHONE, THE ONE HE used for boys. "How did she get this?" he moaned as he flicked it open.

"Do you remember the Dubrovka Theater in Moscow?" she said. "When it was attacked by Chechen Islamist terrorists?"

"You ruined me," he moaned. "You *ruined* me."

"My parents were there, at the theater. To see a play," she said. "And they were among the hundred seventy people who died . . . Do you remember now?"

"You ruined me . . ."

"Do you also remember the assault rifles and explosives the terrorists used? Do you remember who the terrorists bought them from?"

"Oh, please, I don't do things like that. Oh God," he wailed at the screen: *$48.19.*

And he still owed $300 million on the U.S. Ukrainian cluster bombs, as well as the $140 million he'd borrowed for the deposit.

How could he close it now? And his buyers, they'd be sending silent men with knives or deadly needles after him . . .

"There's a Russian saying," Anna said. *"If you pray for revenge, God will turn a deaf ear.* But I don't pray for revenge. I take it."

"**THIS FRIEND OF YOURS,**" Isaiah King said. "Nachin?"

"He's not my friend," Ross said. "He's only alive because Turk didn't kill him."

"From what our Hong Kong office can find out, Nachin's payments came from an outfit in Taiwan. Called, suitably enough, Taiwan Provisions."

"How'd you find this out?"

"Unbelievable, what computers can do to each other, these days."

"Like people," Ross commented.

"But Taiwan Provisions doesn't exist."

"I'll find them."

"No, you won't. Not only have they gone, but they've wiped out their past. They never existed."

"And Nachin?"

"Going to spend lots of time thinking about things. In a Kalimantan jail."

"What about his daughter, Moonlight?"

"She's fine, as long as she stays in Mongolia."

"**IT'S ALL GLOOM** and doom at *The Times*," Ian Hamilton said. "They never bothered to fact-check my tip, just did their attack piece on Rawhide. And now they're mad, though I told them I'd gotten the tip but hadn't run it down . . . They just took the hook because the president's people told them to attack Rawhide."

"They should have known better."

"Know what? I think I'm happy the *Times* fired me."

"Good, you have your life back," she murmured. "What are you going to do with it?"

"By the way, I hired an attorney. She says they can't steal my retirement."

"Good."

"Would you stop *saying* that!"

She chuckled. "What next?"

"Rome."

"Rome?"

"I was a classics major – I never told you? Spent my junior year in Rome. All my life I've dreamed of going back. Hanging out in the ruins and reading Pliny. I've found an apartment six blocks from the Forum."

"That's fabulous, Ian –"

"And you, my sweet, you're free too. What's next?"

"We haven't decided."

"*We?*"

"I've met someone, we're taking a trip."

"A lucky guy."

"I think we both are."

EASTPAC ENERGY WENT INTO FREE FALL AFTER THE FAKE *TIMES* HIT job on Rawhide. In EastPac's attempt to buy Rawhide they'd increased their stake to 21.7 percent, despite poison pill attempts by Mitch Carter to dilute it. Though this wasn't enough for any type of control, it struck fear in everyone's heart.

But when the *Times* article hit, plus the president's tirade against Ross, Rawhide's stock fell to new lows, and every day EastPac's 21.7 percent was worth less. As in many takeover attempts, EastPac had borrowed against their assets to buy their Rawhide shares. Thus they owed far more than what the stock was now worth.

Their own investors, mostly Chinese banking groups, were getting nervous: what if Ross's poison pill counterattacks *did* stave off East-Pac? If so, EastPac would be left holding a bag of bad apples, and their own lenders were starting to swallow lots of anti-acids to keep their worry down.

As more investors realized the risk, EastPac's own stock began to fall. It lost seven percent on Tuesday, and another eleven percent on Wednesday. The company's Singapore office stopped answering journalists' calls and were burning the night lights looking for a face-saving solution.

"I don't give a damn about their management," Ross told Lily. "I want their assets."

With a takeover of EastPac, Rawhide would expand from the world's fifteenth-largest energy company to the ninth. It was an audacious move; the financial analysts would attack it – but what did *they* know? If they were smart they'd be rich, and they weren't rich at all, earning a living by talking crap for some media front.

At first, Lily was shocked, then surprised, then excited. "If you can pull this off . . ."

"If their stock goes down another four percent, we have them. They're not expecting it; we'll blow them right out of the water."

After midnight in New York, before the Singapore 8:30 a.m. pre-open, Ross, Mitch, Isaiah, and Rawhide's investment team placed orders to buy fourteen percent of EastPac. Fifteen minutes later they'd increased their orders to thirty-one percent. At the 9:00 a.m. Singapore open, they bought another twenty percent.

Rawhide now had the controlling interest in EastPac Energy.

THE NEW YORK POST RAN IT FIRST: *"THE* TIMES *HAS ISSUED NO apology, but their website has deleted every negative article on Rawhide, citing 'ongoing new information.' In the meantime, many short sellers have lost millions and once again the* Times' *business news has come up wrong."*

Other media followed in minutes: "The *Times* tried to cover its ass," chortled *Fox News*, "but its ass is too big and the cover too small . . ."

Ross grinned at Lily. "How the hell you learn to do all this?"

"*Xiào lǐ cáng dāo.* A dagger, hidden in a smile."

48

THE BUTTON

"WE HAVE A MATCH," Elodie said, "for the DNA you took from the Wuhan sub. But it's not what you thought."

"Shoot," Turk said.

"He's American."

He shivered, as if having made a dangerous mistake. "Not possible."

"It's in a special database we can access. You might even have crossed paths with this guy. A Navy diver. But there's no longer a trace of him, other than DNA. He's vanished."

"What's his name?"

"He doesn't have one. Not in the database. But he was there. He's real."

"There's a mistake," Turk said. "Somewhere."

"Sorry to deliver such news," Elodie said.

"No." He swallowed. "You did right."

"We'll send you all the data. People will try to fight it, but it's, what you say, incontrovertible."

This couldn't be. All along all the clues had led first to Indonesia, then China, then Russia. But the US?

We didn't do this kind of thing.

Or did we? Hadn't a covert U.S. Navy team blown Nordstream? Hadn't the Prez himself promised to do it? Hadn't the secretary and undersecretary of state and other Pentagon officials boasted about it afterward?

Hadn't we, contrary to every treaty, been putting missiles and bioweapons labs on Russia's borders? And more recently sending enough weapons and cash to fight Russia till the last Ukrainian was killed?

And hadn't the same U.S. government agencies and media been the ones hunting Rawhide down?

According to the UN and international courts, the sabotage of the Russian-German pipeline in their own territorial waters was an act of war. If they'd blown Nordstream, could they have blown his platform too? His refinery?

He loved his country. A place where you could become who you were, go after what you wanted. And where if you worked hard, you might get it. True, we'd done a lot of harm, too, killed millions of people – Vietnam, Iraq, Afghanistan, Syria, Central America, so many other places. But still, nearly everyone wanted to come to America.

But how could this same country, for which he'd risked his life, blow up the gas platform of an American company, kill 131 people, and destroy the savings of millions? How could it then attack a refinery in the heartland of America?

Not possible.

But America wasn't one country anymore. Like a rabid dog tearing its own guts.

And the Navy had other teams like the one that blew Nordstream – guys who didn't even know each other's real names.

But *who* above them had sent down the orders?

Were they the same ones who ordered the explosion of Nordstream?

For them, blowing Nordstream had been a resounding success. For the U.S. oil industry, it destroyed the expanding sales of low-cost Russian natural gas in Western Europe, thereby impoverishing European industry and creating a new multi-billion market for high-cost American liquified natural gas. It torpedoed economic links between Western Europe and Russia for years to come, perhaps forever. It wrecked Europe's economy and kept the dollar artificially strong. Even better, it vastly increased American weapons sales worldwide. Best of all, it guaranteed decades to come of sorrow and hatred between Russia, Ukraine, Europe and the US, and thus many years of escalating worldwide "defense" profits.

The only downside? It brought us all to the edge of nuclear war.

IT WAS SNOWING IN SWEETWATER. NORM CASSIDY LAY IN THE darkness watching the snow rise up the bedroom windows, Shirley breathing softly beside him. For a moment, he was stunned that they'd left the comforts of Newport Beach for this snowy, freezing outback. But his beloved wife beside him, a wry smile on her sleeping face, her private knowledge of many things, her clarity and wisdom – did she prefer it here?

Since they'd left California the worry lines in her face had faded, her half-sleepless nights, her silent pacing in the living room to avoid waking him.

Wyoming was a beautiful place, and most of the people lovely too. Ranchers, truck drivers, farmers, teachers, refinery workers, folks in the county office, grocery stores and "family diners" like Enoch's . . . nearly everybody worked hard and took care of everybody else – wasn't this how to live?

The kids had almost instantly liked the new school, the stern, warm-hearted teachers who took them on field trips to dinosaur digs and battlefields and buffalo herds or read stories aloud that made them love books.

It had been Lyle who'd enticed him here. Once you met Lyle, how could you want to work for anyone else? Now could *he*, Norm Cassidy, be the same? Be that good?

Lyle had been twenty-six years older, but to Cassidy more an elder brother than father. Cassidy had his own father, a wonderful guy who lived with Cassidy's mom in the Seacliffe trailer park in Newport

Beach amid families of all races and backgrounds, with many heartfelt relations between them. A constantly renewing clan who watched out for each other too.

So Lyle as an elder brother was someone you listened to, competed against and even fought, but always loved. Because their first thought was always for you. Lyle and others like him had learned the magnificent truth that Cassidy'd learned from his own father. If you want peace in the world, love people.

When he left for the office three hours later, the blizzard had eased. Two feet of new snow soft and feathery as goose down atop the hard crust of previous days. Stomach full of pancakes, bacon and coffee, he'd waded to his cruiser, grabbed the brush from the back seat, and cleared the windows, slipped inside, and sat wincing at the frigid seat under his thighs, started the engine then the defroster and watched the ice crystals slowly vanish from the glass.

The car was reluctant to move, finally cracking its way through the crust to the county road and unwillingly along it to town. At the office, the Channel 2 news truck was already there, the camera guy and cheery young reporter drinking coffee and warming their hands at the woodstove. *His* office, the one Lyle had bequeathed him.

"Cut the crap," Lyle snapped. "You earned this job fair and square."

The Channel 5 folks showed, then Channel 7. "There's jelly donuts on the conference table," Cassidy told them. "And more coffee."

"Okay, Sheriff," called out Steve Daniels of Channel 7, "stop buying us off. What's the good news?"

Cassidy finished his cherry donut and coffee. "Before he died, Lyle was working with federal agencies investigating the sabotage of our refinery, but also with an investigative and legal company hired by Rawhide Energy. Lyle would be pleased we've now learned a lot about the four individuals allegedly involved, based on multiple airport cameras and on the travel documents they used. They drove from here back to Denver then flew to Los Angeles and Singapore then Myanmar and may have crossed into China somewhere on its 1,300-mile border with Myanmar."

He halted to pour another coffee. "The Chinese government says the four are not their citizens or even known to the government. Nor did they ever enter China. But it's apparently a very porous border, part of it very mountainous, and it's easy to buy your way across."

"So where are they?"

"The Chinese don't know if they're still in Myanmar, which is in the midst of a civil war, so it's hard to know. But strangely, in another intelligence database, two of the four individuals match former Taiwanese Military Intelligence Bureau operatives. But the Taiwanese say he's unknown to them."

"Who is he, then?"

"That's what we're trying to find out."

"But why," asked the lovely Channel 2 reporter, "would *Taiwan* attack *us*?"

He smiled. "They weren't attacking the US, remember. They were attacking Rawhide."

"NUCLEAR WAR IS ON OUR DOORSTEP," ANNOUNCED THE Bulletin of Atomic Scientists in a worldwide plea to governments everywhere "to avoid the coming apocalypse. As a final warning to humanity, we have lowered to Doomsday Clock to 5 seconds before midnight. Please, may every person on earth and every government find a way to stop before it's too late . . ."

"We've lost our ability to see the truth," Lily said.

Did we ever have it? Ross wondered, but didn't say.

"YOU SITTING DOWN?" TURK GROWLED.

"We're having breakfast," Ross snapped back. "That okay with you?"

"The guys who blew your platform? It was us."

"Us?"

"The DNA from the Wuhan sub DNA is an American Navy guy. Who's now completely disappeared. All we have is his fucking DNA . . ."

"You're saying the people who blew up the platform," Lily cut in, "are American? *Our* Navy?"

"The data's clear."

Ross thought, incredulously, of calling the president to ask him was it true. "Has to be a mistake."

"No chance. I took the swab from the sub's cabin, where the pilot sat."

Ross took a breath. "So this Navy guy was the pilot?"

"And the other guy was American too, the one whose latent FPs show up in the bomb blast, and with a bit of his DNA on the shark-bitten dive gear, he was the one who taped the bomb onto the vertical gas pipe. But other than that, we don't know who he was either."

"The one who didn't make it back to the sub . . ."

"But there was maybe a third guy," Turk added. "His FPs are from the same area of the sub as the pilot's. But they're on the hatch, too, as if he'd gone out with the other diver. A normal two-man sabotage unit, with a minisub waiting . . . He's a Caucasian male, we can draw you a picture, but we don't know who he is."

"Where are you?"

"Liz and I are still in Brussels."

"You should both get back here. You can stay with Lily and me."

"Ground zero? Nowhere else we'd rather be."

"Stay on the line while I call Senator Hollit."

It was 6:05 a.m. in D.C., and Hollit answered instantly. "What you doing?" Ross said.

"Damn cardio exercises. I hate'em."

"Guess who blew our platform?"

"I don't care, Ross. Goddamit, we're *not* going to war with China —"

"*We* blew the platform! *We,* the U.S. fucking Navy!"

"*Hell* we did!" Hollit snarled.

"We have proof," Turk said. "It will hold up in court."

"Oh my God," Hollit muttered when Turk explained . "And these 'latent FPs,' they're really proof?"

"Unfortunately, yes."

"Given all the president's attacks on Rawhide, it's clear he's tied to this," Hollit muttered. "This can bring him down."

"He'll find a way to deflect it," Ross said. "He always does."

"Escalating somewhere to divert everyone's attention?"

"Does he think a nuclear war won't happen?" Turk put in.

"He doesn't know what he thinks these days. Or maybe he thinks he's saving the world from iniquity. The iniquity of knowing what he's done . . . Oh fuck."

"We have to find a way to stop this," Ross said. "Or he'll kill us all."

"Give me a minute," Hollit said. "Let me think."

"Only one way. The 25th Amendment."

"What about the Veep? You want *her?*"

"We'll have to bypass her too. Like the Dems did with Nixon and Agnew."

"No matter what you do, you're not going to pry his finger off the button."

49

DEFCON 1

DURVON ST. MILES SAT WEEPING in his palatial living room, rocking back and forth on the silk settee. How *could* this happen? What had he done to deserve it?

Over and over, he looked for a way out. He could borrow maybe a billion, but that wasn't near enough. Even if he sold this beautiful town house he loved so much, the site of so many illicit pleasures, that wouldn't even come close.

Even if he sold them all: the Cotswold castle would bring ten million, the 16th century place on Île de la Cité another twenty . . . But that was not even a month's interest on any debt he could structure. What if he took out a huge life insurance policy, then somehow "died" and it went to someone who would secretly pass it to him? A joke.

His chest was crushed. All the cocaine and single malt in the house couldn't ease this sorrow. All the years he'd built it up, this money, all gone.

Lord Durvon St. Miles? He hated himself with a deep ruthless fury for being so naïve and credulous as to believe it might happen.

You're their enemy, kid. They will always take you down.

Anna – how had she gotten this phone, the one he used for his private pleasures?

He tried to think of any enforcers he'd used in the past who he could hire to kill her. But who of them would go to Moscow now?

And now with the Ukraine weapons final payoffs coming due, where was he going to find all that? How could they charge him so much for what the Americans had given them free? Then the damn Sudanese wanting forty percent or else. And all the intermediary whores with their stilettos and guns. It wasn't fair.

He needed a little thrill to get his mind off the tragedy that had befallen him. From the locked bottom drawer of his ebony desk, he took out his *Book of Boys*.

LIKE AN EXPLOSION, THE WUHAN SUB DNA NEWS WAS SUDDENLY everywhere. Even the president's media coughed it up – *"Alleged DNA tied to supposed sub linked to poorly maintained gas platform explosion,"* said the *Times* – a caption which the paper's old guard considered a rousing success against their younger inquisitors. Or another – *"Rawhide Seeks to Spread Blame for Platform Explosion,"* snickered MSNBC.

But most of the media, for once, covered the actual story. The word was coming down that now it was okay to go after the president, and this was a good knife to do it.

The news stunned Rawhide's board. "If this is true," Jim Burleigh said in the split screen, but couldn't finish.

"It can't be," Deborah said, shaking her head.

"There's a lot of this going on," Asa Chomsky said. "Off-radar. Eliminating enemies, rewarding friends. Every government does it."

"You have four paths to follow," Isaiah told them. "And you can win all four. The *first* is legal: we can cut their balls off twenty ways. The *second* is financial: you do this right, you can make billions. The *third* is political: you can kill off most of your political enemies. And *four*: with the publicity you'll smell like roses forever."

"IT'S GRATIFYING," Turk said as he scanned the living rooms of Ross's Mad Ave penthouse, "that you have enough space."

"I once told him," Lily laughed, "that he could use the kitchen for a basketball court."

"You can have your own suite," Ross added, "with a jacuzzi and sauna."

"How different," Liz said. "Turk's been showing me all his favorite places . . . sleeping on frozen sheepskins in the back of a Mongolian truck . . ."

"It wasn't *that* bad –"

"Or hanging out by the Yangtze, going shopping in the basement of the Central Park Mall in Jakarta?"

"You got yourself into that," he stated.

"I heard," Lily said, "that you escaped that hospital in Jakarta but the Marine at the Embassy wouldn't let you in?"

"I threatened his family jewels –"

"That usually does the trick."

"EDITH'S ON BOARD," Senator Hollit told Ross fifteen minutes later. "As National Intelligence Director, she can put a leash on the Agency *and* the FBI."

"Fantastic."

"It's delicate, her and the Prez, given what she knows about all his overseas deals. You're lucky they hate each other. Or she'd ignore you."

"She's seen the evidence?"

"Her minions have," Hollit responded. "She says the DNA and explosives data is amazing. But that it can't be us, so it must be Russians."

"Russians? Why would they blow up my damn platform –"

"False flag. She says like they blew Nordstream."

"*We* blew Nordstream. You've seen the report. The president and his handlers were even stupid enough to boast about it."

"She says they've checked this DNA against all their databanks," Hollit replied. "There's no U.S. Navy match."

"Because they're looking in all the wrong places. This is some war machine group."

"No matter what, the media will stonewall the DNA & explosives data, call it a conspiracy theory."

"We've had everything analyzed four more times," Turk interrupted. "In France, the UK, and twice at top-secret U.S. labs. It all checks out."

Hollit said nothing, then, "I never expected this."

"She's doing this just to bring down the president?" Ross answered. "Because they fear he might lose the election to someone they don't own?"

"Not just her. He's got lots of enemies."

"I've got lots of enemies too. And they're all going down."

"Jesus," Hollit huffed. "You like the taste of blood?"

"I do now."

"Be careful, some of it may be yours."

ROSS CALLED MITCH AND ISAIAH. "The Agency is off our backs."

"The president'll reverse that," Isaiah said.

"Not with Edith in charge."

"She's only the director of national intelligence. He can fire her."

"Not with the 25th Amendment," Ross replied. "If he tries to fire her, she'll reveal all his crooked deals, get him impeached. Which is even worse for his legacy than the 25th."

"I don't see it happening," Isaiah said.

Ross glanced out the window at the lines of traffic on Mad Ave. "Somebody's going to pay. For all the lives . . . *How* do you try to pay for the loss of a person's life?"

"There's a fucking algorithm," Mitch growled in his sandpaper voice.

"We've tracked down one of the guys who blew the cracker," Isaiah added. "All the way to Taiwan."

"Don't make sense," Mitch muttered.

"Yes, it does," Ross said. "It's part of the puzzle." He shut off, watching the traffic, imagining the millions of miles of traffic jams on the billions of miles of freeways and roads all over this tiny, congested earth, thought again of the fish traps in Makassar Strait. To save yourself, you have to swim against the tide.

But how was this world – nine billion warring, murdering, craving, fornicating, polluting and pillaging humans on the verge of nuclear holocaust – how were they going to recognize the trap?

Let alone get out of it?

NORM CASSIDY SLAPPED HIS HAT AGAINST HIS THIGH TO SHAKE OFF new snow. The cemetery drifts were over his boots, and his ankles and knees were already wet and cold.

"Mornin, Chief," he said when he reached the grave. "Just dropped by to say we have arrested Tom Hogan's killer. Name of Ricardo Contrayo, a Mexican *pollero* – a *coyote* – one of those guys who smuggle illegals across the border –

"Stop interrupting, Chief. I'll explain . . . A week before Tom got killed, this Ricardo Contrayo drove from El Paso to Cheyenne in a Chrysler 300C. Then in Cheyenne he bought a used Subaru Forester using cash and a fake ID, and drove to Sweetwater. He got there at 21:15, entered the hospital at 03:25, and left at 03:51. He drove the Subaru back to Cheyenne and abandoned it and drove the Chrysler 300C back into Mexico –

"*How* do we know all this? We started tracking all the out-of-state plates on every camera we could find, then narrowed it down by type of vehicle. The 300C is the ride of choice for these scumbags, so it didn't take us long to find it.

"You think that was easy? First, we chased down every image of that car on every camera between here and Mexico . . . We had Ricardo's prints from the Subaru and plenty of good facials, his DNA for that matter . . . But what blew our minds as we put all this together, is *wow*, the stupid fuck is coming back, bringing another bunch of illegals across – we got him easy a hundred yards inside the border . . .

"*Who* got him, you askin, Chief? I went down there personally, and with a couple of good old boys in the Border Patrol and a couple of Texas deputies, we restrained the gentleman, arrested him in Texas and expedited his travel back to Wyoming . . ."

More snow was coming down, blotting the view. Cassidy realized his feet were freezing. "Be quiet, Chief, let me tell you the rest. Where is he right now? Well, he's languishing at our expense in Wyoming's most exclusive resorts in Rawlins . . ."

Cassidy shivered and drew his coat tighter. "That's right, he's looking at a death sentence. But Wyoming hasn't had an execution since 1992 . . . heck, you know that. We scared this bastard so bad he coughed up the folks who hired him . . . You guessed it: Singapore, then China, then strangely back to Albuquerque then El Paso. But there the trail goes dead."

He nodded. "You're right: that don't bring Tom Hogan back."

He put on his hat and waded through the snow back to his cruiser, turning one more time. "And with you, too, Chief."

And smiled as he climbed into the car, at Lyle's answer:

"Dammit, don't call me Chief. *You're* the Chief now."

"OUR NATION'S EXISTENTIAL ENEMY," THUNDERED THE president, "is Russia. All the good things about them you see on television or hear on the record player – the radio, I mean, they're lies! It was the Russians, mind you, who blew up that plat . . ." He bent down to peer at his teleprompter. "Just like the Russians blew up that Northwest . . . you know, that thing. Who in *our* beloved country could imagine *our* government caught up in such a nefa – nefari – bad scheme? And that an American company could blame *us* – the United States Government – for this crime – what does it tell us? It tells us that company – I mean Raw . . . Rawhood . . . isn't really *American* at all . . ." He raised his eyes from the teleprompter and faced the camera. "So since Rawhood isn't American, who are they really working for?"

He raised both arms, a religious, inclusive gesture. "We *all* know the answer: Rawhoud's refusal to obey our sanctions. Their refusal to stop working with our enemies . . . And now their allegitations" – he held the front page of the *Times* up to the cameras – "have emboldened Russia. As I speak, Russian tank columns are moving toward the Estonian border. Estonia is their start of their destruction of Europe."

He looked into space. "You know, years ago, when I was an Air Force pilot, we knew you couldn't talk to the Russians –"

"Mr. President, when were you an Air Force pilot?" the *Wall Street Journal* correspondent called out.

He ignored her. "Many times," he continued, "I've tried to reach out to the Russians. But they refuse to answer." He bowed his head, raised it, and stared toward the camera. "As a result . . ." He bent to his teleprompter. ". . . with great reluct . . . with great relush . . . *reluctance*, I have been forced to raise our defense readiness to DEFCON 1."

The camera swept the audience of journalists and White House staffers solemnly rising to their feet and clapping their hands.

50

AMENDMENT 25

"**D**EFCON 1," Turk said, "is the urgent, last-minute warning when a nuclear attack is imminent or already happening. Telling us to fire back."

"I can't believe the Russians would be so stupid," Senator Hollit murmured.

"They're not," Ross said.

"The Prez is always accompanied by a military officer with a brief-case of the codes to launch our nuclear missiles," Turk said. "So when the Prez asks, the officer gives him the codes. Supposedly the secretary of defense has to agree."

"What if the secretary disappears," Ross said, "like last year?"

"No problem. And even if the secretary is there to disagree, the Prez can instantly fire him or her and insert someone else who does agree. It's already worked out beforehand, so it only takes seconds."

"That's true," Hollit said.

"The codes instantly go via National Command Authority – NCA," Turk added. "And to NORAD and all our missile launch sites world-wide and all Air Force, Navy and Army commanders, ordering them to prepare to launch their missiles. By now, many of the missiles have already been triggered. Others are unpinned, armed, and ready to be launched. At this point, it's hard to turn back."

"So to stop this now?" Ross said.

"Under Section 4 of Amendment 25," Hollit said, "to remove the president from office, the Veep has to get a cabinet majority to tell the House and Senate that the Prez is no longer able to fulfill his duties. Then she takes over."

"Holy Jesus, then *she* has the nuclear codes?"

"Eventually we'll have to pull an Amendment 25 on her."

"Christ, that will take time!"

"As third in line," Hollit continued, "the speaker of the House becomes president."

"In the meantime," Turk said, "the Russians know we've gone to DEFCON 1, and I'm afraid they'll launch their missiles in retaliation –"

PETER MIKHAILLOV PULLED OUT PHONE #3 AND CALLED ANNA. "You still up?"

"I answered the phone, didn't I?"

"I have an answer to your first riddle."

"Which one?"

"Who you are."

Her voice turned husky. "You think so?"

"The girl in the pinafore. That summer you were five and I was seven, and our families had villas next to each other on the Black Sea. You've never changed."

"You think so?"

"And the second riddle . . ." He glanced at the new snow tumbling past the window. "It's very cold outside. And very warm inside. Like you."

She said nothing, then, "How do you know?"

"Because you're that same girl."

"The third?"

"Why you are incomplete? Because each of us alone is incomplete. But together we form a whole."

Her voice grew warm. "You think so?"

"I know it. And so do you."

Anna listened to his deep, kind voice and felt a warm sensation up her spine. So long alone. A father dead, a mother. She may have avenged them, but they were still dead. *Pray for revenge and God will turn a deaf ear.* Year after year of battles for money, another tick up the crude price, another trophy or defeat.

It's October in Moscow," she whispered. "Come warm me."

He sat back, amazed. The Ice Maiden he'd revered since boyhood, the scrappy little girl with the buck teeth who had become this lovely, brilliant and kind but very fearsome woman, who had built a crude empire out of her fantastic mathematical mind – had he truly answered her three riddles?

He took the elevator down to the garage and leaped into his red 911.

God willing.

"THE DEMS ARE WITH US," Senator Hollit said when he called Ross and Turk back. "Most of them, anyway."

"They'll vote for 25?"

"Senate and House both."

"How soon?"

"Tomorrow."

"Too late. Has to be today."

"Not yet. The White House saw this coming and just announced a one o'clock presidential address to the nation. Supposedly a plea for worldwide peace and understanding." Hollit exhaled. "So we have to wait, see what this brings."

"He's delaying," Ross said. "Trying to reassure the Russians while telling our generals to arm the bombs."

"When they're armed, can we reverse it?"

"Not easy," Turk answered. "They're now live till you use them."

"You mean we can't turn back?"

"It's not in the manuals."

"I'll call you back, five minutes." Ross switched phones and punched in Anna's Moscow number. It rang six times before she answered.

"Can't talk now," she gasped. "I'm fucking in the hot tub –"

"Anna, we've gone to DEFCON 1."

"Against us?" Water splattered as she sat up. "Why?"

"The president says you're invading Estonia."

"Not true!" a man yelled in the background.

"Oh my God . . ." Anna said.

"Who can you reach, at the top?"

"Anybody. Who you want?"

"The boss."

"Stay on," she said, "We'll call him."

Ross paced, phone to his ear, heart pounding. She came back on. "He's in the field. For security I can't reach him. You guys keep trying to kill him."

"Our president says he's trying to reach him."

"Not true. We keep trying to contact *your* White House. They don't answer. Wait, I have Lavrov –"

"The foreign minister?"

"He who used to love your country."

"What's going on?" A man's gruff voice, in English.

"It's me, Sergei," Anna answered. "I have the Rawhide guy, Bullock, on the line. He says in an hour the American president is going to claim we've invaded Estonia."

"Estonia? Who the fuck would be that crazy?"

"*Call* the UN! Show satellite data, prove it's not true! We only have an hour before he announces this. Call the Estonian president, make a joint statement. Please do it!"

"How does this Rawhide guy know all this?" Lavrov fumed.

"He's an insider with top security connections. Has opposed the president for a long time."

"First they say we want to put nuclear missiles in space? Everyone is already doing this. And now Estonia?"

"The good news," Anna said, "is the top is worried about how far the president's pushing this. They can't control him anymore. Want to get rid of him, but can't figure what to do with the Veep."

"I could not figure that, either."

"But the president's fighting back, deflecting it by pretending there's a Russian threat."

"From *us?* He's crazy! Why would we risk nuclear war? Killing everything on Earth?"

51

SHELTER

"*I*N A NUCLEAR ATTACK, FIND SHELTER *at once. Do not look at the blast. Immediately get inside the nearest building and move from the windows –"*

Preceded by a loud beeping sound, this FEMA Presidential Emergency Alert hit every television, radio, cable program and fixed and mobile phone. It came seven minutes after the UN, the Russians, Estonians, and other European governments issued urgent statements that there was no Russian advance toward Estonia.

– *"If you are caught outside, hide behind any protection. Lie face down to protect exposed skin from the heat, radiation, and flying debris . . ."*

"He thinks he can still turn back," Hollit said. "That this's a good strategy, for his reelection."

"But he's making the Russians escalate too." Ross hit Anna's number. It rang and went dead.

"I'll call you back," Hollit said and clicked off.

Anna called back breathlessly minutes later. "You're at DEFCON 1! *I know!* What can we do? If you're launching missiles, we launch ours too."

"I'm not sure we are." He felt powerless because he didn't know. "Maybe not."

"Call *your* crazy president! Does *he* even know? *Our* president has many faults, but he loves Russia. He does not want to destroy us."

"What's Lavrov say?"

"He too loves Russia. He used to love your country also. His daughter, she graduated Columbia University. Now she is telling him, *watch out, they may do this.*"

"We may do what?"

"Nuke us."

"No," he gasped, "can't be." Then he realized it could. "Yes, we might."

"Our president's decree is we can only use nuclear weapons in response to a nuclear attack against us –"

"– Or if the very existence of Russia is endangered."

"For us, they are the same. And now, in response to your DEFCON 1, we've moved from our third level of combat readiness – *Military Danger* – to our final level – *Maximum Combat Readiness.*"

Ross felt the chill of certain death down his spine. "You're going to fire?"

"Unlike you, where your president can push the button all by himself, in Russia three people must decide: the president, the chief of general staff, and the defense minister."

"Will they now?"

"They're watching real-time by satellite. The instant you fire, we do too."

"IT WILL BE DONE," Senator Hollit said, "by the end of today."

"Who's talking to the Russians?"

"You are."

"No, I mean who officially!"

"We burned all those bridges long ago. You and Anna are now our best connection."

"That's tragic." Ross kept pacing, acid burning his gut, then turned to Lily. "They don't know what they're doing."

She nodded, face in her hands, glanced up at him. "Tell them."

Hollit broke in. "The officer with the briefcase has just been ordered to move away from the president."

"Without the codes, the Prez –"

"Can't nuke anybody."

Ross felt a wave of exhausted release. He switched to the phone with Anna. "Tell Sergei that our president no longer has the codes. They're with the Strategic Air Command or the National Command Authority, still ready to use, but the irrational danger from our side is controlled. You do the same."

"We'll see." She clicked off.

"IN A HISTORIC MOMENT NEVER BEFORE SEEN IN AMERICAN politics," the *Times* breathlessly revealed, "both the House and Senate have agreed almost unanimously with the President that the Vice President should be removed from office."

"What the hell?" Ross said.

"Wait and see," Hollit answered.

Twenty minutes later, both houses of Congress *in extremis* voted to impeach the president, totally astonishing him. "This is treason, beaver dams, pure as factories," he mumbled to his press corps as he was led from the White House to an armada of limousines and taken "for evaluation" to Ward 71, the presidential suite at Walter Reed National Military Medical Center.

"Who did this?" the president yelled.

"You did, sir," a Marine answered.

NO ONE WAS MORE ASTONISHED BY HIS SUDDEN ASCENDANCE to the presidency than the new president himself. As speaker of the house, he'd been too busy to even think about being third in line – a bizarre possibility that under normal circumstances he would never have wished for.

"I've always had a good relationship with our new president,"

Senator Hollit told Ross. "If anyone can get us out of this mess, he can."

"On Ukraine?"

"He's been opposed to it from the start. Opposed to all those years of our inciting Russia, going back on our word. 'We're creating an enemy where there was none,' he said recently . . ."

"Once you create enemies," Ross countered, "they don't go away. You're walking around with a scorpion in your pocket, waiting for it to sting."

IN HIS FIRST MOVE, THE NEW PRESIDENT FLEW TO ICELAND TO meet with the Russian president. The first subject was an immediate stand-down from nuclear confrontation, stepping back from DEFCON 1 by the U.S. and from Maximum Combat Readiness by the Russians. Also on the table were a resolution to end the Ukraine war, limits to NATO expansion and sanctions, stopping the Middle East wars, and a serious plan for an international ban on nuclear weapons.

"It's only the nuclear threat that keeps us from world war," wailed a spokesperson for Honeywell, one of the war machine's biggest contractors.

"We've been living in a house of dynamite," the new president answered. "Waiting for each other to light the first match. That's insane, and we're going to stop it."

"While these initial moves may seem positive," warned the Bulletin of Atomic Scientists in a third release, "the risk remains very high of a nuclear conflict resulting in the destruction of life on Earth. Those industries opposed to weapons controls, principally the defense industries of the U.S., will continue to battle for more weapons development, faster and more dangerous nuclear missiles, and more deadly conventional weapons. They are a very powerful, very rich, and very well-connected network that includes many major companies, banks, politicians and government agencies. It will be very hard to overcome. For this reason, we have maintained the Doomsday Clock at five seconds before midnight, the closest we have ever been to nuclear war."

52

DARWINIAN

A SEA OF HAMMERED SILVER spread to the horizons. The setting sun threw the sailboat's shadow far across the water. A light wind filled the jib, driving them forward. The waves hissed along the hull, rocking it gently.

Turk had never felt so alive. Liz was so much fun, so closely connected, so alive, so kind, that being with her reminded you constantly of how little time is left.

She lashed the wheel and came forward. "Heading?"

He thought a moment. "Oh, okay. Who's our closest neighbor?"

"At this moment Martinique. And soon to be St. Lucia."

She put an ice bucket of rosé d'Anjou and two tall slender glasses on the table. "It's perfect, this wine, with the salt air."

"It's perfect, this life, in the salt air."

He glanced up at a vapor trail high above them.

Yes, they both thought. *For the moment.*

THE WINDOW TABLE AT THE JULES VERNE GAVE A VIEW HALF A thousand feet down the side of the Eiffel Tower to the brilliant panoramas of Paris up and down both banks of the Seine.

Ross eased back into his chair, into the soft joy at the bright city lights, the effervescent brevity of life, when every instant is worthwhile, tantalizing and deep.

"When you bet me this dinner," Lily said, "I never thought you'd win."

"I thought I might." He shrugged. "Their case against me wasn't that good."

"Only because you revealed his deals."

"The evidence was piling up. Everyone was figuring it out."

"The Kompromat?"

"The Ukrainians had him by the balls for every deal they gave him. And he ended up destroying their own country and killing most of their young men."

She shook her head as if one could free it of this unforgettable sorrow, and squeezed his hand. "We still have each other. What shall we do?"

"We have this week in Paris. Then home and try to stop this war before it's too late?"

"And at the same time, you think you're going to run Rawhide plus your recent acquisition of Asia Pacific?"

"I'm asking Mitch to take over."

"Mitch?"

"So I can try, full-time, to stop this war . . ."

"Once we stop throwing billions at Zelenskyy, we can find peace."

"The war machine doesn't want peace."

She glanced at the remnants of her chocolate soufflé. "How insane that at any moment we can all be atomized. By a few people who control the life and death of everyone else, the entire Earth. How did we let this happen?"

The elevator down was windy, cold, and empty. They took a path through dark trees past a glistening pond and along Avenue de La Bourdonnais toward Rue de Monttessuy and their apartment. Although it had not rained, the sidewalk was damp, slippery with leaves. The air was cold and misty, their steps hushed. *We're happy,* Ross thought. *How long do we have?*

A taxi with a green roof light turned the corner and came at them with a huge roar. He dove with her behind a concrete planter box as bullets ripped through cars, shattered windows, and smashed off buildings.

In a sudden silence two car doors clicked open – the shooters were coming, on foot.

Twenty feet ahead was a red-fronted restaurant with a sign, *"Le Bon Acceuil, The Warm Welcome.* Feet were running toward them. Ross and Lily sprinted into *Le Bon Acceuil* past stunned and screaming customers and out a back alley, clattering over trash bins and broken pallets.

Gasping, they halted, listening. The street at the end of the alley seemed bright and empty. They ran for it. The taxi with the green roof lights shot past, then backed up fast.

They dashed back up the alley and into the restaurant as the taxi came screaming up the alley.

Out the restaurant's front door, a waiter was holding a taxi door open for an elderly couple. "We're coming too," Ross yelled as he shoved Lily in beside them and jumped into the front beside the driver. "Go! Go!"

The taxi raced up Rue de Monttessuy to La Bourdonnais. "Take us to the police!" the old man quavered.

"Yes," Ross said. "Fast!"

"You saved our lives," Lily gasped to the old man, who looked at her uncomprehendingly.

"Put on your seat belts," the driver said.

Police cars were screaming through the streets toward Monttessuy, blue lights flashing. The taxi sped the other way on Quai d'Orsay toward the precinct station.

"They stole our taxi!" the old man lamented at the precinct station to the young black policewoman behind the bullet-proof glass.

"They tried to kill us!" Lily yelled. "Bastards tried to kill us!"

The policewoman glanced at the two old people. *"These* two?"

While Lily tried to explain, Ross called Isaiah. "I should have guessed," Isaiah muttered. "Where's your damn security?"

"Gave them the night off." Ross felt fury at himself for putting Lily at risk. "Have to go under."

"I'll call DGSI."

This was the French internal intelligence agency. "Where are *they* in all this?"

"Not like the Feebies. They'll get you to your plane. No, not yours. I'll get you a rental."

Two hours later, he and Lily sat side by side in a fast Dassault headed to La Guardia, where a chopper would take them to a guarded compound in the Berkshires that Isaiah had suddenly dredged up from German intelligence.

"I'm not going to live like this," Lily said.

He eased back into the leather couch. "Depends who they were, tried to kill us."

"Tried to kill *you!*"

"I can pay for good security."

"Bullshit."

"Even if I die, my love, there's no choice."

"Yes." She digested this. "There's no choice."

THE BOY STOOD IN THE LOBBY FACING THE SECURITY CAMERA. AN Asian tilt to his face, beautiful wide blue eyes, golden hair, and a naked Viking chest . . . Between eleven and fourteen, maybe, just as the dark web site had advertised . . . "Tell me your name," St. Miles said.

"Shalom." A voice still high, on the point of cracking.

"When I press the buzzer take the elevator to the top."

The boy appeared a minute later in his lobby camera. "Take off your clothes," St. Miles said.

The boy undressed to his silky shorts. Glorious as a god, his penis long and thick hanging down below the shorts. Like a sword about to strike.

St. Miles made MaiTais and they sat in the living room, the boy naked with his huge dick hanging out of his shorts, his other clothes bundled on the couch beside him, St. Miles masturbating softly as he watched him.

When he offered cocaine, the boy shook his head. St. Miles realized he'd hardly said a word. *Doesn't want me to know where he's from.* "Where are you from, Shalom?"

"Palestine."

"But you have a Jewish name –"

"Not my real name. I am wishing the Jews goodbye." Shalom stood in front of him, his clothes in one hand, the huge dick hanging down. "Turn around and bend over."

This was new. Usually he, St. Miles, made the rules. But it might be fun to try.

He bent face-down over the couch. "Give me your hands," Shalom said. "I want to hold them."

St. Miles slipped his hands behind his back and tilted up his pelvis. The boy quick-clipped cuffs around his wrist. "Hey!" St. Miles yelled.

This could be exciting.

The boy slipped a slender stiletto from the back elastic of his shorts, raised St. Miles' left arm, and drove the blade through his heart.

ROSS WALKED OUT INTO THE STARLIGHT. DEEP IN THE Berkshires, he and Lily were safe. For the moment. And the world-ending cataclysm had not yet hit. The horror, the Earth-destroying nightmare, had not cleaved down upon us.

Not yet.

In the north, from far above in the Constellation Cygnus, came a sudden pulse, an instant's brightness. From one of its stars, Wolf 1069, a red dwarf with a livable planet called Wolf 1069b, only thirty-one light years from Earth . . . Had some Being there realized these silly humans had almost destroyed their world?

And still probably would?

Silly humans.

All the better, said the Being from Wolf 1069b. As these silly humans would say, it's Darwinian.

THE END

ABOUT THE AUTHOR

Mike Bond is a former war correspondent, intelligence expert, U.S. Senate candidate, diplomat, conservationist, investment banker, and international energy company CEO. Considered one of the world's foremost experts on crude supply and oil refining, he is also a Russia and Eastern
Europe specialist.

Author of twelve best-selling novels, he has been called *"The master of the existential thriller"* (BBC), *"One of the 21st century's most exciting authors"* (Washington Times), *"One of America's best thriller writers"* (Culture Buzz), and *"A master of the storytelling craft"* (Midwest Book Review).

Based on his own experiences, his novels are set in the world's most perilous places, deadly landscapes, political conspiracies, wars, and revolutions, making *"readers sweat with their relentless pace"* (Kirkus), *"in that fatalistic margin where life and death are one and the existential reality leaves one caring only to survive."* (Sunday Oregonian).

He and his wife, undersea explorer Peggy Lucas, have climbed mountains on every continent and trekked more than 50,000 miles in the Himalayas, Mongolia, Russia, Europe, New Zealand, North and South America, and Africa.

Mike Bond Website: mikebondbooks.com

For film, translation or publication rights,
or for interviews contact:
Meryl Moss Media
meryl@merylmossmedia.com or 203-226-0199

ALSO BY MIKE BOND

REVOLUTION

The 1968 Tet uprising plunges America deeper into the abyss of Vietnam. Martin Luther King is shot, and riots rage in 130 burning American cities. Students protesting the War take over American universities, and street battles in Paris nearly topple the French government. Senator Eugene McCarthy enters the Democratic presidential race against Lyndon Johnson, followed by Bobby Kennedy, who goes on to win the California Democratic primary.

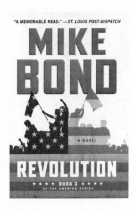

Revolution puts you into this turbulent cultural change as if it were today.

FREEDOM

From the war-shattered jungles of Vietnam to America's burning cities, near-death in Tibet, peace marches, the battle of Hué and the battle of the Pentagon, wild drugs, rock concerts, free love, CIA coups in Indonesia and Greece, the Six Days' War, and Bobby Kennedy's last campaign and assassination. *Freedom* puts you in the Sixties as if it were now.

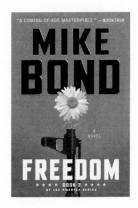

AMERICA

America is the first of Mike Bond's seven-volume historical novel series, capturing the victories and heartbreaks of the last 70 years and of our nation's most profound upheavals since the Civil War – a time that defined the end of the 20th Century and where we are today. Through the wild, joyous, heartbroken and visionary lives of four young people and many others, the Sixties come alive again. *"An extraordinary and deftly crafted novel."* – MIDWEST BOOK REVIEW

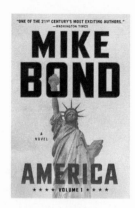

GOODBYE PARIS

Special Forces veteran Pono Hawkins races from Tahiti to France when a terrorist he'd thought was dead has a nuclear weapon to destroy Paris. Joining allies from US and French intelligence, Pono faces impossible odds to save the most beautiful city on earth. Alive with covert action and insider details from the war against terrorism, Goodbye Paris is a hallmark Mike Bond thriller: tense, exciting, and full of real places, and that will keep you up all night. *"A rip-roaring page-turner."* – CULTURE BUZZ

SNOW

Three hunters find a crashed plane filled with cocaine in the Montana wilderness. Two steal the cocaine and are soon hunted by the Mexican cartel, the DEA, Las Vegas killers, and the police of several states. From the frozen peaks of Montana to the heights of Wall Street, the Denver slums and million-dollar Vegas tables, Snow is an electric portrait of today's America, the invisible line between good and evil, and what people will do in their frantic search for love and freedom. *"Action-packed adventure."* – DENVER POST

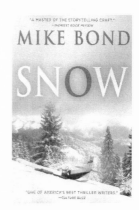

ASSASSINS

From its terrifying start in the night skies over Afghanistan to its stunning end in the Paris terrorist attacks, Assassins is an insider's thriller of the last 30 years of war between Islam and the West. A US commando, an Afghani warlord, a French woman doctor, a Russian major, a top CIA operator, and a British woman journalist fight for their lives and loves in the deadly streets and lethal deserts of the Middle East. *"An epic spy story."* – HONOLULU STAR-ADVERTISER

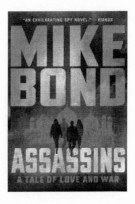

KILLING MAINE

Surfer and Special Forces veteran Pono Hawkins quits sunny Hawaii for Maine's brutal winter to help a former SF buddy beat a murder rap and fight the state's rampant political corruption. *"A gripping tale of murders, manhunts and other crimes set amidst today's dirty politics and corporate graft, an unforgettable hero facing enormous dangers as he tries to save a friend, protect the women he loves, and defend a beautiful, endangered place."* – FIRST PRIZE FOR FICTION, NEW ENGLAND BOOK FESTIVAL

SAVING PARADISE

When Special Forces veteran Pono Hawkins finds a beautiful journalist drowned off Waikiki, he is caught in a web of murder and political corruption. Hunting her killers, he soon finds them hunting him, and blamed for her death. A relentless thriller of politics, sex, and murder, *"an action-packed, must read novel ... taking readers behind the alluring façade of Hawaii's pristine beaches and tourist traps into a festering underworld of murder, intrigue and corruption."* – WASHINGTON TIMES

THE LAST SAVANNA

An intense memoir of humanity's ancient heartland, its people, wildlife, deserts and jungles, and the deep, abiding power of love. *"One of the best books yet on Africa, a stunning tale of love and loss amid a magnificent wilderness and its myriad animals, and a deadly manhunt through savage jungles, steep mountains and fierce deserts as an SAS commando tries to save the elephants, the woman he loves and the soul of Africa itself."* – FIRST PRIZE FOR FICTION, LOS ANGELES BOOK FESTIVAL

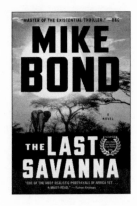

HOLY WAR

Based on the author's experiences in Middle East conflicts, Holy War is the story of the battle of Beirut, of implacable hatreds and frantic love affairs, of explosions, betrayals, assassinations, snipers and ambushes. An American spy, a French commando, a Hezbollah terrorist and a Palestinian woman guerrilla all cross paths on the deadly streets and fierce deserts of the Middle East. *"A profound tale of war... Impossible to stop reading."* – BRITISH ARMED FORCES BROADCASTING

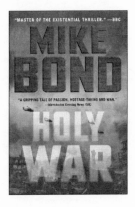

HOUSE OF JAGUAR

A stunning thriller of CIA operations in Latin America, guerrilla wars, drug flights, military dictatorships, and genocides, based on the author's experiences as as one of the last foreign journalists left alive in Guatemala after over 150 journalists had been killed by Army death squads. *"An extraordinary story that speaks from and to the heart. And a terrifying description of one man's battle against the CIA and Latin American death squads."* – BBC

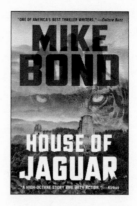

TIBETAN CROSS

An exciting international manhunt and stunning love story. An American climber in the Himalayas stumbles on a shipment of nuclear weapons headed into Tibet for use against China. Pursued by spy agencies and other killers across Asia, Africa, Europe and the US, he is captured then rescued by a beautiful woman with whom he forms a deadly liaison. They escape, are captured and escape again, death always at their heels. *"Grips the reader from the opening chapter and never lets go."* – MIAMI HERALD

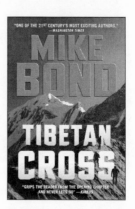

THE DRUM THAT BEATS WITHIN US

The tradition of the poet warrior endures throughout human history, from our Stone Age ancestors to the Bible's King David, the Vikings of Iceland, Japan's Samurai, the Shambhala teachings of Tibet, the ancient Greeks and medieval knights. Initially published by Lawrence Ferlinghetti in City Lights Books, Mike Bond has won multiple prizes for his poetry and prose. *"Passionately felt emotional connections, particularly to Western landscapes and Native American culture."* – KIRKUS

JOY

First published by Lawrence Ferlinghetti in City Lights Books, Mike Bond is an award-winning poet, best-selling novelist, ecologist and former war and human rights correspondent. His previous poetry collection, *The Drum That Beats Within Us* received high praise and has been a best-seller repeatedly since its publication in 2018. This new collection draws from his extensive poetry on love, wilderness, wisdom and fate, on our everyday lives and the infinite and eternal universes in which we live.

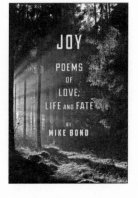